☑ YO-AGB-501

PRAISE FOR
BARBARA ROGAN . . .

"A shrewd observer and a passionate writer. . . ."
—*The New York Times*

"Barbara Rogan has already mastered the essence of the storyteller's art: the creation of an absorbing and compelling world peopled with characters the reader cares for deeply."
—Wendy Smith, *Cleveland Plain Dealer*

"Her style is utterly engaging, with a lighthearted, confidential tone that works beautifully. . . ."
—Gerri Cobren, *Christian Science Monitor*

"Rogan is no minimalist and comfortably packs her [stories] with complications and characters so that her readers are quickly enmeshed and will be staying up all hours to see what happens next."
—*Library Journal*

. . . AND HER TRIUMPHANT
NOVEL
A HEARTBEAT AWAY

"An absorbing book that never lets down for a moment."
—Barbara Hodge Hall, *Anniston Star*

"Entertaining . . . graphic, spiced with wit . . . spirited storytelling."
—*Publishers Weekly*

"Extraordinary . . . absolutely authentic . . . a tour de force. . . . Barbara Rogan has a winner."
—*Roslyn News* (Long Island, NY)

A HEARTBEAT AWAY

BARBARA ROGAN

POCKET BOOKS

New York   London   Toronto   Sydney   Tokyo   Singapore

This book is a work of fiction. Names, characters, places and incidents are products of the author's imagination or are used fictitiously. Any resemblance to actual events or locales or persons, living or dead, is entirely coincidental.

POCKET BOOKS, a division of Simon & Schuster Inc.
1230 Avenue of the Americas, New York, NY 10020

Copyright © 1993 by Barbara Rogan

Published by arrangement with William Morrow & Company, Inc.

ISBN: 0-671-89087-5

First Pocket Books printing October 1995

10 9 8 7 6 5 4 3 2 1

POCKET and colophon are registered trademarks of Simon & Schuster Inc.

Cover art by Joseph Danisi

Printed in the U.S.A.

Years of cruel neglect by our nation's leaders have devastated the inner cities of this country. The war against poverty has been subverted, gradually and inexorably, into war against the poor. The victims, as always, are the weakest among us, those least able to defend themselves: children, the elderly, the disabled, and the sick. This book is dedicated to those who sacrifice personal advancement to fight despair, disease, and death: the doctors, nurses, and staffers of our cities' emergency rooms.

Dedicated, too, to Lesley, Liz, and Ellen.

ACKNOWLEDGMENTS

• • • • • • • •

This book could not have been written without the generous assistance of many people. I am particularly grateful to the magnificent staff of the Montefiore Medical Center Emergency Room. In opening their doors to me, Fred Yaeger, Montefiore's press manager, and Dr. Robert Wyman, medical director of the ER, displayed a well-placed confidence in their staff. Dr. Timothy Simpson, Lewis Gelabert, Dr. Joe Testa, Dr. Wendy Graae, Jan Marie, Kathleen, Dr. Heidi Cohen, Anita Porco, Chris Dykema, Dr. Celia Shmukler, and Enrique Barrientos were particularly helpful. Dr. Ellen Haig provided me with invaluable technical guidance and her patients with intelligent, compassionate care. Dr. Stuart Apfel was generous enough to read the manuscript, correcting my errors and providing valuable insight into the workings of the ER. Any remaining inaccuracies are due entirely to the author's stubbornness. Dr. Zachary Apfel and Dr. Morton Salomon also shared their expertise. My thanks to all.

And finally, a deep bow to Jane Austen, the inspiration for much that is contained herein.

A
HEARTBEAT
AWAY

1

·······

A man draped in sackcloth climbs onto a chair and spreads his arms as if to fly. "In the midst of life, we are in death. Repent ye, for the kingdom of God is at hand." Though he is a striking figure, with his long, tangled beard, dreadlocks, and a fervid gleam to his one good eye, no one in the room looks at or in any way appears to notice the speaker. Intent each on his own misery, in various degrees and attitudes of despair they sprawl across plastic bucket seats clamped to the floor.

Murchison, the ER guard, lumbers up to the man. "Tell you one last time, Preacher," he says, not unkindly. "Keep it up, you gonna find yourself repenting out in the rain. These folks got their own problems. They don't need you."

"Judge not that ye be not judged, fool."

"Sit that ye be not sat on!"

If the medium is the message, Murchison, at six feet three inches and 220 pounds, has a way with words. Preacher sits. The weather is wicked, a driving cold rain that blasts the windows and rattles the sliding glass doors of Mercy Emergency Room. Outside, the world is liquid gray; the autumn sky hovers just out of reach. The day is prematurely lost.

Murchison retreats to his desk beside the door separating the ER waiting room from the treatment area. The door opens, and Crow trundles backward into the waiting room, pulling her cleaning cart behind. Standing beside Murchison's desk, hands on hips, she surveys the waiting room, like a Civil War battlefield, littered with wounded. Another observer might notice signs of bygone grandeur in the waiting room's proportions and marbled arches; Crow's trained eye sees mud, and falls accusingly on the ranks of the homeless gathered around the coffee machine like a hearth.

"Least they could do is wipe their damn shoes," she says. "You know I mopped this room three times this shift?"

The guard shrugs. "What you gonna do, throw them out on a day like this?"

"Ain't you the bleedin' heart."

"You so tough, let's see you toss 'em out."

Crow looks over at the homeless, then out at the rain. She grumbles, "You gonna move those feet, or I gotta mop over you?"

Murchison grins. "Mop away, my shoes could use a shining." But at the last moment he leans back and rests his big feet against the desk. His blue uniform pants are crisply creased but stained dark at the cuffs. The floor beneath his desk is splotched with blood.

On the other side of the door, Pilar Johnston sits on her throne behind the triage window. A young, pregnant Hispanic woman rests both arms on the counter and answers questions in a whisper, while a steady trickle of blood drips down her legs and collects in a puddle between her feet. Crow signs to Pilar, who makes a sour face but leans over, looks down, and quickly shifts gears. Moments later the patient is ushered into the treatment area.

Starting at the hospital entrance, Crow erases the woman's red trail, ending up at the nurses' station. "How am I suppose to know?" Pilar scolds, not looking up from her triage log. "People 'spect me to read their minds. . . . Stands there like a little mouse, does she tell me she's bleeding? Je-sus."

"Quiet day, anyhow," Crow observes.

"Hush your mouth, girl. That's just asking for trouble." Sixteen years in the ER, twelve as head nurse, have taught

Pilar the importance of guarding one's tongue. Even as they speak, the Emergency Medical Service's direct phone rings behind the counter.

The ER clerk answers. Moments later the call goes out on the intercom: "Dr. Blue to ER stat, Dr. Blue to ER. Four incoming." Dr. Blue is Mercy's code for ATR, acute traumatic resuscitation.

Crow flattens herself against the counter and tucks her bucket in between her feet. Seconds later the stampede begins. Dr. Thomas Graystone, the ER's medical director, leads the herd of residents and nurses. Pilar bellows for a nurse to take over triage and sets off down the hall. In motion she looks like a lumbering brown bear, with meaty forearms and a body that bulges out of her size-16 uniform, but for all her bulk, she can fly when she needs to. Now she reaches the ambulance door just as the first siren chokes off in midwail.

Graystone stands out in the rain, holding an umbrella, triaging the patients as they arrive. First is a middle-aged white woman, unconscious. Multiple trauma, lacerations of the face and head, and shock—for starters. Graystone orders a neurological consult and passes her on to Daniel Bergman, the ER's other attending physician, who grabs the stretcher from the attendant and sprints down the hall toward crash room A. Another multiple trauma arrives, this one a black male, conscious but groggy. Graystone hands him over to Calvin Wang, the senior resident. From the same ambulance, the attendant brings out a small child. "Found this little guy strapped in a baby seat next to the man. Vitals are fine, kid seems okay." The baby screams lustily as he's borne off by a nurse. The final ambulance disgorges a white teenage male, conscious and oriented, with superficial lacerations of the head and arm.

Pilar checks his vital signs, calling them out to Graystone. "Pulse one-ten, BP . . . on the low side but not bad."

The boy grips her arm. "Where's my mother?"

Pilar looks inquiringly at the senior paramedic, who juts his chin toward the crash rooms. "She's here, the doctors are looking at her now. Suture?" she asks Graystone, but now it's pro forma. The boy looks good, his accelerated pulse natural under the circumstances. Graystone's eyes track the multiple injuries down the hall.

"Right." He bends down to the boy. "We'll be with you as soon as we can, son, but it's going to take a while."

"I'm okay," the kid whispers. "Take care of my mom."

Afterward, Crow comes to mop the floor inside the ambulance bay. There's a lot of blood, which fortunately doesn't bother her as much as other things. Like patients who spit on her clean floors, drunks who vomit in her bathrooms (if they make it that far), the stench of some people, the infested clothing she has to dispose of—these things make her wonder what she's doing with her life. But the blood, that's natural.

The paramedics are hanging around the ambulance bay, waiting to find out about their patients. Percy asks Crow what's happening. She says, "Two in the code rooms, one in Suture, the baby's okay."

"Ten'll get you one the white lady checks out," says Vinnie, a new guy from Bensonhurst. "Swear to God, I thought she was gonna crump right in the wagon." It's his first year in EMS, and he's still self-conscious about the lingo. Patients never die in ambulances, or in emergency rooms, for that matter. They crump, code, lose it, check out, or go south.

Percy ignores his partner. He ambles over to Crow and smiles a pleasant, gap-toothed smile. "Hey, darlin', check this out." Beneath his white paramedic's jacket he wears a red T-shirt with the motto YOU MAUL 'EM, WE HAUL 'EM.

Crow laughs. Encouraged, Percy comes closer. "What's happenin' with you, little darlin'?"

She snorts. "Don't you little darlin' me, Mr. Married-with-Four-Children."

"Now who told you that? Vinnie, you been telling tales?"

"I didn't say nothing—what do I know how many kids you got?"

"Nobody has to tell me. I know what I know." Crow leaves them to go change her water. On her way to the equipment closet, she glances into the suture room. The teenage boy who came in on the ambulance lies facing her. His eyes are closed and his skin is pasty, with green shadows. His head lolls over the edge of the gurney. A doctor stands at his side.

The doctor looks up. Deep-set crystal-blue eyes meet Crow's. Crow is startled; she's never seen this man before.

"Fetch a resident quickly. The boy's bleeding from a ruptured spleen."

She can't believe he's talking to her. Working as a housekeeper in the ER is the next-best thing to being invisible. Crow's so low on the totem pole, most doctors don't even see her. She glances over her shoulder, but there's no one else in sight, and the doctor's looking straight at her. "Move it!" he barks.

She rushes down the corridor, zigzagging to avoid a patient handcuffed to a stretcher and bracketed by a pair of cops. Just outside crash room A, nurse Alice Straugh is working the hall alone, relaying orders from the doctors inside. Crow calls out, "That kid in Suture needs a doctor."

"He'll have to wait. We've got two multiple traumas, and this one's shaping up to code."

"The doc said stat, the kid's bleeding inside." Crow feels fraudulent, as if she's reciting someone else's lines.

Alice worries her lower lip. Pulling a doctor out of a crash room is bad enough; doing it on the say-so of a housekeeper is sheer folly. But Crow's never cried wolf before. Alice makes up her mind and opens the door to crash room A. "I need a resident stat, we've got a bleeder!"

Graystone himself emerges. His eyes sweep unseeing over Crow, fasten on the nurse. "Where?"

"Suture."

Crow trots behind him down the hall. When they reach the room, the patient is all alone. Even from the door, it's obvious he's gone sour. Graystone rushes in, bends over, and raises the patient's eyelids. He checks the name on his chart and hollers, "Peter! Wake up, Peter!" He sounds angry at the patient, though in fact his fury is directed inward. It was he who triaged the boy out.

No response; no one home.

Graystone wheels around. He marks the absence of anyone useful before he takes in Crow, malingering in the hall. "Get me some bodies!" he commands.

Twice in one day: record visibility.

The nurses' station, depleted by the car crash, is staffed only by a student nurse, a blond little girl who looks terrified at the specter of mop-wielding Crow bearing down on her like a Fury but responds appropriately, stat-paging reserves from the rest of the hospital.

The next time Crow passes the suture room, the patient is lost to view amid a scrum of white-coated bodies. She procrastinates, scrubbing the spotless floor of the corridor outside. Crow's no rubbernecker, but, as the doctors say, she's got an investment in this kid.

Because both code rooms are occupied, they work on him right there in Suture. Perched on a stool overlooking the two residents and three nurses surrounding the patient, Graystone pours out a steady stream of orders and instructions. "Let's get that IV going. Set up an automatic BP, sixty-second intervals. Dr. Kraven, ABG stat. Nurse, call X Ray and see if we can get a portable unit."

Elsa Kraven paints the inside of the patient's wrist with antiseptic, straps it to the table, and plunges a twenty-three-gauge needle deep into his wrist. She winces sympathetically, but the boy doesn't stir, a very bad sign. The blood-pressure monitor beeps: Pressure is falling rapidly. The patient's elevated pulse rate and profuse sweating point to hemorrhagic shock. "Where the hell is he bleeding?" Graystone mutters.

Outside, Crow raises her head as if to speak, then lowers it.

Elsa Kraven peers into the patient's ears. "No sign of blood behind the eardrums, no indication of fracture."

"BP still dropping," a nurse says nervously.

"Get a crash cart in here. Call Anesthesiology and alert OR. If this guy doesn't calm down, we're going to have to do exploratory."

Word comes back from X Ray: The portable unit is broken; they'll have to wheel the patient in. Graystone mutters under his breath. They still haven't located the source of the patient's problem, nor have they stabilized him. "Check his leg pulses again. Maybe an arterial bleed."

"Normal, both sides," Kraven calls after a moment.

The doctors and nurses pause, eye each other with dismay, and resume the protocol with an air of discouragement.

Shit, thinks Crow. She clears her throat diffidently. "It's his spleen. It's ruptured."

Five pairs of flashing hands stop in midmotion. Graystone swivels on his stool. The faces of the doctors and nurses turned to Crow wear identical expressions of astonishment: It's as if a chair had spoken.

"What did you say?" Graystone asks.

"I'm just telling you what that doctor said."

"What doctor?"

"The one who sent me to fetch you."

Graystone stares at Crow as if he's never seen her before, as indeed he hasn't, though they've worked in the same department for a year. "First thing we looked for," Elsa Kraven says dismissively. "There's no bruising, no sign of rib fracture." Graystone gets off his stool, approaches the patient, and presses down firmly on the left upper abdomen. The patient moans and draws up his knees.

"He's guarding," he says in a wondering tone. "Let's draw some fluid."

The nurse hands him a 60-cc syringe. Graystone inserts the needle and draws up the plunger. Blood fills the syringe.

"That's it. Is that IV going?"

"We're in, both lines," Kraven replies. They start pumping fluids into the patient and watch as his blood pressure slowly rises. After thirty minutes, it's stabilized enough for him to be rushed into surgery.

When Graystone returns to crash room A, he finds the boy's mother in cardiac arrest. The room is crowded, Anesthesiology having been called in to assist with breathing and Neurology to evaluate the head injury. Dan Bergman is running the code. He looks up from pumping the woman's chest, his long hair plastered to his forehead, glasses slipping down his nose. "It's getting real old, Tom. We crank her up, she maintains for a minute, then quits on us."

Graystone frowns at this familiarity in the presence of nurses. "Carry on, *Dr.* Bergman. Where do you want me?"

They crack her chest, but it's no good. After thirty minutes, Bergman calls the code. The neurologist says it's just as well, considering the extent of the head injury. The anesthesiologist stalks out in disgust. Everyone's on edge, pissed off. Patients aren't supposed to die in ER. She could have held out for ICU, or at least made it to the operating room. Then others would have had to deal with the hassle.

The husband arrives, wearing a gray sweat suit, looking like they pulled him out of a gym. Nevertheless, it's apparent at a glance, by the hundred-dollar haircut, the winter tan, and the Rolex watch, that only an accident could have brought *this* man to Mercy. He strides up to the triage desk, a man accustomed to instant responsiveness. "I'm Julian Royce. Where are my wife and son? I want to see them right away."

Dan Bergman steps forward, takes the husband into the ER administrator's office, and shuts the door. The others stay as far away as they can, which isn't far enough. Royce can be heard bellowing impatiently, "Where are they? Why can't I see them?" Bergman says something unintelligible, and the other falls abruptly silent. The doctor's voice murmurs on. After a while, the husband begins to cry, awful hoarse sobs escalating as his resistance crumbles.

Death given voice is an unmodulated moan, like the sweep of wind over a desolate prairie. Loss of a spouse is a primal wound, erasing boundaries not only of race and class but even of species. The mournful cry that issues from the throat of this stricken man differs in no way from a wolf's howl of desolation as it stands over the body of a fallen mate. Listening, Crow feels her own throat constrict in empathy. The sound seeps under the door, filling the corridors and treatment rooms of Mercy Emergency. Patients stir uneasily, but the staff goes about its business as if tuned to a different wavelength, sustained by the syncopated heartbeat of the ER's systems, the steady hum of its monitors and pumps, the rhythmic drips and beeps of life support.

After the nurses finish tidying up the woman, it's Crow's job to clean the crash room before the husband comes in to view his wife. She enters, bucket in hand. On the gurney, a white sheet conceals an absence, a void. Out of respect, Crow circles around the body, not turning her back.

When they open them on the table, it makes an awful mess. She mops the floor, wipes down the walls, and disinfects the gleaming stainless-steel surfaces, taking care where she lays her gloved hands. The doctors and nurses are supposed to dispose of needles themselves, depositing them in a special container; but when things get hot, they don't always take the time. The one thing Crow doesn't want to do is prick herself in that ER.

She works quietly, efficiently. The silence in the room is a respite from the storm, a welcome relief from the chaos without. After a year in the ER, she's not bothered by one little corpse. The first time was different. When Pilar first ordered her to clean a room with a body in it, Crow nearly laid down her mop and quit. "No way," she told Pilar.

The head nurse folded her massive arms across her chest and looked her up and down. "What's the matter with you, girl? Ain't you never seen a corpse before?"

"I've seen enough, thank you," Crow said.

"He won't bother you. They're model patients."

"Nobody said this was part of the job."

"Goes with the territory." With a firm but not unfriendly push, Pilar propelled Crow into the room and shut the door behind her.

She had to make herself look. The body, covered with a clean sheet, lay like a forgotten sack of laundry on the table. Inert, inoffensive, feeling no pain.

Never since then has Crow feared the vacant company of the dead. In many ways, being dead in the ER beats being alive. For the sake of survival, patients are tortured, torn from their loved ones, cut, pricked, spliced, and forcibly intubated, all without anesthesia. Dealing with pain is the last item on the agenda. A screaming patient, they say in Mercy, is a live patient.

The dead, at least, are left in peace.

The thing that lies now upon the gurney is less animate than the room's furnishings, its quiescent monitors. The space the body occupies is like a hole cut out of a picture. Its presence in the room, its aggressive nonexistence, deepens

Crow's sense of aloneness. Yet she senses a kind of lingering attention in the room, a hovering awareness, an odd remnant of life.

It's not the first time. Once, cleaning up after the staff failed to save a young accident victim, Crow glimpsed, or thought she glimpsed, a man in a white coat sitting in the corner of the room, his face buried in his hands. But when she looked directly at the recording nurse's chair, it was empty. Imagination, she told herself. Nerves, a trick of light. Yet the hair on her arms stood on end, her stomach flip-flopped, and it was all she could do not to bolt the room.

Crow has no truck with ghosts or demons, heaven or hell. Her faith is the faith of the streets: What you see is what you get. And what Crow sees—what the ER has shown her—is that dying is a process, not a finite act. Like most things, it takes some folks longer than others.

The woman who now lies beneath the sheet is stiller than still, deader than the steel gurney she lies upon; yet the air about her stirs uneasily. Crow, a mother herself, knows why.

"That boy gonna be all right," she says out loud. "They got to him in time. He's safe now; that boy is just fine."

Does she sense, at that moment, a palpable lightening of the air, an easing of tension? It seems so; that was her aim, yet Crow refuses to credit it. As far as she's concerned, she's just whistling in the wind.

When the room is spotless, Crow goes out to the nurses' station. Pilar looks up from the medication log. "You done in there?"

"I'm done." Casually Crow asks, "How's that boy doing?"

"What boy?"

"You know, her son. The suture room."

"He's okay." Pilar narrows her eyes. "What you asking for?"

"A person can ask, can't she?"

"Girl, you know the form. Once a patient leaves the ER, they don't exist no more. You don't call, you don't ask, and you don't follow up."

Pilar is nobody's fool, she's fond of saying. Half the patients they get in Mercy ER are hopeless, and the other half are crocks, people who walk in with a sore throat or a low-grade fever and claim they're dying. Pilar's like Missouri: "Show me" is her motto. Her stern face, carved in flint, could serve as a figurehead for the institution unaffectionately known throughout Brooklyn as Merciless. But Crow has eyes and ears, and knows what she knows.

"I hear you," she says. "I hear you making your calls, too, when you think no one's listening."

"You hear too damn much, Little Miss Tippy-toes." Pilar looks at the door of the administrator's office, and her broad brown face closes in on itself. She knocks and enters without waiting.

A small group of residents and nurses has gathered near the nurses' station. Someone tells a joke; a burst of laughter rises up and surrounds them like a vapor barrier. The administrator's door opens, and Pilar and Bergman emerge with the husband between them, no longer weeping but pallid and sweaty. The bereaved man walks with his arms crossed high across his chest, like a patient nursing an incipient heart attack. As he passes, the staff fall silent and avert their gazes. All except Crow.

Eight that evening: Weary Crow is in her utility closet, finishing up for the day. She rinses out her mop, sets out supplies for tomorrow, and throws her coverall into the laundry basket. Suddenly the hall light dims. She turns to find Dr. Graystone looming in the doorway.

Although gossip is the oil that lubricates the ER, Crow knows little about its head. Graystone is tall, as black as she, though only, Crow suspects, on the outside. His lean, dark face is handsome but austere; he affects a mannered formality incongruous in a man his age. Unlike his gregarious friend Daniel Bergman, Graystone does not hang out at the nurses' station between customers, flirting and gossiping. His friends are chosen from among his peers. He does not date nurses; and if he has a life outside the hospital, he keeps it there.

"Ah," he says, in lieu of her name, which he does not know and has not thought to ask, "it *was* a ruptured spleen." The voice is upper-crust Long Island.

Crow takes her purse from a small gray footlocker in the corner of the room and straps it around her waist. "Uh-huh," she says.

"The patient's doing fine now."

"That's good."

She's ready to leave now, but he won't go away, stands blocking her way. Crow sets her feet apart, hands on hips. She's bone tired, she's just put in three hours' overtime, and her baby's waiting for her. If she doesn't leave now, she'll be too late to kiss Joey good night.

Graystone looks at her and sees, as if for the first time, a slim woman of indeterminate age, dark-skinned, with pronounced cheekbones and watchful eyes too large for her face. He gives her a rare smile, which she doesn't return. The smile fades. He asks, "How did you know?"

"Doctor, I wouldn't know a spleen from a tonsil. That other doctor said."

"How'd he know?"

"You're asking me?"

"What doctor? Who was he?"

"I don't know. I never seen him before."

"What did he look like?"

She casts back in her mind. "White man in his fifties. About your height, thin, gray hair, very blue eyes." It's funny: She remembers his words, but not the sound of his voice.

Frowning, Graystone asks, "If you didn't know him, how did you know he was a doctor?"

"He wore a lab coat and stethoscope."

"Anyone can put on a lab coat and stethoscope."

Crow casts up her eyes. "If it looks like a doctor and acts like a doctor and talks like a doctor, then far's I'm concerned," she says, "it *is* a doctor."

12

2

· · · · · · · ·

CROW

The rain has stopped. Black streets glisten; pulsing neon lights reflect off sidewalks studded with puddles. Heads emerge from doors and windows, black faces and brown, peering upward. The night looks like a Miles Davis composition.

Just outside the project I stop in the bodega to buy milk and juice. In the alley, a huddle of men pass something hand to hand. The smell of crack drifts out to the street. A man's voice calls out to me: "Hey, baby, come on over." I don't look his way, but damned if I'll cross the street. Deepside's too goddamn tough to show fear. White folks, repairmen, even cops are scared to come in here, with good reason. But this is my turf, these streets are my element. I glide through this city like a dolphin through water, wakeless.

Inside the project, people call out: "Yo, Crow, how's it going?" "How they treatin' you, girl?" It's late and it's damp, but there's still little kids running around, watched by their mamas, aunts, and grandmas. I check the sliding ponds, benches, and walls for signs of trouble in the gang graffiti, but nothing's changed, no names X'd out.

Whoever built this project gave no thought to acoustics, or maybe they did and just didn't give a damn. Fifteen apartment houses twelve stories high set round three tiny little squares with cement benches and a floodlit, fenced-in playground.

Sounds from the five clustered buildings converge in the central courtyard. Hearing my own name echo through the concrete cavern, I look up at my apartment, sixth floor of building E, and see Joey waving from the window.

I wave back and start running, cradling my shopping. Our stoop is colonized by homeboys, Mokie, Ray, Jamal, and their buddies. They hang out, smoking, fooling with their girlfriends, waiting for trouble. Flattop haircuts, baseball caps turned backwards, gold chains, ghetto blasters blaring. Don't mess with us, the getup says; we are tough motherfuckers. But I baby-sat for half these tough motherfuckers, and I don't take no lip from them now. "Move it," I tell them, and they do. Mokie says, "Yo, Crow, you bring me something from the hospital?" I slap him upside the head and they laugh.

Elevator's working for a change. I check the mirror before getting in. I ain't scared, but I'm no fool, either. There's evil people about.

When the elevator door opens to the sixth floor, Joey's waiting in the hall, dressed in his teddy-bear pajamas and dancing from foot to foot. "Mommy!" He flings his arms around my knees. Every morning I go off to work, and every night I come back, but Joey always greets me like the long-lost love of his life. I scoop him up and bury my face in his hair, inhaling his odor of baby shampoo and talc. Joey favors his daddy. Blue's mixed blood shows in his soft brown curls, narrow nose, those sweet little lips like ripe berries—made for blowing a horn, Blue used to say. Joey's complexion's halfway between Blue's café au lait and my bitter chocolate. "What you doing out here without your slippers?" I pretend to scold.

"My feet said they were too hot from those stupid old slippers."

"Well, you tell your feet to watch their mouth."

"I told him put them on." Selma stands in the doorway, watching the nightly reunion. "He don't listen to me."

I can smell roasting meat and potatoes, and my mouth waters. "Come on in, baby," I say, and I carry the boy on one hip, the shopping on the other, into the apartment.

Selma locks the door behind us with chain and dead bolt. "Time for bed now," she tells Joey.

"I want Mommy to tuck me in."

14

I carry him into his little room and tuck him in. Right away he starts. "Mommy, sit with me. Mommy, rub my back. Mommy, read me a story. Mommy, sleep with me."

"Mommy's hungry," I tell him, but Joey wraps his little arms around me and won't let go. He's worn out, though, and it's not long before he falls asleep with his head on my lap.

"You spoiling that child," Selma says when I come blinking out of his bedroom. "You just encouraging him to carry on."

I say, "What that child's been through, Selma, there ain't enough I can give him." We go on into the kitchen, plain and simple but, as always, so clean you could lick the linoleum. Selma keeps the place like it was her own. Spends more time here, too. She don't like being alone.

Suddenly feeling my own weariness, I sink into a chair. The table's set for one. Selma goes to the stove, starts heaping pot roast, carrots, potatoes, and corn bread onto a plate. "Ain't you eating?" I ask.

"I ate with Joey. You really think that child remembers?"

"How's he gonna forget?"

"He was a baby!"

"Three years old," I remind her.

"He don't talk about it."

"No, he just cry every time I leave him."

She puts the plate in front of me and takes a chair. I dig in fast. Selma's a first-class cook. For thirty years she made her living at it, cooking for a series of restaurants and diners till the arthritis got her. Now she just looks after Joey and me, except once a week on Sundays she limps down to the soup kitchen in Bed-Stuy and cooks up a stew for the homeless.

She laughs at me, and I slow down, ashamed of myself. "It's good," I tell her.

She waves her hand. "Eat, eat."

"You sound like the lady from the hospital cafeteria." I try on her Hungarian accent. "That's all you're eating? Such a skinny *malink*, like a regular crow you are. Take more! Eat, eat, my dahlink."

Usually my imitations make her laugh: Selma always said I have a wicked good ear and a tongue to match. But this time she don't crack a smile. She's surely got her mind wrapped around something tonight.

"Johnny Deacon called," she says.

Now that gets my attention off my plate. "They're back?"

"Not yet. He called all the way from Paris, France. Said they're coming home next week, opening Saturday night at the Cellar, and he expects you there."

I haven't seen Deacon and the boys since the funeral. Haven't thought about them, neither. No point reopening old wounds. I tell Selma, "I'm working Saturday."

"You don't have to. That's just overtime. I'll sit with Joey."

"Thought you didn't like Deacon and them."

"Never said I don't like 'em. Just said they ain't your kind. Person's got to stick with her own."

Selma always says, Stick with your own kind. Move up, but not too far. Her own daughters married steady union men, a mailman and a garbage collector. They're out of the project and into the two-family houses six blocks from here. That's the range of Selma's ambitions, for them and for me. Time was I used to argue, but not anymore. I ask her, "So how come you're saying I should see him?"

"That old man can't do you no harm. Do you good to get out."

"I need the money."

"There's needs and needs," she says cryptically. "Crow, we got to talk."

I sigh but say nothing. Selma want to talk, there ain't nothing gonna stop her.

"You got to get yourself a job," she says.

Selma's not my mother, but she acts like it. I figure she's entitled. My mama died when I was fourteen, and since I didn't have no father to speak of, the state would have got me but for Selma, our good neighbor. She took me in and raised me with her own two daughters.

"I got a job," I say. "You think I'm volunteering my services at that hospital?"

"I mean a real job. A job with a future."

"My job's got a future. I'm working my way up to brain surgeon." I'm doing my best to amuse, but she doesn't crack a smile.

"You got your high school diploma, you got two years' college, you got languages, and you just throwing it all away like it was

16

nothing. Girl like you got no business spending your days mopping up other people's filth."

"It puts bread on the table," I tell her, pushing away an empty plate. Selma starts getting up to refill it, but I shake my head.

She says, "There's fifty ways to put bread on the table, all better than that. People spend their whole damn life trying to get out of this project. You got out, you made it; now you're trying to crawl back in. There's plenty other things you could be doing. You could go back to school. You got that insurance money."

"That's put aside for Joey's education," I say, with a look even she don't dare answer. "'Sides which, I like what I do. It pays well. It's a good job."

"What you talking about, a good job?" Selma's voice is thick with scorn. "It's the worst job in the whole damn hospital."

"Somebody's got to do it."

"Somebody. Not you. You want to work in that crazy place, at least get yourself a office job. You're qualified."

"I don't want a fucking office job!"

"You watch your mouth, Crow. Don't you talk that street trash 'round me."

"Sorry, Selma," I say.

She takes my hand in hers, rubs her thumb over the gold band on my wedding finger. Her voice goes soft. "I know what you're doing. But I am here to tell you, baby, it is time to get back in the world. You got to get on with your life while you still a young woman." She sits back in her chair, arms crossed, and waits for me to answer.

It makes me nervous when my Selma goes soft on me. I need her anchored firm and fast. "I'm a hard woman," she always used to say, "and I'm raising my girls hard. Woman don't watch out for herself in this world, ain't nobody gonna do it for her." Looking at her now, though, she don't look so tough, with her thick black hair all streaked with gray and that sorrowful cast round her mouth.

She's waiting on my answer, but I have none. How can I explain to Selma what I can't explain to myself? It's true Mercy is a terrible place; not for nothing it's called Merciless in the 'hood. Shit happens all the time; ain't a day passes without shootings, knifings, falls off roofs and subway platforms. Rapes, don't ask how many. Child abuse. There's times I think if I see one more beaten, burned, or tortured child, I'm bound to explode.

First week I worked in the ER, I had a nightmare. In the dream, I'm drifting alone in a boat on a evil sea, and the boat's leaking; but what seeps inside isn't water but a thick red liquid, reeking and foul. I've got my hospital pail and mop with me, and I'm bailing as fast as I can, but the muck keeps oozing in, not only through the seams, but through the very pores of the boat.

I woke up determined to quit that job. But I couldn't. Something holds me fast to a place where the city's hidden wounds are exposed, where masks are discarded and people show what they really are. Mercy ER is life stripped of illusions. It's where I belong.

Once I heard a old nurse tell a young one, "Leave that shit alone. Don't touch it. You're a nurse, not a damn housekeeper."

I get no respect in Mercy, but what Selma don't grasp is that I want none. Once my life was full of respect; love, too. Times like that the world expands; then, like a child's balloon, it bursts. My opinion, God's a damn Indian giver. These days I don't want nothing I can't afford to lose. I just want to stop where I belong, do my job, and be left alone.

It's useful work. More than useful: essential. Without Crow and her trusty mop, without Crow's finger in the dike, those doctors and nurses would be up to their knees in filth and gore.

I know what Selma thinks. She thinks me working in the hospital's something to do with Blue and how he died. I say what difference does it make? A woman's got to do what a woman's got to do.

3

·······

"Something strange happened at work today," Alice says.

"Did it, dear?" Her mother angles her compact mirror, studying her face. "Richard, why didn't you tell me my lipstick was smeared? No wonder everyone was staring at me."

Her husband gives her a besotted look, none the less sincere for being practiced. "They were staring because you were far and away the most beautiful woman at the benefit."

Dasha fixes her lipstick, gives the mirror a little nod of satisfaction, and closes the compact. She is fifty-five years old, but nature, art, and science have so conspired in her favor that she is often taken for her daughter's sister. Tonight Dasha wears a strapless black sheath, size 8; her graceful throat is set off by a thick silver band of Zuni design. Sitting beside her on the couch, Alice in her hospital whites feels frumpish.

Dasha says, "You should have come, darling. The dancing was divine, and the champagne wasn't bad, either."

"The champagne was first-rate," Richard amends. "I'll say that for the BAM benefits: They take you for an arm and a leg, but you get your money's worth."

Alice murmurs apologetically. She enjoys the ballet and approves of the evening's cause, money for AIDS research, but she feels terminally awkward among her parents' society friends. "And what do you do, Alice?" they always ask, for times have changed, and young women of their class are expected to have careers. "I'm a nurse," she replies, and their eyes glaze over. Her profession is an embarrassment to her parents, who, perceiving Alice's early bent toward the helping professions, had urged her toward medical school. They were horrified when she insisted on becoming a nurse, could not conceive that a daughter of theirs would rather carry out orders than issue them—unless, of course, the orders were theirs. Worse yet, the job at Mercy, of all places. Dasha, disguising her unease with overkill, introduces her daughter to friends as "Darling Alice, toiler in the urban vineyards, the Florence Nightingale of the inner city." Alice is applauded, her dedication admired, but afterward no one speaks to her except to relate the story of a relative's catastrophic illness or ask for medical advice.

"Well, you should have made the effort," Dasha says now. "There were at least three men there I wanted you to meet. It's no good barricading yourself in here." She looks about her daughter's home with an air of dissatisfaction, though in fact it was she who chose, paid for, and furnished the spacious brownstone. Alice's apartment, a wedding present that has outlasted its occasion, is set high on a hill in Brooklyn Heights amid a warren of winding, hilly streets, bistros, boutiques, and stately old homes. It's a charmed neighborhood, an island of moneyed gentility surrounded by the real Brooklyn, producer of the human mulch, Mercy ER's never-ending gruel of victims.

"I wasn't barricading myself," Alice replies. "I was working."

Dasha sniffs. "And why in God's name must you work overtime? Surely there are nurses who need the money."

"Not enough. We're chronically short-handed."

Some people manage to get away. We met a doctor from your hospital at the benefit. Charming young man, very attractive; looked a lot like that actor, what's his name: Kevin Kline."

"Dr. Plummer," says Alice, making a face. Though the doctor works upstairs on Ob-Gyn, Plummer lore abounds throughout Mercy. He is the worst sort of ladies' man, spiteful toward women who refuse his charms and contemptuous toward those he seduces; he also abuses nurses. Just this morning Alice heard a story about an OR scrub who assisted him in a hysterectomy. Plummer asked for one instrument; she, mishearing, handed him another. Plummer nicked her hand with a scalpel. "Have I got your attention now?" he asked.

The nurse complained and there was a hearing, but the balance of power being what it is, nothing came of it. Plummer claimed he nicked her by accident, and no one could prove otherwise. But the nurses know.

Dasha regards her daughter critically. "A very personable young man. And single, one gathers."

"I'm not his type."

"He was very complimentary about you." She raises a perfectly arched eyebrow. "Don't tell me he's gay?"

Alice snorts. "No such luck. I meant he likes his women very young, very innocent, and very pretty. Right out of nursing school, for preference."

Which, to Richard, sounds sensible enough. "Better to sow one's oats before marriage than after, eh?" he ventures.

Dasha shoots him a warning look. The ostensible cause of Alice's divorce had been excessive fidelity: her husband's to his longtime mistress. Though it began with every possible advantage—a Tiffany registry, a Givenchy gown of ivory lace, an elegant Plaza wedding, and a more-than-presentable groom—the marriage had lasted less than a year. When she first met Charlie Wheaton, he was the youngest partner in Richard's law firm, blessed, not only with brilliance, but also with rugged good looks. Despite the disparity in their fortunes, Alice was generally considered lucky to have snared him, and a fool to have turned him loose over such a trifling matter.

It is one of her parents' conceits, which Alice has never challenged, that she was mortified by Charlie's infidelity and has yet to recover from the shock. In fact, her discovery of the affair came as a blessed relief to Alice, providing acceptable grounds to divorce a man whom everyone agreed was perfect for her. It was not that Charlie abused or mistreated her; it was just that, once the wedding was over, he saw no point in pretending to love her.

Alice bears him no ill will for that. She's simply not a very lovable person; and perhaps she should have understood from the start the nature of the deal Charlie offered. Instead, by foolishly mistaking courtship for love, she brought disappointment upon herself.

Now Dasha shrugs her bare shoulders. "Just because a man dates that kind of girl doesn't mean he'd ever marry one. Don't write this Plummer person off, Alice."

"Mother, I know the man."

"You always do this. No sooner do I mention a man's name than I get that *look*. Your problem, darling, is that you don't give people a chance."

"Not true, Mother. Charles was one of your finds. I gave him a chance."

Her parents exchange a glance. Overt references to Charlie, Alice has learned, lead reliably to a change of subject. Dasha gives her a mollifying pat. "Tell us about the strange thing that happened at work."

A stranger might detect a note of condescension in Dasha's tone, the willed cheeriness of a mother asking her child about his day in school, but Alice does not hear it. She brightens at once.

"A housekeeper saved a patient. We had two codes going at once, everyone was tied up, and Crow insisted that I pull out a doctor to look at a boy who'd already been triaged out. And she was right, the kid had absolutely gone sour, and if Dr. Graystone hadn't got to him when he did, we'd have lost him."

"Doesn't sound so strange to me," Richard says. "Sounds like the woman deserves a medal."

"The weird part is that she insisted a doctor had sent her for help, but when Dr. Graystone got there, there was no one around."

"So he left the hospital."

"That's what I thought, but then where did he go? He'd have had to pass me to leave the treatment area, and I didn't see anyone. Nobody knows who it was; Crow didn't recognize him."

Richard snorts. "'The Case of the Disappearing Doctor.' Elementary, my dear Alice. The girl made him up."

"Crow? Why would she do that?"

"Would you have pulled a doctor out of an emergency on the say-so of a domestic?"

Alice says slowly, "I'd have told her to get the nurse from triage."

"Would the delay have mattered?"

"Yes."

"There you go. The maid sees a patient in distress, she knows no one's going to listen to her, so with great resource-fulness she gives you the only thing that will induce you to commandeer a doctor: orders from another doctor."

"Except Crow didn't just know the patient was in trouble. She knew what was wrong with him."

"How long has she been working in the ER?"

"No, Daddy," Alice says firmly. "It doesn't work like that. You don't just pick it up by osmosis."

"My dear girl, you've been working there what: five years?"

"Seven, actually."

"You can't tell me you're not infinitely more experienced and competent than those residents they run through there every few months."

She closes her eyes. They've had this discussion many times before. "If you were going in for open-heart surgery, would you rather be operated on by a cardiac surgeon or the OR nurse?"

"It's not the same thing. How many resuscitations have you worked on over the years?"

"I don't know. Hundreds."

"And you're telling me you couldn't run one yourself, better than young Dr. Bubblegum fresh out of med school?"

"Of course she could," Dasha says loyally. "A dump like that, what kind of doctors do they get? Probably all foreign-ers."

Alice's eyes fill with tears. "For once I wish you'd come right out and say it."

"Say what?" they ask in unison.

"You want me to quit my job."

Her mother pouts. "Darling, have we ever suggested such a thing?"

No, Alice thinks. You just burrow away, patient as a mole, undermining the foundation. But she doesn't say it; even the thought feels disloyal.

Dasha takes her hand, turning it over to expose the roughened palm. "It's just that we hate seeing you work so hard, darling. Taking orders from every Tom, Dick, and Harry."

Alice sighs. Her mother always makes it sound as if Alice were a barmaid in a seedy saloon. Her parents don't understand what she does, but whose fault is that? She's never found the words to explain what binds her to Mercy. And if she could explain, if she could talk to them about the grinding poverty, the awful bottomless need of the people they serve, still they would never understand; they would mistake her words for some kind of reproach, when in fact Alice had nothing but admiration for her parents' charitable work.

Her family is one pole of Alice's world, her work the other. The two are incompatible. When she and they were younger, Alice tried to bridge the gap, to draw her world together. Time's passage has impressed upon her the folly of that effort. Better to perform a kind of psychic surgery on herself, to sever the link between the poles. One world need not impinge on the other. A person can lead two lives.

4

•••••••

During a lull the next day, a small group gathers at the nurses' station, which backs up to the front-desk reception and triage area but faces inward toward the treatment area. The talk turns to the mystery of Crow's disappearing doctor, and Alice Straugh is questioned again. "I don't know," she says, flustered by the attention. *"I* didn't see him."

"Maybe it wasn't a doctor at all," Elsa Kraven says. "Maybe it was some relative floating around."

"Crow said he was wearing a stethoscope."

"Anyone can put on a stethoscope."

"A paramedic, then."

"No way," Pilar says. "Crow knows the paramedics."

"Maybe an LMD," says Calvin Wang, a third-year resident. Local medical doctors occasionally show up in the ER, summoned by those few of their patients who have private physicians.

Alice makes an unaccustomed joke: "Maybe she saw Elias."

After a moment's startlement, everyone laughs. Just then Crow comes around the corner. She stops in front of the nurses' station, plants her mop like a staff, and fixes Alice with a stern gaze.

"Crow," Alice stammers. "We were just talking about you."

"I heard."

"We were trying to figure out who that doctor was."

"I heard that, too."

Alice is getting more nervous by the minute. Crow's not smiling, and she's not moving away, either. Pilar and Elsa Kraven exchange a puzzled look.

Crow says, "I heard what you said about maybe I saw Elias. Well, let me tell you something, Alice Straugh: I didn't see any damn ghost, and I don't appreciate you going 'round saying I did."

"It was just a joke," Alice mumbles, mortified, blushing to the roots of her frizzy red hair. She swivels her chair and buries herself in patient files. An awkward silence ensues. Then Pilar comes out of the station and walks Crow, sans mop, through the waiting room toward the coffee machine.

"What you come down so hard on her for?" Pilar speaks softly but maintains a bruising grip on Crow's arm. "She didn't mean no harm."

"Where's she get off dissing me, making me out to be some kind of goddamn superstitious pickaninny?"

Pilar throws her head back and laughs. "Listen to the little street tough. 'Dissing me!' You got the words and the rhythm, Crow, but it ain't your song. Not to mention you're wrong about Alice. She's okay. Shit, girl, you got some kinda burr up your ass today. If I'd of said that about Elias, you'd of laughed."

"Maybe," concedes Crow. "But she's just too damn white to talk like that about me."

Pilar gives her the Look that's struck fear into the hearts of generations of interns. She breathes heavily through her nose, saying nothing.

"Know what came into my head when I heard that shit about 'Maybe Crow seen the ghost'? Buckwheat. Remember him, from the Little Rascals? All the time seein' spooks, and every time he saw one, his nappy hair would stand on end, his knees would knock, and his eyes would get all round and shiny-white. 'Feets, don't fail me now!' That's what I thought of."

"Girl, I ain't got time for attitude in my ER. Alice didn't mean it like you took it, and that's a end to it." Even after Crow nods, Pilar's not satisfied. She surveys the waiting room with the jaded eyes of a longtime wrangler assessing the herd; they'll keep, she decides. Angry looks, pleading gazes bounce off her stony face. She buys two cups of coffee from the machine and lowers her bulk slowly into one of the bucket-shaped molded-plastic chairs that line the wall.

Crow accepts a cup, sits beside her. "What's the story on this Elias cat, anyhow?"

"You don't know about Elias?"

"Some ghost is all I know. Something goes missing or a file gets lost, folks say maybe Elias took it."

Pilar shakes her head. "I can't believe you here a year and nobody told you the story. Elias Glass was head of ER when I first started here, sixteen years ago. Fine doctor, good man. Wife was dead, didn't have no kids, pretty much lived here in the hospital. Late one night, just as he was walking out the door, the paramedics brought in a infant girl. Baby'd bit a loose button off her mama's dress and choked on it. She was blue in the face, no breath sounds at all. Elias does a Heimlich but it don't work, the button's wedged too tight. He runs her back to room one, hollers for a trach kit, and grabs his scalpel. Just then, some asshole starts shooting out in the corridor—there'd been a fight earlier and the damn paramedics brought both parties here. The bullet ripped through the wall, hit Elias in the base of the skull, and penetrated his brain."

"You were there?"

"As close to him as I am to you." Pilar's breaking her Styrofoam cup into little pieces, stuffing the fragments into what's left of the cup.

There's a silence between them. The story feels unfinished. Crow wonders about the baby, but Pilar's face stops her from asking. "Jesus," she says.

"Yeah," says Pilar. "I seen a lot of shit go down in this ER, but nothing like the night Elias died."

Crow drains her coffee. "So why the jokes, all that shit about 'Elias took this, Elias did that'?"

Pilar shrugs. "Makes a good story, something to tell

young residents pulling their first night shift. Besides, some folks don't think it's a joke. Some folks believe it."

"Get on," scoffs Crow.

"They say he haunted this damn place alive, so why not dead?"

"Not you."

"I figure if anyone would've seen him, it'd be me. I knew him. I was holding him when he died. And I never." Pilar tosses her mutilated cup into the trash and lumbers to her feet with a groan. "That's it. Break's over."

Crow trails her back inside. As she passes the nurses' station, Alice Straugh looks up anxiously. Crow winks at her.

With a deep sigh, Alice sinks back into her chair. She still doesn't know what she did, why Crow was so offended. That old chestnut about Elias's ghost has been around longer than either of them, despite the lack of any evidence. Whatever credence the legend has comes from staffers' perception that any hospital as old and layered with tragedy as Mercy *ought* to be haunted.

For Mercy is nearly seventy years old, a dinosaur of a hospital. Although its fortunes have risen and waned with the ebbing tide of its Brooklyn community, decades of deterioration have not wholly effaced the traces of its former glory. The vaulted ceiling of Mercy's main lobby, its ornamental cornices, arched passageways, and marble floors are remnants of an earlier era of optimism, a period when beauty was presumed to matter.

When Mercy was founded in 1921 by a private consortium of doctors, Deepside was a community of wealthy old WASP families with connections on Fifth Avenue and Philadelphia's Main Line. By 1945 their brownstone mansions had been converted into flats and the WASPs had disappeared, leaving Deepside to the immigrant Jews and Italians who, a scant generation later, would themselves decamp before a wave of blacks and Hispanics. By then most of Mercy's patients carried no insurance and were unable to pay for care. On the verge of closing its doors, the hospital was purchased by the city and expanded into a small but full-service municipal medical center.

Since then, Mercy has been hostage to the city's fluctuating fortunes. Like the child of whimsical parents, it is alternately plied with treats—hideously expensive CAT scans, state-of-the-art neonatal equipment, spanking-new ICU monitors—and punished without cause.

Its problems are exacerbated by a chronic lack of staff. Even when funds are available, candidates are frightened off by the Deepside location and by Mercy's spotty reputation. After trying for months to hire a staff surgeon for the ER, Graystone finally snared a good one, a Downstate grad who craved the variety and action of Mercy's ER. The man was offered the position and accepted it. Coming to work his first day, the young surgeon was mugged at knifepoint in the doctors' parking lot. He turned around and went home. The following day Graystone received a note. *Sorry to let you down, but at the risk of being thought a coward, I prefer a working environment where I wield the scalpel.*

Dan Bergman suggests issuing white flags and armbands to all staff and prospective staff. More seriously and privately, he suggests jumping ship. "You and me," he woos Thomas Graystone as they lunch in the doctors' lounge. The lounge is windowless but large, with space enough for bunk beds along the far wall, a sink on the wall, and a conference table with six rickety folding chairs. The tiled floors are worn down to an indeterminate color, the flaking walls decorated with annual group photos of the ER house staff. "A nice little walk-in clinic," Bergman says, "strictly cash-and-carry. We could call it Ebony and Ivory. A guy I know in the Bronx, used to work at Columbia-Prez, he opened a place. You know what he netted the first year?"

"Don't tell me."

"Two hundred and fifty grand, and that's after taxes and insurance. Two fucking fifty, Thomas. A man's got to think of the future."

They're munching on sandwiches, tuna for Bergman, roast beef for Graystone. In theory they're entitled to an hour lunch break; in reality there's never time even to run up to the cafeteria. Rather than go hungry, the doctors send out or brown-bag it.

Graystone says, "I *am* thinking of the future. You want to

spend the rest of your life treating sore throats and pulling splinters?"

"Nothing wrong with that," Bergman replies quickly.

"Bo-ring."

"Yeah, well, I could live with boring. You want to spend the rest of your life in the Knife and Gun Club?"

"I don't know about the rest of my life. Right now it's what I want to be doing. What's eating you, Dan'l?"

Bergman shoves his glasses back up his nose. "That kid I had yesterday, fifteen, sixteen years old, gutshot? Pilar shears off his clothes and I see a neat line of stitches all up his chest. The handiwork looks familiar, so I look at his face, and sure enough, this same kid was in maybe three weeks ago, slashed from sternum to clavicle. You sew 'em up, send 'em out, and two days later they're back. What's the point?"

Bergman is a tall, lanky man, loosely fitted into his body. His blond mane is shaggy, not quite shoulder length but long enough to impact negatively on his waiting time in restaurants. Under his white lab coat, presently sprinkled with potato-chip particles, he wears khaki-colored dungarees, an oversized checkered flannel shirt, and L. L. Bean desert boots. The residents, the nurses, and even the clerks call him by his first name.

Graystone, on the other hand, has never appeared for work without a starched white shirt, a dark tie, and broughams polished to a high sheen. His black hair is clipped short, close to the scalp. His manner is distant but unfailingly courteous; he addresses his nurses as Ms. So-and-So. Anyone who screws up is taken aside; Graystone's reprimands are fierce but private. Humiliation is not one of his teaching tools; neither is camaraderie. Residents and nurses alike call him Doctor, or sir.

Despite appearances, however, Graystone is the artist to Bergman's technician. Graystone's fingers have eyes; he operates by touch, and his diagnoses are informed by a laying on of hands. Bergman is analytical, with a dogged, checklist style of diagnosis. Though neither one is a surgeon, doctors who cover small ERs have to become jacks-of-all-trades. Serious surgical cases are shunted up to OR, but the minor stuff they handle themselves. Like childhood sweethearts who marry straight out of high school, Graystone and Bergman have adapted to each other's styles.

They're longtime friends, a relationship that goes back to Columbia med school. When Graystone was made chief of Mercy's Emergency Department, his first official act was hiring Dan Bergman away from Downstate. He's always assumed they'd go on as they were forever. Lately, though, Daniel's been restive.

"We couldn't just walk out," Graystone says. "This place would collapse without us."

"They got along without us before, they'll survive without us after."

"How?"

"Not our problem, my friend. Look, think about it, okay? Don't just say no."

The door opens, and Douglas Plummer enters without knocking. The gynecologist is a handsome fellow in his early thirties, with slick dark hair, a well-tended mustache, and supercilious eyebrows that waggle at the sight of Graystone and Bergman huddled together. "Am I interrupting something?"

"Do bears shit in the woods?" Bergman asks.

"Love you, too, babe. Which of you guys sent for me?"

"I did," Graystone says. "Room four, thirty-eight-year-old black woman, twelve weeks pregnant, incomplete abortion."

Plummer rolls his eyes. "For this you called me? Treat her and street her, dudes."

"She's bleeding to beat the band. Probably needs a D and C, maybe got some other problems."

"Who's her attending?"

"Hasn't got one."

"Like I didn't know. No insurance, either, I presume?"

"What's it to you, Plummer?"

"Forget about a bed. If she needs surgery, we'll do her straight out of ER."

"Since when are you full up?" Graystone growls.

"One bed left, but I've got an elective coming in this P.M. Private patient, incidentally, not your usual dreck."

"Dude's got a serious attitude problem," Bergman says as the door swings shut behind Plummer.

"Racist asshole."

"Think of it, Tom. We blow this joint, you never have to set eyes on that scumbag again."

"Now *that's* tempting. On the other hand, Dr. Treat'em-and-Street'em could end up head of ER."

"An ob-gyn? No way."

"Some clone, then. Plummer's got a big mouth, but what he says plenty of others believe. I'd have to know who would come after me."

"You can't control what happens after you leave. They could hire the greatest guy in the world to replace you and fire him the next week. It'd be out of your hands."

"That's why I can't let go. We've got a tiger by the tail here."

"You realize what you're doing, Tom? You're making us hostages of the system. You're condemning us both to a life of involuntary servitude."

Graystone smiles at his friend. "Not both. You're free, white, and over twenty-one."

Alice Straugh is holding the patient's hand and talking with her when Dr. Plummer enters room 4. He does a double take when he spots Alice, then gives her the full 250-watt, perfectly capped smile. "Alice."

"Doctor."

"Met your parents the other evening at the BAM benefit. Lovely people."

Alice hands him the patient's chart without comment. He accepts it without taking his eyes off her. "You the twelve-week incomplete abortion?" he asks the patient.

"No, sir," she replies with dignity. "I am the woman just lost her baby."

"Same difference," Plummer says with a wink at Alice. He washes his hands and moves to the foot of the gurney. "Let's take a look."

The patient clamps her knees together. "Would you mind introducing yourself to this end first?"

For the first time, Plummer glances at the patient's face.

He sketches a sardonic bow. "Dr. Plummer, staff physician, ob-gyn. May we proceed now?"

"Can I help you, Doctor?" Alice asks.

"Thank you, love."

She joins him at the foot of the examination table, gently places the woman's legs in stirrups. Blood gushes from her vagina, spilling from the table onto the floor. "Jeez, what a mess," Plummer mutters.

"Sample for Path, Doctor?"

He hesitates. The woman is, after all, uninsured. But Graystone was right, the bleeding is abnormal, and even uninsured patients can sue for malpractice. "Yeah, all right," he mutters. Alice fills a vial, labels and bags it for Pathology.

Plummer inserts a speculum roughly. The patient groans. He shines a light and peers up inside her. "Can't see a damn thing. I'm gonna clean that out a bit. Get me some swabs, dear."

Alice fetches the swabs, long sticks with absorbent cotton on the end. Dear indeed, from this pipsqueak. She'd like to stick those swabs where the sun don't shine. But nothing shows on her well-trained, good-humored face.

Without a word of warning, Plummer widens the speculum opening and thrusts a swab deep inside. The patient screams and jumps three feet straight up from the table.

"Did that hurt?" Plummer asks.

She cannot speak. She wraps her arms around herself and sobs.

Plummer winks at Alice. "You know what we call that?"

"No, what?"

"The chandelier response."

Alice is so angry she nearly chokes on the words caught in her throat. She tells herself her silence is a matter of professionalism, but that's a crock. Alice has never talked back to any doctor, any time.

"Get away, butcher," the patient sobs. "I want a real doctor."

The doctor withdraws the speculum, strips off his gloves, and drops them on the floor. "This is ridiculous. I was hoping to spare you the surgery, but so be it." He signs the admittance papers and leaves the room with one last, soulful glance at Alice.

The woman clutches Alice's hand. "What surgery? Why'd he hurt me like that?"

"They've got to do a D and C. That means they're going to clean out your uterus, just to make sure nothing's left inside that could cause an infection."

"Not him. I won't have that doctor from hell touching me again."

Personally Alice would rather take a coat hanger to herself than open her legs to Plummer. But with no insurance, this woman has to take pot luck. She's lucky Dr. Graystone caught her case to begin with. If it were up to Plummer, he'd have sent her home without the operation.

Alice pats her hand. "You'll be asleep, you won't feel a thing. It won't hurt, I promise." She goes to the foot of the bed and releases the woman's feet from the stirrups. At once the patient pulls up her knees, groaning. "Why'd he do me like that?"

Because he doesn't care, thinks Alice. Silently she strokes the woman's forehead till her quivering subsides.

5

• • • • • • • •

Saturday night, Thomas Graystone arrives early at the Village Cellar, an hour before the first set. Johnny Deacon is back in town for the first time since Blue Durango bought the farm, and Graystone wants to check out the new tenor sax, a Lester Young throwback named Billy Mason. He holds out a twenty, and the kid on the door says, "One?" though Graystone is manifestly alone. "One," he replies, and takes a seat behind the piano, where he can watch Deacon work.

Slowly the room fills, couples straggling in two by two, like Noah's beasts. Graystone, too, used to bring dates on these weekend crawls, but he gave it up as unfair, on them and him, too. The women felt obliged to comment on the music, and usually their comments missed the mark. Afterward, however hard he tried not to, he felt differently about the women. Graystone doesn't approve of wasting good women, and he despises his own intolerance, but there's not a thing in the world he can do about it except to come alone.

The Cellar is hung with photos of jazz musicians who've played the club, which is everyone of note. From where he sits, Graystone sees shots of Charles Mingus, Thelonious Monk, Sweets Edison, McCoy Tyner, Johnny Deacon, Coltrane, Charlie Parker, Ella, Lester Young, Cecil Taylor.

Here and there the odd white face—Borah Bergman, Ran Blake—Sam Roth's nod to equal opportunity. Interspersed among the pinups and nearly obscured by the smoke are red No Smoking signs, his sole concession to city ordinances. "I'll hang 'em," Sam once told Graystone, "but fuck me if I'll enforce 'em." No one else bothers. Even city inspectors recognize limits to their power. Graystone detests the smell of smoke, won't tolerate it in his hospital or his apartment, but it's as much a part of the clubs as the music. Besides tobacco, there's a whiff of marijuana in the air, and some awful stink emanating from the kitchen. The Cellar's cuisine is as foul as it is expensive. No one eats there; Sam uses the food to exterminate rats and tourists.

Graystone's waitress happens by. College girl, by the look of her. "Help you?" she asks in a discouraging tone. He orders a Dewar's, praying his beeper doesn't sound tonight. He's off call, but that's no guarantee.

Johnny Deacon materializes onstage, just sits down at the piano and starts picking at the keys. The audience pretends not to notice, it's not cool to applaud, but Graystone gets a knot in his stomach at the proximity of those blessed hands, the grizzled head, the rangy back in an old tweed jacket. The same jacket, by all appearances, he wore twenty years ago, the first time Graystone heard him play.

Memory floods over him. He's seventeen years old and on the prowl. A warm spring night—he's with his buddies Mickey Weiss and Jeff Rigo, and they're hoping to get laid. They hang around Greenwich Village, score a few drinks with their fake IDs, strike out with a few older women. They're hanging just outside the Cellar, trying to decide what to do next, when someone opens the door and a wisp of music sizzles upward, like steam escaping from a subway grate, like a whiff of perfume. Graystone turns and reads the placard on the window. "Johnny Deacon's playing. Let's go in."

"No way," says Mickey, tossing back his blond hair. "The night's still young, my friend, and there's better fare on the streets."

"You're joking," says Jeff. "Waste a beautiful night like this in a murky cellar?"

But Graystone is hooked. That one sweet lick did it; he can no sooner resist that tantalizing sound than he could have refused a houri.

"You go on," he tells his friends. "I'll catch you later."

While they stand around arguing, a couple of hot-looking unaccompanied blondes squeeze past them into the Cellar. Jeff and Mickey suddenly discover an unsuspected affinity for jazz. They pay the cover and go downstairs.

For Graystone that night, the music comes as a revelation; he hears voices speaking in a tongue he never learned but understands perfectly, and what those voices say, they say to him. The music flows unimpeded from the players to him. It enters his ears, bypasses his brain, and descends directly to his heart, his gut, and his groin. It's not the first time Graystone's heard live jazz. His mother's brothers, when they were still allowed to visit, used to play. But they weren't in Deacon's league, and, anyway, Thomas was too young. *This* music grabs him by the balls.

Mickey and Jeff manage to pick up the blondes, who turn out to be from Great Neck, so everybody's happy. But it's a different order of happiness for Graystone, who, by the end of the evening, would have followed Johnny Deacon anywhere.

That was the summer of his first infatuation, not with a woman but with jazz. After that night, Graystone took to sneaking into the city like an addict bent on a fix. He feasted on Miles Davis, John Coltrane, Dizzy Gillespie. At first it all seemed miraculous, but as he listened he learned, and as he learned he began to discriminate. It wasn't always great music, but the thing about it was, you never could tell when it might be. Sometimes nothing special happened. But once in a while, if he got lucky, there came a moment when the musicians started hoisting each other higher and higher, piling on the riffs and egging each other on till they were playing better than mortal men have any right to play. There were times when Graystone expected them to levitate right off their chairs; there were times he felt he was flying himself. That music carried him places he couldn't get to any other way.

Like all great love affairs, this one met with staunch

opposition. His mother hated it. She didn't mention her brothers, whose offense was never revealed to Thomas, though surely it was connected to the time the cops came knocking on their door, looking for his uncles. Instead, she spoke in generalities about *those kinds of people, that kind of music*. In desperation she presented Graystone with his own personal subscription to the Philharmonic, which the un-grateful boy promptly exchanged for an open ticket to the Greenwich Village Jazz Festival. On the general scale of rebellion, this act surely ranks low; but in the Graystone household it stood as a direct shot across his mother's bow. Elvira was furious. Graystone went out and got himself a summer job loading trucks to pay her back; but he kept the ticket and saw every group that played in the festival.

Now a strident blare of tenor sax brings Graystone back to the present. One by one the band has drifted onstage to join Deacon. As they tune their instruments, the buzz of conversation fades. A casual nod from the leader and they're off. Graystone sees at once that it's going to be one of those nights. The room is transformed.

The piece is "Night Rumble," a Deacon staple. Starts with a blare of brass, trumpet challenging the tenor sax, a jostling, elbow-poking scrap laid over jittery percussion. Trumpet dies, protesting, borne out by the bass; sax is left alone. An eerie, wraithlike tone rises, twisting through the smoky air. Blue Durango used to play this like a vampire, milking the silence, sucking the blood from his listeners' veins. Hearing the remembered notes, Graystone goes cold all over; but the new man doesn't blow like Blue. He's got his own style, a prettier tone, a kinder, gentler sound: a Bush-league musician, Graystone thinks, though he tells himself it's not the man's fault whose footsteps he's treading in. The sax fades, and Deacon comes in on piano, doing something dire with his left hand while his right races across the upper registers. His music's changed since his partner bit the dust, grown darker and deeper. The left hand undermines the right. Don't you believe that right-hand jive, it says. I'm telling you the truth.

Graystone's transfixed by those hands, whose long brown fingers seem to sink into the keys, entering rather than depressing them. The music is born of the intercourse between fingers and keys; there's an intimacy to Deacon's touch, a voyeuristic pleasure in watching. Graystone, like most physicians, is a material man, a concrete thinker, a dyed-in-the-wool cause-and-effecter. Ask him where the soul resides and he'll laugh to scorn: What he can't excise with his scalpel doesn't exist. Nonetheless, his experience of this music is that it emanates from Deacon's soul, somewhere within his solar plexus, and flows outward through his fingers. The soul, in its essence, of a black man.

The last notes of "Night Rumble" fade. There's a brief pause, a kind of shiver, then the room explodes with applause. Deacon swivels on his stool and bows his head. Maybe there's a sardonic glint in his eye, maybe it's Graystone's imagination. "Buddy Jessup on drums," Deacon rumbles, "Mack Holloway on bass, Jordan Reese on trumpet, and I'd like to introduce our newest member, Billy Mason on tenor sax." He starts turning back to the piano, but on the way his eye is arrested by something. Deacon's sudden stillness alerts the others, still linked by the music's umbilical cord. They follow his eyes. Graystone, too, turns around to see someone emerging from the dimness, weaving through the crowded tables: a black woman in a satiny white blouse and dark trousers. There's something careful yet graceful in the way she sets her feet, like someone accustomed to walking on thin ice. She sits at the table reserved for the band. Her profile is oddly familiar to the doctor, who can't quite place it. Is she a singer, a musician, perhaps a patient he once treated? "'Bout time, Missy," Deacon rasps; then, to the audience: "Here's a little piece I wrote for my old buddy, Blue Durango. We call it 'True Blue.'"

It's no dirge. Or if it is, it's the New Orleans variety, a foot-stomping, wake-the-dead boogie-woogie. "True Blue" embodies Blue's life, not his death, and it sets the band to howling and the audience to dancing in their seats. Johnny Deacon kicks away his stool and bends over the piano, pounding the keys. The drummer breaks a stick but doesn't miss a beat, the sax shrills and dips, and the trumpet swings the band. It sounds like twelve people up there. The music hits one climax after another, and just when it seems it can't go any higher, it stops.

Just stops.

In mid-riff.

Stunned silence from the audience.

Deacon turns and spreads his hands. "That's where it's at," he growls. "Don't look at me. I didn't write the script."

The woman at their table stands up and starts to clap. After a moment, the audience joins in. Deacon retrieves his stool, and the set continues.

When the band breaks, Deacon leaps off the stage and sweeps the woman, who has risen to meet him, into his arms. Over his shoulder, her face turns toward Graystone. Now Graystone knows that he knows this woman, but he still doesn't know from where.

CROW

From the steps outside, I hear them playing "Night Rumble," and I like to die. Deacon wrote the piece all right, but Blue made it his own, and hearing it unexpected like that feels like the time a couple months after it happened when I was walking down the street and suddenly a block ahead of me I saw a man walking Blue's walk, wearing a beat-up old leather jacket just like his. I ran up to him, grabbed his arm, spun him around, and saw: a stranger. An imposter. Nobody.

It don't seem right. Deacon should've retired that piece when Blue died. He's got no business handing it over to some Johnny-come-lately: "Here's Blue's soul, try it on." Standing on the steps, I think of turning 'round and going home, I almost do it, then something strange happens. This feeling comes over me, a kind of tingling on my neck, and I get the idea that Blue's standing behind me, and if I just turn around real fast I'll see him there, hopping from foot to foot, anxious to go in to the music and the warmth. "Let's hear what the boy can do. Come on, Crow, give the kid a chance." 'Course I know damn well Blue wouldn't want them retiring that piece, no way in hell he'd stand for that. He always said he learned to blow like he did by perching on the shoulders of giants, and I reckon he'd figure now was his turn to be the shoulders. So I go in.

Sam, perched on a stool by the door, does a double take, nearly falls over his own paunch getting to me. "Long time no see, Crow," he says. We touch cheeks. Mine smells of disinfectant, his of tobacco. "Where the hell you been keeping yourself?"

"Brooklyn," I say.

"Oh, *well.*" He shrugs as if I'd said Mozambique. "Deacon said you might be in. There's a table up front." Sam starts escorting me, but I tell him I know the way. Deacon spots me halfway across the room. His eyes glint; he calls out, "'Bout time, Missy." Then he introduces a new number: "True Blue."

A fine old wild-and-woolly piece of honky-tonk it is, hot licks on the piano and some trumpet and sax riffs sound like cats mating on a tin roof. And just when you think the Cellar's own roof is about to fly off, the piece ends, just stops dead in its tracks like Blue did, no winding down, no easing off, just hit the peak and die. And maybe I should be crying, but I'm laughing inside, because Deacon got him down so right: If you could turn a man into a piece of music, that piece would be Blue Durango.

The audience is silent, peeved at how it ended, not understanding that that's just the way it went down. But Deacon don't care what they think, he's looking at me, and I get to my feet and beat my hands together to tell him what I think, and wouldn't you know the audience follows like sheep. Doesn't matter: Deacon's looking at me and I'm looking at him, both of us grinning like pure fools.

Nobody knew Blue like we knew him. People always had the wrong idea about him on account of his name, which was stuck on him by some newspaper writer when Blue was first coming up. Blue saved the review; he showed it to me once. "Joe Durango played tenor sax, a fiercely talented young musician, but monochromatic: everything he plays comes out a shade of blue." 'Course he was wrong; Blue had no limitations. He could play a tune that'd make you laugh till you cried or dance like a soul possessed; he could play a riff so deep-down raunchy he had all the women and half the men comin' in their seats. But it's fair to say that left to itself, his music just naturally drifted toward the dark side. His sound sprang from life's underbelly; it bore witness to the hard, jagged truth of things. There's times, working in the ER, when they wheel in an accident victim and I glimpse white bone peeking through torn flesh, or I look into a bereaved parent's eyes and see the future stretched out long and bleak and hopeless, and then I wonder how Blue would have played this. Because that's where his music came from, that vestibule between life as we pretend it is and the real thing.

So the name stuck: Blue, a useful moniker, not unfair, but misleading. Folks who knew his music and who watched him onstage, intense and often scowling, took Blue for a hard man. That's true of his music but not of him. Blue surely had a hurtful childhood, bounced from foster home to foster home, abused along the way; things happened he didn't talk about, but he poured all that pain and suffering into his music, freeing himself for joy. I never knew a sweeter man, or a gentler.

After the set ends, Deacon and the boys come over. Deacon lifts me out of my seat and takes me in his arms, and with my eyes shut and my cheek pressed into that old tweed of his, suddenly I'm back at the wedding. Johnny Deacon was Blue's best man, and soon as the service ended, he grabbed me so fast that later Blue complained he never got a chance to kiss his own bride. Deacon hugged me. "Take care of my boy," he rasped in my ear, in that subway voice of his. "Make him happy, Crow."

I open my eyes, and the club swims back into focus. Many faces are turned toward us but one stands out, a man's face studying me. I know that face, but it takes me a moment to figure it out, because it's someone who don't belong in this world of mine, someone from my after life. Then it comes to me: It's Dr. Graystone.

I am not pleased to see him. If there's one thing I don't want, it's getting my before life mixed up with my after. It's surely not that I'm ashamed of what I do now. It's just that they got nothing to do with each other, and that's how I want to keep it.

When Deacon finally lets me go, Buddy steps up and gives me a shy peck on the cheek, Jordan and Mack follow, and then Deacon introduces the sax player.

Boy shakes my hand. "Ma'am, I surely was a fan of your husband. Best damn sax I ever heard, bar none. Hope you don't mind me taking his place in the band."

"You can't take his place," I say real quick.

His face clouds over. "No, ma'am."

"But you got your own sound, and that's just fine." He brightens up then, and we all sit down. Max sends over a round of drinks. "Looks like Crow's got an admirer," Buddy says after a bit. "That cat ain't taken his eyes off of you."

I turn my head toward Dr. Graystone. He's still staring, but I can see from the puzzled tilt of his head that the penny hasn't dropped yet. With luck it never will. "You know him, Crow?" Deacon growls, still looking after Blue's interests.

"Just someone from the 'hood." I give Graystone a fraction of a nod, then shift my chair so he can't see my face.

Deacon raises his glass. "To absent friends," he says.

43

6

. . . .

The child on the examination table doesn't make a sound. His right arm is broken, and there's a large contusion on his left cheek; he's alert, fully conscious, certainly in pain, and yet he doesn't cry. "What a brave boy," Alice Straugh says. "How did you get hurt?"

"He fell," his mother replies.

"What's your name?" asks the nurse.

Again it is the mother who answers. "Noah," she snarls, pacing the tiny examining room like a caged bear. Anger is endemic in the ER, a natural by-product of interminable waiting, but this woman's over the edge. Either she's a psych case, Alice decides, or she's several hours past her fix.

"How old are you, Noah?"

"He's five."

"Can he talk?" snaps Alice.

"'Course he can talk. Kinda dumb-ass question that?"

"Then let him. How did you fall, Noah?"

The child watches his mother. In a soft voice, he says, "I don't know."

"He fell off a chair," the mother says.

"I fell off a chair."

The woman runs her hands through her hair. "Where the hell's that doctor? Keep a person waitin' all day."

44

"I'll go see," Alice says. She goes in search of Graystone, finds him in a treatment room with Calvin Wang, staring at the ECG of a ROMI, a rule-out myocardial infarction. "Looks pretty good," Graystone is saying, "but let's wait for the labs." He glances at Alice and immediately gives her his full attention. "What's wrong, Ms. Straugh?"

"Baby-basher."

"Tell me."

"Room six, Noah Berry. Five-year-old black male, spiral fracture of the humerus, contusions on the opposite side of the face. The mother says he fell."

"You don't believe her."

"No, sir."

"Why not?"

"The boy doesn't cry. He won't talk. He's scared. When I undressed him, I found old bruises all over his body."

"Kids do get hurt. And hospitals are scary places," he says without much hope.

Alice just looks at him.

Graystone sighs. "Okay, I'll have a look. Have we seen this kid before?"

"The mother says not. I'm not sure, but I think I remember them from a few years back."

"Did Radiology do a full workup or just the arm?"

"Just the arm."

"Check with Records, tell Radiology we're sending him back for the works, and call the social worker. Who's on, Ms. Goldblossom? Fill her in. Tell her to put on a lab coat and stethoscope and join me. After I examine the boy, I'll take the mother out, and she can have a shot at him."

"The mother won't leave him."

"Oh, no?" Graystone says grimly. They part at the corner; Alice turns left, toward the records room. Graystone watches her a moment; her back is stiff, and she walks gingerly as if the floor were paved with eggs.

Entering room 6, he sees the woman bent over her son, speaking urgently. At the sound of the door opening, she wheels around.

Graystone introduces himself to the boy, who doesn't answer but fixes the doctor's face with a bright, intent gaze.

Though Graystone has long since grown adept at seeing patients strictly in terms of their symptoms and diagnoses, he can't help noticing this child's eyes, warm and sweet as melted chocolate. He pats the boy's cheek, then turns to the X ray clipped on the screen. The break jumps out at him, a clear spiral fracture of the humerus. Spiral fractures are caused by force applied in a rotary motion. Such an injury might result if, for example, a child's arm were simultaneously wrenched and twisted by a much larger person.

"Let's take a look," he says, bending down to examine the boy's arm. It's bruised and swollen, but not abnormally so for this kind of fracture. Graystone checks first of all for circulation problems. The boy's pulse is strong under his arm, in his elbow and wrist; the arm is warm to the touch, and the color in his nail beds is normal. He manipulates the arm as gently as possible, but cannot avoid inflicting pain. Tears gather in the boy's eyes and roll down his cheeks in eerie silence.

Graystone glances at the mother and sees a coiled spring of a woman, thirtyish, with filthy, matted hair, dull eyes, and muddy skin. The child is lighter in hue and his features are sharper, more Caucasian. Both mother and son are too thin: malnourishment or disease.

"Mrs. Berry, we're going to need some additional X rays, and I want Noah to be seen by a pediatric orthopedist. The bone in his upper arm is fractured. The good news is that circulation appears unimpeded, but we will have to keep him under observation for a while to make sure. How did this happen?"

"I already said. He fell."

"From where?"

"Off a chair." She stares, daring him to disbelieve.

Graystone's face reveals no trace of his thoughts. He unties the boy's hospital gown. The mother stirs uneasily.

"What you doing? It's just his arm's hurt."

The youngster's thin body bears a chronology of abuse, mottled yellow, green, and purple bruises, old burn marks. Though he was forewarned, the severity and extent of bruising catches Graystone off guard; for just an instant, he allows himself to envision the torture that must have gone into the making of those marks. Then, quickly, his mind veers away. He veils his eyes from the mother, but she's in his face, crowding the table, a dark and angry presence.

"I see you've had other accidents," he says to the boy.

Again Noah seeks his mother's eyes. "No, sir," he murmurs.

"Boy's a fighter," the woman says indifferently.

Lorraine Goldblossom, the ER social worker, sweeps into the room, dressed in whites and wearing a stethoscope. Graystone holds the boy's gown open long enough for her to see the bruises, then closes it. "Spiral fracture," he murmurs. They exchange a look. Graystone goes to the door and holds it open. "Mrs. Berry?"

"I ain't going nowhere without my boy."

"He'll be fine. I need some information from you so we can treat that arm. It will take only a few minutes."

Mrs. Berry doesn't want to leave but can't quite summon the nerve to defy the doctor. She glares suspiciously at Lorraine, who returns a bland smile. As soon as the door closes behind them, Lorraine pulls a chair up to Noah's side. She is a woman of a certain age, wife to an orthopedic surgeon in private practice on Long Island, mother of three grown sons. Her hair is frosted, her makeup precise, and her shoes and clothes are quietly expensive. Noah shifts to the extreme edge of the table, as far away from the white lady as he can get.

"Your name's Noah, isn't it?" she says pleasantly. "That's a beautiful name."

The boy says nothing.

"My name is Mrs. Goldblossom, but the children all call me Mrs. G. I work here in the hospital. What do you do, Noah? Do you go to school?"

"Sometimes I go to kindergarten."

"Really! My grandson goes to kindergarten. He loves to paint. What's your favorite thing to do in school?"

His lips purse as he thinks it over.

"Lunch," he says.

Lorraine looks at his toothpick arms and sighs. "What do you like to play with?"

"Blocks. I can build a really tall tower. Taller than the ceiling."

"That's pretty tall."

"Even taller," he boasts, leaning on his good elbow.

"Wow. Do you build towers at home, too?"

"No, I ain't got no blocks at home."

"Who do you live with, Noah?"

"Mommy."

"Just you and Mommy?"

He nods. "Sometimes I stay with Grandma."

"Do you know where you are now?"

"In the hospital."

"Why are you here, Noah? Do you know?"

"My arm."

"That must really hurt," Lorraine says sympathetically. "How did it happen, Noah?"

At once his eyes go to the door. "I fell. Off a chair."

"Who was home when you fell?"

"Mommy."

"Was she in the room with you?"

Clattering footsteps approach; voices are raised in the corridor. Noah clutches the front of his hospital gown, working the fabric. "I don't know."

Lorraine moves into his line of sight. "Listen to me, Noah. I'm going to tell you something very important. Are you listening?"

He nods.

"I know that right now your arm is hurting a lot, but the doctors and nurses are going to fix it so it's good as new. What you have to know is that this is a safe place. No one can harm or punish you here. If anybody hurt you outside of here, no matter who it was, we can stop them from ever hurting you again. We can keep you safe, but only if you talk to us. Noah, can you tell me exactly how your arm got hurt?"

His eyes look trapped. "I fell," he whispers.

"Did somebody tell you what to say?"

The doorknob twists. Noah's chest begins to heave. "You leave me alone, or my mama's gonna hit you."

"Does she hit?"

"Only if people is bad."

Then the door opens, and the mother rushes in, her face twisted with rage. Lorraine turns and spreads her arms. Beyond Mrs. Berry, she glimpses Alice Straugh, Dr. Graystone, and Henry Murchison, the security guard, all converging on the room.

Noah begins to scream: "She don't hit me, she never hit me, swear to God I didn't say nothing, Mama, I didn't tell, don't be mad, I'll be good I'll be good I'LL BE GOOD!"

Long ago, before Pilar's day even, the ER nurses had a lounge all their own. It was a cozy, comfortable room, furnished with armchairs, a Naugahyde sofa, a small refrigerator, and an electric ring for boiling water. No such room exists now, of course. The ER in its present incarnation has no space for luxuries. Nowadays if a nurse needs to drink a cup of coffee or just escape the chaos for a few minutes, she must take her break either at the nurses' station, under the wrathful eyes of patients who've been waiting for hours, or in the staff ladies' room. That's where Lorraine Goldblossom finally tracks down Alice Straugh.

"There you are," she says; then, noticing Alice's reddened eyes: "Are you all right?"

"Why shouldn't I be?" the nurse says gruffly. "I've seen a million of these kids."

Lorraine's voice is smooth and poised, a finely calibrated professional tool. "It's okay to feel hurt, Alice. We're not machines here."

Blotting her face with a paper towel, Alice avoids the mirror. She's a mess: eyes and nose bloodshot, hair in fiery disarray.

"Spare me the I'm-okay-you're-okay cant, okay? I don't need permission to feel bad."

"Of course you don't," Lorraine says.

The door swings open, and the two women look up. But it's only Crow with her cart.

"I don't want to hear you're giving that boy back," Alice says fiercely.

"We've put him on direct relief," the social worker says, stroking Alice's arm. Direct relief is hospital code for protective custody. "In the end, though, as you know, it's not our call. Child Welfare will decide."

Alice snatches back her arm. "What's to decide? You saw the kid's body."

"Saw the X rays, too. Radiology confirms two old breaks. I spoke to the mother, and her story's bullshit. But that doesn't necessarily mean she's the one."

"You heard the boy!"

"He *said* she didn't do it."

"And begged her not to do it again. For heaven's sake, Lorraine."

"It's not a matter of what you or I happen to believe. It's a matter of interventive appropriateness."

"You're copping out."

"No, *you're* getting too invested."

Alice bends over the sink, splashes cold water on her face, then rubs it briskly with a paper towel until her fair skin glows.

Lorraine draws a deep breath. "A case like this," she says, "you've got to choose between two evils. You take the boy from his mother, he gets fed into the child-welfare system. Foster care's no picnic, and the system is nobody's friend. The best thing for the child, if we can work with the mother, try to raise her self-esteem—"

A loud bang interrupts her. Crow has just slammed her mop against a porcelain washstand. She's shaking her head, muttering under her breath.

Lorraine arches an eyebrow. "Is there a problem, er . . ." She looks at Alice, who mouths the name. "Is there a problem, Crow?"

"Me, I've got no problem," Crow says without looking up. "That little boy's got a problem."

"Yes, he does, and we're trying our very best to resolve it."

Her tone is patronizing. Alice glances nervously at Crow, who straightens and plants her hands on her hips.

"Yeah," she says, "by raising that bitch's self-esteem."

Lorraine blinks. "It so happens that all the current research points to low self-esteem as the primary cause of child-abuse syndrome. That means . . ."

"I *know* what it means. I may not be up on *all the current research,* but at least I've got the sense I was born with."

The social worker looks as if she just swallowed a toad. "Meaning I don't?"

"Meaning if the shoe fits . . ."

Alice intercedes. "What would you do, Crow?"

"I'd stop her."

"How?"

"I'd teach her that what goes around comes around."

"What, break her arm?" bleats the nurse.

"Did she do that? Absolutely break her arm. Be the last time she ever raise it to a child."

"Barbaric," mutters Lorraine. "Totally inappropriate."

Crow regards her from somewhere deep behind her eyes. "No ma'am. Beating babies, now, *that's* inappropriate."

"Crow's right," says Alice.

"Where's your compassion?" Lorraine asks.

"I got plenty," says Crow. "For the child."

"Hear, hear," Alice mutters.

Lorraine flashes her an exasperated look. "I would expect *you* at least to understand the psychosocial complications of poverty. Think where this woman's coming from. Poor, black, a single mother—"

"I'm poor," says Crow. "I'm black. I'm single. Does that mean I'm not responsible for what I do? There ain't nothing that girl been through hasn't happened to me and worse— but I'd cut off my hand before I'd raise it to my boy."

Alice applauds fiercely.

Suddenly the door bursts open. "Jesus Christ," says Pilar in disgust. "Is this a hospital or a damn convention hall? Alice, I got an ER full of pissed-off customers, two nurses out, and here you are contemplatin' your navel. Lorraine, CWA is looking for you."

They leave, Alice with a tentative smile at Crow, and Crow is left alone to work in peace. Just as well, because if she'd had to listen to any more jive about the self-esteem of baby-bashers, she'd have treated that condescending honkie liberal to a taste of home-style justice. When some white lawyer and his crackhead girlfriend beat their white child to death, that's a scandal, a disgrace, and a crime; but when a working-class black woman does the same, it's "What can you expect, consider where she's coming from." If that's not racism, Crow would damn well like to know what is.

She attacks the floor with a vengeance, then moves on to the sinks and mirrors. By the time she finishes, the ladies' room is gleaming: anger transformed into cleanliness, Crow's version of immaculate conception.

Having not yet seen this child who reduced Alice Straugh to tears, Crow detours on her way to the waiting room, nudges open the door to room 6, and peeks inside. Surprisingly the little boy is all alone, a tiny figure dwarfed by the adult-sized examination table. He's sleeping calmly, both his arms strapped down, an IV feeding into the left hand. As she watches, his eyes suddenly fly open and connect with hers. Crow smiles from the doorway. "How you doing, baby?"

Solemn eyes regard her warily. "Okay."

Crow looks up and down the hall, then steps inside the cubicle, leaning her mop against the wall. "I got a little boy just about your age. How old are you?"

"Five. How old's your boy?"

"He's four."

"I'm bigger than him."

"Yes, you are." But he's not. This child's scrawny, bones no thicker than a chicken's leg, half the weight of her son, fattened on love.

The boy's eyes dim, his eyelids flutter shut as he falls back under the spell of the sedatives. Crow watches him a moment longer. Such a sweet-faced little thing; well-spoken, too. How could his mama do him like that? As she turns to go, her eye falls on a figure standing motionless in the far corner of the room.

Crow gasps, clutching her chest. "Damn, you scared the life out of me!" In quick succession she sees that it's a stranger, a white man, a doctor, the same doctor she saw the other day.

He fastens a deep blue gaze on her. "Look under Jackson," he says.

"Say what?"

"Jackson."

"Who are you?" Crow demands, taking hold of her mop.

"He's been here before."

"Wait right here," she says, backing out of the room. "Don't move."

She runs to the nurses' station. Pilar is on the far side, triaging a customer. Crow hisses.

Pilar looks back over her shoulder. "That you, Crow? What you want?"

"Could I see you?"

"Not now, I'm busy."

"It's *him,*" she whispers desperately.

"Him who?"

"Him, that doctor I saw the other day, remember the boy with the busted spleen?"

"*That* him." Pilar moves with her deceptive speed across the nurses' station to Crow's side. "Where?"

"Room six."

She tears down the hall, Crow on her heels. Room 6 is empty save for the patient.

Crow says, "I swear to God. He spoke to me."

"What'd he say?"

"He said the boy's been here before. He said, 'Check under Jackson.'"

Pilar's eyes narrow. "You shitting me?"

"Hell, no. He was here."

They return to the corridor. A bored-looking cop leans against the wall, guarding a prisoner handcuffed to a stretcher. "Anybody come outta this room?" Pilar demands. The cop shakes his head. Pilar strides down the hallway, opening every closed door. Crow sticks to her like a skinny shadow. There's no sign of the intruder; no one else has seen him. The last door connects the Emergency Department to the rest of Mercy General. It is kept locked and can be opened only by punching in a code.

"He must've gone through there," Crow says. "It's the only possibility."

"There's one more possibility."

"What's that?"

"You need your head examined." But Pilar regrets the words even as she speaks them, because she sees this is no crock; the unflappable Crow is truly spooked.

As soon as she gets a moment, Pilar goes over to records. Under the name of Jackson, she finds eighteen patient files: eleven for females, six for adult males, and one, dated two years back, for a three-year-old black male named Noah Jackson who presented with second-degree burns on the palms of both hands.

She skims the file with a practiced eye. The mother claimed the baby accidentally touched a hot stove, but the depth and extent of the burns indicated that his hands had been in contact with the heat source for about ten seconds. The resident also noted contusions and bite marks on the patient's body.

Child Welfare was called in. The ensuing investigation turned up nothing conclusive. The mother finally admitted that the child had been abused, but she blamed the abuse on a boyfriend who could not be found. Ultimately CWA released the patient to his mother's care.

There are photographs, a little blurred but good enough. The face is younger, still unformed, but the huge, hurting eyes are unmistakably those of Noah Berry.

7

· · · · · · · ·

Alice balances two grocery bags on her hip, unlocks the door, pushes it open, enters, and kicks it shut behind her. There's a whiff of cigar smoke in the air, and the television's on. "Daddy?" she calls.

"We're in here," her mother's voice trills from the living room. Alice turns the other way, into the kitchen.

The room is cold, the stove unlit. Muttering under her breath, Alice sets the oven to 450°, shrugs off her coat, and unpacks the groceries: feta cheese, olives, romaine lettuce, carrots, plum tomatoes, pine nuts, new potatoes, mint jelly, milk and juice for the children, beer for her sister's husband. Brooke and her family are in from Chicago this week, and Alice has offered them dinner; her parents invited themselves. She takes the leg of lamb she marinated yesterday out of the fridge and puts it on the table, spreads two sheets of paper towel on the countertop, and starts peeling carrots.

Her mother enters in a cloud of *Magie Noir*. "Hello, darling. We let ourselves in."

"Mom, I asked you to preheat the oven for me."

"Did you? Sorry, I forgot."

Alice's back is unresponsive. Dasha plants a kiss on top of

her head and sprawls gracefully in a kitchen chair. "You look tired, darling. Hard day at Merciless?"

Not for the first time, Alice wishes she'd never shared the hospital's nickname with Dasha. Where is it written she had to tell her parents everything? The question makes her think of Noah. Pilar always says you can't bring the job home, and Alice knows it's true; yet she can't stop worrying about this kid. What will become of him? If CWA doesn't hand him back to the mother, which they are perfectly capable of doing, then they'll feed him into the system, and Lorraine was right about one thing: Foster care is no picnic. Without the dubious protection of maternal love, the little ones are so helpless, so vulnerable. And Noah is pretty. In the world outside this apartment, bad things happen to pretty children.

She chops the head off a carrot and remembers Crow saying "Absolutely break her arm." An eye for an eye, a bone for a bone: Street justice meets biblical justice, and both come out on top. Something about the housekeeper fascinates Alice. Crow always seems so sure of herself, so solid. Lorraine had been foolish to patronize her. There's an aura about Crow, not only of intelligence, but also of subterranean danger, a hidden precipitateness. She's like an off-duty gunslinger in a saloon: not there to do you any harm, but you wouldn't want to rile her.

"Alice?" her mother says. "You look a thousand miles away."

"Just planning what to do. I have to finish the vegetables, make the salad . . . I haven't even showered, and now I have to wait fifteen minutes for the oven to heat up before I put the lamb in."

"Poor baby. Can I help?"

"You could set the dining-room table."

"Of course." Dasha looks around vaguely for the plates, as if expecting them to materialize.

"First the cloth," Alice says, as if to a child. She points with the peeler: "Then plates, napkins, silverware, and glasses." There was a time when she found Dasha's ineptitude in the kitchen charming; it is, after all, the only place where her mother defers to her. Lately, however, she's been unable to resist the subversive observation that there is method to Dasha's vagueness. A woman who once cooked an eighteen-pound turkey with the plastic wrapping intact cannot be expected to pull her fair share of KP.

Dasha wanders from the kitchen to the dining room carrying a couple of plates or a handful of silverware each trip, telling a complicated story about friends who are getting a divorce. Alice makes sympathetic noises and tunes out. The peeling, chopping, and garnishing are automatic, even soothing; they occupy her hands while her mind hovers in the space between the ER and home. She sprinkles the lamb with one last pinch of thyme, puts it in the oven, and lowers the temperature to 350°. Should be 325°, but it's too late; she's got to cut corners.

Her father's voice, full of disgust, booms in the living room. "Jesus Christ, what an asshole."

"Hockey," Dasha says, rolling her eyes.

At work Richard never speaks an ill-considered word, but at home he cuts loose. Alice admires but cannot emulate this linguistic faculty, which her sister Brooke shares. When they were kids, Brooke tried to teach her.

"Repeat after me: Freddy Renier is an asshole."

"Freddy Renier is . . ." Her mouth worked. *"Freddy Renier is an . . . Freddy Renier is . . ."*

"Spit it out!"

"Freddy Renier is an idiot!"

With the lamb safely tucked into the oven, Alice goes in to greet her father. He raises his face for her kiss without taking his eyes off the screen. "Do you believe these bums?" he groans.

"Rangers losing again?" Alice asks, pretending an interest she doesn't feel. It's not that she's unwilling. Her father's favorite sport is football. Alice has tried to learn the game, not because she liked it, but for his sake: He had no son to watch with him. Once, Richard took her with him to a Giants–Forty-Niners match. She sat in his box, and for the first quarter all went well. Her father explained the strategy, and Alice began to perceive an odd grace in the game. Seen from high above, the complicated patterns woven by the players resembled a quadrille danced by buffalos.

Early in the second quarter, a Giants receiver was flattened by two San Francisco steamrollers. When the play was whistled dead, he lay still on the field. At once, Alice's nursing instincts kicked in. "Immobilize him!" she screeched at the field. "Get his vital signs!" She started toward the door; Richard had to grab her arm.

She turned on him. "Did you see that? Did you see those two big bruisers crash right into him? They could have snapped his spine, the fools."

"It's part of the game, dear," he said, but Alice continued to fret about the injured player long after he had returned to the game. At halftime her father took her home: the end of Alice's football career.

She leaves her father and climbs the winding staircase to the master suite. Stripping off her uniform, she steps into the glass-enclosed shower. By the time she emerges, Brooke's family has arrived. She hears them downstairs: the children shrieking in the backyard, John's deep voice remonstrating. Alice dresses quickly in jeans and a cotton pullover and blow-dries her hair to its natural state of anarchic frizz.

As she descends, Brooke's gurgling laugh rises up to meet her. "Of course, three's ridiculous these days," she's saying in a tone of self-mockery.

Her sister sits on the sofa, bracketed by their parents. Like their mother, Brooke is a beauty. Firstborn, she'd claimed the best of both parents' features: their mother's almond eyes, their father's wide, firm mouth and brow. Bright and social, an early talker and incorrigible flirt, Brooke so delighted her parents that they vowed never to have another child. "Why tamper with perfection?" they'd asked one another. Besides, they were so busy, Dasha with her charities and social calendar, Richard with his law firm.

Thus Alice was and has always known herself to be an unplanned event ("but not an unwelcome one," Dasha always trills at this point in the story). Born three days before Christmas, she was brought home on Christmas Eve and laid in a carry cot underneath the tree.

"Look what a lovely Christmas present we've brought

you," her parents had cried, as four-year-old Brooke pranced into the room.

Brooke knelt beside the cot. Gently she lifted up the filmy pink blanket that covered the infant. "A baby!" she cried, hugging herself in ecstasy. "A real, live baby! Oh, Mommy, can we keep it?"

"Forever and ever," Dasha said, smiling fondly at her firstborn. "She's your baby sister."

Brooke bent close to the cot, examining the baby closely. Slowly the excitement and joy faded from her face. Her little eyebrows drew together in a worried frown, and she caught her lower lip between her teeth.

"But Mommy," she said at last, looking up, "she's so ugly."

This story has become a cornerstone of family lore, a set piece trotted out each year together with the tree decorations and eggnog cups. And though Alice always smiles and laughs with the others at Brooke's adorable drollery, privately she thinks the story would have been a lot funnier if she'd grown up to be beautiful, or at least pretty. But, Brooke having had the pick of the familial genes, Alice was stuck with the leftovers. She was not ugly but ordinary, her face good-natured but plain, her complexion muddied with freckles. In Alice, Dasha's sleek auburn hair had degenerated into a dire red, the kind of Orphan Annie crop that incites perfect strangers to address one on the street as "Red." Still, some advantage might have resulted if Alice's temperament had matched her hair color, but as it turned out, she was a troglodyte in a family of swans: slow and deliberate in everything she did, a cautious child, generally tractable though given to odd bursts of unshakable stubbornness, the very opposite of her mercurial sister.

It must be understood that such a child, unbidden, unwished for, and unfortunate, came as a disappointment to parents accustomed to perfection. Dasha and Richard were so careful not to play favorites that it was obvious they had one; and neither Brooke nor Alice ever doubted who it was.

Even in the matter of the baby's name, they deferred to

Brooke. Dasha liked Chloe, and Richard favored Caroline; but Alice was Brooke's adamant choice, based on her recent acquaintance with Lewis Carroll's classic, and she prevailed.

Alice. Such a dull name, so fatally suitable. Although she cannot remember a time when she did not loathe her name, Alice has never blamed its bestower. Sibling rivalry is pointless in a contest so uneven; thus the sisters lived in harmony. Throughout grade school, Brooke had assumed the role of Alice's protector, enveloping her sister in the mantle of her own popularity. Adolescence was not kind to Alice, who by the age of twelve had achieved her adult height of five-six. Gangly as a green colt, Alice could not hide in the shadow of her petite sister. One day in the autumn of her freshman year, they were walking through the lunchroom when a voice, intended to be heard, spoke behind them. "Look, guys," it said, "Beauty and the Beast." After that, Alice transferred to an all-girls' prep school: in terms of self-esteem, a classic case of locking the barn door after the horse has escaped.

"Guess what Brookie's gone and done again," Dasha calls out now, as Alice enters the room. Brooke smiles beatifically.

"All on her own?" asks Alice, bending down to brush her sister's cheek.

"With minimal help," Brooke says. "Hello, Alice. Didn't realize you were home."

"You thought perhaps dinner was cooking itself?"

"Good point. What is that luscious smell?"

"Roast lamb. It's going to take a little while. I hope you're not starving."

"Mea culpa," Dasha says, striking her chest. "I forgot to turn on the stove."

Brooke casts up her eyes. "How do you put up with her?"

Alice smiles. "Did I get it right? Congratulations are in order?"

"By this time next year, you'll be an aunt of three."

"Boy or girl?"

"Too early to tell. Besides, I don't think I want to know this time. Takes all the suspense out of it."

"Have you told the kids?"

"Oh, *they*'re thrilled. They're fighting over whose room it's going to sleep in."

"You're not?" Alice ventures.

"I don't hate the idea. John's delighted, of course. He's not the one who has to give birth."

Dasha says, "But you're so good at it, darling. People should do what they're good at."

"Somebody's got to supply the grandchildren," Richard puts in. "Alice certainly isn't holding up her end."

Brooke and Dasha laugh, Brooke a bit uneasily, but Alice sits dumb as a post, unsmiling.

When they were children, it was always Brooke who wanted a career, she who wanted a family with lots of children. Then they grew up, and Brooke dabbled for several years in publishing before settling gratefully for domestication; while Alice, married and divorced without issue, made her work her life.

But though she'd given up on marriage, she never—and shouldn't her mother *know* this?—never stopped wanting children. Alice stares down at her lap until the laughter dies an uneasy death.

"Just a joke, darling," Dasha says. "Don't be so *serious.*"

The French doors fly open, and John and the children blow into the room on a blast of autumn wind. Their racket, the laughter and chatter of the adults, create a cozy, noise-filled space. The children converge on Alice, who hugs them and slips Hershey bars into their hands: "For after dinner."

"What's for dinner?" Jason demands. "I'm starving."

"Roast leg of lamb, rice, and a Greek salad," Alice says proudly: not bad for a Monday night.

"Yuck! I want a hamburger."

"Jason!" his parents cry simultaneously.

Three-year-old Amanda pipes up, "I want peanut butter and jelly."

"I better check the roast, or we'll all be eating peanut butter," Alice says, but as she rises, the children launch themselves at her, knocking her down onto the floor. Laughing, she gets on all fours to wrestle with them.

Dasha pulls her feet in and looks on bemusedly, with the

air of an anthropologist amid cannibals. Brooke remonstrates lazily, without measurable effect. It's John who comes to Alice's rescue, lifting Jason and Amanda by the napes of their necks and carrying them across the room toward the television. They struggle at first, but as soon as the screen comes alive, they float to the floor like autumn leaves. John returns to the adults and offers Alice a hand. "Wonderful invention, the television. Turn it on and the kids off, all in one switch."

They kiss. John's a big-boned man, six-three, with huge, competent hands. Though Alice often feels uncomfortable with large men—Charlie, her ex-husband, was six foot two and looms even larger in her nightmares—she likes John's natural courtesy, his easy, gentling manner. He's a man she could imagine working with horses or building a canoe; and in fact he does work with his hands, though in nothing so rustic; he's a dentist in Chicago.

The oven timer chimes, and Alice hurries into the kitchen. John ambles in after her. She puts him to work slicing the roast while she tosses the salad. The bone in the middle makes carving tricky, but John is handy with a knife.

"How's business?" she asks.

"Thriving. Bit of a turnover, though."

She looks a question.

"Lot of AIDS patients," he says, tasting the lamb. "Yum."

"How come?"

"I don't seek them out, that's for sure. It's just, a lot of dentists won't treat them, so those who will get stuck with more than their fair share."

"Does it worry you?"

"Let's put it this way. The first bill I pay each month is my life insurance." He raises a shoulder, lets it drop. "You do what you can. I get regular blood tests, take all the precautions, and hardly ever have sex with my patients."

Sputtering, Alice takes a jar of mint jelly from the refrigerator, spoons it into a cruet.

"How about you?" he says. "How's life in the ER treating you?"

In hospital hierarchy, top rank consists of heart surgeons, neurosurgeons, and transplant specialists. Dentists don't even register on the physician's scale of machismo; and don't they know it. "Same old same old," Alice answers deprecatingly.

"Any interesting cases lately?"

"The usual mess. Today we had this homeless woman, presents with pain in her left ear. Turned out she had a live—"

John raises a hand. "Please, not before dinner. I meant the good stuff, the six-o'clock-news stuff. You must get plenty of trauma. You're right on the front line."

"We get our daily trauma fix. And you're right, it's a war zone."

"Lot of drugs?"

"Drugs, and all the other poverty-related illnesses. Everything you can imagine. Last week I had a fourteen-year-old girl with abdominal pain, big as a house, swore on the Bible she wasn't pregnant and went on swearing it till I laid a six-pound baby boy in her arms. You send 'em home, knowing they'll be back."

"Well, I guess you double as the neighborhood clinic."

Alice sprinkles cherry tomatoes into the salad and tosses it with unwonted vigor. "You've got that right. And of course practically nobody's got insurance. You can tell who does and who doesn't just by how they approach the triage desk. Patients with insurance come strutting up, demanding service like they own the joint. The others slink in like stray dogs expecting to get kicked. Meanwhile, the government plays with our funding like a kid with a yo-yo, and we end up subsidizing patient care out of our own operating budget, which reduces the amount of care we can provide. It's nuts. And no one in Albany gives a darn."

"A damn," John says.

"Whatever."

8

· · · · · · ·

By Friday afternoon the emergency room is overflowing. Every seat in the waiting room is occupied; the treatment slots are full, and patients on stretchers clog the corridors. With no free beds in the medical and pediatrics wards, the ER backs up even more. Carla Esperanza, the unit manager, is tearing her hair out, trying to foist patients on other hospitals who'd rather not, thank you. The triage pile keeps growing.

At seven the night shift comes on. Pilar sits in the nurses' station in front of a large mounted blackboard that lists patients' names, slot numbers, and assigned nurses and residents. She's going over charts with the night charge nurse, Maria Viscotto. "Crash room one, we got a twenty-six-year-old white male, motorcycle versus lamppost, multiple trauma, stabilized, awaiting surgery. Crash room two, a seventy-three-year-old Latino male, stroke. Neurology say he blew a vessel in the right parietal area; they're working on a bed upstairs. Room three, forty-four-year-old black female, febrile, white blood count off the wall, sudden onset, etiology unknown. ID's is all jammed up; Carla's trying to transfer. Room four, the catch of the day, ready for this? White male, twenty-eight, presented with his penis stapled to his abdomen."

"What the . . . ?"

"Don't ask. Room five, eighteen-year-old black male, brought in by EMS, unconscious, in rapid A-fib. Underlying path probably drug-related. Cardiology said they sending someone, but that was a hour ago."

"I'll call them." Maria makes a note.

"Room six, sixteen-year-old black male, shot in the foot. On line for surgery. Room seven we're trying to transfer: six-year-old black female, double pneumonia. Eight, you got Preacher."

"Not again. Is he Jesus?"

"I guess so. He called me Martha and told me to wash his damn feet. Lorraine was trying to line up a detox, but I don't think she got anywheres. Then you got four in the hall. Three-A, black male, twenty-four, concussion, head versus baseball bat, waiting on neurology. Four-A, thirty-four-year-old Latin female, AIDS and active TB. Six-A, five-year-old black male, spiral fracture of the humerus."

"Noah? Is he still here?"

Pilar nods. "No beds upstairs, and we can't release him to the mother. Don't let her near him."

"Got it."

"Seven-A, twenty-one-year-old white male brought in by EMS with seizures. No history of seizures. Pending lab work, assume drug-related. EKG indicates possible MI; Carla's working on transferring him, too."

"Bet they're standing on line."

"Right. Also you got a couple emergents in the triage pile."

"Jesus, what a zoo."

"Yeah, well, it's that time of month."

They exchange a look. There's a saying in the business: Full moons fill emergency rooms. Maria says, "Remember when a harvest moon was romantic? Go on, get out of here."

"That's okay, I'll stick around till you get up to speed. Oh yeah, your housekeeper called in sick."

Maria smacks her forehead. "Damn her, that's the fourth time this month."

"I think ours is still here."

"Be an angel, will you?" Maria gathers up the charts with a harried air.

Pilar lumbers to her feet and goes off in search of Crow.

Crow is in the doctors' lounge, mopping the floor. It's not part of her daily routine, which usually ends with one last pass through the corridors, but tonight the ER halls are so crowded she can't even see the floors, much less wash them. The lounge is empty when she begins, but soon after she gets started, Drs. Graystone and Wang come in. They sit at the table in the middle of the room. Neither greets Crow, not out of rudeness but simply because they don't notice her. Even when they lift their feet for her mop, the doctors don't see her. Crow doesn't mind. She enjoys the privileges bestowed by invisibility. In her presence, people talk as they would in perfect privacy.

Graystone is signing out to Wang, going over the patient roster. "How the hell did he manage that?" Wang asks of room 4, the stapled penis.

"Lovers' spat. Guy spread it around too thin, so his boyfriend decided to teach him a lesson."

"Kind of a New Age chastity belt." Wang is having a hard time containing his laughter. Graystone is fair with his residents, doesn't feel the need to inflict on them the agonies he suffered as a resident, but there are some things he won't tolerate. Mocking patients, even behind their backs, is one of his taboos.

There's a tap on the door, and Alice Straugh peeks in. "Okay if I feed Noah in here?"

"Sure," they reply in unison. In a short time, little Noah has become the ER pet. Alice wheels him in, strapped in a wheelchair, his right arm in a sling. He ought to be walking, there's nothing wrong with his legs, but they can't have a child running around underfoot in the ER; so until they can transfer him upstairs, Noah is confined to a chair during the day, a stretcher at night.

"How're you doing, champ?" asks Graystone.

"Hot to trot," says Noah. "Mean and lean." They laugh; he basks in their approval. Most patients diminish in the hospital, losing vitality when they shed their street clothes;

but away from his mother, this child seems to flourish. Alice sits down beside him and starts cutting up his meat, putting food on the fork and the fork into his left hand.

"Aren't you off, Ms. Straugh?" Graystone asks.

"I signed out. It's just such a madhouse tonight, I figured no one would have time to sit down and feed Noah. And he likes company, don't you, Noah?"

He nods, his mouth full.

"How's the food?" Wang asks.

"Great," the boy says fervently. "They give you a lot. Hiya," he says to Crow.

"Hi yourself," Crow replies. She's finished the floor and is dusting off the doctors' desk and the photos of the house staff on the wall. Suddenly she freezes. Staring at one of the group portraits on the wall, she polishes the glass with her dust rag and brings her face up close. "That's him. Jesus, that's him!"

Alice looks up. "Who?"

"That doctor. The one I saw. The one who told me about the kid's busted spleen and that other thing." She glances at Noah and away.

In a moment, Alice and Graystone are beside her. "Which one?" asks Graystone. Crow points to a tall gray-haired man standing in the center back row of a group shot. A young man in the front row holds a hand-lettered sign: MERCY ER HOUSE STAFF, 1976.

"Who is he?" asks Alice.

Graystone squints at the captionless photo. "No idea. Before my time. Maybe Ms. Johnston would know. I think she was here then."

"Did I hear somebody taking my name in vain?" says Pilar, entering the room. "Crow, I been looking all over for you. Maria asks can you stay on a while tonight, night housekeeper's out sick."

"Pilar, look. It's that doctor." Crow points, laughing with relief.

Pilar looks from the photo to her and back again. Her eyes narrow. "You saw *him?*"

"Yes!"

"You never."

"What you talking about, Pilar?"

"I'm talking about you're full of shit is what I'm talking about." She turns to Graystone. "Don't you know who that is?"

He doesn't reply. He's staring at Crow.

"Come on, Pilar," Alice groans. "Tell us."

"It's Elias."

The room is silent, except for the steady clink of Noah's fork against his plate.

"Who's kidding who?" Crow says.

Pilar removes the photograph from the wall and turns it around, revealing a caption pasted onto the back. She points. "E. Glass. Elias."

"Good one, Crow," says Alice with a thin laugh. "You really had us going."

"Yeah, real funny." Pilar's eyes declare her unamused.

Crow says nothing.

"Elias?" calls Dr. Wang from the table. *The* Elias?"

"The one, the only, the late," Pilar says grimly.

Crow takes the photo from Pilar, turns it over, studies the face. Blue eyes meet hers. The doctor has a pleasant face, not smiling, but warm nonetheless. His hair is gray, his eyes deep-set, his eyebrows bushy, his gaze the same as when she saw it last: intense, personal, and focused on her. She returns the picture to Pilar.

"I made a mistake," she says flatly, then turns and walks steadily out of the room.

Alice turns at once to Pilar. Her face is so pale the freckles stand out in bas-relief. "That was no mistake."

"She was shitting us."

"Uh-uh. No way. I saw her face. I thought she was going to faint."

"She was shitting us," Pilar repeats emphatically.

"Why should she?"

"Who the hell knows."

"It's a joke," Dr. Wang says, his accent more pronounced than usual. "A practical joke. To stir things up, to get some attention."

"Crow's not like that," Alice says. "She wasn't joking. You could see she wasn't."

"So what is your idea? You believe in ghosts?"

"Of course not."

"Then what just happened?"

No one answers. They turn as one to Graystone, who still hasn't said a word. "What do you think, sir?" Wang asks.

Graystone doesn't hear him. He's staring after Crow, at the closed door; and he looks stunned, as if he's the one who'd seen a ghost.

CROW

I don't believe in ghosts, that's the first thing. A person believe in ghosts, she be all the time looking over her shoulder. That ain't no way to live. I can't afford to believe, because if there's such things as ghosts, then Blue's a ghost; he's out there somewhere, drifting, all alone. That cannot be.

I don't believe in ghosts. But I saw Elias Glass, not once but twice. I didn't imagine it. I didn't even know he was a damn ghost till I saw his name on that picture, but once I saw it I knew, no room for doubt. It don't make sense, but it's a fact.

I keep thinking I ought to feel more scared than I do. At first I was shocked. I was shaking so bad inside, it was all I could do to leave that room without letting it show. All them people gaping at me.

I go hide in the supply room. I pull my knees up to my chest and breathe deep like they teach you in birthing classes. After a while my head stops spinning and I feel better. I ask myself, Why me? Why should I be the one? I got nothing to do with the doctors here. Their world and mine don't even touch. I'm invisible to them, and I like it like that; invisibility suits who I am now, it accords with my nature. And yet when Pilar said his name, I was struck dumb, not from fear, but with a stunning lack of surprise. I felt, *Of course.* Of course I see him. Of course I'm the one. Ain't I got one foot in that camp myself? Don't I know how close we are, the living and the dead?

That close we are, a breath, a heartbeat, a blink away. A person can be sitting with a person's head in her lap, awash in his blood; a person can be looking in a person's speaking eyes and suddenly the light's extinguished, like someone pulled the plug:

One moment he's altogether there, next moment he's altogether gone and her left holding an empty shell. And a person can cry out, Come back, come back! in a voice to compel, to draw the other back; a person can hold the shell tight in readiness and scream a person's name, knowing he's near 'cause she can feel it, and besides, how far could he have got? a person can know that somewhere just beyond her grasp there's a word, a tone, a way of looking that will bring him back, but she can't find it and with every passing moment he's slipping away, slipping away, oh Lord.

I put my head down and weep: for me, for Blue, for the one-way door, for the irreversibility of time. Then I quit, 'cause I learned a long time ago that crying don't do no good.

So it makes some kinda sense, me seeing Elias, but it ain't altogether natural. And now I know what he is, I feel nervous thinking he might pop up anytime. When the door opens I jump a foot, but it's only Pilar, looking for me. She shuts the door behind her. Her face is calmer now. "Were you kidding, Crow?" she says. "Tell the truth and nothing bad will happen. We'll have a laugh and forget about it. But I got to know."

"Sure I was kidding," I tell her.

Her face goes all crafty. "How'd you pick him out of that picture?"

"His name was right there on the back."

"How'd you know that? Did you take the picture off the wall?"

"I must have, mustn't I?"

Her eyes bore right through me. "You seen him, didn't you."

"Pilar," I say, "if there really were ghosts in the world, this place would be crawling with them. You wouldn't be able to walk down the hall, they'd be so thick. You had it right the first time. I was pulling your leg."

"I seen your face. We all seen your face."

"Forget about it."

"Girl, don't you tell me forget about it. This is my ER. Ain't nothing goes down here but it's my business. How'd you know about that kid's spleen? How'd you know Noah's other name?"

I ask her: "Did Elias have a brother?"

"No, he didn't have no goddamn brother. You *did* see him. Sweet Jesus." Pilar plumps down to the floor. Her hand, the size of a catcher's mitt, clamps my shoulder, squeezes, and lets go. We sit for a while in silence. I'm not sorry for her company.

Finally she asks the question: "Why you?"

"Takes one to know one?"

She thinks it over. She nods. Makes sense to her, too, which scares the shit out of me. Sometimes I wonder how much Pilar knows about me.

"You say one word, I'll deny it on a stack of Bibles," I warn her.

"You crazy, girl? Think I want to lose the few nurses I got left?"

"All right then."

It's time to get back to work. I stand up and give Pilar a hand, haul her to her feet. At the door, she stops and gives me that head-nurse look again.

"What?" I ask.

"I don't believe in no damn ghost." She looks round as she says it, just in case.

"Well, shit, me neither."

"I don't believe you seen Elias. I ain't saying you're lying, but you could of imagined."

I look at her and wait.

"I don't believe you seen him," she says. "But if you ever see him again, you tell him Pilar say she's sorry."

"Sorry for what?"

Pilar plants her hands on those wide hips. "Is that your business?" she says. Then she turns and stalks down the hall, shaking her head and muttering to herself, "Lord, the nerve of some people. Next she be asking to read my mail."

9

·······

On his way out of the emergency room, Thomas Graystone is shadowed by Calvin Wang, who trots to keep pace, his bobbing head level with Graystone's shoulder.

"Dr. Graystone, Dr. Graystone," he bleats.

Graystone looks at him impatiently. "What is it?"

"What happened in there? Did she truly see Elias, that girl?"

Graystone halts, assaulting Wang with so fierce a look that the smaller man slithers to a stop and takes two steps backward.

"Woman," Graystone says. "Person. Housekeeper. Take your pick. Not girl."

"That housekeeper, then: Did she truly see him?"

"Of course not. Don't be an ass." Graystone strides on through ER doors that part for him like obedient servants. He is halfway to the doctors' parking lot when suddenly he stops and looks back. Wang is gone.

"Of course not," he repeats to himself. Then, walking briskly toward his car, he dismisses the matter of Elias's ghost once and for all, turning instead to the greater, the profound and inexplicable mystery of Crow's own identity. For he knows her now; he has recognized in her the regal woman in white satin from the Cellar, Johnny Deacon's guest. Though the musicians had clustered about her, gazing in admiration, she was no one's lover, he was sure of that. There had been no possessive arm slung 'round her chair back, no hand on her shoulder; she was there in her own right, and when she left (he knows because he waited), she left alone.

Often in the weeks since then he's caught himself thinking about that woman, seeing her face, not beautiful but striking, a weirdly congruent mixture of lady and urchin. Her walk had dignity, and there was in the set of her head a pronounced air of self-possession, as if she was what she was in a way that Graystone, outside the hospital and without his white coat, is never quite sure he is. Though it is no conceivable business of his, he has puzzled over her relationship to Deacon, who's old enough to be her father but clearly isn't. Anyway, what would any daughter of Deacon's be doing scrubbing floors in a hospital?

And Graystone had been so sure he knew her, though until an hour ago he couldn't place her, and even now he doubts himself. If the woman from the jazz club is actually the ER housekeeper whom he sees every day, how could he have failed to recognize her sooner? Yet even as he poses the question, the answer presents itself: He did not recognize her because it is so very improbable. As unlikely—the image comes to mind—as the glass slipper fitting Cinderella's foot.

It's not merely a matter of context but of substance; Graystone cannot draw a line connecting the mysterious lady of the Cellar with the cleaning woman who mops the floors in his department, whom he had never previously noticed and never would have had it not been for the odd business of the disappearing diagnostician. It's not her, he thinks, as he starts his car and drives out of the doctors' parking lot. There's no reasonable way the two women could be one. But when he stops at a light, he sees, projected in the glare on his windshield, the profile of a woman passing alone and erect through a crowded room. This image gives way to one of Crow as she stands in the harsh fluorescent glare of the doctors' lounge, her face stern and shuttered; and though his mind still harbors doubt, his heart makes the connection.

A car honks behind him, and he realizes that the light is green and has been for some time. Graystone takes the Brooklyn Bridge, then crosses lower Manhattan to the SoHo loft that is his home.

From the outside, the building looks like the warehouse it used to be, but inside it's deceptively well secured and comfortable. There's a gallery on the ground floor, two apartments on the second floor, and Graystone's duplex on the third. Raw space when he bought it seven years ago, over his mother's strenuous objections. ("A good investment," he'd argued; but Elvira had clucked her tongue and answered, "Long Island's Gold Coast is an investment. Westchester is an investment. *This* is a crapshoot.")

He bought it anyway. Afterward, to make peace with his mother, he let her design it from scratch. Elvira, having long ago reached the design-saturation point in her own home, took on the task with enthusiasm. Architects, contractors, painters, and craftsmen rolled through the loft; for months Graystone never knew who or what he would find when he came home. Though the process was tedious, the result he thinks rather fine: a soaring, open duplex done in earthen tones, with a bedroom, bath, and study on the upper level. The fixtures are terra-cotta, the floors bleached oak with scattered Navaho rugs. The furniture, clean-lined, Scandinavian, is upholstered in raw linen, and the art is original, purchased from the gallery downstairs in which Graystone has a small interest. Michelle, his current lover, says the place is cold and needs livening up with some flowering plants and brightly patterned scatter pillows. But Graystone at home wants responsibility for no living thing, and he likes his place just the way it is, quiet and restful, without a hint of red or other stressful colors. The one detail he personally insisted on was soundproofing to block out the sirens, horns, and cries of the street.

Graystone locks the front door behind him and goes directly to the kitchen. He tosses his coat onto a chair, extracts a pasta dish from the freezer, and pops it into the microwave. He climbs the staircase to the bedroom. The counter on his answering machine announces two messages.

The first voice is his mother's. "Thomas, are you still at work? It's past eight already. I keep meaning to ask about Thanksgiving. You and Michelle are coming to us, aren't you? Since you're never in, I called Michelle, and she said she thinks you're planning on it. What a sweet, lovely girl she is, Thomas. I hope you realize your good fortune. Of course you do. See you both next week, darling. Bye-bye."

Where did she get Michelle's number? He certainly hadn't given it to her. Last thing he wanted was those two talking him over.

The second message is from the lady herself. "Hi, stranger," she murmurs, with a tinge of irritation beneath the sexy contralto. Graystone hits the Stop button. Michelle's message will keep till after dinner. He's hungry, and guilt is a lousy condiment.

The microwave beeps, summoning him back to the kitchen. The fettuccine Alfredo is bland and watery, but a glass of champagne improves the meal. Like most bachelors with disposable income, Graystone indulges himself with small luxuries. Champagne is a chief indulgence, never overdone, just a split with dinner, for Thomas Graystone is a man of moderation: moderately comfortable, moderately pleased with his life, and somewhat more than moderately successful with women.

This last is due to no particular virtue of his. Graystone regards his success with women merely as a function of economics, a matter of supply and demand. There's a dearth of single black physicians on the market. He knows perfectly well that the women he dates, Michelle included, wouldn't look twice at him if he were a clerk in the ER instead of its head. The knowledge does not offend him; rather, it exonerates and appeases his conscience. The accessibility of lovely women is a side benefit of his profession, a bonus all the more welcome after the years of painful adolescence.

Strange, given his present status and success, how his thoughts with a perverse nostalgia tend to revert to those early days. Though Graystone is now lord of his own small fiefdom, still his heart is stamped by old feelings of loneliness, otherness, ineradicable difference.

The loneliness wasn't for lack of friends. Buddies, guys to hang with, he had aplenty. In high school, it was cool to be friends with "the black dude"—no further definition needed, as he was the only one. Often he was invited to parties by kids he hardly knew, his blackness valued as a sign of his hosts' urbanity. On these occasions, he usually found himself the only black in attendance, excluding the help. Graystone was used to this and minded less than when, in an excess of consideration, his hosts invited Wanda Maston on his account.

Maston, aka the Mastodon. A *big* girl. Barrel thighs, straightened hair, and a passion for field hockey. Wanda held no charms for Graystone, nor he for her; but as the only two blacks in their school, they were expected to gravitate together at parties and school functions, the way small children find each other in a crowd of adults. Given a choice, Graystone preferred staying home.

In his set was a white girl who seemed to like him. Cass was pretty: enormous blue-green eyes, silky blond hair, a body to die for. She painted. Invitations to view her work were hard currency among the boys who circled her like sharks. None of his friends had had her yet, though several were working at it. The girl pretended ignorance of their rivalry and turned her eyes on Graystone instead.

He tolerated her flirtation, certain she was using him to goad the others but not minding, in view of the collateral benefits. They talked at parties, sometimes on the phone. She told him she was a rebel, permanently at odds with her parents. "No one tells me what to do. No one makes my choices for me." In those days, Graystone used to play the harmonica. He carried it around all the time, whipped it out whenever he got the urge to play. Cass said she loved his playing. She said he was a real musician.

One night she was walking out of a party just as he arrived. He walked her home, taking two hours to cover five blocks. They held hands; hers had paint chips under the nails. On the corner of her block, she said good night and held up her face. His lips touched down on her cheek and traveled to her mouth. It was a long, slow kiss. Cass tasted different from the few black girls he'd kissed. They were standing under a street lamp. Graystone kept his eyes open. He felt as if all the windows in the houses were eyes watching them.

His friends caught the drift. Go for it, man, they told him. Graystone had never dated a white girl, never even asked one out, disliking rejection on any grounds. But he asked Cass, and she accepted. Twice they went to movies together, meeting at a friend's house and going on from there. Graystone chose theaters far from their homes. Standing on line, he felt the flicker of eyes shifting from him to her and back again. Cass pretended not to notice.

On the way home from their second date, he stopped and parked. They started off talking in the front, ended up in the backseat. More than the feel, the sight of his black hands on her white breasts set off a succession of feelings, like a chain of firecrackers: He was frightened, ashamed, triumphant, and finally enraged at all the complications displacing simple lust. Despite his excitement, he never lost his head. When she said stop, he stopped at once. Part of him remained alert and uninvolved, a watchful sentry posted just outside the car.

The next day, Cass missed school. The day after that, she sought him out. "We have to talk," she said. Her eyes were bloodshot. They ducked into the gym and stood under the bleachers. "I can't see you anymore."

"Why not?" he asked, as if he didn't know.

"Parents," she said. "Some goddamn busybody saw us at the flick."

"Thought you were a rebel. Thought you made your own choices."

"So did I." Tears seeped from her eyes, leaving trails of mascara along her cheeks. "They say if I don't stop seeing you, they'll send me away to boarding school."

He gave her his best Humphrey Bogart sneer. "It's your call, babe."

She said, "Can we still be friends?"

"No," he replied.

Black hands, white skin. The next time he touched a white woman, it was as a doctor, a resident on rounds. Even then it felt illicit, dangerous. All eyes, it seemed, were on his hands, his face, seeking out signs of hesitation or embarrassment. In response he turned his face to stone. The patient shuddered at his touch. "Cold hands," she said.

After Cass, he never again wasted time on white women. The world is full of beautiful black women, and Graystone had his share and then some. Lately, though, he'd slowed down. There comes a point in a man's life when dating is more a chore than an adventure. Graystone is thirty-seven years old. That's a lot of women under the dam.

His friends are all married, and most have children. He thinks it must be fine to come home to people who are glad to see you. For the first time, Graystone is beginning to feel the pull of domesticity.

He pours another glass of champagne and goes up to the bedroom. The red light on his answering machine glares reproachfully, like an unwalked dog. Graystone averts his eyes. He knows what "Hi, stranger" means. It means, Why haven't you called me? It means, What's happening with us anyway? It means, Get off the fence, son.

His involvement with Michelle has lasted six months, nearly a record. Thoughts of marriage have crossed his mind fleetingly but have taken up residence in hers. Last time she spent the night, she rearranged his living-room furniture, hiding his favorite lounge chair in an alcove, replacing it with a beautiful but hideously uncomfortable Shaker ladder-back chair. His mother also hated his poor chair, a squat, overstuffed, buff-colored recliner, the only holdover from his old apartment and the ideal venue for watching football. Graystone sensed a conspiracy. As soon as Michelle left, he moved his old chair back.

His lover is an interior designer with a small business of her own, a bright woman, ambitious, socially intelligent, dynamite in bed. His parents adore her. His friends covet her. She's a natural hostess and loves children. Graystone's mind tells him that Michelle would make a perfect wife. But his heart lurches another way.

For Graystone, though he's no romantic, has long harbored the notion that when the right woman comes along, he will know her instantly. His mother claims that love is something to be built up over time, not fallen into. Maybe so; yet he never imagined himself choosing a wife as coolly and methodically as he'd chosen a medical school. Graystone is fond of Michelle, but when he's not with her, he has difficulty picturing her face. The most he can manage is a quick flash before her image merges with the faces of previous lovers.

Love affairs, the doctor has observed, follow a certain set pattern, with stages of variable duration but fixed order. In this they are not unlike infections. Each begins with a period of flirtation, a cluster of inconclusive, nonsystemic symptoms, a kind of stirring of the blood. In the florid stage, the affair or infection is in full bloom, with all bodily resources brought to bear. Then a crisis point is reached: The body rejects the intruding bacteria, the heart its encroaching lover; the organism begins to regain its integrity. Finally there is a period of recuperation.

Sometimes, of course, patients don't recover from infections. Some affairs never end; men fall in love and stay there. Graystone has long since resigned himself to the knowledge that he is not one of those men. He seems somewhere along the line to have acquired an immunity to the chronic strain of love.

The affair with Michelle is coming to a head. They both sense it; hence his silence, her probing call. Given a choice, Graystone would let nature take its course; he enjoys her company and would not precipitate a break. But he may be given no choice. Michelle came into the relationship fully aware of his reputation with women. The first time they went out, she put her position on record. "I know all about you, Dr. Heart-of-Gray-Stone, and I am here to tell you this is one heart you are never going to break." Her sights were set on marriage, and he for one couldn't blame her; at their age, the biological clock ticks faster for women than for men. If he asks her, she will come tonight. She'll warm his bed and cook his breakfast. But sooner rather than later, he'll have to pay the piper.

When the phone rings, he hesitates, but it's only Bergman.

"What's up, Dan'l?" asks Graystone.

"Risa wants you to come to dinner Saturday. I told her I see more than enough of you at work, but she insisted. Michelle, too, of course, which is some compensation."

"Just for the record," Graystone asks, "is this strictly a package deal?"

Silence; then, in Daniel's most portentous tone: "This girl's a keeper, you realize. Schmuck."

"Have you been talking to my mother?"

"You're not seriously planning to lose this one, are you? 'Cause if so, I just might have to take up polygamy."

"The shoe's on the other foot. The lady's looking for a commitment."

"Smart girl. Can I ask you a question?"

"Would it matter if I said no?"

"What are you waiting for? A sign from heaven? Neon lights flashing 'She's the one!'?"

Graystone rubs his brow. "Dan'l?"

"Yes, Thomas?"

"Mind your own damn business."

"Yeah, baas."

They talk shop for a while. Graystone, having failed to attract an acceptable ER staff physician, has decided to offer the job to one of the third-year residents. The choice has come down to Calvin Wang or Elsa Kraven. Bergman favors Kraven, but Graystone has his doubts. "She's soft," he says. "I've seen her cry during codes."

"So what?" says Bergman. "She's a good blade. Sensitivity's no crime."

"It's no asset, either."

"You're full of shit, Tom. Underneath that icy exterior of yours, you feel as much as anyone."

"No, I don't, and I don't want to. What good is a surgeon who feels sympathy pains every time he cuts someone, or an ob-gyn who goes through labor with his patients? Let the nurses hold the patients' hands; we've got a different function. I'm not saying Elsa's not good. But she winces each time she sticks someone."

"She goes ahead and sticks 'em anyway."

"Will the others take instruction from a woman?"

There's a pregnant silence. "Gee, I don't know. Will they take it from a black?"

"Screw you," Graystone says amicably. "By the way," he adds, a bit slyly, "what do you know about the ER housekeeper?"

Daniel takes a moment to shift gears. "Crow? Nothing. Why?"

"I ran into her a couple of weeks ago. At least, I think it was her. She was with Johnny Deacon and his band."

"So the chick's a jazz groupie. What's so strange?"

"You don't get it. She was no groupie. She was Deacon's honored guest. He played to her all night. Sam, the club owner, served her personally. She was somebody, a personage."

"Whereas at work she's nobody?"

"Well, yeah."

Bergman laughs. "You jerk."

"I mean, I never noticed her. Did you?"

"Ah, Thomas, are you suffering that nose disorder again?"

"What nose disorder?"

"The one where your nose gets stuck so high in the air you can't see what's happening below."

Graystone sighs. "Is that a yes or a no?"

"Sure I noticed Crow. You'd have to be blind not to."

"Why, you think she's attractive?"

"Let's just say she's noticeable."

In the background he hears Risa's voice: "Who's noticeable?"

Bergman sighs. "Now see what you've gone and done? You've got me in trouble."

"What you get for marrying a nurse, brother."

"Now you tell me."

"What's her family name?"

"How the hell would I know?" After a moment's pause,

Bergman says in a different voice, "You're not actually interested in this girl, are you?"

"Just curious."

"Watch it, man. You know what killed the cat."

"No fear," Graystone says. After all, he's got Michelle to protect him. When he calls her, she answers on the first ring. They have a cozy, intimate chat, but Graystone doesn't ask her over and pleads fatigue when she invites herself. That night he dreams that a crow has flown into his loft, and in its panic it crashes about, smashing fixtures, shattering treasures, weaving a trail of chaos through his ordered world.

10

· · · · · · · ·

Selma stands in the hall outside the bathroom, watching Crow apply makeup. "Where you going, all dressed up?"

"I'm not sure. Deacon's picking me up."

"Johnny Deacon?"

"Do we know another Deacon?"

"What's he up to, hanging around you?"

Crow raises her eyebrows. "Aren't you the one said I should see him?"

"Once, I meant, for old times' sake, not make a habit of it. Deacon's got his life, and you got yours. A person's—"

"Got to know where she belong. I know. But he called three times, and you know how hard it is saying no to Deacon."

Selma snorts. "That old man always did have a feeling for you."

"A paternal feeling," Crow says.

"You call it that if you like."

The doorbell rings. "I'll get it," Selma says, closing the bathroom door. When Crow comes out, Selma and Deacon are sitting side by side on the couch. Deacon's wearing a somber look, but this changes to a broad smile as he sees Crow. "Don't you look sweet," he says, coming forward to meet her. Inside his tweedy bear hug, Crow flashes back to

83

Paris: a glimpse of light slanting through louvered atelier windows, the sound of five men arguing, laughing, making music. She opens her eyes to Selma's unguarded face, nervous and defiant.

"What you two been conspiring about?" Crow says.

"We're *conspiring*," Selma says, drawing out the word, "to steal your money and do you in. What else would we be *conspiring* about?"

Deacon laughs deep in his throat. "Now don't irritate Selma, Crow, or she'll be sending you to bed."

Crow curls up in an armchair. When Deacon sits back down beside Selma, the sofa sags. It's possible no man has sat on it since Blue died. The room looks small with Deacon in it.

"I been telling him all about your job," Selma says.

"Goddammit, Selma—"

"He's got a right to know."

"How I make my living's no one's concern but my own." Crow looks at Deacon. "The way she goes on, you'd think I was peddling my ass on Times Square."

"You're not alone in the world," he says reprovingly.

"Deacon, darlin', you know I love you, but what I do is none of your damn business."

Laughing, he turns to Selma. "Hear that? Only woman in the world who'd dare talk to me like that."

"Always did have a mouth on her," Selma replies, shaking her head sorrowfully.

"Tell you one thing, Crow," says Deacon. "You are never gonna be a boxer till you quit leading with your chin. And another thing: You are dead wrong, baby. It *is* my damn business, and I can't see you in a job like that. That's not who you are."

"Who I am is not who I was. Why should it be? Things change. Besides which, since when is good honest labor something to be ashamed of? Old-time leftist like yourself's got no business disapproving."

"Politics is politics," he says decisively, "and life is life. I dislike the thought of Blue Durango's widow mopping floors. It offends my sense of order; it makes me uncomfortable, and anything that makes me uncomfortable is wrong."

"Oh, is it, Your Majesty?" Crow says with a laugh, for that's what the band used to call him when he got on his high horse: "Yes, Your Majesty," and "No, Your Majesty," and "What you say, Your Majesty."

But Deacon is not to be waylaid. "And why the hospital—the damn emergency room, of all places?"

"Why not? A job is a job."

"A job is never just a job."

"But sometimes a cigar is just a cigar."

"Don't you start cracking wise on me, girl. She do this to you?" he asks Selma.

"All the time."

He shakes his head. There's a silence, which all seem disinclined to break. After a while, Deacon asks, "Where's little Joey? I brought something for him."

"Sleeping," Crow says.

"Well, then, you give him this for me." From the deep pocket of his jacket, Deacon produces an unwrapped rectangular box, eight inches long. He hands it to Crow, who lifts the lid and catches her breath. Inside the box lies an old harmonica, a vintage Hohner, well preserved.

"Oh, Deacon."

"It's Blue's."

"I know that. I wondered where it got to."

"I found it with some equipment when we packed up in Paris. Put it aside. Figured I'd deliver it in person."

"So you will," Crow says. She closes the box, hands it back to Deacon, and leaves the room. A few minutes later, she returns, leading Joey, pajama'd, blinking, and sleepy-eyed.

"Hello, young fella," Deacon says, enveloping Joey's little hand in his huge one. "What a fine-looking boy you're getting to be. Do you know who I am?"

Joey nods. "You're the greatest piano player in the whole wide world."

Deacon throws back his head and roars with laughter. "That's wonderful, that's just grand. Who taught you that, son? Mama teach you to say that?"

"It's his own opinion," says Crow.

"Why not, he's as good a critic as any." Deacon lifts Joey

onto his knee. The child sniffs the lapel of his jacket, then snuggles into it like a weary pup. "Aside from being the greatest piano player in the whole wide world," says Deacon, "I was also your daddy's closest friend, and he gave me something to hold for you until you reach the ripe old age of four. So when you turn four, I'm going to give you a very important present."

"I *am* four," Joey says, wide-eyed.

"Are you really? Is that right, Crow? This boy is four years old already?"

"Yes, he is."

"Well then, I guess I got to give it to you now." Once again Deacon produces the box, once again it is opened. Joey takes the harmonica into his hands and turns it over and over, examining it from all angles. At last he brings it up to his mouth and blows tentatively.

"Like this, son," says Deacon, reversing the instrument. "You blow in this side."

This time, Joey produces a note.

"That's real good. Next time I come, I want you to play me a tune. Will you do that?"

"I don't know how."

"Just fool around with it, that's all. Find out what it can do. Your daddy learned to play on that harmonica."

"Really?" Joey looks down at the instrument with awe.

"Yes, sir, and he loved that harmonica, carried it with him wherever he went. But there's one thing he loved more."

"What?"

"You, son. He loved you."

Joey looks up into Deacon's face. "Really?"

"More than anything in the whole world, he loved you and your mama."

With a serious look, Joey places his arms around Deacon's neck and plants a kiss on his whiskery jaw.

The old man's arms tighten around the little body; then he hands the boy to Selma, who carries him off to bed. Crow says, in a husky voice, "He'll never forget this."

"Crow," Deacon says, "let's you and me go paint this old town red. I am celebrating tonight."

"I can't stay out late. Work tomorrow."

"We'll catch the early set. Joss Merkin's playing at the Vanguard."

"Damn bus comes when it feels like," she says apologetically as they ride down the elevator. The subway's closer, but Crow doesn't do subways anymore.

"Taxi would be faster," says Deacon.

"In this neighborhood?" She laughs.

"You never know." Just outside the project gate stands a yellow cab with its off-duty light on. Deacon takes Crow's arm and guides her to it. He opens the back door. *"S'il vous plaît, madame."*

"You kept this cab waiting all the time you were inside?"

"I hired it for the evening."

She looks at him in amazement. "What'd you do, Deacon, hock the family jewels?"

He laughs and settles in beside her. Without a word being spoken, the driver cuts a U-turn and heads back toward the city.

Deacon cuts loose a long, deep sigh. "That child, I look in his face and I see Blue. Does he remember his daddy?"

Crow's face ossifies. "He remembers what happened. He has dreams about it."

Deacon presses his palms together. If he could comfort her, he would, but some things are beyond solace. The manner of Blue's death and his son's witnessing of it belong to the order of unassuageable grief.

"I do, too," he says. "Not about his dying; about *him*. The other night, I dreamt the band was rehearsing, and after we pack it in, Blue says, 'I don't know about you cats, but after two years of omelets and baguettes I am dying for a hot pastrami sandwich, New York style, six inches thick with plenty of mustard.' I wake up thinking, I gotta take Blue to that old Jewish deli down on East Broadway, best damn pastrami in the city if it's still there. You dream about him, Crow?" he asks with a sideways glance.

"Every night."

"Every night. Well, you must love going to bed."

"I do," she says. "It's waking up that's hard." Then she's

sorry she said it. Blue used to say that Deacon had God's own eyes: They saw too much. She changes the subject. "What are we celebrating, anyway?"

"My new record deal."

She rounds on him. "Is that right? Ah, Deacon, that's good news. I am pleased for you, darlin'."

"I know you are, baby. And I'm pleased for you."

She looks at him quizzically. He roots through his voluminous jacket pockets. "I know I got it somewhere. Here we go." He extracts a crumpled white envelope and places it in Crow's hands.

Inside is a check made out to her name and signed by Deacon. The amount is more than she earns in six months at the hospital. Crow stares at it for a moment, then lays it on the seat between them. "What's this?" she asks in a cool voice.

"Blue's share of the advance."

"Blue's not playing on this album."

Deacon waves a hand. "He collaborated on the arrangements. It's all material we worked on in Paris."

"If this money comes from the record company, how come you're giving me a personal check?"

"They signed with me. It's none of their business how the money is split. Blue and I had an understanding."

"I can't accept this." She thrusts the check at him.

His right hand, annealed by decades of day-in, day-out playing, clamps her wrist. He is no more smiling now than she is. "Blue wouldn't have refused. He knew he had it coming."

"I don't buy your story, Deacon. Thanks for trying, but we don't need your charity."

Deacon's the sweetest-tempered man in the world as long as things go his way, but on the rare occasions when he's crossed, Crow's known him to go off like a barrel of firecrackers. He's got that pre-explosive look about him now.

"Fuck charity," he says, taking her hand and slapping the check into it. "You are Blue's widow, and you're having his share whether you like it or not. Tell you somethin' else, little darlin': There's gonna be more where that came from."

"You're doing this for Blue. You feel some kind of cockeyed obligation to look after Blue's widow and orphan."

"Hell with obligations. Sinful old man that I am, never had much use for 'em. God knows I loved Blue, but dead is dead, darlin'."

"Then why . . . ?"

"You're not listening, girl. He *earned* that bread. For me to keep it would be like stealing the pennies off a dead man's eyes. So just say thank you and shut up."

"Thank you, Deacon." Crow turns her face to the window. She doesn't move or make a sound. Deacon doesn't know she's crying till he sees her reflection in the glass.

He touches her arm. "Now what is it?"

"I wish Blue could see this. I wish he could see what you're doing."

"He wouldn't bat an eye," Deacon says irritably. "He'd give me that respect."

"I know there was nothing in writing. I went through all his papers. You didn't have to do this."

"Now you're insulting me. Since when does a deal have to be in writing for Johnny Deacon to honor it?"

She grasps his hand. "Deacon, I didn't mean to dis you. You just took my breath away."

The anger fades from the old man's face. "Least now you can quit that damn housekeeping job, find yourself something better."

"Like hell I will. One thing's got nothing to do with the other."

"Shit, Crow, you are the stubbornest damn woman I ever did know. You are stubborner than my third wife, and that's going some. How do you think Blue would feel if he could see you scrubbing floors in a hospital?"

Crow grunts softly, like a boxer struck under the belt. Then, disregarding Deacon's advice, she sticks out her chin. "He'd be proud of me."

"It'd break his heart," Deacon declares.

They enter the Brooklyn Battery Tunnel. Crow gazes out the window at her own spectral reflection. She remembers Elias, and a chill runs through her. "Deacon, do you believe in life after death?"

"I never was much of a churchgoing man. I believe in the gospel music, though, leastways while it's playing. Blue ever tell you about that gospel singer we heard down in Baltimore?"

"I don't think so."

Deacon chuckles. "Me and Blue were walking home from an all-night gig one Sunday morning when suddenly this voice comes out of a church, grabs us by the ears, and marches us inside. Up on the pulpit stands this big old black mama, liquid gold pouring out of her throat. Six in the morning and the church is packed. Lord, to hear that woman sing 'Swing Low' was to lay down your head and weep. Time she finished, Blue was on his feet shouting 'Hallelujah!' Later on I ask him, I say, 'Blue, you ain't getting religion on me, are you, son?'

" 'No way,' he says, 'you know me, Deacon.'

" 'So what's all that Hallelujah and Praise-the-Lord jive you were spouting in church?'

" 'Hell,' says Blue, 'I'll praise anyone made a voice like that. Besides, there ain't nothing wrong with a little salvation. I been saved twice myself.'

" 'Get on,' I tell him, 'what you talking about?'

" 'God's own truth,' he says. 'First music save me from the street; then Crow come along and save me from music.'

" 'That's fine, Blue,' I say, 'but now who's going to save you from Crow?' "

Deacon laughs till the tears roll down his cheeks. Crow digs him with her elbow, but she's laughing, too, as their cab pulls up to the Vanguard.

CROW

Deacon steps out, and all at once he's a different man, cloaked in his public persona: dignified, gracious, a little aloof, as royalty must be. Arm in arm we make our entrance. Deacon works the room, dispensing smiles and handclasps. I greet old friends. Crow, they say, where the hell you been keeping yourself?

Every seat is taken, but for Deacon they produce a table and set it up in the front row, just behind the piano. It's past ten and the band is onstage, about to begin. The brass players dip their horns to Deacon, and Joss, warming up the ivories, tips an invisible hat. Then he nods to the band, and they are off.

Deacon's eyes don't stray from Merkin's hands. Halfway through the piece, he leans over to me and says in a tone of satisfaction, "His right hand's slowed down some." I smile. Blue told me that in the old days these two used to duke it out like musical gladiators in Harlem's after-hour joints, playing as if the loser would be fed to the lions. Joss don't seem slow to me. With Deacon's eyes warming up his back, he's playing like the devil is on his tail.

Joss is like Deacon, he likes his music to tell a story. I close my eyes and let it lead me through the streets of the city where the real folks live: Harlem, Bed-Stuy, Deepside, the barrios of East Harlem and the Bronx. Along the way, I hear echoes of Ellington's "Caravan," bits and pieces cribbed from the master. No shame in that; they all do it, borrow and embellish riffs, then toss them back in the pot. Joss grew up in Harlem, and the 'hood is in his music: sharp-edged, real, yet transfigured by love. Amidst the blare of traffic and the wailing rise and fall of radios, I hear the shrilling of young girls, the crowing of homeboys, the deep-throated cries of women left alone.

The piece ends and the clapping begins, but it's more respectful than ecstatic. The old Harlem crowds used to sing out their pleasure: "Yeah, Daddy," they would cry, "swing that thing." When the spirit moved them, they would get up and dance. But this downtown crowd is maybe a third black; the rest are tight-assed honkies impressed as hell with their cultural liberalism, who sit like they're in Carnegie Hall, listen with pinched, attentive faces, and applaud politely, without comprehension.

Am I unfair? Blue always had a large white following, and I used to wonder what those folks got out of his music. I thought it must be as foreign to them as Chinese music is to me, but Blue said not; he always claimed they're not so different from us as I thought.

Joss plays a few more numbers, then swings the band into his version of "Summertime." When the sax moves up to center stage, I close my eyes, the club fades away, and I'm in the Paris flat, leaning weary as a beat dog against the open door of Joey's room. It's three in the morning, and I've been walking the baby all night long. Every time I lay him down, he resumes hollering.

Blue comes up behind me. I feel his calloused fingers kneading my shoulders, and I sag against him. "Go to bed," he says. "I'll take care of Joey."

I go down the hall and fall into bed. Blue comes in, takes his sax, and goes back out. Then the music starts, soft and sweet: "Summertime." Tired as I am, the music draws me out of bed. I creep down the hall, quiet as a mouse, but I needn't have bothered; Blue's lost in the sultry lullaby. Music streams from his body, passes through the instrument, lifts our baby from his crib, and rocks him gently in its currents: Blue's song is our child's cradle.

Joey quiets; he coos; his little hands dance in the air. Even after he falls asleep with a smile and a sigh, Blue plays on, unable to stop the music that flows from him like mother's milk.

The piece ends; I open my eyes reluctantly. First thing I see is a man staring at me from across the room. I look away, but it's too late; this time he knows me. Throughout the rest of the set I feel him watching. Soon as the band breaks, he comes to our table and waits for me to acknowledge him.

"Dr. Graystone," I say.

"Hello, Crow." He holds out his hand. I shake it. It seems to me he hangs on a moment too long. Deacon's looking at me expectantly. Last thing I want is to introduce these two. It is necessary to keep the two halves of my life separate, because if I tried to put them together they wouldn't fit; there'd be a gaping hole in the middle. But Deacon's waiting and Graystone seems content to stand there all night, stiff and dumb as a post. I introduce them.

"An honor, sir," Graystone says to Deacon with a little bow. "I'm a lifelong fan." He turns his eyes back to me.

"Would you like to sit down?" I say, willing him to leave, willing the earth to open up and swallow him.

"No, thank you. I don't mean to intrude." Still, he doesn't leave. I can't figure out what he wants.

"How do you two know each other?" Deacon asks.

"We work together," says Dr. Graystone.

I laugh at this description. Deacon's eyebrows meet across the bridge of his nose. He puts his hand on my shoulder and looks Graystone up and down. "I hope you people realize what you've got here."

"I believe we're beginning to," Graystone says.

Only when Joss Merkin approaches our table does he withdraw. "Sorry," I whisper to Deacon. "I don't know what he thought he was doing."

"Speaking as an old bird-dogger, I'd say it was obvious."

I laugh. "Deacon, he's head of the department."

"So?"

Deacon doesn't understand. How could he? I pat his hand. "He probably wanted your autograph and was too embarrassed to ask."

11

• • • • • • •

At 7:00 A.M. Monday morning Graystone enters the ER and strides down the hall to his office along a path strewn with greetings. "Good morning, sir"; "Nice weekend, Dr. Graystone?" He passes the utility closet just as Crow backs out, pulling a cumbersome cleaning cart. They collide. "Excuse me," Graystone says, startled to see her in her drab brown uniform.

"My fault," says Crow. "I ought to signal." Before he can think of a way to detain her, she is halfway down the hall.

During morning rounds, he keeps his eyes open, but though he is newly attuned to signs of her passage—wet floors, gleaming stainless-steel surfaces, things he never noticed before except in their absence—he sees nothing of Crow. It almost seems she's avoiding him; several times he spots her leaving a room just as he enters. These glimpses are enough to arrest his attention, even in midspeech, as his eyes follow her disappearing back.

Later that morning, returning from a meeting upstairs, Graystone enters the ER through the back door and surprises the housekeeper plying her mop on the floor. His legs carry him straight to her, then stop. He says nothing, having no idea what he wants of her.

94

She glances up. "You're in my way, Doctor."

"I'm sorry," he says, but he doesn't move. His feet feel as if they've been trapped in tar, and his tongue, too. What can he say to her? "Nice floor"? "Did you get a load of Mr. Martin's EKG?" They work together but have nothing in common. All he can do is stand and sway.

Hand on hip, she regards him. He searches her eyes for a reflection of their encounter at the Vanguard but finds only impatience and a tart amusement, as if she's thinking, What's this fool want from me now?

At last he says, "Did you enjoy the music Saturday night?" his voice a shade too hearty in his own ears.

Her eyes close, then open. In the pause between his question and her reply, he understands that he has erred, bringing the outside in; in some obscure way he has offended.

Crow dunks her mop in the large tin bucket and wrings it out. "I always get a kick out of Joss. Now, if you'll excuse me, I've got a floor to wash."

He retreats to his office and sits behind his desk, legs splayed out, chair tilted perilously backward. He has a budget proposal to do, a useless but unavoidable bit of bureaucracy. He's convinced no one upstairs reads them; they just send him back his old budget, less 5 percent. For years he's been agitating for a separate pediatric ER, without success. In the end it all comes down to the bottom line. The hospital's pediatric ward upstairs operates at near capacity; therefore the administration sees no need to fill beds by investing in a separate pediatric ER. Graystone doesn't even have a full-time ER pediatrician. Children who come into the ER are treated by the regular ER staff, backed up, theoretically, by the pediatric attending upstairs. They'll fight over it again this year; as always he'll marshal his figures and studies, compare Mercy to other hospitals, appeal to their sense of pride. As always the brass (all white males at that level, not that it matters, he tells himself) will listen with sober, sympathetic faces, shake his hand, compliment his presentation, and vote it down.

Waste of time, really, especially given the city's current deficit. As it is, his staff haven't had a raise in two years, and rumors abound of a week's unpaid furlough for doctors and nurses.

Graystone takes out a file full of statistics and data, and another with previous years' budgets. He spreads the papers out, takes a fresh white pad from his desk drawer, and uncaps his pen. Starts doodling. The margins fill with geometric figures, triangles shaded in intricate patterns. He tries to fix his mind on the budget, but it keeps slithering away. Crow's snub is a thorn in the side of his tender self-esteem.

What was it she said? "I've got work to do—" as if he hadn't, as if he had nothing better to do than to stand around gossiping with her. And her tone of voice, like a mother telling her child to quit fooling around and start his homework. The nerve of the woman is extraordinary, but nothing compared to his own gross stupidity. Getting slapped down by the skivvy was just punishment for sticking his nose where it didn't belong. What had possessed him?

Not infatuation, he assures himself, but rather curiosity, always his quickest emotion. What snags his interest is the complicated equation between two seemingly mutually exclusive entities, Johnny Deacon's Crow and Mercy's. Each so at home in her own skin, each so solidly what she was. The woman is a chameleon, and Graystone feels a boy's fascination with exotic animals. More than anything, he would like to be a fly on her wall, to see her transform herself, change her skin before his very eyes.

Dan'l was right, of course. He should stick to his own. Crow's story is no concern of his. In any case, however perplexed his own feelings might be, the woman has made hers perfectly clear. She wants no part of him. She gives him nothing but the glassy edge of her politeness, like the back of her hand.

He *will* stick to his own. He will forget the blasted woman, he will cease to notice her, he will return to his pre-Crow consciousness. Resolving thus, Graystone is shocked by a fierce contraction of the soul: regret for something that never was.

After a perfunctory tap on the door, Pilar pops her head in. "We got us a real SHPOS."

"A *what?*"

She enunciates precisely: "A SHPOS. A subhuman piece of—"

"I know what it means." Graystone's face does not so much change color as give the impression of doing so.

The battle against dehumanizing nomenclature in the ER is as hard-fought and constant as the fight against disease. Emergency rooms have their own private language, shorthand descriptions of procedures, diagnoses, medication, personnel, and departments that offer the dual advantage of saving time and facilitating talk in front of patients. Since most conversations are conducted in initials anyway, it's a short step to using the same method to describe patients. Designations run from the relatively mild GORK (God Only Really Knows), GOMER (Get Out of My Emergency Room), and PIA (Pain in the Ass), through the gruesome (Crispy Critters for burn patients is a particular nonfavorite of Graystone's), to the contemptuous (and, in his ER, totally unacceptable) SHPOS. Recognizing the need for stressed-out ER staffers to let off steam, Graystone has been known occasionally to turn a deaf ear to some of the milder epithets. But he will not and cannot tolerate the expression he just heard from Pilar.

Now he rises, scowling, and says, "I never thought I'd hear that kind of gutter filth from you, of all people."

She comes in, slamming the door behind her. Pilar and Daniel Bergman are the only ones in the department wholly unawed by Graystone's august ways. "Believe it," she says. "Cops just run him in. White male, forty, well nourished, well dressed. They say he's the asshole scum been doin' those little black boys in Bed-Stuy."

Graystone shuts his eyes. Over the past six months they've treated four young molestation victims of the man the press has dubbed the Bed-Stuy Stalker. Two of the patients described a pudgy white man with wire-rimmed glasses. The third child was too traumatized to speak, the fourth too young.

"Why us? Why not Bellevue? They're equipped for this sort of thing."

"We're closest. Bunch of ladies caught him walking off with a little boy, four years old. Man's got lacerations of the face and scalp, bleeding like a pig." Pilar doesn't say it, but by the looks on the faces of the two arresting cops and the state of their knuckles, she guesses they got in some licks of their own. No skin off her back if they did. On the long list of Pilar's hates, child molesters rank first, second, and third.

"Who's with him?"

"Murchison. They're in Suture."

"Violent?"

"Vicious," Pilar says shortly. "I'm not putting any of my nurses on him. I'll do him myself."

Graystone knows what she wants, but he doesn't want to do it. "Get the attending," he says.

"Bergman's on an MI, Wang's got an acute asthma, Kramer's admitting a prolapsed uterus, and I don't think you want to expose any of your baby docs. Also, I would like to get this lowlife out of here before the press arrives."

He accompanies her to the suture room. Outside, two cops hold up a corridor wall. "Hope your knife slips, Doc," says the black one pleasantly. Graystone opens the door for Pilar. As he follows her in, the patient groans: "Oh Lord Jesus, not another fucking jungle bunny."

He has plump pink choirmaster cheeks and maniacal eyes behind wire-rimmed glasses. His wrists are manacled to the pull-out extensions of the examination table, his ankles and head bound by linen strips. This cruciform position together with the blood trickling down his face confer an unwonted Christly look. Graystone takes his time pulling on his latex gloves, adjusting to the atmosphere in the room. He nods dismissal to the hospital guard standing behind the patient's head.

"I'll stay, sir," Murchison says firmly.

Pilar wheels over the suture supply cart. She and Graystone take their places on opposite sides of the patient.

The way he's bleeding they could have used a third pair of hands, but neither of them suggests it.

The patient struggles against his restraints. He curses them, calls them niggers, coons, and black morons, and threatens them with awful reprisals if they touch him. "I am acting under orders from the highest authority, do you hear? The very highest authority."

"Did you call Psych?" Graystone asks Pilar.

"They're sending someone ASAP." Their eyes meet in the silent communion of colleagues who've worked shoulder to shoulder for years. There are only two time frames in a hospital: stat, which means immediately, and ASAP, which means sometime in the indeterminate future if nothing else comes up.

They throw a sheet over the patient and work on him as if dissecting a cadavar, neither asking his name nor addressing him. Insulated by gloves and masks, still they avoid unnecessary contact. Nothing they do or say acknowledges his existence in any way except as a collection of discrete lacerations.

Graystone says, "Set up an IV, Nurse. Any drug allergies?"

"Couldn't get a history."

He hesitates, but there's no way around it. In the loud, distinct voice he would use on the hard-of-hearing or comatose, he asks the patient if he has any allergies.

"Yeah. I'm allergic to jigaboos."

"Patient uncooperative," Pilar notes on the record. Graystone orders penicillin and immobilizes the patient's arm while she starts the IV. Although it's hospital legend that Pilar can spear even a junkie's wasted vein blindfolded and one-handed, she takes several painful jabs finding this man's.

The doctor shakes his head at her. He brings the light down low to explore a bloody gash on the patient's scalp. "The edges are jagged."

"Gonna have him a nice scar."

"Slut came at me with a bread knife," the patient says in a suddenly calm voice. "They're animals, you know. Throw a litter a year, like bitches. Genetically useless material. Sterilize the lot of 'em, I say. Save the taxpayers' money."

Graystone swabs the laceration and flushes it with saline and Betadine solutions. He addresses the air above the patient's head. "I'm going to suture the wounds now. The more you squirm, the more painful it will be." Murchison steps forward to stand opposite Pilar, while Graystone positions himself behind the gurney.

The patient sees the needle and thread, and his eyes open wide. "Hey, wait a minute. Where's the shot? Where's the fucking anesthesia?"

Graystone smiles. "Big tough guy like you doesn't need anesthesia." He nods to Pilar. She immobilizes the patient's head between her strong hands while Murchison lays across his chest, pinning him to the table. Graystone inserts the needle into his scalp.

The patient screams. His body arches, lifting Murchison to his toes.

"Goddamn nigger bastard!" The patient's mouth purses; he's about to spit in Graystone's face when suddenly his cheeks are clamped between iron fingers. Pilar's broad face comes down so close that her breath mists his corneas. A thick-gauge endotracheal tube dangles from her free hand.

"Now you shut that evil mouth, 'cause next time I see it open, I'm gonna shove this tube right down your throat, help you with your breathing." Then she lets go.

The patient swallows his spittle and clamps his jaws tight.

Graystone finishes the job in silence. While Pilar cleans up, he strips off his gloves and signs the patient out to the arresting officers, joined now by a plainclothes detective from sex crimes, Sal Feducci. Feducci's an overweight, middle-aged man, barrel-chested, with a flattened nose and a cauliflower ear, relics of a short but honorable career as a boxer. His bulging body and lumpy face give him the look of a comical, rather dull-brained bear. Children talk to him, suspects routinely underestimate him: a good, effective cop.

He and Graystone have struck up a strange sort of friendship over the bodies of abused women and children. Now they shake hands, and Graystone says, "He's all yours."

Feducci peeks into the suture room. "Aw, jeez, would you look at that bandage."

"What's wrong with it?" Pilar asks indignantly.

"His own mother wouldn't recognize him, all wrapped up like a mummy. I was gonna put this guy in a lineup. Doc, any way you could maybe reduce that thing?"

"I just put twelve stitches in his scalp and six in his jaw. The dressing stays. But he won't need it longer than three, four days if you want to postpone your lineup."

"Seems I got no choice."

Graystone can't resist asking. "Is he really the Stalker?"

"No doubt about it. We searched his place. Asshole made videotapes. He'll do serious time if he don't walk on a psych pass. So whaddaya think, Doc—is he nuts?"

All three cops regard the doctor anxiously.

"I'm not a psychiatrist."

"But . . . ?" prompts Feducci.

"We see lots of patients who are truly delusional. This guy's a little too organized about his mania, too deliberate with the provocations."

"You're saying he's faking it."

"I'd say it's a good possibility."

Feducci claps him on the shoulder.

A few minutes later, Graystone and Pilar stand side by side at two sinks in the doctors' lounge. Without speaking, they scrub till their hands are raw.

"What do you think," Pilar says presently, as she dries her hands. "Think he'd of bled to death without treatment?"

"No. The lacerations weren't that deep. They would have clotted eventually."

"Well, that makes me feel a little better at least. There's some lives don't want saving."

He snorts. "You talk a good game, but you do your job."

"I *always* do my job. Only sometimes my heart ain't in it." She nods good-bye, but Graystone with some reluctance points to the table.

They sit facing each other, Pilar heavy and solid as a boulder, Graystone on the edge of his seat. Looking into her ponderous face, he remembers the first time they met. He was a first-year resident starting his ER rotation; Pilar was head nurse. Halfway through his first week, Pilar caught him reprimanding one of her nurses for some petty misdemeanor. She took him aside.

"Here's how it is," Pilar said. "Forget what they taught you in med school. In real life, the nurses run the show, and on this turf I run the nurses. I was here before you, and I'll be here after you."

"Blessed be thy kingdom," he replied unwisely, having had no sleep in thirty-six hours.

"Respect," she said, wagging a finger under his nose. "Respect's what makes the world go round and this place function. You respect me and I'll . . . allow you the benefit of the doubt."

Almost he expected her to jump up on a desk and belt out an Aretha Franklin imitation.

He does respect her, and over time Pilar has come to reciprocate. Graystone's ascension to power was tricky at first, what with the seniority on her side, the authority on his, but gradually they negotiated a delicate coexistence, tacitly mapping out areas of sovereignty. The arrangement has worked well, eliminating skirmishes in all but disputed border territory.

Now approaching no-man's-land, Graystone dons his stuffiest manner. "Ms. Johnston, did I hear you threaten a patient with bodily harm?"

"A little discomfort," she answers modestly. "I noticed you're kinda tight with the anesthesia yourself."

"There's a budget crunch on."

"Uh-huh. And those sutures didn't half smart."

"That's not the issue. The point is, threatening patients with unnecessary procedures as punishments is not what we do here."

Pilar, indignant, takes on a massive quality, a Mount Rushmore solidity. "The man was fixing to spit in your face. You want to share bodily fluids with that piece of work?"

He sighs. "No."

"Well, then." They lock eyes. Graystone's the first to break. He doesn't even have to ask himself if he would have used anesthesia on another patient; he knows damn well he would have.

Pilar says, "Is that all, Doctor?"

For the second time that day, he finds himself inexplicably tongue-tied, scuffing the floor with the tip of his polished shoe.

"About Crow," he mumbles.

"Crow?"

Why should he feel guilty? Graystone wonders. Whose ER is it, anyway? "Who is she? Where does she come from? What's her last name?"

Pilar fixes him with a beady eye. "What do you want with Crow?"

"She works in my ER. I like to know something about the people who work here."

"Since when?"

"Forget it. A passing curiosity. Not worth the fuss."

"Something wrong with her work?"

"No, nothing like that."

She crosses her arms. "I *know* what you want with her."

"You do?" he asks slyly, hoping she'll tell.

"Yes, I do, and I'm warning you right here and now: I won't stand for it."

"You won't?"

"No way," she says. "You're not firing the best damn housekeeper I ever had."

Speechless, he gapes at her.

For the first time, Pilar's air of certainty wavers. "You're not planning to let her go?"

"Why would you think that?"

"That thing with Elias . . . she didn't mean nothing by it."

It takes him a moment to remember, then he shrugs. "I never took that seriously."

Pilar falls into a considering silence, while Graystone wishes he'd never mentioned Crow's name.

He says, "Forget it."

Pilar says, "Durango."

"Durango?" Like a puzzle solved in fast motion, the

pieces fly together in Graystone's head. "As in Blue Durango?"

"Blue who?"

"Blue Durango, Johnny Deacon's sideman. Crow's the widow?"

Pilar raises a shoulder and lets it fall. "All I know's what people tell me. Crow's not a talker."

"That's not all you know."

"Ask *her*," she snaps, "you so certain it's your business."

Alice prides herself on never rejecting a patient, no matter how abusive, infested, or contagious. There are nurses she knows who shun the purple stigmata of AIDS, others who cannot abide burn or psych patients. Not Alice. She cares for youngsters strung out on crack or crazed with angel dust as if they were her own flesh and blood; she bandages the wounds of murderers and comforts thieves. She is a nurturer, a born hand-holder, a runaway empathizer from her earliest years, when she established a doll hospital for the neighborhood children. But when the police deliver the child molester, Alice meets Pilar's inquiring eye with a defiant glare: Not this one, says her look; not for me.

Pilar is notoriously hard on her nurses. She runs them ragged and doles out words of approval as if they were gold nuggets from her own personal treasury. But she doesn't ask them to do what she wouldn't do herself, and now she doesn't argue with Alice; she just shrugs and takes the patient herself.

With Pilar occupied, Alice takes over triage. The task imposes its own mind-set; she turns brisk and businesslike, holding empathy at bay as she assigns incoming patients to one of the three basic categories: emergent, urgent, and nonemergent, or crocks, as Pilar calls them. For an hour, Alice works steadily, chipping away at the long line of people waiting to be seen. "Next," she barks, like a postal clerk. "Next; step up to the counter."

"Yo, Alice," a small voice says.

She knows his voice even before she looks down. "Noah!"

she cries, absurdly pleased. "You've come back to see us." For he promised solemnly to visit when he was released, two weeks ago, into his grandmother's custody, and somewhere in the back of her mind Alice has been waiting.

"No, ma'am," says the boy's grandmother, brown and tough as an acorn. "We're here on business." She takes Noah's arm in her gnarled hand and turns it over, revealing two fresh, round burns, each the exact circumference of a cigarette.

Alice looks at the arm, then at the grandmother. She calls another nurse to take over triage and, grim-faced, marches the boy and his grandmother back to an empty treatment room.

It's wrong, against all protocol. There's a waiting room full of people hurt worse than Noah. Though surely painful, the boy's burns are not life-threatening. The urgency abides in Alice.

"What happened?" she asks the old woman.

"Don't you look at me like that. My daughter came back, that's what happened. I told 'em she would, and how am I suppose to stop her? I bar the door, she take it right off the hinges. They wouldn't listen. Now look what she's gone and done." She shakes the boy's arm accusingly. They stare at the burns, two women with a single expression.

Noah stares down at the floor.

"It's the crack. That shit just rot the heart right out of them. She comes into my home, sits in my chair, tells the child, 'Fetch this, do that,' and when he don't move fast enough for her . . ."

"You didn't stop her."

The woman glares. "I tried." She pushes back the hair that falls over her forehead, revealing a swollen purple bruise. "There's the thanks I got for my trouble."

Alice approaches to examine the bruise, but Noah's grandmother waves her off. "I can't take it no more. I ain't saying I don't care about the child. He's family and I want to do right by him, but I didn't sign on for no package deal. Long as he's with me, she gonna come around. You hear what I'm saying?"

"Wait," says Alice. "It may take a while. Just you sit tight." Just to be sure, she stations Murchison outside the door while she hunts up Dr. Graystone.

Graystone is leading the resuscitation effort on a cardiac arrest, a seventy-five-year-old male brought in with V-fib and no measurable pulse. A fresh batch of med students watch wide-eyed as he runs through the drill: two 200-watt shocks, CPR, epi drip, lidocaine. They get some pretty rhythms, but nothing close to life-sustaining. Graystone puts in a transvenous pacer but gets no capture. Finally he calls the code. Alice nabs him on his way out the door.

They talk, and then they look for Lorraine Goldblossom. The social worker is alone in her tiny office. Alice tells the story. "The grandmother won't keep him anymore," she concludes.

"I'll speak to her," Lorraine says briskly. "If necessary, CWA can try for a restraining order to keep the mother away."

"A restraining order for a crackhead?"

"If she violates it, she goes to jail."

"You know crackheads don't think that far ahead. The only hope for that kid is to get him far away from the mother."

"The grandmother's stable. CWA isn't going to foster that child out when there's a viable family home for him to go to. The mother agreed to seek help. I know they set her up with a program. Much as I sympathize, Alice, this one's not our problem."

"It's *not* viable. The grandmother can't protect him, and the mother's still on crack." Alice appeals to Graystone, who asks if there's a father in the picture.

Lorraine shuffles through her notes and says in a bored voice, "Mother claims she doesn't know his name but said he was a 'muh-fuckin' white devil,' quote unquote."

"I'm admitting him," Graystone decides. "We'll give CWA time to consider their options."

"Utilization review's gonna love that," Lorraine says.

Graystone shrugs. Noah Berry's admitting diagnosis won't be the first he's fudged. The review committee always bitches about dispositional admissions, and with good reason, since inevitably Medicaid balks, and the hospital ends up eating the cost. But they know and he knows that without his ER, half their beds would stand empty.

From Lorraine's office, he and Alice go to talk to the grandmother. They find the boy alone, huddled in a far corner of the treatment room.

"Where is she?" Alice demands of Murchison.

The guard spreads his hands. "You said make sure the kid stays. I got no authority to detain the old lady if she don't want to stay."

"She left me," Noah says, dry-eyed. "She say she can't keep me no more. She don't want me. Nobody cares about me."

Alice kneels beside him. She takes him in her arms.

Noah clings to her neck. Beneath his skin she feels bones, no meat at all. An urge comes over her to walk out right now, take this boy home and feed him. It seems the right and obvious thing to do. She rubs his back, and suddenly Noah dissolves in sobs. It amazes her that he can open his arms to her, lay his head on her shoulder, cry, and be comforted; that after all the rejection and pain this child has suffered, he still has it in him to trust another human being. It tears her apart. She cannot bear to think of what lies ahead.

In her years in Mercy ER, Alice has seen everything. Children have died in her arms, and parents have lunged for scalpels, desperate to follow them. She's treated battered babies, adolescent suicides, victims of torture and other atrocities, all the flotsam and jetsam of the city's malevolent tide. Outsiders talk of shattered lives and broken hearts as if those things were metaphorical, but those whose job it is to sweep up the shards know better. Agony in all its forms is the raw material of their craft. In order to help others, one must first survive. On aircrafts parents are advised, in case of a sudden drop in air pressure, to adjust their own masks before assisting their children, a principle viscerally understood in the ER. Alice has evolved a mental shield, an imaginary Plexiglas sheath through which she can reach out, but no one can reach in.

Noah's tears penetrate the sheath. They soak through her

uniform, through her skin, through the walls of her arteries. They mingle with her blood and make their way into her heart.

She holds the child close; she cradles his head. The words "flesh of my flesh" come into her mind. "*I* care," she whispers softly. "*I* want you."

12

·······

CROW

Percy and Vinnie just ran in a multiple trauma, little girl hit by a car. I scramble to make way for the streams of doctors, nurses, and techs converging on room one. On his way out, Percy sees me, but for once Mr. Sweet Tongue's got no smile nor joke. "How's she doing?" I ask him. He shakes his head, turns thumbs down. Hysterical screams from the waiting room mark the mother's arrival. I hurry away to my closet. It's near to quitting time, and I want to make one more pass through the halls before I go.

First I do the corridor by Records and the doctors' lounge, then round the corner to the treatment rooms. Most everybody's working on the little girl, and I got the hall to myself, except for one doc with his nose pressed against the window of the trauma-room door. Even from the back, it's plain he's itching to go inside, but he can't. It's the first rule of the ER: no nonessential personnel in the trauma room. Like Selma say, too many cooks spoil the broth.

Bad sounds come out of that room. Someone hollers, "Clear!" Dr. Kraven yells, "Come on, little girl, breathe!" One part of me's grieving for the child and her mama, wailing up a storm in the waiting room. Another part's thinking that if they open her up on the table, I am never gonna get out of here tonight.

The doctor at the crash-room door don't notice me coming

with the mop—they never do. Normally I'd just work around him, but he's standing in a patch of blood. "Excuse me," I say. He jumps and turns to me with a look of shock.

I drop my mop. I cross myself. I'm no Catholic, but it can't hurt.

He's as spooked as I am. To look at him, you'd think *I* was the ghost. I get a hold of myself and say firmly, "Doctor, a word with you."

Elias isn't having any. He turns his face to the window.

"I know who you are," I say. "If you don't come now, I'll scream the place down." I don't know what makes me think he'd mind, but it works. Reluctantly he comes my way. Without taking my eyes off him, I pick up my mop and lead him to my supply closet. I wait a second to see if he'll pass right through the wall, like ghosts in the movies, but he just stands with his hands behind his back, waiting for me to open the door. It's like he's kind of embarrassed by his ghosthood, like he don't care to flaunt it. I let us in and shut the door.

We study each other. He looks like his picture: tall and lean, with that stoop-shouldered posture they get from years of bending over patients. Gray hair, bushy eyebrows, a little pale, but all in all he don't look bad for a man's been dead fourteen years. Liver-spotted hands fiddle nervously with his stethoscope. I notice he's got one of those little teddy bears attached to it. What I see looks solid as a rock: nothing misty, moldy, or translucent about this ghost. If you didn't know, you'd never guess, but knowing, you can feel the difference. There's a kind of emptiness where he stands. If I closed my eyes, I'd think I was alone.

There's something else. The ER's full of smells, mostly foul. Blood, shit, vomit, infection, the acrid stench of fear and death, and set against those, my countersmells: disinfectant, ammonia, chlorine. A whole tapestry of odors with a hole in the middle, that hole being Elias. People, living people, exude odors, products of their animal presence. Elias has none.

Me, I'm so scared I'm sweating like a pig. Flashes of old horror movies race through my head. I wonder what I'll do if Elias suddenly decides to take his head off or transforms himself into some oozing horror. But he don't seem the kind of ghost who'd do that to a person, which, even if he was, oozing horrors are pretty much our stock-in-trade. Meanwhile, he looks shakier than me.

"It's okay," I tell us both. "It's cool. Let's just remember who's who here."

He doesn't answer. I don't know if he can.

"I don't want to be rude," I say. "I don't mean to hurt your feelings. But I got to tell you right up front: I don't believe in ghosts."

"Very sensible," Elias says. "Neither did I."

His voice sounds rusty, like water running through a disused pipe. Except for that, and his lips moving slightly out of synch, it could be anyone talking.

"Dead is dead," I say, though I kind of hesitate to use the word. Working in a hospital, there's all kinds of protocols about what things are called. Deaf ain't deaf; it's hearing-impaired. Blind is vision-impaired. So what's the proper term for Elias's problem: existentially impaired?

Anyway, he don't seem to mind. "Absolutely," he says.

"People believe in ghosts, they just superstitious fools, far as I'm concerned."

Elias nods.

"There's just one problem," he says.

"What's that?"

"Who're you talking to?"

He's got me there. When it comes right down to it, I'd sooner believe in him than doubt myself.

What I really want to ask him takes some leading up to. First, to be polite, I ask him about himself. "What's the point of hanging around this place? Haven't you got someplace better to go?"

He shrugs, frowning down on me. For a moment, it looks like he's going to pull rank, which wouldn't be hard. 'Round here, a dead doctor outranks a live housekeeper any day of the week. I say, "I ain't trying to tell you your business, you being the deceased one and all, but I read how when people die, there's this tunnel with a bright light at the end you go through, and all your loved ones are waiting for you on the other side. So what happened to you?"

His long face sags. "The usual thing, I suppose. Unfinished business."

"What kind of business?"

Those bushy eyebrows reach for the ceiling. "What's it to you?" they're saying.

"I'm not just being nosy," I say. "I happen to have a strong personal interest in the matter."

"My dear young woman, I know no more than you. They don't give out guidebooks, you see. There are no rules posted."

"Why am I the only one that can see you? How come I'm so lucky?"

As soon as I ask the question, I can tell he's not pleased about it. I see myself in his eyes: black face, brown uniform, that's all he notices. Pilar said he was a good guy but even the best of them are puffed-up little godlings. Can't hardly help it, the way they're treated. It offends his dignity, being seen by me. No doubt he figures if he's going to be seen at all, it ought to be by the department head, or at least an attending physician.

"Damned if I know," he says.

"I'd watch the language, a man in your position."

There's a commotion in the hall. From the screams and weeping I guess they lost the little girl. Elias turns toward the door. I see I won't have him much longer, and I still haven't got to the point.

I stretch out a hand to hold him, then pull it back. "Just one more question, please."

He looks back at me with a doctor's shallow patience.

"Do you know my husband?" I ask. "Have you met Blue Durango?"

A condescending look comes over his face, the look I used to try and keep off my own face when folks in Europe asked if by chance I know their aunt or cousin or nephew who lives in New York.

"No," Elias says. "I haven't had the pleasure." Then he stands aside for me to open the door for him, which I do.

13

· · · · · · ·

He's off on Thanksgiving, but force of habit wakens him at dawn. Michelle is sound asleep beside him. In repose her face seems sweeter, her beauty less contrived. She has kicked off the quilt and lies naked to the waist. A magnificent chassis, Graystone thinks; expensive to maintain, though. A sharp November chill leaches through the open window. He draws the quilt up to her neck.

In her own space, Michelle is obsessively tidy, but in his apartment her belongings are strewn all over. She seems to him to be staking out territory, the way wolves leave scent markers on trees. He takes a small, silver-wrapped box from his night-table drawer and places it on the pillow beside her face, then goes off to shower.

When he returns, she is sitting up in bed, wearing the top half of a pair of his pajamas. Crumpled bits of silver paper litter the bed, as if an impatient child had snatched at it, and in her cupped palm a pair of gold and ruby earrings sparkle. She looks miserable; but when she sees him, she smiles.

"Happy birthday," he says, sitting beside her on the bed.

"They're lovely, Thomas. Thank you."

He touches her cheek. His finger comes away wet.

"They're wrong, aren't they? What I get for picking them out myself."

"No, baby, they're beautiful."

"Then why the tears?"

She lifts her eyes to his. "Do you really want to ask me that?"

No, he doesn't. He doesn't want to be having this conversation at all. At this point, though, there's no way out.

"Of course I do."

Michelle says, "They're rubies."

"Rubies are bad?"

"Rubies are wonderful. But I was hoping for a diamond. Not a big one. Just one little diamond, in a ring."

"Hate diamonds. Insipid things. Try those on, why don't you? I think they'll suit you." Graystone hears himself babbling but can't stop. What a fool he was, raising her hopes with that little box. Should have known better. Women and birthdays are a volatile mix.

Sure enough, the tears begin to flow. He puts his arm around her. Michelle lays her head against his chest and says, in a muffled voice, "I know what suits me. You know, too. I'm thirty-six years old, and I want to have babies, Thomas."

"Darling, we've been having such a good time together, why rock the boat?"

She pushes him away. "Good time? *Good time?* Is that all I am to you?"

"Not *all,*" he says.

Michelle looks stricken, then angry. "What are you looking for? Open your eyes, fool: You are never going to find a better woman than me if you search till you're old and gray. This is *it,* darlin'. We are perfect together."

It's true. Had he met her in a butcher shop, she would have had a sign pinned to her front: PRIME WIFE CUT. When he's with her, he basks in the envy of other men, and when he's not, she never enters his thoughts: the perfect doctor's spouse. What are you waiting for, Daniel had asked, a sign from heaven? Of course not, Graystone had scoffed, but Daniel wasn't far off the mark. Despite aspersions cast by certain disappointed ladies, Graystone is no Don Juan. He sees himself rather as Don Quixote, taking to heart that cautionary tale: A man who sets off in search of a dream ends up dying alone, without issue.

He hesitates, and the woman hangs on his silence. Graystone stares, seeking an answer in her face, but her beauty is a barrier he can't penetrate; it draws him in, it shuts him out. Then a strange thing happens. Even as he watches, Michelle's features seem to blur and re-form. In her place, he sees another woman, someone as wrong for him as Michelle is right, as unsuitable as any woman could be; yet this imagined face, with its angular, self-contained intelligence, its hidden judgments and heedlessness of him, is stronger and more immanent than the lovely, eager face before his eyes.

Crow is not a partner for him. As a medical man, Graystone knows that the strange, obtrusive images of her that plague him at the oddest moments are mere mental tics, born of fatigue and stress. They convey no pertinent information—other than the sudden peripheral yet certain knowledge that he does not and will never love Michelle.

He takes her hand and rubs his thumb against her silky skin. "I can't lie to you, baby. I'm not ready to get married."

"You mean you're not ready to marry me."

He doesn't deny it. She opens her eyes and lets him see inside. Graystone feels like a monster; he'd like to bash his head against a wall. What is wrong with him?

"Michelle," he says helplessly, "you're a stunning woman."

At once she's out of his bed, dressing so fast it makes his head spin.

"Don't do this, baby," he pleads. "Let's have coffee. I can't fight before coffee."

"Who's fighting?"

"You can't leave now. My mother's expecting us for dinner."

Michelle tugs on her tight leather boots as if she's late for a train. "Don't forget the pie," she says. At the door, she tosses the earrings to Graystone, who snags them reflexively.

"Nice catch," she says. "But that's you, isn't it: The hand is quicker than the heart."

"Could you take the earrings, please, Michelle? Could you just take the goddamn earrings I spent hours choosing for you?"

"Save 'em for the next fool, baby. I told you from the start: I can't be playing games."

Elvira's eyes peer past him into the darkness. "Where's Michelle?"

"Couldn't make it." He drops a kiss on her head. "Happy Thanksgiving. What's that wonderful smell?"

This diversion has all the efficacy of a cobweb stretched across the path of a speeding locomotive. "What happened?"

"She decided to go to her own people."

"She *told* me she was coming here."

"A change of plans, Mother."

Her lips constrict. "I see," she says.

Thomas walks down the hall, past the grand staircase, past the dining room with the cherrywood table set for six, sparkling with crystal and silver and bone china, into the living room. The occupants rise to greet him: his father, Dr. Harold Graystone, Harold's brother Marcus, and his wife, Claudette, a dusky beauty from Guadeloupe via Paris. Claudette kisses him on both cheeks, then on the lips. Her scent, dark and sultry, wraps itself around him. In her heavy French accent, which ten years' residence in the States has not eradicated or even lessened, she cries, "Darling Thomas, why we never see you?"

He murmurs an excuse.

In the dining room, Elvira makes an ungodly racket removing one place setting. Then she appears in the doorway, her smile bracketed by tight little lines. "It seems Michelle couldn't make it."

"What's the matter, Thomas, you lose another girlfriend?" Claudette teases, not without a trace of malice. His uncle's second wife is twenty years younger than her husband, three years younger than Thomas. For as long as he's known her, she has flirted outrageously with him, kissing him on the lips with Gallic abandon, flaunting her splendid little breasts and tight bottom in formfitting dresses, while her fond and foolish husband smirks like a man displaying a sleek black panther on a leash. And for her trouble, she has had nothing but the occasional box of chocolates, which she eschews, and a collection of treacly Hallmark cards, exceptional in their blandness. *"To a Dear Aunt on Her Birthday . . ."*

"Not lost, only misplaced," says Graystone for the sake of peace, temporary as it must be.

Dinner is served by Mary, Elvira's housekeeper. Unextended, the table seats ten; their party of five seems attenuated. Harold sits at the head of the table, Elvira twelve feet away at the foot. Beneath her gracious hostess's manner may be heard a faint ticking sound. While his father and uncle argue amicably about investments, the value of various mutual funds, and the direction of interest rates, Thomas drifts back to an earlier time.

Childhood Thanksgivings were celebrated with his mother's family: Thomas's grandparents, uncles and aunts, a baker's dozen of cousins. In convoy these Metzgers set out from Brooklyn, a wagon train of battle-scarred old Caddies and ancient Studebakers braving the hostile stares and unnumbered streets of suburbia.

Thomas's city cousins spoke a language of their own that was Greek to him. They knew groups and dance steps he'd never heard of, and people with names like Flo the Ho, Candyman, and Freak Runner. The older kids called girls "bitches" and each other "nigger," a taboo word, a *nonexistent* word in the Graystone household. They were intimates of truant officers, beat cops, dope sellers, numbers runners, and other arcane types Thomas had only read about. Sex was no mystery to them; they all, even the youngest girl, knew more than he did and teased him for his ignorance. Thomas was awed by his cousins and envied their lives, shot through with adventure and risk.

His uncles had several vaguely defined daytime occupations, but by night their true identities emerged: They were blues musicians. Like cops, even off duty they kept the tools of their trade close at hand. After dinner, stuffed to bursting, drunk with food, they all gravitated to the living room. Uncle George sat at the piano, fooling with the keys; then Uncle Zach ambled over with his bass, and Uncle Ham produced an old twelve-string guitar that shone with age and care; and soon without a word to each other they'd ease into playing. Thomas always worked his way around the room to stand behind George. His uncle's long, stained fingers flew over the keys, loving that staid old Singer, teasing out sounds Thomas never knew were in there.

Not only music came with the Metzgers but also magic, transformation. Most remarkable of all was the change in Elvira, who in her brothers' company shed her everyday self. Through sheer determination, Thomas's mother had eradicated all traces of Brooklyn from her speech, which by now differed from that of their white Long Island neighbors only by a slight excess of refinement, a certain stiffness of diction and tone. But under her brothers' spell, her voice loosened, her vowels lengthened, her sentences curled up at the end, her tone turned husky blue and full of laughter. Another Elvira emerged, one who danced sinuously and sang to her brothers' accompaniment the old songs, blues from the Delta passed down from mother to child, generation upon generation in an unbroken chain.

These uncles were towering, robust men, taller than his father, so tall their heads were shrouded in clouds of smoke, or so it seemed to Thomas, himself a puny lad of nine when they were banished forever from the house.

He was never told why, but he didn't need telling: He had witnessed the scene that led to their banishment.

It was a hot summer afternoon, in the dead zone between the end of school and the beginning of camp. They had just moved into the big new house on Long Island's Gold Coast, the first black family in the community, and Thomas had made no friends. He was sprawled across his bed, reading comics, when suddenly he heard a siren approaching their house. The wailing rise-and-fall grew louder and louder until it filled the house and rattled the books on his shelves. Brakes screeched to a halt; the siren quit in midshriek. Thomas raced downstairs to find his mother standing inside the screen door, talking to a pair of cops. Their holsters were unstrapped, and their hands rested casually on their guns. Across the street a knot of neighbors gathered, white ladies in soft summer dresses. "Where is he, Elvira?" one of the cops demanded in a loud, rude voice.

No one called his mother Elvira. In the shops, in her husband's medical office, on the street, it was always "Mrs. Graystone." Thomas clenched his fists and squeezed past her. "Don't talk to my mother like that!"

The cops laughed. The one who had spoken before said, "You got a license for this little bulldog, Elvira?" and they laughed again.

His mother gripped him, her palms damp against his arms. "Thomas, go upstairs!" she ordered, and gave him a push. No one spoke as he mounted the steps. Thomas slammed his bedroom door, crept back to the head of the staircase, and strained to decipher the murmur of voices below. His uncle George's name was mentioned several times. Also the words "fight" and "fugitive." His mother's words were inaudible, but her fear resounded like a stone dropped into an empty well.

Shortly after the police car drove away, Thomas's father arrived home, and his parents closeted themselves in their bedroom. Thomas, ear pressed to the door, heard wild weeping. His mother's voice cried, "We're ruined in this neighborhood. All the stereotypes, all their worst fears . . . 'What do you expect?' they'll say. Damn him, damn him!" Dr. Graystone's reply was steady, deep, and comforting.

Elvira didn't appear for dinner, but that night she came to Thomas's bedroom. "It was all a mistake," she told him. "The police came to the wrong address." The way she said it, he could tell he wasn't required to believe her, only to pretend to.

Several months later, on Thanksgiving morn, Thomas ran downstairs barefoot and in his pajamas. His mother was in the kitchen, kneading pie dough. Already the room was full of mouth-watering aromas. "When will they be here?" he demanded.

His mother didn't look up. "Who?"

"My cousins!"

"They're not coming."

He was stunned. "Why?"

She wouldn't look at him. She wore an old housedress, but her face was carefully made up. Thomas had rarely seen it naked: In the mornings Elvira rose, washed her face, brushed her teeth, and put on her makeup before emerging from her bedroom. Her strong hands worked while her lips shaped careful words.

"It's no kindness to celebrate our good fortune in the presence of those who have much less. It hurts their feelings; it leaves a bitter taste. Your uncles would not feel comfortable in this house."

"Did you ask them?"

Her eyes, bright and small as a ferret's, narrowed to slits. "No."

"My cousins wouldn't feel uncomfortable. We always have fun together."

His mother motioned for him to sit opposite her. "Thomas," she said, punctuating her words with fierce pushes and proddings of the dough, "you remember when we packed up the old house, we told you: Take only what you need, what you use. This move, it's more than just a new house. It's a new life, a world of opportunities. But what you've got to understand, baby, is nothing comes from nothing. You gain something, you give something up. You don't carry dead weight along."

"My cousins aren't dead weight, Mama."

She gazed past him out the window, where great expanses of manicured lawn, unmarred by sidewalks, stretched down to the road. The street was narrow and winding like a river, canopied by great oaks.

"You're old enough to understand," she said. "Your cousins have their world, and you have yours."

"Wake up, Thomas, and pass the gravy." Elvira is shaking his arm. "Your uncle asked you twice. What *are* you dreaming about?"

"Thanksgivings in the old days, with your family. Remember, Mother?"

Elvira glances quickly round the table and trills a social laugh. "How nostalgic, Thomas."

"Whatever happened to my cousins?"

Elvira shrugs and turns to Marcus on her other side.

"You're not in touch at all?" he persists.

"You know what Tom Wolfe said, darling. You can't go home again."

"You can phone. And it's Thomas Wolfe. Tom Wolfe wrote *Bonfire of the Vanities.*"

"You know what I mean. People grow apart. Life-styles change." She smoothes her hair, which needs no smoothing. Sleek and black, it falls to just below her chin and there curves under obediently. "He understands me," she confides to Marcus. "He just loves catching people out on their words. I always said he should have been a lawyer."

Graystone laughs. "Listen to her. I should have been a useless parasite."

"Talking about lawyers," his father says, "which we shouldn't on Thanksgiving, I heard a story. What's brown and white and looks good on a lawyer?"

"What?"

"A pit bull."

Mary clears the china under her mistress's watchful eye. "Who wants ice cream?" Elvira asks. "Just plain vanilla, I'm afraid. *Michelle* was bringing the cake, before her change of plans."

Graystone winces. "She baked a pie! Pecan, no less. I totally forgot. Sorry, Mother. *Mea culpa.*"

She looks at him and says, "I had no doubt whose fault it was."

Sixteen miles and a world away, Selma, her daughters and their families, Crow and Joey, and Johnny Deacon are all gathered in Selma's apartment. The adults sit in the living room at a foldout aluminum picnic table that sags beneath the weight of roast turkey, sweet-potato pie, collard greens, dumplings, glazed carrots, cranberry sauce, and the enormous honey-baked ham Deacon brought. The room, long and narrow, is papered in a faded floral pattern and furnished with a green brocade couch enveloped in plastic slipcovers, a rose-colored armchair, and a huge old-fashioned television console. A montage of family photos, framed in gilt, hangs on the wall beside a painting of a black Jesus on the cross, gazing upward in agony.

The guests crowd around the table; they hold their elbows in but can't help jostling as they pass food and reach for seconds. The children sit separately in the kitchen, presided over by the oldest girl.

Between dinner and dessert, the grown-ups pause to catch their breath. Crow, glowing from Deacon's champagne, proposes a toast: "To absent friends."

They drink; then Deacon stands, refills their glasses, and lifts his own. "To endurance," he says. "To getting on with business." He looks sternly at Crow. "To the future."

14

• • • • • • •

Don't, oh please, don't do that."

Alice says, "Squeeze my hand, honey. She'll be done in a moment."

Elsa Kraven looks up from the foot of the table. "I'm sorry, Trina. Just a couple more stitches. Try not to move."

"You're hurting me. Mama, oh, Mama."

Alice strokes the head of the pretty child, fourteen years old, found beaten, cut, and raped in an alley beside her house, waylaid on her way home from school. Under her hospital gown, she wears the top half of a parochial-school uniform. "Easy, honey," Alice croons. "Breathe deep. We're here to help you. Good girl, good. Almost done now."

"I want my mama."

"She's here, and she'll be in to see you soon as we finish."

Kraven steps back to study her handiwork. Though deep, the vaginal laceration was clean-edged and with stitches should heal completely. She worries more about disease. The rapist cut this child before he raped her, as if determined to infect her with whatever he had. With months, maybe years, of uncertainty to endure, there is no way for this girl to put the trauma behind her. And though Kraven tries to insulate herself from her patients' suffering—"It's not my pain" is her mantra—this time it doesn't work. Her hand is steady, but her gut clenches with each stab of the needle into lacerated flesh.

She snips the thread and checks the rape kit. They have everything but the pubic hairs, which have to be plucked, not cut—the last, painful indignity. At the head of the table, Alice is holding the girl's hand, talking softly. Kraven catches her eyes. The nurse nods, slips behind the patient, and grasps her shoulders.

"This is the last thing, Trina," Kraven says. "We've got to take a few hairs. It's going to sting just a little, but then we'll be all finished, and you get to see your mom."

The girl keens softly, talks to herself. "Mama gonna kill me. She told me don't go down that alley."

"No, honey," says Alice. "Your mama's gonna hold you and hug you and comfort you. She's not angry at you; she's angry at whoever hurt you."

For the first time, Trina looks directly at Alice. Her golden brown eyes brim with tears. "In my building, most the girls got babies already, but I ain't never been with a man. I was waiting for somebody special. Now look what happen. He didn't even know me. Why'd he do me like that?"

Over the girl's draped body, the women's eyes meet. Alice squeezes Trina's shoulder. "I don't know, honey. One thing I can tell you for sure, though: It wasn't anything you did."

Later, in the hall outside the ob-gyn room, Elsa Kraven leans against the wall, arms crossed over her chest, hands jammed under her armpits. She weeps silently, denying her tears. Blond tendrils have pulled loose from her bun; spiky with sweat, they frame her face like the petals of a disaffected sunflower. "I hate this place," she says.

Alice proffers a Kleenex. "This place or this city?"

"Tell you one thing. They better not bring in the asshole who did her. I get my scalpel into him, I'll do the world a favor."

"They ain't never gonna bring him in," says Pilar, gliding by. "Police never gonna find him. You see any reporters standing out front? You see the mayor or the chief of police? This just some poor little black girl got raped, not your white yuppie stockbroker."

Elsa goes off in search of Trina's mother. Cradling the

clipboard with the patient's chart, Alice sags against the wall. Her feet are swollen, her legs ache, her whole body feels used and abused. After seven years, it's getting old, or she is. No one does seven years in the ER—no one except Pilar, Woman of Steel, beside whom Alice feels perpetually soggy, bloated with the city's woes. Because try as you might to keep your personal life separate from your work, inevitably there's seepage. After a while, you start seeing the world as one vast emergency room. You catch yourself triaging people you meet on the outside: This one's a crock; this one's in real trouble. You start perceiving through a cop's eyes, from the bottom up: the world divided into victims and perps.

It's not as if options don't exist. The temptation is always there. With the dues she's paid, Alice could name her beat: obstetrics, pediatrics, surgery. And one day she's going to do it, she promises herself. One day she's going to throw in the towel, hang up her gloves, retire to a nice quiet medical ward. But Alice looks forward to that day with all the enthusiasm of a superannuated tightrope walker descending to sell popcorn: Because if Mercy is a circus, and there are many in the community who call it that, then the emergency room is its high-wire act, performed without a net. The thrill of miraculous saves, spiced by the constant danger of a plunge into fatal error, is an addictive brew. Why should she ground herself, why bow to the malevolent wind that blows over the city?

Screams and the sound of a violent ruckus rouse her suddenly. Alice runs toward the nurses' station. Rounding the corner, she skids into Dr. Graystone, Henry Murchison, and Crow standing all in a row, their backs to her, staring at something or someone she can't see. Graystone is saying, "Let her go."

"Fuck you, Dr. Oreo."

Alice can't see the speaker, but the voice is familiar. Crow steps forward. "Listen up," she says, her voice gone thick with the accent of the ghetto. "You still got the chance to walk out free and clear. Nobody gonna stop you. Nobody gonna come looking for you. Keep this shit up, you gonna land your skinny ass in jail—and you know that boy be gone by the time you get out. What you want with that useless little white girl anyway? She don't know shit; she ain't no good to you."

"I want my boy," the voice screams. "He's mine!"

"You *know* you ain't gonna get him like this. Walk away, sister, whilst you got the chance."

"You fetch me my child right now, or I swear to God I'll cut the fucking white bitch throat."

Now all at once Alice knows this voice; and in the moment of knowing, her body responds without conscious thought or intention. Shouldering past the two men, she thrusts herself forward. Crow's rapt, astonished face turns toward her, but Alice has eyes only for the intruder.

The woman stands at bay, her back to a row of filing cabinets. Her left arm is wrapped tightly around the neck of their student nurse, Jennifer Caprizzi; her right hand holds an eight-inch-long serrated knife to Jennifer's throat. The nurse's eyes are closed; her lips move soundlessly, in prayer or supplication.

All this Alice absorbs in a moment's practiced glance; then she is blinded by a rage far beyond her control, an outpouring fed by the blood and pain of a thousand victims. Their anguish gathers inside her; their voice breaks through her as she cries with passionate indignation, "Get out, get out. This is not your place!"

Noah's mother fixes her bleary eyes on Alice. "I know you. You the goddamn sorry-ass trouble-makin' cunt started all this shit."

"And I know you," says Alice.

"I come for my boy, and I ain't leaving without him."

Alice's face is ashen, save for two florid patches on her cheeks. "You *animal.* You think after what you did to that child we're going to give him up to you?"

"The fuck you calling a animal, honkie bitch?"

"Did I say animal? No way. Animals care for their young. You tortured your own child. They haven't got a word for what you are."

Staring at Alice, the Berry woman jabs the knife tip a fraction of an inch deeper into Jennifer's throat. Little droplets of blood form around it. Jennifer sags at the knees.

Crow curses, and the men cry out in frustration; they dare not move.

"Coward!" cries Alice. "Why don't you try it on someone your own size?"

"You my size," says the other, and suddenly she shoves Jennifer away and charges Alice. Then several things happen very quickly. Murchison and Graystone jump at the woman, collide with each other, and fall to the floor. Jennifer crashes into Crow, knocking her down. Crow shoves her mop into Berry's path and hollers, "Run, Alice, run!"

The intruder leaps over the mop. She crouches before Alice with her knife held low in a street-fighter's stance. Still holding the clipboard, Alice raises her hands above her head. As the knife slashes upward, her arms descend. The board's metal clip slams into Berry's forehead.

The knife clatters to the ground, and Berry staggers backward, clutching her head. Blood wells from between her fingers and streams down her face, but she doesn't retreat; she regains her balance and lunges again at Alice.

Alice waits until she feels the woman's hot breath upon her face, then ducks beneath her arms and jabs upward. Her right fist lands squarely on Berry's jaw.

Berry's head jerks back; she topples like a tree. Murchison dives on top, pinning her arms, but there's no struggle. Noah's mama is out for the count.

CROW

I'm scrubbing the floor in the last stall when Alice comes in. I see her in the mirror, but she don't notice me. She turns on the cold water, holds her right hand under the tap. While it runs, she stares at herself in the mirror, turning her head this way and that, making all kinds of faces. Then she turns off the water and steps back from the sink.

"Pick on someone your own size," she sneers. Crouching like a boxer, she jabs upward. "Pow!"

Then I step out of the stall and Alice wheels around, clutching at her throat. "Crow, my God, you scared me."

"You?" I scoff.

"I didn't realize anyone was here."

I can clock the exact moment she recalls her little war dance: Her face turns pink. I would hate like hell to be white. Black person blush, can't nobody tell.

"Pretty tough for a white girl," I say.

She gets right in my face. Says, "Have I ever called you a black girl?"

Now this is a bit surprising coming from little Miss Don't-Make-a-Peep, Don't-Raise-Your-Eyes. I mean this a girl, doctor tell her to cut her wrist, she'd ask, "With what?" Always wearing this worried look, like she's constantly losing her panty hose; she's even scared of me, or was. Alice used to remind me of those preppy kids work down at Selma's soup kitchen serving stew (which they wouldn't eat to save their lives, though Selma made it herself, and it's good as can be) and gaping at the poor black folks like tourists in a Third World country. But she didn't look like no tourist today, facing down that bitch. Standing there all dressed in white with her pale face haloed by fiery hair, she looked like some kind of avenging angel or angry prophet. When she raised up her clipboard, I recalled an illustration in a book my mama used to read me: picture of Moses coming down off of Mount Sinai, holding the tablets above his head and glaring down at those fools kneeling to a golden calf. Now that don't exactly jibe with the Alice I thought I knew. What we got here, I'm thinking, is a whole new-and-improved Alice.

"Pretty tough for a white *woman*," I say.

She grins. "Thanks. You weren't bad yourself."

"I figure the woman look at me, least she knows what she's gettin': someone from the 'hood, someone who knows where she's coming from."

"Do you? Know where she's coming from?"

I shrug. "Piece of me felt sorry for her, sure. Somebody took my baby away, I'd lose it, too. But I ain't forgetting what she did to that child."

"Noah." Alice rubs her cheek. Her knuckles are red and swollen.

"You want to soak that hand," I say.

"Are you licensed to dispense medical advice?" she asks with a smile.

"I'm licensed to dispense common sense." My face has got a will of its own: Damn thing's grinnin' back at her like she some kind of friend of mine. "Where'd you learn to fight like that?" I ask.

Smile fades; back comes her usual anxious look. "I never did. First time in my life I ever hit anybody."

"You must've been a saintly child." (Wouldn't of lasted long in my neighborhood.)

"It just never occurred to me I could."

"Now you find out you're a natural."

"I shouldn't have done it."

"No, you definitely should have done it. What you mean is you shouldn't've enjoyed it."

Again she blushes—nature's own confession. "It's not like me," she says. "I'm not like that."

"So what got into you?"

Alice stares into the space between us. "Everything. This place. Seven years. You get a view of the world. We live in a city of sheep and wolves, predators and prey. It gets too much. Comes a time the sheep need to stand up."

I say, "Welcome to the fold."

15

·······

"Tuna salad," says Daniel Bergman. "Garden pasta. Cottage cheese and fruit. Jesus Christ, Thomas. Remember when a man could get a cheeseburger and fries in this joint?"

Graystone selects a pasta dish from the rack and puts it on his tray.

"Consuela, my love," Bergman says, "my kingdom for a slab of red meat."

"Raw?" asks the cook.

"Medium will do fine."

"An' you call yourself a surgeon," Consuela sneers, slapping a patty onto the grill. In the gleaming backsplash behind the grill, Graystone catches a reflection of Crow, sitting alone at a table for four. She is the reason he's forgone his usual sandwich in the doctors' lounge. He hadn't counted on Daniel tagging along.

When the hamburger's done, Consuela slides it across the countertop, and the two doctors push their trays down to desserts. "Jell-O," Bergman grumbles. "Low-fat pudding. Frozen yogurt. And these labels: Who the hell wants to know the fat content of dessert? What we have here, Thomas, is a not-so-subtle exercise in mind control."

"You don't think you're taking this too personally?"

"Absolutely not. Big Brother is watching us eat. Probably

got the layer cake rigged to deliver a shock if you touch it."
Nevertheless, he takes two portions, shrugging off
Graystone's quizzical look. "What the hell, got to keep my
strength up. I'm eating for two now."

They nod to the cashier and walk by. Suddenly Graystone
stops, turns to his friend. "What was that?"

"You heard me."

"You mean Risa . . . ?" He traces a convex curve,
stomach-high.

"Give the man a cigar."

"All right, Bergman! Who'd've thought you had it in you!
How's she feeling?"

"Terrific. No morning sickness, nothing."

It's one o'clock, and the hospital cafeteria is filling up.
There's an empty table near the condiment stand, but
Graystone ignores it, heading for a table just beyond
Crow's. Bergman nods pleasantly to the housekeeper as he
passes; but Graystone stops.

Crow glances up from her book, eyebrows raised, smile
pending.

"Hi," he says.

"Hi yourself."

There's a silence. "Good book?"

"Excellent." She turns it over to show the title: *Things
Fall Apart,* by Chinua Achebe. Then, with a mischievous
glint in her eye, she asks, "Are you surprised to see me
reading, Doctor?"

He realizes she's joking, but like all good jokes this one
cuts close to the bone: because yes, dammit, he is surprised,
and it galls him that she sees it. But then everything about
the woman surprises him, every exchange comes laden with
embarrassment. Daniel would have known how to answer
her; he'd have teased her back with that patented mock-
flirtatious manner of his. Graystone hasn't the knack.

"Of course not," he says. "Enjoy your lunch." And
hurries on, stiff-necked with the effort of not looking back.
He's certain she's laughing at him. The woman has no sense
of who he is, what they are relative to one another. Her
attitude, unfailingly polite on the surface, lacks that whisper
of subservience that has come to seem a natural adjunct to

Graystone's hospital persona. She watches and gives no sign of what she's thinking; or else she laughs behind her eyes.

He slides into a seat across from his friend, facing in Crow's direction. "Given the circumstances," Daniel says, "a man gets to thinking."

It takes him a moment to remember the circumstances. "What about?"

"Life, death, the future, all that shit." Bergman segues into a set piece on his dream walk-in medical clinic, and Graystone nods and murmurs but soon loses the drift. Crow, he notices, has returned to her book. What the hell is wrong with him; what does he want from the blasted woman? She's not interested in his feelings about Blue Durango; for her the tragedy was personal, and she's taken pains to keep it that way. Never asked for his sympathy, or anyone else's, as far as he's aware. Somehow that makes him feel it more.

Ever since he learned Crow's identity, Blue Durango's death has been on his mind. Or rather, his discovery of it: For thus we recall the great and lesser events of our time, by their impact on our lives. Durango died on a Saturday night. On Sunday morning, Graystone was lounging in bed with a woman (Yvonne, or maybe it was Joyce then), drinking coffee and sharing the *Times*. The photograph on page B-1 caught his eye immediately.

In it a woman knelt on a concrete floor, cradling a man's head, both of them splattered with blood. The man appeared dead or unconscious. The woman's face was upturned, her mouth open. Her scream animated the photo, imploding the space around it like the scream in Munch's epochal painting. Behind them stood a small boy, his eyes wide with horror, his hands covering his mouth. It didn't take the sign on the wall ("Union Square Station") to know the picture was taken in the subway. That grainy heat and smoke, that dingy airlessness could only belong to the underground.

Even before he read the caption and knew whose blood had been spilled, the picture caught Graystone's attention the way a foreigner, hearing his own language spoken in a crowd, automatically tunes in: for the woman's desperate look was in the vernacular, her cry of anguish uttered in the native tongue of Graystone's own ER.

A lucky shot for some amateur photog, some Johnny-on-the-spot with an eye to the main chance, not even knowing whose death he was documenting. For days the photograph haunted Graystone. The local television news, newspapers, magazines, even the tabloids, ran it, not because Blue Durango was so famous—few people outside the iconoclastic world of jazz even knew who he was—but rather because of the way the photograph captured the dying man's agony, the woman's grief, the child's terror. Set against the grime of the underground, it was a tragic portrait of the city, an urban Pietà.

The stricken man was Blue Durango. The woman, he now knows, was Crow. Just two days before the saxophonist's death, Graystone had gone to hear Deacon's band. Good as they all were, Durango outshone them all. His solos had a richness and complexity far beyond anything Graystone had heard from him before, and he'd been following the saxophonist since he first came up. That Sunday morning, after reading the caption and accompanying article, Graystone locked himself in the bathroom and wept for the death of the man and his music.

Now, knowing what he knows, the proper and necessary thing to do is to march over to Crow, sit himself down, and pay his respects. But something stops him. Looking around the cafeteria where he has eaten hundreds of times, Graystone sees for the first time how seating is segregated, not by sex or race, but by caste. Doctors sit with doctors, nurses with nurses, aides with aides. The housekeeper sits alone.

It shouldn't matter, but it does. If he approaches her here, people are bound to notice. They'll misunderstand. They'll see: black man, black woman; they'll jump to all the wrong conclusions, because in white people's eyes, the one thing Graystone and the housekeeper have in common signifies more than all that separates them.

Not in his, though. For Dr. Graystone, there can be nothing personal about his interest in Crow. He sees her dispassionately, first as a member of his staff, second as

Blue Durango's widow, third as an intellectual puzzle. The woman is full of contradictions, truly a chameleon. Even her speech adapts to her surroundings. Dealing with the Berry woman, she used the accent and diction of the projects; but with Deacon she was a different woman— cultured, refined, amused and amusing, a denizen of a larger world. He can't help wondering in what voice she talks to herself.

Daniel, clucking, passes a hand in front of his eyes. "Earth to Graystone: Where are you, man?"

He shakes his head. "Sorry, Dan'l. Where were we?"

"Man, you haven't heard a word I've said." Bergman follows his line of sight, then turns back with a bemused expression. "You were staring at Crow."

"Why would I do that?"

"What's going on, Thomas?"

"Nothing."

"Better be nothing. Michelle finds out it's something, she'll have your ass in a sling."

Graystone scowls. "Don't be ridiculous. Besides," he says, addressing his pasta salad, "Michelle's out of the picture."

Bergman stares over the top of his glasses. "More fool you."

"Took herself out. Walked out on me."

"*She* walked out on *you*? Why?"

"Didn't like her birthday present. Women." Graystone shrugs.

"So get her back, you ninny."

"No point. She's better off moving on. Girl wants to get married. Can't blame her."

"I thought you were going to marry her."

"You and my mother. I don't know why. I never said it."

"Just seemed like it was in the cards. She's a great gal."

"Yes, she is," Graystone says testily, "and she's gonna make some man a great wife, but I am not the man. And now that you've vented your feelings on the subject, Daniel, maybe we can get back to remembering whose life it is."

Bergman shakes his head and finishes his hamburger in silence.

Though he tries to resist, Graystone can't keep his eyes off Crow. Now and then she takes a bite of sandwich or a sip of coffee without looking up from her book. She seems to have forgotten their brief exchange, but Graystone knows full well the subtlety of women. Is she truly unaware of his interest, or is her show of oblivion a kind of backhanded flirtation, an attempt to draw him in?

A trio of white-clad student nurses emerge from the food line bearing trays. They search the crowded room for seats together, hesitate a short moment by Crow's table, then in unspoken consensus move on. Her uniform sets her apart, defines her, confines her; only Graystone knows who she really is. (Or thinks he does; or wishes.) Simplest thing in the world to go over and offer his condolences, belated but sincere; yet he hesitates.

From afar he hears Bergman's voice. "Piece of cake?"

"Not really," Graystone replies distractedly. "It's tricky." Then, noticing Daniel's outstretched hand and the proffered dessert plate, he lowers his head to his hands.

Bergman looks alarmed. "Come on, Tom, talk to me. Something's going on."

"Coffee," Graystone croaks, escaping with his cup. On the way back from the coffee bar, he pauses at Crow's table.

"May I?" He takes a seat without waiting for an answer.

She looks at him with not a glimmer of flirtation or invitation in her dark eyes, just a straightforward inquiry: What do you want?

"I know who you are," he says.

"I should hope so. I've only been working in your department a year."

"You're Blue Durango's wife."

Crow looks down at her hands, folded on the table, and Graystone studies her. Against the cheap polyester of her uniform, her skin, the color of rich loam, glistens darkly. Her breathing is fluid, like the rise and fall of a saxophone. Graystone thinks of Blue Durango's music, how it changed and deepened in the years before his death; and it comes to him that the change sprang from Blue's possession of this woman. The notion that she is limned in his music comes out of nowhere, as if he were strolling through a gallery and suddenly came upon a nude portrait of the woman. At once embarrassed and aroused, Graystone stirs in his seat, crosses his legs, and lowers his eyes before her. At the same time, a separate part of his mind registers the fact that people are looking at them. Though speculation wafts about the room like an errant breeze, Crow is unruffled. He has never seen a woman sit so still.

"His widow," she says at last, raising her eyes.

"I wanted to tell you how much I admired his work. I heard him play many times, the last time just two days before . . . He was a great musician. His death was a loss and a sorrow to the world."

"Thank you," she says, and holds out her hand. He wants to ask after the child; he wants to ask what she's doing, working as a housekeeper. But her handshake, though gracious, has a feel of finality.

He is compelled to stand. Walking back to Daniel, Graystone knows he should feel relieved. He's done what needed to be done, and now it's over. But he lacks a sense of closure; his palm burns with the imprint of her small, hard hand, and he can't keep from dragging his heels.

"Speculum, please," Douglas Plummer says. "Heard about your little escapade."

"Seems everyone has," Alice replies, handing him the instrument.

"Very gutsy."

"Thanks," she says coolly.

"Rather a quixotic effort, of course. Kid's a lost cause from what I hear."

"You hear wrong," she cries, stung into her first-ever contradiction of a doctor.

"Anyway, you showed great presence of mind, not to mention an impressive right hook. We could use you upstairs, Alice. *I* could. Just say the word."

"Thanks, I'm fine where I am."

"Relax, dear," Plummer tells the patient, a slender Latino woman who gave her age as thirty-something. "Swab."

Alice hands him a swab.

He pokes inside; the patient whimpers, then Plummer withdraws the swab and wipes it across a culture disk. "That'll do it." He removes the speculum. Alice helps the patient free her feet from the stirrups.

"What do I got?" the woman asks.

Plummer ignores her, turning his fine dark eyes on Alice. "Send those off, will you, love?"

"Yes, Doctor."

"We'll hold her pending labs. Page me when they come in."

"Yes, Doctor."

"Looks like your garden-variety UTI, though. Might as well start her on IV penicillin while we've got her."

"Yes, Doctor." Alice enters his order onto the chart.

"Meet you at your place, sevenish."

"Yes, Doc . . . What?"

With a magician's flourish, Plummer produces a pair of tickets from his vest jacket. "Just you, me, and *The Barber of Seville.*"

Alice looks from the tickets to his expectant face. Her cheeks turn as crimson as her hair. "Thank you, but no."

He smiles charmingly. Beneath the trim black mustache, his mouth is full and red. "Did I forget the magic word?"

She bags the lab specimens and labels them. "No, I just . . . don't care for opera."

Plummer looks at the tickets: third-row orchestra seats, one hundred bucks a pop. "Neither do I," he says, and rips them in half, tossing the pieces over his shoulder.

"I *love* the opera," says the patient as fragments drift down onto her draped body. "Anyone asked me, I'd go in a second."

"A play, then," he says. "Your choice."

"No, thank you."

"Nurse?" The patient crooks a finger.

Alice goes to her.

"What's wrong?" the Latina whispers.

"We'll know for sure when the lab tests come back, but the doctor thinks it's a simple urinary-tract infection."

"Not with me. With *him.* He's married, right?"

"No."

"So what you got to lose? Okay, he got a bedside manner from hell, but objectively speaking the man is hot."

Then Plummer draws Alice away into a corner of the room. She inhales the odor of Old Spice, the same cologne Charlie used to wear. "Ballet?" he says. His fingers caress her arm. "Dinner out? Dinner in? I do a dynamite spaghetti carbonara."

"I'm busy."

"I'm not," the patient calls out hopefully.

"You know, I get a bad rap around this place. Try me, you'll like me."

"Excuse me, Doctor . . ." Alice edges past him and out the door.

He waits until she's out of sight before gathering up the pieces of opera tickets and stuffing them in his pocket. Then he hurries down the corridor, catches up with Alice, and pins her against the wall with an arm on either side.

"Alice, you're driving me crazy."

"Crazy with desire?"

For a moment he looks uncertain. "Yes."

"Funny how it came on so suddenly, just about the time you met my parents."

"Don't put yourself down, Alice. Underneath that starched white uniform, there's a hell of an attractive woman."

"I wasn't putting myself down, Dr. Plummer."

"Call me Doug," he murmurs. "I really want to see you."

Crow trundles by, pushing her cleaning cart. The women's eyes meet, Crow's amused, inquisitive, a touch disdainful.

Flushing, Alice places a work-hardened hand against Plummer's chest and says, "Frankly, Doctor, I'd rather eat worms." She shoves him back and strides down the hall to the social worker's office.

Lorraine Goldblossom is on the phone. She waves Alice to a seat, finishes her conversation, and hangs up. "I'm going nuts," she tells Alice. "Three geriatric dispos, no insurance, families don't want to know, and all my nursing homes are full. Place is turning into a damn Pop-drop. What am I supposed to do, take them home with me?"

"I want the boy," Alice says.

"The boy?"

"Noah Berry."

"CWA called earlier. They're taking him today."

Alice folds her arms over her stomach and leans forward. "I want him. I visit him upstairs, we talk, we're friends. There's a bond."

"Are you a certified foster parent?"

"No, but I'll do whatever I have to do to become one."

Lorraine looks doubtful. "It takes six months. And even then . . ."

"Why, because I'm single?"

"Oh, no. That doesn't matter anymore." She whispers: "Wrong color."

"What?"

"They used to cross racial lines. Not anymore. Black kids go with black families, white with white."

"What difference does that make?"

"Personally," the social worker says, "I'm color-blind. But that's the policy these days."

"He's half white."

"Says who?"

"The mother."

"That might help. Still, he's been raised black."

"What if he chooses me? Doesn't he have a say?"

Lorraine comes around her desk and takes the other visitor's chair. She puts a manicured hand on Alice's knee. "It's natural to feel an attachment. You've got a lot invested in this patient."

"His name is Noah."

"But, Alice, dear, be practical."

Alice removes the hand. "I want him. I care for that boy, and he trusts me. Doesn't that count for something?"

"Not much," says Lorraine.

16

· · · · · · ·

Crow's alone in her closet, rinsing out her mop, when a discreet cough sounds behind her. She wheels around. "Jesus Christ, don't be sneaking up on me like that!"

"Sorry," says Elias. "Next time I'll rattle a chain."

"Can you really do that?"

"Of course not," he says huffily. "I was joking."

"Ghost humor." Crow sniffs. "What do you want?"

"The patient in seven—"

"*Shit.* Not again."

"Multiple stab wounds. That Chinese fellow missed a wound in the upper-right quadrant. The lung's punctured."

"Look. Doctor. Folks already think I'm nuts here."

Icy blue eyes regard her steadily. "Do you want to discuss your personal problems, or do you want to save that boy's life?"

"Fine." She turns off the water, props her mop against the wall. "I'm going. But then you owe me."

"What?"

"Wait here, okay? I'll be right back."

The halls are jammed with gurneys. Relatives of patients mill about; patients moan and cry for attention; nurses dart from room to room, tight-lipped and glassy-eyed. Finally

Crow finds the head nurse seated in the nurses' station, writing up a chart. "What is it?" Pilar says impatiently.

Crow relays the message.

"Says who?"

"A little bird."

Pilar squints up at her. "Better be right, girl. You're pushing it." She levers herself out of her seat and, feeling for her stethoscope, hustles down the hall toward seven.

Returning to her closet, Crow is surprised to find Elias waiting. She shuts the door.

"Wang's careless," he says fretfully. "Graystone ought to be told."

"Don't look at me. I can just see me going to the suits. 'Scuse me, Doctors, but in this housekeeper's opinion, Dr. Wang don't know a hole in the chest from a hole in the wall.'"

"It's not your opinion, it's mine."

"And I'm supposed to tell them that?" She hoots.

"So you phrase it differently."

"Don't matter how I phrase it, Elias, it just ain't my place. You want 'em told, you tell 'em."

"Don't you think I would if I could?" he says, tugging at his gray hair. "I try and try. But they refuse to hear me; they act as if I don't exist."

Seeing the frustration on his face, Crow surprises herself in an impulse of pity. It's different for him. Born and bred to command, he could hardly be expected to welcome his new status as she had. "It's not so bad, being invisible," she says kindly. "Once you get used to it."

"How would you know?"

"Me?" She laughs. "I'm the unseen hand that disinfects the sinks and tables; I'm the wind that sweeps away the dirt."

Elias waggles his bushy eyebrows like Groucho Marx. "Graystone sees you," he says.

Crow scowls at the ghost. Bad enough him hanging around, second-guessing the medical staff; damned if she'll put up with him meddling in her affairs. "That's on account of Blue, my husband," she says stiffly.

"The one who died."

"You sure you never seen him? Heard him, maybe? Best tenor sax in the universe, your side or mine."

"I don't have time for music."

"Seems to me you got all the time in the world, now."

"It's so damned annoying," Elias says, sitting down in her one chair. "I scream in their faces. I wave my arms and shout. Nothing, no response. As if I don't exist."

"Have a seat, why don't you."

"I'm persona non grata in my own damn ER. The only one who hears me is a . . ."

"A black housekeeper," she finishes for him. "Life's a bitch, ain't it."

"Death's the bitch," he says.

"Look at it this way, Elias. You ain't exactly my first choice in ghosts, either. Seems we're just stuck with each other."

Elias looks up. Somethng in her voice reaches him. His eyes take her in and smile.

"Seems we are," he says.

"You're a third-year resident," Graystone says. "No one expects you to know everything. What I *do* expect you to know are your own limitations. If something's unclear, if you're not sure, then ask for help, goddammit; don't fake it!"

Calvin Wang sits stiffly in the torture seat in Graystone's office. His mouth is set in a thin, taut line.

"I didn't fake it," he says. "When I listened, his breath sounds were normal. Sir."

"Really. Yet half an hour later when Ms. Johnston happened by, the patient was in acute respiratory distress. Another half hour and he'd have drowned in his own blood. So unless you're claiming that someone came along and stabbed him in the interim, his breath sounds *couldn't* have been normal."

"I heard what I heard."

Graystone blows his breath out sharply. "Wang, you're a senior resident; you're my eyes and ears out there. I can't be looking over your shoulder. I've got to be able to trust your judgment. Now you missed the upper-quadrant puncture, God knows how, and you misread the breath sounds, a combination of errors that could have cost that kid his life. I will not have patients dying of carelessness on my watch. Worst of all, as far as I'm concerned, is your denying it ever happened."

Wang's temples are bathed in sweat; his face is very pale. For a moment, he's silent; then his mouth opens like a dam and words come pouring out.

"Do you know what it's like out there? Do you have any idea? At the same time I'm treating this patient, I have two other stabbings, a gunshot, a sixty percent burn, and an unconscious OD, and those are just the emergents. Also I am supervising three first-year residents. How is a man supposed to function in this madhouse without making mistakes?"

"You call up the reserves. Me, Dr. Bergman, the other attendings. You have the authority. Don't whine, Wang. We all know it's a tough job." Graystone regards the younger man contemplatively. "What did you hear when you listened to that kid's chest?"

"Nothing," Wang says sullenly. "There was so much noise in the ER I couldn't hear a thing."

"So you let it pass and went on to the next patient."

"Yes."

"Doctors make mistakes," Graystone says, leaning forward. "Medicine, especially emergency medicine, is an inexact science. Now and then, conscientious doctors make errors of judgment. We make false assumptions, fail to ask critical questions, flub diagnoses. You, however, did not err in judgment. You made two careless mistakes that could have cost a fifteen-year-old boy his life, and carelessness is something I will not tolerate."

"Sir—" cries Wang, but Graystone silences him with an upraised hand.

"I'm not firing you. You've been conscientious up till now, and I'm willing to believe that this incident was an aberration. Was it an aberration, Dr. Wang?"

"Yes, sir!"

"Then go and sin no more." Graystone walks Wang to the

door and watches him scoot down the corridor like a kid let out of the principal's office. He wonders if he came down too hard on the man. Wang's not the best senior resident Graystone's ever had, but he's far from the worst; not imaginative, but dogged and thorough. And now lucky. If Pilar hadn't gone in when she did, Wang's career could have ended before it began. A patient who shouldn't have died nearly did. No, he decides; he wasn't too hard.

The shifts are changing, and the halls are full of white uniforms and lab coats. The shifts are identifiable at a glance: the day-staffers drooping like squeezed lemons, the night-staffers primed and ready for battle. Among the mill of faces, Graystone's eye is drawn to two. Crow and Pilar huddle in a doorway down the hall, heads together in earnest colloquy. Graystone can't hear their words, but their faces look intent, and their stillness amid the bustle imparts an air of conspiracy.

He stares at Crow. They haven't had a conversation since that day in the cafeteria, a week ago; and not for want of trying on his part. "Good day, Crow," he says each morning when they meet; "Morning," she replies, rushing past. In the evenings it's the same; and in between, though his mouth goes dry and his feet falter at the sight of her, he can think of nothing to say.

His intentions are mysterious but benign. He wants to be her friend, to what end he cannot say. There is unfinished business between them, though the nature of the business eludes him. Certainly, despite Bergman's innuendoes, his interest is not romantic. He and Crow come from different worlds—she knows it as well as he. His feeling for her is of dispassionate goodwill and respect for her refusal to court or even tolerate sympathy. He wishes her well—wishes it with rather startling intensity; yet surely this is an emotion suited more to friendship than to love.

Nevertheless, inexplicably, Crow counters his every friendly approach with the same cool, straightforward, inquiring look: "Yes, what do you want?" The more pointed his attentions, the more stolid her response. He can't get behind her eyes, can't see what she's thinking.

* * *

"What the hell's *he* looking at?" Crow mutters in the doorway.

"Who?"

"Graystone."

"Don't change the subject," Pilar says. "I want to hear about this little bird o' yours."

"No, you don't," Crow says.

"Let's not forget whose ER this is, sister."

"Did you tell, Pilar? Is that why he's staring?"

Pilar turns and fixes Graystone with a withering look. He disappears into his office. "I don't know *what* his problem is," she says. "'Course I didn't tell. I just let on I was passing by and noticed the patient in distress."

"Thanks," Crow murmurs fervently.

"Yeah, so now I'm the big hero, when it wasn't my doing at all. I don't care for it, Crow. The whole thing don't sit right. What's he playing at?"

"Who?"

Pilar lowers her voice. *"Him.* Elias."

"Why ask me? You knew him; you were there when he kicked."

"Man in his condition's got no business hanging 'round."

"You said the man never knew when to go home."

Pilar's gaze turns inward. "Damn fool probably blames hisself."

"For what?"

"Tell him, Crow—tell him Pilar says it wasn't his fault, no way was it his fault. Will you?"

"I'd remember better if I knew what you were talking about."

Pilar elevates one massive shoulder, like a drawbridge slowly rising. "It ain't *my* story. Ask him, you so curious."

Then she puts her great warm hand on Crow's shoulder and squeezes, and they part, Pilar to sign over to the night charge nurse, Crow to her closet, where she finds Elias ruminating in her chair with the face of a forlorn bloodhound.

"Uh-uh," she says. "No way. It's Friday night, and I am out of here."

He rises at once. His long, pale face seems etched in loneliness; his white coat, in need of a laundering, exudes a fine dust of discouragement. "I only came to thank you. Well done, Crow."

Crow feels ashamed of herself. The man hasn't talked to a soul in fourteen years. It's like kicking a stray dog.

"Stay if you want," she says. "You're not bothering me."

Elias resumes his seat. Crow removes a sweater and a pair of jeans from her locker, unbuttons the top two buttons of her uniform, then stops.

"Turn your back," she says.

He turns his face to the wall, laughing. "I *am* a doctor," he says.

"You're not *my* doctor."

"It's a moot point anyway. There is life after death, but no sex, my dear—not even the odd erection."

"Did I ask you that?" Crow scolds. "Do you think I want to hear that shit?"

"Pardon me; I thought you said you had an interest."

"You want to hang out in my closet, Elias, you keep a decent tongue in your head." Crow zips up her jeans and pulls her long black sweater down over her hips. "Anyway"—she studies her face in the mirror—"maybe you just haven't met the right ghost yet."

"That's funny," Elias says. "You're a funny girl, Crow."

"You can turn around now. Pilar said to tell you it wasn't your fault."

"What wasn't my fault?"

"You tell me."

He grunts. Then a knock sounds at the door. Crow opens to find Graystone standing in the doorway, looking grim and determined.

"May I come in?" he asks, striding past her.

"Why not? Join the crowd."

He glances around. "Nice."

Crow sputters with laughter.

An agonized look comes over his face. "I mean in the sense of neat. Tidy. Sort of cozy."

"Have you come to admire my closet, Dr. Graystone?"

"No," he says, then falls silent, looking at her with perplexity.

"Tell him about Wang," prompts Elias from his seat in the corner.

"Hush," she hisses.

Graystone looks surprised. "I didn't say anything."

She turns her back on Elias. "How can I help you, Doctor?"

"I was wondering . . . Caspar Harte's playing at the Cellar tonight, and I wondered if perhaps you'd care to go hear him."

Crow stares. Graystone shifts from foot to foot like a schoolboy.

"With you?" she asks.

"Yes."

"Why?"

His answer sounds rehearsed. "Usually I go to hear jazz alone. I thought it would be pleasurable for once to share the music with someone who really knows it."

Crow sneaks a glance at Elias, who sits cross-legged on her chair, hands on thighs, following the conversation like a spectator at a tennis match. She turns back. "Thank you. But I don't think that's such a good idea."

Graystone nods with brusque approval. "I also thought it would be inappropriate at first. But then I reconsidered. What it comes down to is two people who work together and happen to share a common love for music. Nothing sinister; nothing . . . personal."

Crow studies him; he bears her scrutiny with fortitude. "Happens I'll be there anyway," she says at last. "Maybe we'll see you."

Graystone backs away with a rictus of a smile. "Good. Okay. See you there."

As the door shuts behind him, Crow swings toward Elias. "Don't you ever, ever do that again!"

"What did I do?"

"Talk to me in public like that. Do you know how confusing that is, hearing voices other people can't? Now I know how schizos feel."

His nostrils flare disdainfully. "Then I am to be seen and not heard, like a good little ghost?"

"That's right."

"Your attitude is not only condescending, it's foolish. I don't know why you can hear me and they can't, but as long as there's an open channel of communication, I am damn well going to use it."

"Who you calling a channel of communication? I'm a person who prefers that other people not consider her crazy. Can't you just do telepathy or something, 'stead of talking?"

Elias draws himself up. "I am not the Amazing Kreskin. I'm a doctor, dammit, not a freakin' psychic."

"All right," she grumbles. "Don't get all bent out of shape."

"You said nothing about Wang."

"No, and I'm not planning to."

"He probably knows, anyway." Elias looks at Crow out of the corner of his eye. "He's a good man, Graystone. Fine doctor."

Crow doesn't answer. She gathers up her purse and jacket.

"I didn't mean to intrude on a personal discussion."

"Ain't nothing personal between him and me. You heard the man. All we got in common's the music."

"Right," Elias says.

17
. . . .

He arrives late, almost doesn't come at all. It's the "we" that devils him. "We" as in couple, group, or unit; "we" as in "not you." "Maybe we'll see you," she'd said; no matter how he parses it, it comes down to we and you, in and out.

He's offended. Graystone prides himself on his adaptability. Possessed of a social mobility lubricated by the simple device of never going where he's not wanted, he is as comfortable with white professionals as with black. But with Crow he is not so much unsure of his welcome as certain of his lack of it. Her coolness miscasts his friendly overtures; where he ought by rights to feel pleasantly condescending, he feels pushy, thrusting.

Cold air frosts the windows of his loft apartment. Outside it's bitter; a raw, wet, umbrella-crunching wind cracks through the city streets. Night like this, she'll never show, he tells himself. The hell with it.

The Cellar's first set starts at ten. That hour finds him lounging in his favorite chair, a glass of champagne in hand, Mingus on the stereo. But the music flows around, not through him, and beneath it he hears the kitchen clock ticking, ticking. . . . What if she does? What if she looks for him and he's not there?

149

At ten-fifteen he throws on his camel's-hair overcoat, wraps a scarf around his face, locks up, and plunges into the night. Head lowered against the driving rain, hands in pockets, Graystone walks the three blocks to the Cellar. On nights like this, the ER fills up quickly with street-dwellers suffering from exposure or just looking for a place out of the wind. The streets are deserted; not even muggers venture out tonight. Dangling Christmas wreaths and silver bunting smack against store windows, and scraps of newspaper wrap themselves around his knees like supplicants. On the corner of Houston and Broadway, he passes a deserted Salvation Army stand.

Warmth and light rise up from the Cellar, bathing its steps in a comforting glow. Graystone unwraps his scarf and waits in the vestibule for the ringing in his ears to subside. Then he goes inside.

The club is thick with smoke and music and the smell of wet wool. "How ya doing, Doc?" Sam Roth shouts. "Some fuckin' night." He starts getting off his stool, but Graystone lifts a hand.

"It's okay," he says. "I'll find a spot." He waits for his eyes, still tearing from the wind, to adjust to the smoky haze. Onstage, Harte's quintet is playing a variation on a Coltrane ballad, "After the Rain." Like a waterfall, sound cascades off the stage and washes over Graystone, cleansing his mind and clearing his sinuses, too. He makes out Will Sanderson on trumpet, Regis Price on tenor sax, and Caspar Harte on piano, backed by a drummer and Johnny Deacon's own Mack Holloway, sitting in on bass.

Regis Price steps forward. Head thrown back, the saxophonist stands bathed in light, horn straining for heaven. His solo is a rising prayer, a soliloquy of concentrated yearning.

When the piece ends, Caspar Harte leans over to the microphone. "We are honored to have with us tonight my good friend Johnny Deacon. Stand up and take a bow, Deacon." (No one rises, but from the back of the room Graystone espies a hand he knows well, ensleeved in frayed tweed, waving a genial acknowledgment. He starts forward, threading his way among the tables.) "We're gonna play a little tune of his called 'Almost Home.' Now listen up good, Deacon, 'cause here's how it's supposed to sound."

Deacon's deep chuckle stands out from the general laughter. Emerging from between two tables, Graystone suddenly sees him: beside him, as expected, sits Crow, and next to her a couple of Deacon's sidemen: Jordan Reese, the trumpet player, and Billy Mason, the new sax. Graystone stops where he is, staring at Crow.

A gray silk shirt flows like water across her breasts. Her hair, which by day falls in gentle waves to her shoulders, is pulled back from her face, rolled and twisted in the back in a French knot. Bared, her neck emerges long and graceful from square shoulders, and her head is stately and proud, with an air of perfect gravity.

"Almost Home" is a Deacon showpiece. Spangled piano arpeggios occupy the upper register; beneath that is a contrapuntal layer of mournful reeds, a poignant hymn to places and times lost but not forgotten. Graystone shuts his eyes, and the music paints a picture in shades of black and white, like an old movie. He sees a figure, dimly lighted, standing by a hotel window. The sax rises and falls, it arches back, remembering. The figure—a woman—stirs, pulls back a curtain with a slender hand, and gazes out, watching dawn break over a strange city. Dreaming of home.

Graystone opens his eyes. Strange, he thinks, how even though these musicians are such masculine men, chauvinistic to a fault from all he's seen and read, so often the voice that emerges from their instruments is female. As if there's a woman's voice or soul trapped inside them, whose only escape is through the music.

Crow sways to the music, her movement sinuous and graceful. Deacon's hand rests casually on the back of her chair. As Graystone watches, the old man leans over and whispers in her ear, and his hand drifts up to clasp her shoulder.

Graystone's heart seizes up. Something changes in that instant, irrevocably, with a painful jolt. For one moment, the doctor believes he's suffering an infarction, perhaps a stroke. Whatever it is has affected his vision. Deacon's hand, which once he would have kissed in gratitude and respect, changes before his eyes into an ape's paw, grasping, lewd, and lascivious.

Crow sees him. She looks up and smiles, and suddenly the air itself is different. In place of the rheumy, greasy smog of Sam Roth's Cellar, Graystone inhales a clarified distillation, clean and pure. God Almighty, he thinks in horror and awe. I'm a dead man.

"You made it," she says.

Deacon turns. His thick eyebrows rise. "Dr. Grayheart, I presume."

"Graystone, actually," he says.

"Sit," says Deacon. The doctor purloins a chair from another table and wedges it beside Crow's. Jordan Reese makes room with a scowl. "Y'all remember Dr. Graybeard," Deacon says.

"Gray*stone,*" says the doctor, certain now the old man's ragging him. A smile tugs the corner of Deacon's mouth.

Billy Mason lifts the fingers of one hand. Jordan Reese nods in his general direction.

"Not too shabby," Billy says at large, making it a question.

Reese pulls a face. "Shit, Will plays that thing like he still ain't cut the apron strings."

"I've heard worse," Deacon says. "Hell, I've played worse."

"That's for sure. Remember that night in Venice?" says Reese. He, Deacon, and Crow laugh. Billy, too, though Graystone can see he's faking it.

Deacon says, "Now if I told you once, I told you a thousand times, Jordan. It wasn't me, it was those damn oysters." Another burst of laughter. Graystone smiles politely.

"Hush up, boys," Crow says, and they obey her at once and fall to listening to the music. The next piece is one of Caspar Harte's own compositions, and it plays like a dialogue in bebop, a wonderful late-night, smoke-filled, slightly-high-but-not-flat-out-drunk conversation among old friends. Crow listens with her eyes half-closed, both hands wrapped around a beaded glass, smiling to herself, laughing softly when the clash between sax and trumpet grows heated. And Graystone does what he thought he'd never do: lets the music get past him and concentrates on the woman. There's a hollow at the base of her throat that he can almost taste. Her ears are exquisite, her skin flawless, her perfume subtle, not flowery or sweet but breezy, like the smell of fresh-washed sheets snapping on the line. This was Blue Durango's woman, thinks Graystone, a daunting thought. If Blue made love the way he played sax, he'd be a hard act to follow.

The set ends and Caspar Harte ambles over, Mack in tow. "Thank you kindly," he says to Deacon. "Ole Mack here plays a mean bass. One of these days I just might steal him for good."

"I don't lock 'em up at night, Cas. Man's free to leave whenever he wants."

"No thanks, boss," says Mack. He leans over Graystone to plant a kiss on Crow's cheek. "Good to see you, Crow."

"Hello, Mack."

"So it was you." Caspar carries her hand up to his lips and kisses it. "Been way too long, darlin'. How's that boy doing?"

"Doing fine now, Caspar. Thanks for asking."

Mack hauls over a couple of chairs and they all crowd around the table. Graystone fends off stiff competition for his place beside Crow. When his thigh brushes against hers, he feels faint. She doesn't seem to notice.

Caspar Harte ends up on his other side. "Now who's this?" Caspar asks. "Do I know you?"

"Friend of Crow's," Billy Mason says.

"Thomas Graystone, Mr. Harte." Graystone holds out his hand. "I really enjoy your work."

"Why, thank you, Tom. Any friend of Crow's . . ." He flashes a dismissive smile and turns away.

Deacon orders a round of drinks. When it comes, Graystone tries to pay. The men look amused, and the waitress shakes her head. "It's on the house."

The conversation is general. While Graystone waits for the discussion to turn to jazz, he prepares a remark or two, not to show off his knowledge, simply to convey informed appreciation. But the subject never comes up; instead, they gossip about people they know, places they've been. Graystone is surprised and disappointed. When doctors get together, invariably they end up talking shop. But music, it seems, is something these men do, not something they chat about.

Much of what they do say goes over Graystone's head, as arcane to his ears as, he supposes, ER lingo is to a layman. Deacon and Harte resume what seems to be a running argument. "Ain't a doubt in the world but what ear cats got it all over schooled cats," Caspar says.

"That's just pure snobbishness," Deacon replies. "Look at Regis: Hell, he was playing in the damn Philharmonic when Miles tapped him. Cat could play an eleventh without even stretching."

"I'll admit Regis has got a spread, but you know what the man said: It don't mean a thing if it ain't got that swing."

"Man, you got a lot of face, talking like that about your elders and betters. What do you think, Crow?"

Crow is animated, the center of attention without seeking it. Graystone observes closely, seeking a clue to relationships here. Although she is the only woman at the table, she shows no sign of discomfort or self-consciousness; from which he surmises that this has often been the case. Although all these men, except for Billy Mason, are older than Crow, her attitude toward them is almost maternal, denmotherly perhaps. Theirs toward her, however, is hardly filial. They are respectful; but Graystone marks the way they look at her when she's not watching. He sees her through their eyes, and his heart aches.

The musicians ignore Graystone; he's a person of no account to them. Now and then Crow murmurs a word of explanation in his ear or addresses a remark to him, but there's no personal component to this. It's mere politeness, a generic kindness that senses his exclusion and objects to it. Her kindness is no use to him.

The doctor's smile grows strained. He's out of place and knows it. Yet he will not leave the table even to visit the john, knowing that his seat beside Crow will be claimed by the time he returns. What he really wants, with an intensity as painful as the desire is hopeless, is to get her alone. To what end, he doesn't know or ask; the need exists outside of reason. He is trying without success to contrive a way when Sam Roth approaches the table.

"Call for you," he says to Crow, nodding toward his office.

She follows him, silence in her wake. The men track her with their eyes. Deacon's face has gone gray.

Moments later she returns. "It's Joey," she says, pressing Deacon's shoulder.

"What's the matter with the boy?"

"Asthma. He's asking for me." She gathers up her purse and coat.

"I'll take you," sing out Deacon, Graystone, Caspar, and Reese in perfect unison, like a barbershop quartet.

Deacon rises. "I'll fetch us a cab."

"My car's right out front," Jordan Reese says.

"That old crate? Probably break down in the tunnel."

"Mine won't," says Caspar. "I'll take you, Crow."

"You've still got a set to play," Deacon growls. "You gonna blow this gig?"

"Hell with it."

"Bullshit!"

Crow says firmly, "I'm not spoiling anybody's evening. I'll take a cab."

"You need a car." Reese avoids Deacon's wrathful eye. "Gotta get the boy to a doctor."

"I *am* a doctor," Graystone says. "And I also have a car."

He's beyond shame. This is too clearly an act of God. In silence they all turn to Crow. Graystone holds his breath. Crow looks from one to another; finally, apologetically, at Deacon. "He *is* a doctor," she says.

CROW

On the way he asks a bunch of doctor questions. Is Joey wheezing, is he complaining of chest pain, has he been sick lately, has he ever been hospitalized? We barrel south on the West Side Highway, heading for the tunnel; this time of night there's no traffic and he's speeding, but not as fast as the BMW will go and not near as fast as I want it to. His voice is overcalm, he's talking to me like I talk to Joey when he's having an attack. It'll be okay, his tone says; no need to panic. But I am sick inside. I can't stand it that my baby's ill and I'm stuck miles away, on the wrong side of the river.

"Who's with him?" Graystone asks.

"Selma," I say. "My friend. Our neighbor."

"Sensible woman?"

"Think I'd leave him with a fool?" Then I'm sorry for the attitude, but he just nods. Back at the Cellar, he seemed lost amidst the players, wearing his dignity like armor, but peering through the visor with bewildered eyes. There's no sign of that confusion now. He's all business.

"Who diagnosed Joey's asthma?"

"His pediatrician. Dr. Vogel."

"How long's he had it?"

"'Bout a year."

He glances at me. I see him figuring back, deciding whether to ask. "When did it start?"

I look down at my hands. I don't want to talk about this. Some things, only way I know to deal with is not to think about them. But this is for Joey.

"He was a sickly baby. Lots of bronchitis, colds, coughing all the time. But no one ever called it asthma till right after Blue got killed."

"Where there's predisposition, emotional trauma's a common trigger," he says. His voice sounds dry, like he's reading from a textbook, but when I glance up I see a pulse in his jaw wasn't there before, and his cheek's gone all hollow, like he's gnawing on the lining.

We hit the tunnel, and the car goes dark. I stare out the window at the tunnel lights flashing by; I feel the weight of the water pressing down, and I'm back in the subway again. Blue's in my arms, hot blood shooting from his chest like water from a fountain, soaking us both. His eyes reach out to mine. "Hold on, Blue," I say. "Hold on, darlin'." He tries to speak. His mouth opens; but instead of words his soul flies out.

Gone. In an instant. One moment he's there, our eyes are talking; next moment I'm holding an empty body. He can't be far, I think. I look around. I can't see him, but I feel him close by.

I lift up my head and howl his name, scream a binding scream to hold him to me. It seems to me that if I get the tone just right, I can reel him in, force him back in his body. "Blue!" I cry, "Blue, come back!" I hold his body tight, ready for him, but he don't come. "Blue!" His name echoes down the tunnel. "Blue . . . Blue . . . Blue . . ."

Then I hear something else. I hear my child choking. I look around and there he is, our Joey. Standing with his back pressed to the wall, clutching his throat. Eyes wide with panic. Breathless. His chest's all sucked in like a old man; he's working hard, but the air's not getting through. I see he is dying of fright.

My heart tears in two.

If I let Blue go, death will take him. This lumpen weight in my arms, these glazed, unseeing eyes mean nothing. I can get him back: If I hold him tight, if I scream his name just right, I can get him back. But my child needs me. Our child.

"Go to him," Blue commands me. I hear him in my heart, not my ears. "Help Joey."

I let Blue go.

We emerge from the tunnel. Dr. Graystone glances at me, then away. My face is wet with blood. I touch it, look at my fingers. Not blood; tears. We come up to the tollbooth and I turn away from the light, ashamed. Graystone tosses a token into the basket, and we speed off. He don't look at me, he don't speak. He just reaches over and grasps my arm. Holds it. Something flows between us, some kind of solace. Flows both ways. I don't know why he's hurting, but I know he is.

I give him directions the last few blocks. He pulls up to the curb and hops out, carrying his doctor bag. He locks the door, starts into the project.

"Hold it," I say. "Mokie, get your ass out here."

Mokie materializes from the shadows. Graystone jumps.

I lay my hand on the car's hood. "Watch it for me, would you, baby?"

"Whass happenin', Crow?" I hear in his voice he's been smoking that shit again.

"Joey's sick. This a doctor."

"Doctor making house calls? Shit."

"Five bucks if you watch it, your ass if it's touched."

"Go on, baby. It's cool."

I grab Graystone's arm and lead him to my building. "I never saw him," he says.

"Project eyes," I answer. I wave at my window, knowing they're watching though I can't see them. Only a suicidal fool stands in a lighted window in this neighborhood. Might as well paint a target on your back.

When we get upstairs, Selma's waiting by the open door. She eyeballs Graystone but speaks to me. "I give him the medicine like you said, and he fell asleep for half an hour, but now he's up, wheezing and coughing."

I walk past her, down the hall. Joey's sitting up in bed. When he sees me he starts to cry. His cry sounds like the mewl of a sick kitten, thin and unnatural. Graystone follows me in. I sit on the bed, put my arms around my baby. "Joey, this is Dr. Graystone."

"Doctor making house calls?" Selma's leaning against the doorframe, looking skeptical.

"Hello, Joey." Graystone sits on Joey's other side, takes out his stethoscope, and warms the metal disk against his palm. "Not feeling so great, huh?"

Silenced by this stranger in his room, Joey shakes his head. He's not coughing now, but his breathing's wrong, too fast and the rhythm distorted in a way I've come to know: quick and choppy going in, long and labored coming out. The doctor listens to his chest a long time. With his free hand he strokes my boy's head. This strikes me strange coming from him, Graystone not being, I'd've said, the stroking type. I notice he's got musician's hands, strong and supple. I see Joey leaning into them.

He takes off the stethoscope and looks across at me. "What did you give him?"

"Proventil."

"Liquid?"

I nod.

"How long ago?"

I look at Selma. She says, "Forty minutes? Right after I talked to you. He really was coughing, Crow."

Graystone nods. "The Proventil's kicked in. He'll be fine now. Think you can sleep, Joey?"

Joey nods and settles back on his pillow. The doctor tucks the quilt in around his shoulders and touches his head once more before he leaves the room. I sit with Joey a while longer. His breathing's evened out. He holds my hand pressed up against his mouth; his breath condenses on my skin. In less than a minute, he's asleep.

Graystone's sitting on the couch. Selma's got her purse and she's waiting by the front door. Soon as I come out, she asks, "How is he?"

"Fast asleep."

"Swear to God, Crow, that child was sick as a dog a hour ago. Scared the life outta me."

I go to her, give her a hug. "I know. It comes and goes real fast. You did right."

"I'll be going now." She nods to Graystone, opens the door, and draws me out into the hall. "Is he really a doctor?"

"Yeah, he's really a doctor."

"What's he doing here, then?"

"His good deed for the day?"

"He don't look like no Boy Scout to me," Selma says. She starts saying something else, then just shakes her head and walks down the hall. I watch her into her apartment, then return to mine.

Graystone's settled on the sofa like he's got no thought of leaving. I ask him if he wants some coffee.

"If it's no trouble," he says.

He follows me into the kitchen. There's a separate little dining area, but the kitchen itself is tiny, no room for two unless they're intimate. I feel him watching me. My hands are shaking as I measure out the grounds. "Sorry to drag you away for this," I say.

"I was glad to come."

"Selma's no fool. If she says he was sick, he was."

"Oh, he was wheezing. I'll leave you a prescription for pediatric prednisone. You give him four teaspoons a night for two nights; that and a teaspoon of Proventil every six hours should head off any more episodes. If he gets worse, though, take him straight to the ER. And you might discuss with Dr. Vogel switching him onto an inhaler. It's a lot more efficient."

He's blocking my cupboard. When I touch his arm, he catches his breath. "Excuse me," I say.

"Sorry," he says, moving aside.

I take out two mugs and fix the coffee. We go back into the living room and sit on the couch. He stares into his cup, his face troubled, almost angry. Something's on his mind that he's not saying. A cold dread inside me grows and grows. I got nothing left I can afford to lose. We finish our coffee in silence. Still Graystone makes no move to leave.

"All right," I say at last. "Let's have it. What's wrong?"

"Wrong?"

"With my boy."

He looks surprised. "Asthma—but you knew that."

I shake my head. "Something else is wrong."

"Not with Joey."

"With who?"

Graystone looks at me. What I see in his eyes makes me turn away. He grabs my wrist and holds it till I turn back.

"I want to see you," he says.

18

· · · · · · ·

Forever bringing home strays," Dasha says. "Dogs, cats, broken-winged birds. Saint Francis of Park Avenue, the doormen used to call her. Old dolls. Remember, Richard, that filthy old rag doll she found in the park?"

"You burned it," Alice says.

"It was infested. But a child! Richard, talk to her."

They are seated in the living room of Dasha and Richard's Park Avenue apartment, the eight-room pied-à-terre they use when they're not in Connecticut. Alice has arrived, unannounced, straight from her interview with Child Welfare. She wears a dark woolen suit, smartly but conservatively cut, and a harried expression. CWA gave her the runaround; Noah's caseworker refused even to divulge his location, revealing only that he had gone, not to a foster home, but rather to some kind of therapeutic live-in facility.

"Dogs," Richard says, bridging his fingers judiciously, "can be taken to the pound. Dolls may be incinerated when no longer of use. Cats can fend for themselves. But a child, my dear Alice, is not something one picks up on a whim. Children are not disposable goods."

"Well put, Richard." Dasha applauds.

"I know what I'm doing. It's no whim. I didn't come to

ask your opinion, Daddy. I came to ask for your profession-al help. I've never asked it before."

"There's no need to take that tone, Alice. You are concerned for a child not of your blood, a child you barely know. How can you deny our right to be concerned about you? You have no idea of what you're getting into."

"It's ridiculous," Dasha breaks in. "Even to think of taking some street urchin, a product of God knows what kind of environment, into your beautiful home."

"He's not a product, Mother. Noah's a child, a very special child."

Dasha waves a bejeweled hand for silence. "We have never interfered in your life. Have we, Richard?"

"Never."

"When, against our advice, you insisted on studying nursing, we sent you to the best nursing school in the country. And when you turned down a dozen desirable job offers to go work in that sinkhole of a hospital, we bit our tongues, did we not, Richard?"

"I still bear the scars."

"Mother—"

"I'm not finished. 'Let her do her thing,' we said. 'Let her work out her problems, get this exaggerated altruism out of her system.' We gave you free rein. All we asked, and it was little enough, was that you preserve a decent distance between that job and your personal life. So that when you have resolved whatever complex drove you to this course in the first place, when you are ready to resume your real life, the door will be open. Was that too much to ask, Richard?"

"Not at all. Perfectly reasonable."

"I've done what you asked," Alice says. "Till now I never minded. But Noah crossed the line. I didn't mean for it to happen, Mother. It just did."

Through narrowed eyes, Dasha regards her daughter. "Does this have anything to do with Brooke?" she asks.

"Brooke?"

"Her pregnancy."

"Of course not! How can you ask me that?" Alice jumps up and walks over to the fireplace, holding her hands out to the fire. At eye level, a framed photograph of Brooke smiles out at her, radiant in her wedding gown, in the arms of her husband. Beside it on the mantelpiece stand two other photos: one of Richard at his study desk, a portrait that once graced the cover of *Fortune* magazine; the other of her mother in formal attire, dancing with President Bush. There's an empty space where Alice's wedding portrait used to stand. When she divorced Charlie, her parents put it away to spare her feelings and never got around to replacing it.

"She's jealous," her mother's voice says. "She's always been jealous, she'll always be jealous."

Her father makes a hushing sound and crosses the room to stand behind Alice. He puts his hands on her shoulders. "It's nothing to be ashamed of, Alice. But you must realize, you're still a young woman. Someday you will have children of your own."

Alice turns and regards him with a dry and steady gaze. "I hope I do. And Noah will be the first."

Dasha throws up her hands. "What is so special about this Noah?"

"Sweetness of spirit. Courage. Hope."

Her parents are stymied. What's gotten into Alice? they wonder. Brooke was always the willful, Alice the biddable child: eager to please, never any trouble, perfectly malleable except on those rare occasions when she's dug in her heels and, like a gentle ox, refused to budge. Dasha, at least, is beginning to sense that this is one of those times.

Her mouth curves bitterly. "What makes you think they'd award this paragon to you? They have hundreds of suitable married couples standing on line to adopt these children."

Alice says, "Not this child."

"And why is that?" Richard demands in his cross-examining mode.

"For one thing, he's not up for adoption yet, only fostering."

"And . . .?"

"Troubled history. Dicey family. Wrong color."

"Wrong color?" Dasha and Richard say together.

"I didn't mention that? That's the reason CWA's giving me such a royal runaround. Noah's half black."

Silence.

Pale as ivory, Dasha's face. "You realize what people will think." By people, she means *her* people. It was bound to happen: One day Alice, out with the child, would run into one of Dasha's friends. Nothing one could say would matter then. People always assume the worst.

"I don't think so," Alice says thoughtfully. "He's a bit too dark."

Her mother rises and walks silently, stiff-legged, out of the room. Richard and Alice stare after her. They hear her rummaging in the kitchen. Moments later she returns with a carving knife that she presents, hilt-first, to her daughter.

"What's this for?" Alice asks.

Dasha throws her head back and opens her arms wide. "You want to kill me, go ahead. All I ask is that you do it quickly. Don't drag it out."

"Now, Dasha," Richard remonstrates, but Alice laughs.

"Bravo, Mother. You missed your calling. All those years on the wrong side of the footlights."

"It's no laughing matter, my girl. How are you ever going to attract a decent man with some little"—she starts to say one word, then substitutes another—*"foster child* hanging on your skirts?"

"This is hopeless," Alice says. "I should have known." She takes her coat and walks out of the room. Richard follows, sneaking glances at his daughter's face. Is this his little girl? At the front door, he helps her on with her coat and puts an arm about her shoulders. Her body is stiff and unresponsive.

"I know how much you care about those less fortunate than ourselves," he says quietly. "In our own way, we also care, Alice. We've done a great deal for the poor of this city, through the appropriate channels. I emphasize the word 'appropriate,' because frankly, my dear, what you're proposing, though clearly well intentioned, is *not* appropriate."

Alice opens her mouth to reply, but Richard raises a hand. "I'm not saying one can't do more, or do it on a more personal level. In fact, I'm giving serious consideration to sponsoring a class. It's a very worthwhile program; I'm sure you've heard of it. Contributors adopt a class of inner-city kids in grade school, mentor them through high school, and pay for college for those who make it. In fact, I had planned to discuss it with you. I can handle the financial commitment, but the mentoring aspect is more than I could take on alone. I thought perhaps you might go in with me."

She shakes her head. "This isn't about saving the world, Daddy. It's not about consolation prizes or channeling Alice's misguided impulses. It's about one little boy, that's all. One kid who happens to need me."

"Go home, Alice. Sleep on it. You'll see things more rationally in the morning." Richard plants a forgiving kiss on her forehead. "You always were a softhearted creature, too good for this world. Wouldn't do in my profession."

Stepping away, Alice reveals to him the face that seven years of Mercy have wrought—shows him, for the first time, the eyes of a triage nurse.

"Nor in mine," she says.

19

·······

In a corner of the nurses' station, hidden between two supply cabinets, Graystone stands with his eyes shut, immersed in familiar sounds. The epicenter of activity is ten feet away, where Daniel Bergman, charge doctor for the day, oversees the junior residents. Graystone hears a babble of voices.

"My OD won't vomit."

"Dan, could you eyeball my CHF? He's loxed out, cyanotic, extremely hypovolemic."

"I don't care if his pressure's thirty by Doppler, he's a DNR."

"No urine in the computer."

"Sixteen-year-old black male, history of asthma, never intubated."

"You owe me big time on that psycho."

"Yeah, yeah, I owe you my life."

"Lots of hip-thrusting. Patient doesn't saturate, drool, or become incontinent. No history of syncope, no post-ictal."

"Probably pseudoseizure. Run him by Neurology."

"Nursing home sent over a ROMI, seventy-eight-year-old female, swollen legs. I ask how long. Would you believe three months?"

166

"Twenty-year-old woman's HYSing it up, total GOMER."

"My concussion wants to know if he can eat."

"Sure, why not, welcome to Dan's ER and Grill."

"My asthma eloped."

"Comes in with a goddamn *diaper rash*. Probably go home with the flu."

Down the corridor, patients in their slots spit, cough, rasp, mewl, and utter reedy cries of "Nurse, nurse!" In addition to the usual, flu season has hit with a vengeance. Graystone himself feels like he's coming down with the virus, but it's only love, which, like any childhood disease, hits hardest when it hits adults. Everything hurts: his eyes when he sees her, his ears when he hears her, his heart when he thinks of her, his pride when he remembers. Additional symptoms, noted with a doctor's die-hard objectivity, include radical mood swings from mindless euphoria to fits of despair. Graystone, with hopeless clarity, diagnoses no good outcome to this affair, which is, in fact, no affair at all but rather a one-sided fiasco.

A rude hand jostles his arm. Graystone opens his eyes to Pilar's broad, exasperated face. "Seeing's how you got nothing to do, how about lending a hand?"

"What's up?"

"EMS is running in a trauma, car versus bicycle."

"ETA?"

"Now. Ambulance drivers witnessed the accident; happened just a block away."

Daniel, passing by with a gurney, winks. "Up for a trauma fix?" With Pilar on their heels, they race down the hall, reaching the ramp just as the ambulance screeches to a halt. The back doors fly open, and Percy hops out. The paramedic's shirt and pants are saturated with blood.

"Talk to me," Daniel says, helping to unload the patient. He's a young Caucasian male, wrapped in a crimson sheet and bloody blanket.

"Riding a bike, car hit him from behind. Kid flew; landed on a picket fence." Percy puffs as they run the gurney down the hall. "We were right there, witnessed the accident. Puncture wound to left thorax spurting like a son of a bitch.

Gotta be the heart. Wore a helmet; no sign of head injury. Airways and breathing clear, circulation stinks, pressure dropping fast. We got a line in."

They reach code room 2. Percy helps transfer the patient, retrieves his stretcher, and leaves the room. The doctors take up positions on either side of the patient's chest, flanked by Pilar and Alice. Jennifer stands just outside the sterile zone, phone in hand. On Pilar's instructions, she calls the code: "Dr. Blue to ER stat." The trauma team begins to converge, doctors, nurses, and technicians streaming in from all over the hospital. A pleasurable excitement grips the ER. So much of what they do is minor-league scut work—cuts, bruises, and infections that belong in a clinic, not an emergency room. *This* trauma is the real thing. Even the patients sense the crisis and cease their constant clamor for attention.

Graystone is senior in rank, but, as charge doctor, Daniel runs the code. On his orders, Calvin Wang intubates the patient and Elsa Kraven starts a second IV line, inserting a sixteen-gauge needle into his wrist.

"I'm in."

"Start him on Ringer's lactate and plasmanate. Jenny, call the lab. Uncrossed match, lots of it."

Two nurses pump the IV bags, forcing fluid into the patient's veins. Blood spurts from the chest wound but slows as his pressure drops.

"OR's ready," Jennifer calls.

"No time; he's bleeding out. What's his pressure?"

Pilar has the automatic cuff in place. "Forty . . . dropping. We're losing him."

"Let's crack him, folks."

A nurse wheels over the crash cart. Daniel nods to Graystone, who makes the incision through striated multi-colored layers of tissue, pausing along the way to tie off blood vessels. Then Daniel inserts the rib-spreader and cranks the chest open. Half a dozen masked heads crane downward. At the bottom of the valley, the patient's naked heart spurts blood through a narrow rent in the right atrium.

A moment of silence, and someone mutters, "Jesus." A

fine mist of blood coats the outside of Daniel's glasses.
Pilar, steadying his chin with a forefinger, wipes them off.

The patient's pallid face, with its wistful mustache and
downy cheeks, floats between life and death. In their rush,
no one has taken time to drape him properly. Gazing down
upon the dying youth, Graystone realizes that he knows
him: He's the kid from Berger's deli, the one who delivers
their sandwiches and coffee when they order in. A likable
boy, full of jokes; once he said he felt at home in the ER
because it reminded him of Berger's kitchen. His name,
Graystone recalls, is Rusty. As if this remembrance causes a
breach in the barricade separating *us* from *them,* the doctor
is suffused, all unwilling, with a dense pity, a sense of shared
vulnerability.

He shudders, and Daniel looks up, catches his eye.
Though most would deny it outside, telepathy is as common
as blood in the trauma room. "Probably on his way here
when it happened," Daniel says grimly.

"Hope EMS saved the sandwiches," Wang says with a
nervous giggle. No one laughs.

At that moment, the patient's heart stops beating.

"Plug it up," Daniel barks. "Pilar: Foley catheter."

Graystone reaches inside and slips his right index finger
into the hole in the heart. It fits snugly; the muscle fastens
on his finger like a hungry baby clamping down on a teat.
With his left hand he grasps the heart, which nestles, warm
and soft, in his palm. Graystone feels a surge of love for this
boy whose heart is in his hand.

"Starting massage," he says.

He closes his fist, and the heart contracts; he releases, and
it expands. Once, twice, three times. Then the heart shudders in his hand and comes back to life. Graystone feels it
sucking on his finger. He's part of this patient's body now;
they're more intimate than lovers.

"It's beating," he says with a catch in his voice.

"Not for long if we don't get the pressure up. Keep your
finger in the dike, Tom. Where's the goddamn blood?"

"Pressure's holding at forty," Alice calls.

A lab attendant races in, panting. "Your O-negative." He
hands the bags to Jennifer, who ferries them to Pilar.

Daniel says, "Let's have the Foley. Alice, thread a needle. O-silk."

Pilar hands over the catheter. Then Daniel locks eyes with Graystone. "Nice and easy now." He slides the catheter into the chest, positioning it just outside the hole in the heart. "Go," he says.

The doctors' hands function as if directed by a single brain. As Graystone's finger slips out of the hole (the heart resists, pulling him back), the catheter, guided by Daniel, takes its place. The patient's heart stutters, fibrillates briefly, then resumes its beat.

"Inflate the balloon," Daniel orders.

The bag on the business end of the catheter fills with air, plugging the hole in the patient's heart. Pilar hooks a bag of blood to the other end of the catheter.

"Start pumping." Daniel holds out a hand for the threaded needle.

He stitches the heart around the catheter, quick as a seamstress, then ties off the sutures and pulls out. Meanwhile Pilar squeezes the bag fast and hard, forcing blood directly into the heart. For a moment, the flurry of activity around the bed ceases. Everyone stares at the pressure monitor.

"Forty-five," Alice reads. "Fifty . . . sixty."

A cheer arises. "All right!" Daniel hollers. He lifts a gloved hand into the air; Graystone slaps him five. When his pressure reaches 80, the patient is rushed upstairs to surgery.

Like a locker room after a winning game, the ER rings with laughter, backslapping, and ecstatic reenactments: "Then I put my hand here, and she did this, and he said that, and I thought, Jesus God, what's he want with a Foley?" Doctors and nurses who weren't in on the code drift down for a firsthand report; Daniel has his back pounded so many times he starts to wincing when anyone comes near, and the code nurses, surrounded by their sisters, glow like brides. Only Graystone holds back from the general celebration. He's worried about brain damage due to loss of circulation; this save will lose a lot of luster if the kid comes out a vegetable.

A couple of hours after they send him upstairs, Harry Provitz, chief of surgery, comes down and buttonholes Daniel in the nurses' station. "You ran the code on the kid from Berger's?"

"Yeah, why?"

"Thought I recognized those dainty little stitches." Provitz laughs. "Great save, Danny; gutsy call. Only what's the story on the Foley catheter? We get him in the OR, take a peek inside, and everybody breaks up."

Daniel shrugs modestly. "Had to stuff up the hole somehow, and Tom wanted his finger back."

"Whatever, man. It worked. Kid's doing real well."

Graystone, spotting Provitz, hurries over. "What's his neurological status?"

"Listen to this. Patient wakes up in recovery sixty minutes post-op, real agitated, saying, 'Old man's gonna massacre me.' We figure he's in cloud-cuckoo land. I get on the horn to Neurology, then go over to calm him down. Kid grabs my arm. 'I dropped the bag,' he says. 'All the lunch orders. Old man's gonna kill me.'" The surgeon beams like a proud father reciting his child's first words. Daniel bursts into laughter. Even Graystone permits himself a broad smile.

"Nice work," Provitz says. "You guys really beat the Reaper on this one."

Afterward, Graystone retreats to his office and shuts the door. Something happened today; something got to him. Maybe it was recognizing the patient; or perhaps it was grasping his beating heart in his hand—because for all his years in emergency medicine, Graystone has never before held a living heart. Whatever the cause, he'd found himself moved almost to tears by the boy's narrow escape, and when he walked out of the code room, he'd had to thrust his hands in his pockets to hide their trembling. After so many years of good doctorly dispassion and practicing the distance he preaches, this sudden emotionalism is worrisome.

Emergency medicine by its very nature tends to be

impersonal. Unlike GPs and internists, who must treat patients as a whole in all their daunting complexity, ER physicians function best when they confine their treatment to specific presenting complaints. This limited interaction with his patients suits Graystone, whose expertise lies with the human body, not the soul. He sees the body as a piece of exquisite machinery, irrigated by the tidal ebb and flow of the blood, powered by steadfast heart and stalwart lungs; he regards himself, accordingly, as a master mechanic. The anatomy of the brain is clear to Graystone, but the workings of the mind perplex him. The human heart is comprehensible; human emotions are opaque.

Including, or especially, his own. How many times has he cautioned his residents against identifying with their patients? In theory, the doctor acknowledges that patients are people, each with his own life, which revolves about him like planets about a sun; in practice, however, patients appear as bit players in the drama in which he and his fellow staffers star.

Such casting is as functional as it is inevitable. "Our job is not to share our patients' pain," Graystone tells his people. "Our job is to heal, and in order to heal, we must often inflict more pain. We must do to our patients what we never willingly have done to ourselves." He teaches not only by exhortation but by example: No one has ever seen Graystone get teary-eyed over a patient. And yet, as he reached into the valley of that boy's chest and grasped his living heart, Graystone was assaulted by a visceral realization that it could have been him, lying on that table; that everyone is vulnerable, no one immune; that under the skin, all men are truly created equal.

Now, such startling subdural equations may be valid, they may even be laudable; but in Graystone's scheme of things, they are not helpful. In some mysterious way, he blames Crow. He is not the man he was a month ago, and that's Crow's doing. The woman has bewitched him.

Graystone is in love, and he hates it. In this he is not unlike some women, pregnant for the first time, who look forward to childbirth as a great adventure, only to find when the time comes that it is nothing but awful, sickening, gut-wrenching pain. For years he has fantasized about finding the right woman; and if his fantasies are informed by the soppy, string-section romanticism of late-night movies, they are nonetheless heartfelt longings for a state he's yearned to enter. It never occurred to him that the right woman might be all wrong, or that it would hurt so much. The scene in Crow's apartment replays itself endlessly, destroying his sleep, invading his work like a computer virus. It comes back to him now, in vivid detail:

They sit on the couch in her tiny apartment, empty cups on the coffee table before them. Crow looks at him expectantly. "What's wrong?" she asks.

"Asthma," he replies—hoping, still, to spare them both.

"No; something else is wrong."

"Not with Joey."

"With who?" she asks.

Then he unveils his eyes and lets them speak for him. Crow draws a quick breath and starts to rise. He pulls her back. It's as if he's playing out moves choreographed long ago. Her skin feels different from all other skin; he feels the blood rushing through her body as it rushes through his. What has she done to him, this devilish Delilah?

He will not speak: he is resolved. She will not force it from him. He will preserve his dignity, keep his wits about him. Eventually the madness will pass.

A voice, his voice, says, "I want to see you."

Her eyes widen, as if in shock. "Impossible," she replies.

Her coyness infuriates him. She cannot be unaware of her power. His heart lies exposed between them and she's toying with it. Anger seizes him; he lets go her arm and with both hands grasps her shoulders. Gasping, Crow tries to pull away. Good, he thinks. Let her fear what she's unleashed. He pushes her back against the couch and presses his lips to hers.

Somewhere in the back of his head, the late-night movie unreels. He knows what will happen next. For a moment longer, she will resist. Then the arms that push against him will slacken, her lips will part, her body melt into his. He will lift her up and carry her to her bed (where is it?).

But Crow doesn't soften, doesn't melt. Her body remains

stiff and full of resistance. She is strong, but he is much stronger. He could force her; and for a moment, to his shame, he thinks of doing it, yes, and damn the consequences.

The moment passes. It's not in him to force a woman; and besides, what good would it do? A kiss (and all it stands for, in the bowdlerized land of fairy tales) is a well-known antidote to enchantment; but it must be willingly bestowed. She has to come to him, she has to want him, for the spell to be broken.

He releases her.

She stares at him, eyes flashing, breathing hard, her unshakable composure shattered at last. Her hair has pulled free of its bun; wild tendrils frame her face. She is so beautiful his heart aches.

"Crow," he says, "I'm in love with you."

She slaps him hard across the face and says, "Get out."

There's a tap on the door. It opens before Graystone can answer, and Pilar's face appears. "You got to see this," she says.

He accompanies her down the hall to the nurses' station. A wizened, gray-haired man, dwarfed by a great white apron, heads a phalanx of tray-bearing waiters. Graystone recognizes Hiram Berger, proprietor of Deepside's last remaining Jewish deli.

The old man addresses him. "Where you want we should put the food?"

The waiters' trays are piled high with mounds of cold cuts, quarts of coleslaw and potato salad, heaps of stuffed cabbage and knishes, pounds of fresh rye bread, jars of half-sour pickles, and steaming jugs of coffee.

"Mr. Berger, who ordered all this?"

Berger waves his hand. "Lunch you didn't get. So I brought a little dinner."

"A little dinner? There's enough here to feed an army!"

"It's not so much. You work hard, you need to eat. Now show me where to put it before my boys here get a heart attack."

Graystone leads them to the doctors' lounge, where the

waiters, supervised by Berger, arrange a buffet on the conference table. A warm, garlicky aroma fills the room and seeps into the corridor, drawing staffers and ambulant patients like flies. "Eat, eat," the old man says, and they do.

"Mr. Berger, you didn't have to do this," Graystone says through a mouthful of pastrami and rye.

"Oh no? You know who that boy is what you saved this morning?"

"Your delivery boy."

"My grandson. So please, don't tell me what I don't got to do. That doctor upstairs, the surgeon, he told my daughter if it wasn't for you people, the boy would be dead with a hole in his heart. God should bless you and keep you always." He picks up Graystone's hand and kisses it, then dabs his eyes with the hem of his apron.

"We did our job, that's all. You can thank God for giving your grandson the strength to pull through. The boy's a fighter."

Berger puffs out his cheeks. "God and me, we go back a long way. With Him I got a bone to pick yet. But you people, you didn't owe us nothing; now we owe you everything. A *bissel* pastrami, a few slices rye, it's not so much."

"Well, sir, we appreciate it." Turning away, Graystone finds himself face-to-face with Crow.

They haven't spoken since that night in her apartment, a week ago. When they meet in the halls she looks right through him, as he used to look through her, and each time it happens he feels a bit of his substance bleeding away. Now she stands before him, not quite smiling, but her eyes do take him in; they *see* him.

"You did good," she says.

Blood rushes to his head. All at once Graystone understands the secret of his identification with Rusty: his heart, too, is in someone else's hands.

20

. . . .

Mercy's executive suite occupies a separate wing on the third floor. Hushed, gently lighted, plushly carpeted and paneled, it's a world apart from the ER. Entering these moneyed halls, Alice becomes a hybrid: half nurse, half her mother's privileged daughter.

Jean Schuyler's door is open. She looks up from her desk, smiles, waves Alice in, and meets her in the middle of the room with a warm handshake and a "Lovely to see you again." Mercy's director of nursing is a trim, vivacious woman in her midfifties, with sparkling blue eyes and weathered walnut skin. She's an avid jogger, skier, and mountain climber. The walls of her office, which Alice has entered only once before, are covered with photographs of mountain views and seascapes.

Jean congratulates Alice on the ER's recent spectacular save, rumors of which have penetrated even this insulated province, then segues into a recent hike she and her cardiologist husband took through the Rockies. Alice, aware not only of the good humor but also of the scrutiny emanating from those exceedingly blue eyes, listens quietly, responds politely, and waits for Jean to get to the point, which can only be Noah. Someone must have blabbed about her efforts to secure the boy; why else would the director summon her? Lorraine Goldblossom springs to mind, but really, Alice tells herself, that's unfair. More likely it was someone from CWA, where everyone she's met seems intent on interpreting her interest in Noah as a malicious, probably racist incursion on their turf. Alice tries not to take it personally. It's the nature of bureaucracies to detest and repel wave-makers. What hurts her is the lack of support, not only from her parents, whose reaction was predictable, but principally from the very people of whom she'd expected so much more: her true family, the ER staff.

Even Pilar disappointed. "I'll give you a recommendation," she'd said, "but between you and me, you ain't doing that boy any favor, takin' him out of his own world where he belong."

"A child needs love," Alice had replied; whereupon Pilar looked at her with rock-steady eyes and said, "Everybody needs love; whose needs are we dealing with here?"

For all it stung, Pilar's a friend; she has a right to talk. Jean Schuyler has none. One wrong word about Noah and Alice is out the door.

But Jean's agenda, when at length it emerges, has nothing to do with the boy.

"Kathleen Brady," she tells Alice, "is retiring early next year."

Alice, who barely knows the head nurse on Ob-Gyn, can't see what this has to do with her. "Oh yes?" she asks.

"Your name has come up as a possible successor."

"You're offering *me* the job?" Alice asks, with a slight but noticeable emphasis on the "me."

"It's yours if you want it."

"Why?"

"Your record is exemplary, you've got ob-gyn experience, and God knows you've paid your dues, all those years in ER."

"I like ER."

Jean reaches across the desk and squeezes her hand. "Of course you do. But Pilar's head of ER nursing, and as far as I know, she's not planning to leave till they carry her out. You've been second-in-command for a long time; you have your own career to consider."

Alice shakes her head, not in refusal but amazement. "I'm flattered, but—"

"No buts. If you can't say yes, say nothing yet. Think it over. You understand we're talking about a lot more authority, a big salary increase, regular, decent hours . . ."

No more night shifts, Alice thinks. More time for Noah.

Jean walks her to the door, arm around her shoulder. "Serving on the front line is valuable experience I like all my supervisors to have. But this is a step up a ladder *you* might very well climb to the top."

CROW

I turn 'round from putting fresh sheets on the bunks in the doctors' lounge and there's Elias, sitting at the table with his head propped in his hands. "Yo," I say.

He jumps half a foot, clutching his chest. It kills me how he always acts like I'm the spook.

"You still here?" I ask.

"Where would I go?" he says.

I wonder about that myself, but it's no use asking him. Elias has got to be the dumbest damn ghost in the world. Good doctor, I'll give him that. But when it comes to the big stuff, life and death and what comes after, he don't seem to know any more than me.

Now he tucks his chin back down to his chest and sighs. I'd sit and talk awhile, but I need to finish this room and get out before Graystone comes in for lunch. I've cooled off some since the night he jumped me, but still the man's a sorry disappointment, and I'd just as soon not see his face. I unhook my bucket from the cart, pour in some Lysol, and carry it over to the sink.

"Saw you the other day," I tell Elias, looking over my shoulder. "Standing outside the trauma room, watching them work. No offense, but you looked like shit. Pale as a ghost."

"I *am* a ghost," he says.

"That ain't the point."

He shrugs. I start mopping the far corner of the room. "I can't stand seeing a child slip away like that," Elias says, real quiet.

"He didn't slip away. They saved him."

He brightens a bit. "So they did. Helluva save. They're some team, Graystone and Bergman."

"What is it with you and the kiddies, anyway?"

Elias gives me that long-nosed look of his, the one that asks, "Are you addressing me, Black Female Minion?"

There's dust balls underneath the bunk beds. I bend down to get my mop all the way under. "Pilar told me how you got hit," I say. "Some of it, anyway. I never did hear what happened to the baby who choked on a button."

No reply. I finish under the bed, straighten up, and turn around. Elias is gone.

Well, *excuse* me. Looks like death's no cure for attitude. Hell with him, I say, and go back to mopping. Suddenly the door opens and Alice Straugh scurries in, tracking up my clean floor. I'm about to lay into her when she hushes me with a finger to her lips.

Out in the hall, a man's voice bellows her name. Alice don't answer. Then the door swings open and that shitheel Dr. Plummer busts in. Good-looking man for a honkie, and if you don't believe me, just ask him. Resembles that actor, Kevin Kline. Wears a black mustache that asks, in all modesty, "Ain't I something?" Man fixes on Alice like one of them smart missiles. "There you are!" he says, oozing toward her.

She sidesteps, keeping the table between them. "Yes, Doctor?"

I hang my bucket on the cart and prepare to leave. Behind her back, where he can't see, Alice signals me with an open palm to stay. They don't pay me enough for this shit, I think; but I take out a sponge and some chlorine scrub and start on the sink.

"Have you spoken with Jean Schuyler yet?" Plummer asks.

"You know about that?"

"Hell, darlin', I recommended you. I trust you accepted the offer?"

She stares at him like he's some kind of two-headed roach. She don't want to discuss it, she says.

"Why not?" he says. "We're alone."

Now I *know* he sees me; I just don't count. Alice's eyes meet mine in the mirror over the sink. Full of shame, as if all the guilt of the entire white race is resting on her head. I'm just sorry for her, sorry for anyone's got anything in common with this pitiful asshole.

I turn around. "Pilar come by, looking for you," I say.

"Thanks, Crow."

But as she walks by him, the doctor grabs hold her arm and finally stoops to noticing me. "Would you excuse us, dear?"

I look him up and down. "I got my work to do, same as everybody else."

Alice says, "Let go."

He glares at me, turns away, and starts soft-soaping her, saying as how he recommended her 'cause she's the best person for the job, nothing to do with his personal feelings, blah, blah, blah.

She lets him run down. Then she says, "Bull."

It ain't "bullshit" but as close as I ever heard her come to cussing. Plummer blinks a few times. "Well, maybe you're right," he says. "You know, I'm crazy about you, Alice. There's a kind of virginal quality about you. You're like an ice maiden, or Rapunzel locked up in her tower. 'Rapunzel, Rapunzel, let down your hair.'"

"Dr. Plummer—" she says.

"Doug."

"Put a sock in it."

He walks out smiling like, but we hear his footsteps stomp angrily down the hall. Alice falls into the seat where Elias sat before and lowers her head to the table. Packing up my cart, I murmur, "Rapunzel, Rapunzel." I know it's wicked; I just can't resist.

Alice raises her head. "You're laughing at me?"

"I'm just kidding with you, girl. What's that fool want with you, anyway? It's clear you ain't buying his shit."

"I don't know," she says. "You think it might have anything to do with the fact that my parents donated fifteen million dollars to New York Hospital last year?"

I *knew* she was a rich girl; I could smell it. Damned if I hold it against her, though. 'Specially considering where she come from, Alice is all right.

"No way, baby," I say. "Must be that virginal quality of yours."

We stare at each other. I see the laughter in her eyes, and I get the feeling she sees into me as well. Another life, another world, her and me might've been friends.

She battens down a smile. "It's not funny. The man does not understand the word no."

"That's 'cause you're applying it to the wrong part of his anatomy," I explain. "Don't you know the old saying?"

"Which old saying?"

"A kick in the balls is worth a thousand words."

She laughs. Just then Pilar clumps in, looking like thunder. "I saw Plummer come flying outta here. What's going on?"

Alice says, "He finds me irresistible."

"Like a ice maiden," I add.

"That jackass been bothering you now? I swear I've had it with that man. Alice, you got to report him."

Her face gets that pinched look again. "I couldn't."

"You got to! The man's a menace. Goddamn, I wish he'd try that shit on me; I'd teach him how to treat a lady."

I eyeball Pilar's bulk, 220 pounds if she's a ounce, and try to feature it. She'd flatten him like a pancake. Alice got her lip between her teeth, trying not to laugh.

"Well," says Pilar, "somebody needs to put him in his place."

"Who would I tell?" Alice asks.

"Graystone."

I can't help but laugh.

Pilar wheels on me. "What's your problem, girl?"

"Talk about the pot calling the kettle black."

She puffs up like a blowfish. "What's that suppose to mean?"

"They're all the same. These doctors think they got a right, like *droit de seigneur.*"

"Dwa de who?"

"You know, those feudal lords who use to get first crack at all the young virgins in their domain."

"Sound like some fancy French perfume. Virgins, huh." Pilar snorts. "Pretty slim pickings around here, I can tell you that. Anyhow, Graystone's not that way."

"Oh, no?"

The head nurse settles herself beside Alice at the table. I figure what the hell and join 'em. Not that I got any interest in Graystone; it's just past time for my break.

Pilar says, "I tell you for a fact that man ain't touched a nurse since he started here, and there's plenty wouldn't have minded a tumble."

Then she tells us about this one nurse, Sondra was her name, worked the ER when Graystone was a resident. High yellar gal, body like Marilyn Monroe, and this sexy little voice. They had to keep her away from the cardiac patients, else you could track her comings and goings by the beeping of their monitors. Doctors was standing on line for a date with her, but she wouldn't give 'em the time of day. She'd set her cap for Graystone, wouldn't nobody else do; and the colder he acted, the bolder she got. One night, 'round two in the morning, it's real quiet, and Graystone's sleeping in the lounge. Sondra sneaks in and shuts the door behind her. They all seen her go in; they heard the bed creak; and fifteen seconds later out he comes, streakin' like the devil's on his tail.

We laugh. "Maybe he doesn't like girls," Alice says.

"He likes 'em just fine. Man's got integrity is all."

"That or a rod up his ass," I say. "Probably just thinks he's too good for nurses."

Pilar gives me a look. Graystone's her boy; far as she's concerned, butter wouldn't melt in his mouth. Me, I know better. I can't lie: Way he acted that night surprised me. Like Pilar, I'd thought better of him. Didn't figure him for the type to go messing with a person's mind. Thought if there's one thing we have in common, it's knowing where we belong.

21

· · · · · · · ·

"This is precisely the time," Daniel says, pacing the length of Graystone's office with his white coattails flying. "This is the perfect opportunity. Would you just look at the numbers, would you do that for me?"

It's the tail end of a hard day, and Graystone slumps behind his desk, rubbing his temples. "It's not the numbers," he says. "It's the idea of deserting the ship."

"Don't give me deserting the ship! How many times do I have to say it: This place is bigger than me, it's bigger than you; it'll survive without the both of us. Long as Pilar doesn't leave," Daniel adds thoughtfully.

"But a walk-in clinic. Man, it'd be like eating cauliflower and cabbage for the rest of our lives."

"Cauliflower and cabbage? More like caviar and champagne, fool. Tom, I'm saying it makes no sense, two Columbia-educated docs ending up in an inner-city Knife and Gun Club. That ain't how the script's supposed to read."

"It has its compensations," says Graystone, thinking of the Berger kid.

Daniel shakes his head. "That kind of save is one in a million. Can't live off of those."

The phone rings. Graystone snatches it up.

"Thomas," Elvira says briskly, dispensing with a greeting, "I've decided to invite Michelle to my Christmas party."

He presses the receiver hard to his ear. "Bad idea, Mother."

"I beg your pardon?"

"I don't think you should."

"Why ever not?"

"This isn't the time to discuss it." Daniel has stationed himself in front of the bookshelf and is pretending to browse, but by the set of his head Graystone sees he's marking every word. "Can I call you back?"

"We're going out to dinner, and anyway, I'm not asking, I'm telling. Will you be seeing Daniel?"

"He's here now, actually."

"Ask if they're coming to the party."

Graystone conveys the question.

"Absolutely, wouldn't miss it for the world," Bergman says.

"He's coming. What do you mean, you're not asking, you're telling? I don't want you to invite her."

"Are you telling me whom I can and cannot invite to my own party? In any case, I'm not asking her for you. I happen to be very fond of that girl. We've become friends."

"Mother, we both know what you're up to. I'm just saving you the trouble; I'm telling you it's not going to work."

"Thomas. Darling. Any man who'd lose a girl like that's a fool, and you know your mama didn't raise no fools."

Graystone runs his hand through his stubby hair. Daniel's shoulders are shaking suspiciously; but there's only one way left to stop Elvira, and, heroically, he takes it.

"I'm bringing someone," he declares.

Dead silence. Abandoning all pretense of tact, Daniel turns around grinning.

"Who?" Elvira demands.

"A woman. You don't know her. So obviously it would be awkward—"

"Who is she?"

Graystone sighs. "The widow of a brilliant young musician. Wait—we've got a code. Gotta run, Mother." He hangs up and raises his eyes to Daniel's.

Daniel approaches, folds his long limbs into the visitor's chair, pushes up his glasses, and waits expectantly. Graystone purses his lips and says nothing.

"The widow of a brilliant young musician?" Daniel prompts.

Graystone shrugs.

"Crow? You're taking Crow?"

"I had to say something." He rises, starts prowling the room.

Daniel swivels to follow him. "So it's a gag."

"Man, get serious. Does it make any sense, me dating a housekeeper?"

"Hell, no. You had me going for a minute there."

"Although," says Graystone with an oblique look, "a man could do worse."

His friend laughs. "A man could do better, too."

"Snob."

"That's rich, coming from you!"

"Aren't you the cat who's always on my case? 'Find yourself a nice girl, Tom. Settle down, Tom.'"

"Right scenario. Wrong woman."

With no trace of amusement in his voice, Graystone says, "What's that supposed to mean?"

"Hey, easy! It's nothing against Crow. I like the girl. But she's not . . . you're not . . ."

"Best quit while you're ahead, my friend."

He can't get near her. The thaw that followed the Berger kid's save was short-lived. Now, every time he approaches, Crow evaporates like a ghost. Graystone can't very well go chasing her around the ER like a lovesick calf. Finally he gets smart. From across the hall, he stakes out a treatment room whose occupant has just been moved upstairs. When Crow arrives to clean it, he follows her in and shuts the door.

She spins, holding her mop before her.

"Sorry," he says, raising both hands. "Didn't mean to startle you."

"What do you want?"

"To talk to you."

"Well, this is a bad time. I've got three more rooms waiting on me."

"You're a hard woman to find, Crow. Should I make an appointment with your secretary?"

"That's very amusing, Dr. Graystone." She turns back to swabbing the floor.

"Here, let me give you a hand." Stepping forward, Graystone lays hold of Crow's mop. She pulls it away indignantly, and he maintains his grip. A childish scuffle ensues, from which Crow emerges victorious, mop in hand.

"Just trying to help," says Graystone in a wounded tone.

"Is that right? How'd you like me barging in on your operations, offering to help and grabbing your instruments?"

"Not much."

Crow nods. "Well, then."

"If I promise never to touch your mop again, will you quit for five minutes and listen to me?"

She puts up her mop, rests a hip against the examining table, and folds her arms over her chest. "I'm listening."

Graystone launches into the speech he has refined over countless sleepless hours. It's a touching little piece, contrite yet assertive, in which he apologizes handsomely for his behavior, accuses himself of insensitivity and poor timing, and blames this lapse on the intensity of his feeling. Such emotion is improper, inconvenient, even embarrassing; he has tried his best to overcome it, he confesses, but to no avail. Her fascination for him remains greater than reason. He can no longer resist it. With a smile every bit as confident as it is charming, Graystone asks for a second chance.

Crow listens without expression. Then she says, "No."

"No?" Graystone is astonished. Though his first attempt had met with no encouragement, he'd attributed that failure to his own miscalculation. He shouldn't have come on so strong, shouldn't have come on at all while she was distracted over a sick child. Also, he had failed to allow for the

disbelief factor. How could he blame Crow for doubting an infatuation that he himself sees as bizarre and inappropriate?

Yet it never occurred to him that Crow might refuse a second, more respectful approach; for surely she has as much to gain from a liaison between them as he has to lose.

In a starched voice, he asks, "Why not?"

"It's a matter of principle."

"What principle is that?"

She hesitates, then juts out her jaw. "I don't believe in mixed dating."

Without actually moving, Graystone draws away. An old, bleak anger shines out of his face. "What do you mean?"

"I'm black."

"And what the hell am I?"

"Black-skinned."

He sucks in his breath. " 'Dr. Oreo.' That's a load of shit. Doesn't make a goddamn bit of difference where a man comes from. Nobody's got a corner on being black."

"Nobody's got a corner on it, but some folks practice it more than others." Her face softens just a bit. "Didn't mean to hurt your feelings. All I'm saying is, you've got your world and I've got mine. Which I thought you knew as well as me."

"You're the one putting up barricades, baby, not me."

"Like they ain't already there! I don't notice you making any public announcement."

Graystone drops his eyes. "Naturally I feel it's best to be discreet. We have a policy about interdepartmental relationships. As head of the department, I'm expected to set an example. . . . My problem isn't with what you do, it's with where you do it."

"Uh-huh," says Crow, arms akimbo. "Well, whatever your problem is, I don't need no backdoor man."

"I've no intention of being your 'backdoor man,' " Graystone growls; though in fact the relationship he rather fuzzily envisions is nothing else. Damn woman's putting him on the spot. Is he expected to jump up on a desk and bare his soul in the middle of the ER?

"Oh no?"

It's her smile that does it, that hard little smile that says, "I know who you are and I know what you want."

He says, "I'm taking you to a party. At my parents' house."

Crow blinks. "Your parents."

"That's right. The Saturday before Christmas. A big party. Lots of hospital brass. Very public." He moves toward her slowly, like a man stalking a bird.

"A million people I don't know, all friends of yours."

"I sat with your friends." Graystone grasps her wrist lightly, as if taking her pulse. "Not scared, are you?"

"Hell no! Just don't sound like my kind of scene."

His eyes challenge her. "You said you didn't want a backdoor man."

"Said I don't want *no* backdoor man. That's how black folk talk."

He bristles at that, till he sees by her half-smile that it's a tease. Somehow, without his quite noticing how or when, they've made that transition. Graystone's not a man who takes easily to teasing. He's never had to; people tend to tread carefully in his presence. Coming from Crow, though, he finds the phenomenon surprisingly tolerable.

"You said you didn't want to come in the back," he says, "so I'm asking you in the front. I'm asking you to a great big formal in-your-face party. The question is, are you man enough to accept?"

Crow gives him a weighing look. "People would talk their damn heads off."

Flinching inside, Graystone says, "Let 'em."

"What are you pushing this for? You're like some fool on a raft heading for the rapids, yellin', 'Faster, faster!'"

"Don't catastrophize, Crow. Attending a party at my parents' is not exactly going over Niagara on a raft." A vision comes to him, of his mother's icy smile and Grand Inquisitor eyes trained on Crow. "Not quite," he says.

She laughs.

"Will you come?"

"I'll give it some thought," she says.

* * *

"You can't," Daniel says.

"I did."

They're sitting in a pub half a block from the hospital, nursing a couple of scotch-and-sodas.

"Don't get me wrong. I'm happy as a clam to see you fall flat-on-your-ass in love. It couldn't happen to a nicer guy. But have you considered the consequences?"

"What consequences?"

"Elvira, for one."

Graystone grunts.

"Anyway," he says, "who's talking about love?"

"Taking that girl to your mother's, that's either love or a death wish; and you never struck me as the suicidal type."

"I knew it," Selma crows. "Minute I saw Dr. Whitebread making house calls, I knew it."

Crow pours herself a second cup of coffee, then sits back down, straddling the kitchen chair. Children's laughter filters in from Joey's room. Selma has brought her grand-daughter to play.

"You knew what?" she says.

"I knew that Dr. Gray Fox was after your ass."

Crow smiles into her cup. "He invited me to a party at his parents'."

Selma's small face puckers in thought. "Devious," she says at last. "You never said yes."

"I said I'd think about it."

"Are you crazy, girl?"

"You're the one said I should get out more."

"Yes I did, but I meant with our own folk. You know my daughters been dying to set you up."

"Ain't he one of us? His skin's black enough."

Selma hisses in disgust. "I'm serious. The man's a damn Oreo, and you know it."

"More like a Hydrox," Crow teases. "Darker and sweeter."

"Tell me if I'm overstepping my bounds," Daniel says. "Let me know immediately. I speak to you as I would to a brother—a younger, slightly retarded brother. Here is my question. What do you call a guy who dumps a beautiful, classy, successful businesswoman to take up with a housekeeper?"

"Daniel—"

"In Jewish you call him a schmuck."

"You're overstepping."

"*Plus*, even if you pull it off, even if you score, then what? Where do you see it going?"

"This is none—"

"Because sooner or later, probably sooner, it's bound to end. And then what? Will you quit? Will she? Or do you just go back to looking through her?"

"I had this dentist when I was a kid. 'Raise your hand if it hurts,' he used to say. Sadistic bastard."

"You don't want to hear, just say the word."

"Which word, Dan'l?"

Daniel lifts his hands in surrender. He waits a decent interval before saying, "Not to mention Elvira."

Graystone raises his eyes to heaven. "I believe you already mentioned Elvira."

"Crow, you have to admit, is not Elvira's kind of woman. You spring Crow on her, she'll code on us."

"Not Elvira. She's a tough old broad."

"Uh-huh." Daniel fishes a pad out of his overcoat pocket and scribbles a few words.

"What're you writing?"

"Memo to myself. Bring. Defibrillator. To. Party."

Selma says, "You think you're in some kinda damn fairy tale, Prince Charming gonna come ridin' up in his shiny new Porsche and carry you off to his castle?"

Crow's eyes grow chilly. "He's no Prince Charming, and I'm sure as hell no Cinderella. And when the day comes that I need rescuing, I'll hang 'em up for good."

"Well, I'm glad you know that at least. 'Cause I don't believe in no fairy tales, and I don't believe in no happ'ly-ever-afters; and you ain't got no business believing in 'em either."

"You forget who you're talking to," Crow says softly.

Reaching across the table, Selma lays her roughened hand against Crow's cheek. "I ain't forgetting," she says. "But, baby, even with all you been through, you're a young woman still, and I'm a old one. I'm tellin' you a man like that ain't lookin' for happy endings, child, not with you. He live in a different world from you and me. Best keep it like that."

"He's not a bad man, Selma," Crow says.

"Then why's he messin' with you?"

22

. . . .

CROW

Quiet conversation, laughter, the clink of silver against china, the hushed, unhurried pad of waiters' footsteps: If I close my eyes, I could be back in Paris, Blue and me sitting knee to knee in the corner café.

Restaurant's in Brooklyn Heights, just a mile or two from where I grew up, but I've never been in here before. 'Course not; the whole thing's about keeping people like me out. Full-course lunch costs more than I earn in a day. Decor is tarted-up English pub: dart boards and hunting prints, leather banquettes and forest-green walls. Clientele very white, very prosperous. Lot of suits, male and female. I draw my coat tighter around my uniform.

She asks am I cold.

"No," I say, "I'm just not dressed for the occasion. Why'd you pick this place?"

Alice looks around the room as if noticing it for the first time. "I come here sometimes."

"I sort of guessed." Maître d' damn near kissed her hand when we came in. How are you, Ms. Straugh? Saw your parents last night, Ms. Straugh. Stopped in for an after-concert bite with friends. Usual table, Ms. Straugh?

"It's quiet," she says.

"Would be, at these prices."

"I wanted to talk to you. Why should all our conversations take place in the ladies' room?"

"Better ambience?" I'm just jivin', but I shouldn't; Alice gets that anxious look of hers.

"If you don't like it, we can go somewhere else."

"No, baby, this is fine."

The waiter approaches. Fox-faced dude with slicked-back hair, looks like they hired him to match the decor. He looks at her, not me. "Are you ready to order?"

"Crow?"

I choose the chicken breast stuffed with wild rice. Alice orders the salmon steak. The waiter bows his head to her and glides away.

Feels strange, sitting here with her. In movies, on TV, you always see black and white folks sitting together in restaurants, laughing and jiving like homeboys, and it sounds so normal. As if they're starting from the same ground, as if they share a common language. Which in my experience they don't. That's gotta be the famous magic of movies they always talk about. In real life, even before you sat down at that table it'd be piled so high with problems, misconceptions, and suspicions, you could hardly see over it. I ain't saying blacks and whites can't be friends. I'm just saying that to get there, they've got to plow through some shit. Movies never show you that part.

Alice don't look any easier than I feel, even though she's the one did the inviting. She goes from torturing her roll to strangling her napkin. "Guess you've heard about me and Noah."

"It's a hot topic," I tell her.

"What do you think?"

I'm kind of surprised by the question. "I think it's none of my business," I say.

Her face sags. "That means you disapprove."

"It's nothing to do with me."

She puts her elbows on the table and leans across it. "I saw something in that boy, Crow. I saw the good, strong, caring man he will become, if all that sweetness isn't crushed and betrayed. I saw so clearly that I could help him, I could give him what he needs. Why shouldn't we get a chance?"

Beats hell out of me why she needs my approval, but it's plain she's asking for it. I don't want to hurt her feelings, but I ain't gonna lie.

"Child's been raised black," I say. "These days, young black men are an endangered species. I don't favor taking them away from the community. It's not good for them, and it's not good for us."

"I don't want to take him away!" she cries out. People sitting nearby turn their heads, but she doesn't notice. "I want to expand his world, not diminish it. I wouldn't want Noah to be a black boy in a white world, to be different all the time. That's sad for a child. He has to have black friends as well as white. And so do I."

"You're talking like you already got him."

"I don't yet, but I will."

"They giving you a hard time?"

"They're trying to." Alice picks up a breadstick, snaps it in two. "Makes me sick the way they talk about these kids, as if they're interchangeable parts. 'Sorry, that one's not available, but how about this pink-cheeked little baby girl, just eighteen months old and already potty-trained!' They act like I'm shopping for a pet. I don't want a generic *child*. It's Noah I care about, Noah I want. *That* child spoke to me."

Love shines in her eyes every time she says his name. I meant what I said to her. Black child raised white has nobody, belongs nowhere. That's a terrible thing for a child. All the same, I've got a mother's heart can't help but feel for any woman loves a child like Alice loves Noah.

It's not like the boy's got much else going for him, I tell myself. Tortured by his own mother, that's the last child in the world you'd want to see fed into the foster-care system. Blue was mauled by that system, and he ain't the only one. Just last month in Mercy, EMS brought in a baby, DOA, scalded to death. Foster mother did it.

Of course, there's decent women out there, just wanting to do some good. Look at Selma. City gave her money for my keep; she took it and put it aside. The day I married Blue, she gave me the bankbook. It was all there, every penny with interest; my dowry, she called it. In my eyes, a woman like Selma is a natural saint, and she ain't alone. But there's also plenty who are in it just for the money. It's a crapshoot, the luck of the draw, and who am I to say the boy's better off takin' his chances than going with Alice? She may be white, but she loves him.

I find myself hoping she gets him. I tell her so.

Way she smiles, it seems to mean something to her.

"He's coming for Christmas," she says. "CWA's not happy, but his grandmother wouldn't have him, and they couldn't justify holding him over the holiday. I have him for three days."

"Good for you."

"You have a son, don't you, Crow?"

All of a sudden I glimpse where we're going. "Yes, I do," I say.

"What's his name?"

"Joey."

"How old is he?"

"Four and a half."

"Noah's five," she says.

I say nothing.

"I want that boy to have the time of his life," Alice says. "I want to take him to the Christmas show at Radio City Music Hall, skating at Rockefeller Center, dinner in a fun restaurant. I know he would enjoy it twice as much sharing it with a friend. And so would I." Alice reaches 'cross the table and grasps my hand. "Would you and Joey come? Would you be my guests for the day after Christmas?"

I look down at our linked hands, pink and brown. If Blue was here, I know what he'd say. "Give the girl a chance," he'd say, laughing at me. "Don't be such a hard-ass." Blue was opener than me, but then Blue was a musician, and music is a great leveler.

This girl is all right. I don't want to hurt her feelings, and I know Joey would love the show. But I got the feeling something more than an afternoon's outing is under discussion here.

In Europe we had white friends, musicians, mostly. Never had any in this country, though. For me it's different here. Not because I buy into that white-devil shit. I got no faith in devils nor in angels, white or otherwise. It's just that, growing up like I did in the project, racists are thick as cockroaches. Most white folk you meet, it ain't a question of "Are they racist?" but "How racist are they?"

Way I see it, in this country there's basically three types of white people. First there's the ones who're open about it, who come right out, call you nigger to your face. In a way they're the easiest, 'cause you know up front what kind of trash you're dealing with. Second kind's the ones who never say the word, but all the time it's lurking right behind their eyes where you can see it clear as day: like the storekeepers who follow you around the aisles, waiting for you to steal something. And then there's the hypocrites, who act nice and talk polite to your face, but they'd eat their houses brick by brick before they'd sell to a African-American. You see it all the time. Black family move into a white neighborhood and the For Sale signs sprout faster than crabgrass.

Blue always claimed there's a fourth kind, white folk who for no apparent reason escaped the general plague. Maybe so, but if such people exist, there ain't no sure and easy way to tell the righteous from the hypocrites. For myself and my child, I'd rather be safe than sorry.

This thing with Alice, though, has me thinking maybe Blue had a point. Damned if I can't help liking the bitch. With her, maybe a person *could* get past the black/white thing. The class thing, though: That's the sticking point. Rich and poor don't make good friends. Different interests, in every sense. Kind o' day she's talking about, Radio City and all, that's a whole week's salary for me. She made it clear she'd pay our way, but I don't care to be beholden. I'm searching for a gentle way to turn her down when all of a sudden it's Graystone's face I see, his voice in my ear. "You're the one putting up barricades," I hear him say.

Then once again I'm looking into Alice's raw, hopeful face, only this time a strange thing happens. Now I got to say, and I know it sounds bad, but to me, white faces never have quite the same reality as black. They look unfinished, not fully formed, like an unbaked pie or an unstained chair. Sort of like masks, almost-but-not-quite faces that don't stick in my mind like black faces do. And that was true of Alice, too, till suddenly now, for no clear reason, her features come together into something unique and individual; her face grows at once more solid and more transparent. It's like that white skin ain't there anymore; the veil is lifted and I can see clear inside her. What I'm saying: All of a sudden, Alice is someone I know.

Still, I hesitate. My life's complicated enough, I'm thinking, without adding complicated friendships. Meanwhile she's waiting on a answer. Her eyes hide nothing. I don't know how a person live in the world with eyes like that.

"We'd be proud to come," I hear myself say.

Alice beams at me. The waiter brings our food. Her salmon looks perfect. So does the chicken, but when I cut into it, my knife sticks. The meat is pink and gamy, way undercooked.

Alice notices at once and summons the waiter.

"Is anything wrong, miss?"

"Look at my friend's chicken," she says.

The waiter's eyes flicker from my plate to my face, then back again to Alice. In that pressing glance I feel the back of his hand, the whisper of contempt. It feels like *déjà vu*, but it's no illusion; I've been down this road before. What's going to happen next is as clear and as inevitable as a car crash seconds before impact. Clear to me and him, that is. Alice hasn't got a clue.

"I see nothing wrong," the waiter says.

"It's raw inside!" she sputters.

"We have a French chef. He cooks meat, he does not cremate it. If your friend likes her chicken burned, try Kentucky Fried Chicken, just down the block."

His words are addressed solely to her. I am the dog she brought in on a leash. One thing I've learned, being black in America: There ain't no middle road. Shit like this come down, either you Tom it or you fight. Me, I don't go looking for trouble; but somebody gets in my face, I'm ready. My fists clench; I scrape back my chair. But my anger is sidelined by Alice's.

She sits up tall. Red patches come out on her cheeks. Her voice as she berates the waiter grows crisper and, though I'm sure she don't know it, more haughty. She don't look like mousy little Nurse Straugh now. Alice is reverting to type.

The maître d' materializes. "Is anything wrong, Ms. Straugh?"

"Raw fowl and insolent waiters!" Ms. Straugh replies.

The maître d' pales. The offending dish and waiter are borne off, one to be replaced, the other never seen again. Alice quivers with indignation. I sit back in my chair and laugh.

"It's not funny," Alice says.

"All that for a piece of chicken."

"Oh, but you can't let them get away with that sort of nonsense," she says expertly. "That kind of thing's intolerable."

"Racism?" I ask.

Girl look at me like she's never heard that word before.

"No," she says. "Bad service."

23

· · · · · · ·

The dress has been worn only once before, on the night the band played Buckingham Palace. When she removes it from its bag, a faint scent of flowers comes with it. Crow slips it on, a rose-colored jersey knit, with off-the-shoulder sleeves, a fitted bodice, and a long, graceful sweep of a skirt. Though she's a bit thinner now than then, the dress fits perfectly. Standing before the mirror, she feels a tingle on the back of her neck, as if Blue's lips were brushing the skin there.

She hugs herself, a gesture devoid of comfort. Desolation weighs her shoulders and bows her long neck. There's a coldness come upon her that owes nothing to the weather, a freeze that radiates from deep inside. Every atom of her body longs for touch, not the ghostly brush of memory but the strong, passionate embrace of a lover: Blue's touch is what she needs, and what she cannot have.

In the year since his death, Crow has grown skilled at sublimation, channeling her thoughts into narrow causeways of here and now: a process not to be confused with healing. When memories burst forth, they carry pain as raw, despair as intense, as she felt on the day of his funeral. Perhaps if the police had caught the mugger who left Blue lying in his blood, then she might have known some sense of closure, might have begun to rebuild her life. But they never did; and though she performs the necessary functions of life—eating, sleeping, earning a living, caring for her child—Crow remains trapped, like Elias, in a limbo of denial and hopeless longing.

Footsteps in the hallway recall her to the living. Quickly she wipes her eyes, straightens her back.

"You look beautiful, baby." Selma leans against the doorframe, her hands on Joey's shoulders. "Jus' beautiful."

Crow turns and smiles at her son. "How do I look?"

"I wish I was a grown-up."

"How come?"

"So I could marry you."

Laughing, she kneels and opens her arms to him. "Come here, baby, and gimme some sugar."

"Don't muss Mama's hair now," Selma warns.

Crow's just looking for a good-night kiss, but the moment Joey's arms close around her neck, fear bubbles to the surface. Not for the child, but, shamefully, for herself: She dreads leaving the safety of the 'hood for the greater world outside.

Outsiders might see her feeling of safety as illusory. Stray bullets carry no names, they might argue, and madness and despair strike at those closest at hand. Crow would not disagree; and yet she knows the shoals and reefs of these her territorial waters, and navigates them daily. Outside are perils of a different, unforeseeable sort. Outside, the cold eyes of strangers judge her.

The doorbell rings, and the women look at each other. Neither moves.

"I'll get it," Selma says.

"I'll come."

"Not yet. Five minutes at least. You got to make 'em wait a bit."

"Behave yourself, Selma."

The old woman limps across the living room and squints through the peephole before opening the door.

Graystone fills the entrance. His overcoat is draped over one arm; the other cradles a brightly wrapped package. He looks surprised to see Selma.

"Come on in," Selma says. "She be out in a minute." She takes his coat and leads him to the sofa, but remains afoot herself.

They are silent for several minutes. Graystone looks about. A modest Christmas tree stands in a corner of the room, trimmed with tinsel and candy canes. The room smells of pine needles and roast chicken.

"You're baby-sitting for Joey?" he asks presently.

"Uh-huh. That child be like a grandson to me. Crow, she be like my own daughter. Mind if I ask you somethin'?"

"Go ahead."

"What you messing with Crow's head for?"

"I beg your pardon?"

"It ain't my pardon you should be beggin'. Don't you know what that girl been through?"

Graystone's look is august and offended. "I'm not taking her to some sleazy dive, Selma. I'm taking her to my parents' home." God help me, he adds silently, wiping his forehead with a handkerchief. Last night he didn't sleep at all, and since morning, his stomach has been churning.

Then Crow comes out, and Graystone, rising, catches his breath. "Crow. You look beautiful."

Crow laughs. "You don't have to sound so relieved."

"That dress . . ."

"Is it all right? Blue bought it for me in Paris."

"Perfect. You'll be the most elegant woman at the party."

Selma sniffs. "Long as she ain't the *only* woman at the party."

"Selma!" Crow cries.

Then Graystone notices Joey, peeking out from behind his mother's skirt. "How're you doing, young man?" he says, holding out his hand.

Joey comes forward to shake it. "Doin' fine."

"What do you think of your mother tonight? Is she beautiful?"

"Selma say she too good for you."

Both women cry out in protest, but Graystone laughs approvingly. "Hey—I brought you a little something for Christmas, but you can't open it yet. Gotta put it under the tree." He reaches behind him for the box, hands it to Joey.

"Oh, man, thanks!" Joey holds the box to his ear and rattles it.

"You didn't have to do that," says Crow.

"No; I wanted to."

Selma shakes her head.

The elevator's broken, so they walk down four flights of stairs. Graystone's taken advantage of his M.D. plates to park in a loading zone right in front of Crow's building. He breathes a sigh of relief to find his car still there and unmolested.

There's an awkward bit of silence in the car. Presently Graystone asks about Joey: How's his asthma? Much better, Crow replies, since he started on the inhaler. "Feisty little fellow," says Graystone, adding, with a sidewise glance at Crow, "Looks just like his daddy."

"You knew Blue?"

"Just from hearing him play, every chance I got. Has Joey inherited his talent, too?"

"Deacon gave him Blue's harmonica a couple months ago. He's teaching himself to play. There's something there, I think. Time will tell."

After a mile or so, Graystone says, "I used to play the harmonica."

"You?"

He laughs at her surprise. "I wasn't bad. Not in your friends' league, of course. But not bad."

"You still play?"

He shakes his head.

"Why not?"

"Don't know. Those days are gone. I'm in a different mode now, I guess."

"A doctor mode."

He glances over to see if she's mocking him. Big mistake; her smile sends his heart surging into A-fib. A dozen times this week he's warned himself to play it slow, but seeing her in that dress, he can't help speculating on his chances (piss-poor, he reckons) of seeing her without it. He notes the outline of her thigh under the jersey skirt, and his palms begin to sweat. Graystone tightens his grip on the wheel and stares resolutely ahead.

By the time they arrive, the party is in full swing. Lincoln Town Cars, Cadillacs, and Mercedes line the street. The house is imposing, a massive brick colonial set atop an acre of manicured lawns and formal plantings. Walking up the cobblestone path, Crow needs to remind herself of who she is. Graystone, at his most austere, offers her his arm.

They enter to a fragrant blast of warmth, light, laughter, music. A maid takes their coats. Graystone's parents hover near the door, greeting new arrivals.

"Mother, this is Crow Durango. Crow, my parents: Elvira and Harold Graystone."

"How do you do," says Crow.

Harold raises her hand to his lips. "One thing I'll say for Thomas: He's got his father's eye."

It's his mother's turn. Taking Crow's hand less to greet than to detain her, Elvira inspects her with X-ray eyes and all the sentiment of an airport security guard. First the dress: a blink of grudging approval there. The lack of suitable jewelry is noted: Crow wears nothing around her throat but a strip of velvet, a dusky rose choker with an ivory clasp. Her complexion is dark, but then so is Elvira's. The upswept hair, the face and figure, are unexceptionable; her hand, however, is remarkably hard, calloused on the pads beneath each finger: the hands of a manual laborer, an artist, or a musician.

Elvira offers up a provisional smile. "Charming girl," she pronounces, though not without reservation. She clears her throat and, without actually moving, gives the impression of rolling up her sleeves. Before the interrogation can begin, Graystone takes Crow's arm in a firm grip and leads her down the hall to the living room.

He pauses in the doorway beneath a sprig of mistletoe tacked onto the lintel. As Crow glances up inquiringly, he places one hand on the nape of her neck, bends his head, and kisses her on the lips.

She stumbles backward, astonished. There's a strange, tingling sensation in her toes and fingertips, as if frostbitten digits were coming back to life.

"Mistletoe," he says apologetically, with a gleam in his eye. "Tradition. Couldn't be helped."

Nearly all the faces in the crowded room are white, a bit of a shock for Crow, though she might have anticipated it. A huge, ornately decorated Christmas tree dominates one corner, and a fire crackles on the hearth. Graystone holds her arm in his as they make their way toward the bar. "Hello," he says. "Good to see you again. Merry Christmas." Crow is introduced to a dozen people. Several are familiar: administrators from Mercy, officials from the city's Health and Hospitals Commission who visit the ER from time to time. None recognize her—impossible that they should, in this setting. They make up to her, pressing her hand, shaking their heads enviously at Graystone.

Crow preens just a little.

Then Dan Bergman emerges from the crowd. "Good golly, Miss Crow," he declares, pressing his palm to his heart. "You look divine."

Graystone relaxes instantly. "Back off, Bergman," he says, laughing.

"Merry Christmas, Dr. Bergman."

"Dan," he corrects her. "Honest to God, Crow, you look much too fine for ole stick-in-the-mud Tom here. Run away with me."

"You can run, but you can't hide," says Risa, linking her arm in her husband's and holding out her hand to Crow. "Hi, I'm Risa Bergman, Danny's pregnant wife."

"Sister," Daniel whispers behind his hand.

"Nice to meet you," says Crow.

"You, too. I've heard so much about you." Voice is friendly, eyes are sharp.

Then a woman's voice shrills, "Thomas, *mon chéri!*" and Graystone is enveloped in a flurry of chiffon and Shalimar. When, at length, he disengages himself, his face is pocked with red. "Jesus, Claudette," he says, dabbing at the lipstick with a handkerchief.

"Oh, what a baby you are! He is lucky I did not catch him underneath ze mistletoe, *n'est-ce pas?*" she asks Daniel.

Crow, finding herself upstaged, studies the woman with interest. She is darker than Crow, nearly as tall as Graystone, model-thin but busty, swathed in a shimmering silver gown with a plunging décolleté and an even lower back. The woman plants a more subdued kiss on Daniel's lips. "Merry Christmas, *chéri.*"

"Be still, my heart," he groans.

Risa digs an elbow into his ribs. "Keep it up, I'll still your heart."

Graystone turns the woman around to face Crow. "Claudette, I'd like you to meet—"

"No, don't tell me—ze lovely Michelle!" Claudette's eyes gleam wickedly. "We have heard so much about you, *ma petite;* it is Michelle this and Michelle that, until one could scream with jealousy."

Silence ensues.

"Oh," she says innocently, "have I made ze little mistake?"

"You have made ze big mistake," Daniel mutters.

Graystone moves around her to slip his arm through Crow's. "Claudette Graystone, Crow Durango. Claudette is my aunt."

Crow laughs incredulously. "Your what?"

"Ce n'est pas Michelle?"

"Knock it off," he growls.

"Pardonnez-moi, I am so sorry. Thomas has so many friends, one gets confused."

"Lucky man," says Crow. "And such fond relations, too. Your aunt, you said?"

"My uncle's wife. Let's have that drink, shall we?"

A short while later, supper is announced, and the party drifts into the dining room. A buffet has been set out along one wall, and in addition to the extended dining table, five or six smaller tables are spaced about the room. Crow and Graystone fill their plates and head for one of the side tables, but are summoned by Elvira's imperious call to join her at the main table. Graystone sits between his mother and Crow. Opposite them, on Elvira's left, are Claudette and her husband.

"At last," says Elvira to Crow. "Now, dear, tell me all about yourself."

"All?" asks Crow, with a little smile.

"Mother, why not let Crow eat in peace?"

"Naughty Thomas," trills Claudette, "keeping his little friend a secret."

Elvira raises her eyebrows. "I am hardly disturbing her dinner, Thomas; I merely asked Crow a question."

"Asked," she says, but in her annoyance it comes out, just discernibly, as "aksed." Crow smiles down at her plate. She has, as Selma's always said, a gift for languages, not only foreign tongues but her own as well: an ear for the accents and nuances of region and class. She had noticed Elvira's careful, overly precise diction the first time she spoke. Her first guess was that Elvira is or has been on the stage; but those inverted consonants are a dead giveaway, a telltale reversion to her roots, which are Crow's as well. Today, Elvira may well serve dinner for sixty on matching china, with silver cutlery and linen napkins, but Crow knows of a certainty that *she* was not born with a silver spoon in her mouth. Plastic, more like.

"Tell me, dear," Elvira says, "where did you and Thomas meet?"

Crow is ready to answer, but Graystone forestalls her.

"I believe the first time we spoke was in the Cellar."

"The *cellar?*" cries Claudette.

"The jazz club."

"I see," Elvira says.

So does Crow, and doesn't much care for the view. She fixes her gaze on Graystone, the man who said, "I don't care what you do. I don't care what your job is." Liar, say her eyes.

He returns a bland smile.

Risa and Daniel Bergman take seats at the table, and the conversation turns general; that is, Elvira discourses on which new books are worth reading and which are commercial trash, bemoans the paucity of decent films, and condemns the dismal state of Broadway. "The dramas are laughable, the comedies depressing. And the new musicals? Pure glitz."

"Come on, Mother," Graystone says. "You know you enjoyed *Les Miz* and *Phantom.*"

"Oh," she replies, rolling her eyes, "one has no choice. In

that kind of production, the audience is seized by the throat and force-fed enjoyment, like roaster hens being stuffed with grain. I'll admit some of the voices are very fine, but at heart these plays are empty spectacles, mere 'sound and fury, signifying nothing.' You can't compare them to the classic musicals: *Camelot,* for instance, or *My Fair Lady.*"

"We saw a revival of *My Fair Lady* in London," says Crow, who's been silent for some time. "My husband loved it. I didn't much care for it."

"Husband?" Elvira says sharply.

Crow flushes. "Late husband."

"I told you, Mother."

"Oh, yes. A musician of some sort, I believe Thomas said?"

"Not a musician of some sort," Graystone says with mounting irritation. "Blue Durango was the greatest sax player jazz has ever known."

"How interesting," Elvira says. "I'm afraid *I* never heard of him. But then, my son has a taste for *that music* which my husband and I do not share."

Crow says gently, "It's our music. Our gift to the world."

"I don't know what you mean by 'our.' No doubt your husband was an exception, my dear, but I must tell you I don't much care for the element involved with that kind of music."

"My husband was no exception, Mrs. Graystone. He was very much of that world, and proud to be. As I am."

The older woman smiles, showing perfectly capped, sharpish teeth. "That would explain then, why you didn't care for *My Fair Lady.*"

"Mother!" Thomas cries angrily.

Crow silences him with a hand on his arm. Her voice takes on a rougher edge, ghetto-tinged. "Wasn't the music or the lyrics, it was the story. I couldn't feature Eliza fallin' for all that Pygmalion shit. What's wrong with being a Cockney?"

Elvira, who has followed every word with frowning concentration, snaps to at the word "shit." Her nostrils quiver. She knows now who she's talking to, knows it with a part of her long buried, though not forgotten. Crow's taking her back to a place she never meant to revisit. She closes her eyes briefly, with the pained look of a lady assaulted by an unpleasant odor but too polite to mention it.

"Clearly," she says, "Eliza wanted to improve herself."

"Improve herself!" Crow scoffs. "Higgins didn't improve her. He taught her nothing useful. All the fool did was swap her accent for his."

"But in England, accent is everything."

"Only in England?"

"Quite right. Speech is everywhere an indicator of class."

"Real class," Crow says, with a glint in her eye, "comes from inside. My opinion, the bitch had no self-respect. The man dissed her, and she bought into it. Person with self-respect don't need to hide where she come from. Don't you agree, Mrs. Graystone?"

Elvira glances at her son, whose face remains impassive. "How fascinating," she says. "Tell us, Crow, when you're not critiquing musicals, what exactly do you do?"

Graystone says, "I see they're putting out dessert. Shall we, Crow?"

"No, thanks," she replies. "I ain't hungry."

Rapt as lovers but joined in contempt, the women look past him, eyes meeting in perfect recognition.

Risa and Daniel exchange a look, and both begin to speak at once.

"What lovely flowers. Who did them?"

"Elvira, you've outdone yourself this year."

She raises a hand without glancing at them. "Children, please: You're interrupting Crow. We were talking about her occupation."

Crow shows her teeth. "I work in Mercy," she says.

"Do you indeed." Elvira studies her thoughtfully. "In what capacity?"

"Housekeeping."

The tension at their table has augmented the natural attention accorded the hostess. General silence greets Crow's announcement, followed by a peripheral babble of polite conversation.

"Housekeeping?" says Claudette. "What does she mean, housekeeping?"

"Sweeping, mopping, scrubbing, that kind of thing," says Crow. "Housekeeping."

If she had said, "Stripping, hooking, the odd spot of blackmail," Elvira's reaction could not have been more marked. She turns eyes expressive of horror upon her son, who pushes back his chair and rises.

"But how wonderful!" Claudette exclaims. "Do you do apartments, too?"

24

• • • • • • •

Siren shrieking, an ambulance streaks up to the ER. Percy wheels out the gurney. On it, motionless, lies a black man with blue lips, naked beneath a gray woolen EMS blanket. His single eye is open and sightless, lashes rimmed with beads of ice, beard and dreadlocks frozen stiff.

Graystone's right there. "What's up?" Then, glancing at the patient, he does a double take. "Jesus, it's Preacher."

"It was," says Percy.

Graystone presses a stethoscope to Preacher's ice-cold chest. Frowns in concentration.

"Nada," says Vinnie, coming up beside his partner. "Ditto BP. Merry Goddamn Christmas, Doc. Whaddya doin' here anyways?"

Not pausing to answer, Graystone takes the gurney and runs it down the hall. Percy keeps pace. "Call come in from Saint Luke's. Pastor found him like this in the manger, curled up in Mary's lap. Damn fool. Ain't suppose to die till Easter, even I know that."

"Couldn't you have at least started a line?"

"What for?"

The doctor glares. "You're ready to declare him? You ought to know the protocol by now: Nobody gets declared till they're warmed up to ninety degrees."

A HEARTBEAT AWAY

Pilar peels off from the nurses' station, takes one look, and hollers for reinforcements. They wheel Preacher into code room 1 and take his vitals: no measurable BP, no pulse, temp too low to register. ER staff begins to converge, the response a bit slower than usual. They're light because of the holiday; apart from Pilar and young Jennifer, the only nurses are per diem agency recruits. Graystone starts chest compressions, Elsa Kraven inserts an IV line, and Daniel Bergman intubates the comatose patient.

"Goddamn Preacher," Pilar grumbles as she wraps a blanket around him. "Gotta pull this shit, ruin everybody's Christmas."

"Warm that first," Graystone snaps at Jennifer, who's about to hook up a cold bag of saline to the IV line. "Hundred and four degrees Fahrenheit." He looks across Preacher's body at Daniel, not liking to correct him in front of the others. Daniel nods and ups the temperature control on the ventilator to 104°.

"Let's push some sodium bicarb," says Graystone. "Nurse, can you start a second line?"

"In what? The man has no veins," Pilar grumbles, but she finds one.

Elsa Kraven calls for more blankets. Two agency nurses look helplessly at each other. Out in the corridor, Crow darts away, returning moments later with a stack. She avoids looking at Graystone, whose attention focuses suddenly on his compressions.

"Give 'em here," says Pilar. Seeing Crow reminds her that she's mad at Graystone, a fact temporarily occluded in the flap over Preacher. Quickly she rearranges her face in a scowl.

She knows, of course. By 7:00 Monday morning, while the residents were still rubbing sleep out of their eyes and the nurses were changing from street shoes to Dr. Scholl's, Pilar, whose sources are extensive and reliable, had already heard about Graystone and Crow. Never one to shirk her duty, she marched straight into his office and demanded, "What that girl ever done to you?"

Graystone didn't bother asking who. "Nothing," he replied, in a voice to send lesser nurses scurrying.

211

Not Pilar, though. "I told you that girl's the best damn housekeeper I ever had. If she leave on account o' you . . ."

"Ms. Johnston!"

"Dr. Graystone!"

"I'd appreciate it, I'd be exceedingly grateful, if you'd mind your own damn business."

"Whatever happen in this ER is my business."

"Nothing happened in this ER!" And that was all he would say, despite three days of Pilar's patented silent treatment. She looks at him now, moving his lips as he counts out his compressions like some kind of greenhorn intern, all to avoid looking at Crow.

Graystone knows he could have saved himself a lot of grief by confiding in Pilar, telling her that it was all over between him and Crow. The madness has been excised, the wound cauterized by shame. Pride keeps him silent, as well as a nagging sense that he is not, perhaps, quite as wholeheartedly relieved as he ought to be.

And this is odd, because Graystone has known from the start that the prognosis was dim. This love affair has ended before it began, and it's a good thing it has. His life is back on track, his reason restored; he has every reason to rejoice. Why, then, does he find himself snapping at hapless residents, growling at nurses, and treating his patients with barely restrained impatience?

Lingering aftereffects, he tells himself, negligible symptoms of a malady that has essentially run its course. He's over her, that's certain; he's as indifferent to Crow as she is to him. And if he weren't, what good would it do him? Things said on both sides make even the thought of resumption untenable. As Graystone thumps methodically on Preacher's chest, the steady, monotonous work sends his mind awandering. The code room fades, and it's Crow's face he sees, lighted by flashes from passing vehicles.

They drive in silence, Crow as removed from him as if a thick pane of glass divided them, he too full of conflicting emotions to speak. At length, as silence threatens to engulf them, he bestirs himself to apologize for her treatment in his parents' home. On his own behalf he offers no apology, for none seems called for.

Instead of acknowledging her own part in the debacle, the hussy curls her lip at him. "Don't blame them," she says. "You set it up."

"What the hell does that mean?"

"Should of told 'em up front who I am, how I make my living."

"I didn't want to prejudice them. I wanted them to get to know you first, the real you."

"The real me!" she hoots. "And who do you think works in the ER, my body double? No, baby, that ain't it. Tell the truth."

"Which is?"

"You're ashamed of me. You're ashamed of being with a skivvy, a menial, a lowly housekeeper. It offends your dignity."

"Not true, I'm not like that." *Graystone rubs his face with the palm of his hand.* "You heard what I said to them. You met my mother, you saw what she is. I know you did, because you called her on it. So was it really absolutely necessary for you to rub her nose in your job the very first time you met?"

"Rub her nose in it! Would you listen to yourself? You're saying my job is shit."

"I didn't say that. I didn't mean it."

"She asked me. I ain't about to lie. Woman think there's something degrading about good, honest work, that's her problem, not mine. I ain't ashamed of what I do."

"Which just happens to be about fifty levels below your capabilities."

"What do you know about my capabilities?" *Her eyes gleam dangerously, but he's too angry to take care.*

"I've seen you with Deacon. I know the world you used to inhabit, the way you speak when you're not determined to sound like a guttersnipe. I know who you are when you're not hiding behind that uniform, that damn mop of yours."

"You're wrong, honey. With Crow, what you see is what you get: a woman from the 'hood, mean and lean and black as the queen of spades."

"That again. You ought to get yourself one of those T-shirts: 'It's a black thing.'"

"I got one."

Graystone snorts. "Just because you grew up in the project doesn't mean you're doomed to stay there. If you don't care about yourself, don't you at least want more for Joey?"

"Don't you talk to me about my son!" Crow sputters. "I don't need you to tell me how to live my life. You want to play Pygmalion, baby, better find yourself another flower girl. I've got my life together, thank you very much!"

She doesn't, though, not even close. The woman is thoroughly unreasonable. Because she cannot cope with her loss, she's throwing her life away, and the boy's with it. Graystone sees it so clearly now. If only he could implement his vision; if only he could sit down with Deacon, two reasonable men reasoning together, and plot out her life.

It would never work, that's what this evening has taught him. Crow wouldn't sit still for it. The woman is so damned unamenable; so given, as well, to turning things on their heads. Her accusations that night, though absurd, still rankle: that he doesn't respect her, that he wants to remake her, that what she is isn't good enough. Though he tries his best, he can't forget the dignity of her response to Elvira, words that recalled to him the woman who sat like a queen amid the nobility of jazz. "True class," she'd said, touching her heart, "comes from *here.*"

Though he knows now that he will never be her lover, Graystone doesn't want to be a man for whom this woman is not good enough. Determined to prove her wrong, he has gone out of his way these past few days to treat her with respect.

Treatment that hawk-eyed Pilar, predictably, misinterprets. For three days she's been on his case. Even now, he returns to an awareness of the room to find her face glowering from across Preacher's inert body.

Graystone is in no mood for attitude. His arms and shoulders ache from doing compressions, so far to no avail. Better-equipped hospitals have automatic compressors for situations like this one, in which CPR must be kept up till the patient's temp rises to a certain degree. Not Mercy, though.

Cocooned in blankets, Preacher is starting to warm up.

Soon they'll know. Percy's lousy attitude notwithstanding, the fat lady hasn't sung yet. Graystone remembers back when he was a second-year resident, a patient was brought in like Preacher, frozen stiff, no sign of life at all. They worked on her for two solid hours, got her temp up to 91° with no quickening, and were just about to call it when suddenly she opened her eyes and cried out for her mother.

Of course, that patient was a child, five, six years old. The prognosis is nowhere near as hopeful for adults; but then, Preacher is a tough old bird. If the street don't kill you, the homeless say, it makes you strong. This man's been living rough since before Graystone came to Mercy.

"Want me to take over?" Daniel asks.

"Yeah, take over." They switch places without missing a beat. Apart from continued CPR, IV fluids, and the passive warming provided by layering, there's little they can do for the patient. Graystone releases Elsa Kraven, and Pilar sends the other nurses out. The three veterans alone remain.

"What happened to him?" Daniel asks. "How'd he get so cold?"

Graystone grimaces. "Damn fool took off his clothes and climbed into a manger."

"Jesus Christ."

"I think that's the point."

"Shit. I knew the poor bastard was crazy, but I didn't think he was *crazy.*"

Graystone circles his shoulders to work the stiffness out. "Holidays, man, they'll do it every time."

"Speaking of which, what are you doing here?"

Pilar looks up from pumping the IV bag. She's been wondering, too, but couldn't bring herself to ask. Senior staff never work holidays. Daniel Bergman's an exception; he comes in voluntarily every Christmas to free up a Christian doc. Pilar's in because Alice is off; no way she's going to leave her ER to a bunch of unsupervised per diem nurses. But for the department head to work on Christmas—that's unheard of.

Graystone shrugs uncomfortably. "Beats the alternatives."

"Ah." Daniel is unsurprised: Thomas's leave-taking the night of the party had been such as, in form and content, boded ill for a pleasant Christmas dinner *en famille*.

He opens his mouth; Graystone flicks him a warning glance.

"Far be it from me to say I told you so," Daniel contents himself with saying.

"Far indeed."

"But you could have stayed home, taken the phone off the hook."

"What's the point? Might as well come in."

Pilar and Daniel exchange a look.

"I see. I'm no shrink, Dr. Graystone, but it seems to me you've crossed the fine line separating eccentricity from total lunacy."

"Very incisive, Dr. Bergman. Perhaps you *should* take up psychiatry."

"I'm thinking of it. That or dentistry." Suddenly Daniel's voice sharpens. "Whoa, baby—think I've got something here."

Graystone presses his stethoscope to Preacher's chest. "Got a beat, got a definite beat!"

Pilar finds a pulse in his wrist. Then Preacher groans. Grinning broadly, Pilar smacks Bergman on the back so hard he staggers. "All right, Danny Magic Fingers!"

25

. . . .

CROW

Doctor come around, knocking on my door. Blue's alive in the dream but he's away. Knowing I shouldn't, I let Graystone in. He don't say a word, just take me in his arms and start kissing me, running his hands on my body. Everywhere he touches me, I burn. Somewhere deep inside there's guilt, but the hunger, the need in me is so overpowering that guilt don't matter. It's like the urge to push in the last stages of labor, a compulsion so strong nothing can stand against it.

Our clothes fall away. When he takes my breast in his mouth, milk flows. My whole body turns liquid. He comes into me, fills me up. My back arches; the world implodes. It's just us two, this moment.

I wake suddenly to the sound of slippered feet. Joey's standing by my bed. "Merry Christmas, Mama."

"Merry Christmas, baby."

He touches my face. "Mama, you're crying?"

"Just a dream, a silly dream." I sit up and feel for my slippers. "Let's go see what Santa brought."

Santa's been good to my boy this year. What else Santa got to spend his money on? Joey gets books and toys, a new winter jacket, a shiny red tricycle. Last of all Joey opens the present Dr. Graystone brought. It's a child-size baseball glove, his first. I never knew he wanted one till he opened the box and saw it lying there, a thick leather mitt like a promise of manhood. The glove's deep pocket cups a softball and a card. Front of the card's a great big, potbellied, brown-skinned Santa. Inside there's a handwritten note, not in doctor scrawl but in clear block letters.

"Read it, Mama," he says.

If I'd had my wits halfway about me, a single cup of coffee running through my veins, I'd have censored it. The boy knows his letters but he can't read yet. I could have substituted something safe, like "Merry Christmas from Dr. Graystone." But my thoughts are scattered and distracted. Though I know a person ain't responsible for her dreams, mine feels wicked all the same. Not only was I cheating on Blue, I was taking such pleasure in it. Worst part is, I still ache.

So without thinking, I read the note aloud. " 'Takes two to play ball, champ. Give me a call if you need a partner. Your friend, Thomas Graystone.' " Followed by his home phone number.

Joey trails me into the kitchen. "Please, Mama, please!"

"I'll play ball with you, baby."

His little-boy face puckers with scorn. "You're a *girl*."

Four years old and already with the attitude. "That don't stop me catching a ball," I tell him.

I see him choosing his words, reaching for tact. "You can play, too, Mama. We can take turns."

Of course it ain't the ball-playing he cares about, any fool could see that. Boy wants a man in his life, and like the song say, if he can't be with the one he loves, he'll love the one he's with. I can't lie: There's a part of me sees this as a betrayal of Blue and a reproach to me. But the better part knows it ain't so. Child's just doing what comes natural. There's a need in him I can't fill.

"Maybe Deacon," I say, though try as I might, I can't feature Deacon playin' baseball. What's important, though: That old piano player's gonna be there for us as long as he live.

Joey's eyes fill with tears. It hurts to see him cry on Christmas, but there ain't nothing I can do. I beat the eggs like they was Graystone's balls. Man's got no right to do what he did, get at me through my boy. Me, I can take care of myself. But a child lost his daddy can't afford no here-today, gone-tomorrow man in his life.

After breakfast I bring Joey over to Selma's and go to work. Never occurred to me that *he* would be there, but ten minutes into my shift, Percy's ambulance comes wailin' up, and a minute later I see them loping down the hall, Graystone and Percy both, bringing poor Preacher in.

Preacher's one of our regulars. Drops in once a week or so with some bogus complaint, hangs around long enough to warm up and cop a free lunch. Only this time, he's wheeled in on a stretcher. I catch a glimpse of his face going into the code room, and it don't look good. Few minutes later, Percy comes out looking pissed, shoving an empty stretcher toward the ambulance bay.

"What's happening?" I ask him.

"Put it this way," he says. "Preacher gonna eat this Christmas dinner at his father's table."

Lump in my throat gets a little bigger when I hear that. I had my share of run-ins with Preacher, what with him trackin' mud over my clean floors, but he's a gentle soul, wouldn't squash a fly if it bit him. Always toutin' God's mercy, though by the look of things God never doled much out on him.

I make my way back to the code room on account of it's him. Just as I reach the door, Dr. Kraven starts calling for blankets. Agency nurses just lookin' at each other, like, "What are blankets?" so I run and grab a bunch from the linen closet and bring 'em in.

Graystone sees me all right. I know by the way he shuts up and starts concentrating on his CPR, moving his lips while he counts—like he couldn't do it in his sleep. I ain't about to say anything. For one thing, Pilar's on my case, watching us all fishy-eyed. For another, standing here with him, I find I can't exactly remember what it was I was going to say. Damn dream comes leaching back at me. I can't look at Graystone, so I look down at Preacher. Man's a pitiful sight, lying there limp as a rag doll, tube down his throat and lines coming out of him. They're working hard on him, but the way it look, I reckon Percy was right. I hand Pilar the blankets and go about my business.

Like always, my work soothes and relaxes me, 'specially the mopping. It's mindless, repetitive, rhythmic, and just strenuous enough; kind of work make me feel like a prisoner on a old-time chain gang, working that pick from dawn to dusk, dreamin' the hours away. After a while, I find my body's in one place, my mind in another. Right now I'm with Joey at Selma's. I can smell the turkey roasting, the fresh-baked pumpkin pie. I hear the duet of their voices as they call out to each other, Joey in the living room with his new cars, Selma in the kitchen.

I'm heading round the corner to change my water when suddenly *he* appears from the other direction. We nearly collide. Graystone puts out an arm to steady me, then drops it. And there we stand.

My whole damn body's blushing. Though I know for a fact he can't know what I dreamt, somehow I'm afraid it shows.

"Merry Christmas, Crow," he says.

"Merry Christmas." With difficulty, I meet his eyes. His face is cold and polite, very head-of-the-department. I got no right to feel disappointed, but I do.

He nods and steps around me.

"Dr. Graystone," I say.

He turns.

"Thank you for Joey's present. He loved it."

His eyes brighten; they shine down on me. "I'm glad," he says.

With an effort, I concentrate my mind on Joey crying in the kitchen. "The card, though," I say.

The light fades from his eyes, leaving a tired wash. "What's wrong with the card?"

"What you wrote—a four-year-old child's gonna read that different from you or me. Thing like that raises expectations that aren't . . . realistic."

"What expectations?"

"He thinks you're gonna come play ball with him."

He draws himself up. "I meant what I wrote. It's got nothing to do with . . . anything else. Giving a boy a baseball glove is a serious business."

A fatherless boy, he means. I do believe I've been unjust to the man, but how can I be sure? It's my duty to protect my child. If I let Graystone befriend him and one fine day he quits coming around, Joey will be devastated.

"You're right," I say. "A very serious business."

He stands without speaking for some time. By now people are looking at us, but he don't notice, or don't care. His face, when I glance up at it, seems remote and perplexed, as if he's puzzling over something that has nothing to do with us: a tricky diagnosis, maybe, or some Latin phrase. At last his eyes come back to me.

"Joey has nothing to fear from me," Graystone says. "I don't make many personal commitments, but I keep the ones I make."

He walks away.

My legs are shaking. I have to get away. Pilar's steaming toward me with a determined look, but before she can nab me, she's waylaid by a patient. I take evasive action.

The supply room has a latch so housekeepers can change in peace. I lock the door and sink into my chair. My heart is pounding. I miss the days of my invisibility.

Damn Graystone. I can't figure why he's being so good to Joey. I mean, the man took a powerful lot of abuse Saturday night. He deserved it, all right, settin' me up like that, but I got to admit he did the right thing in the end. Prettiest sight all evening was Claudette's face when he called her a useless imbecile, unless maybe it was his mother's when he stood up, took my arm, and said, "We're leaving."

Never thanked him for that. Wish I had.

Don't matter anyway. The man couldn't have made it any plainer that his kindness to Joey don't translate to interest in me. Probably gone back to Michelle, whoever the hell she is.

Although there was a moment, at the end, when I wondered. His words seemed laden with subterranean freight; he seemed to watch me closely. But what could it mean? He spoke of commitments, but he never made any to me.

Somebody pounds on the door.

"What?" I yell.

Pilar's voice hollers back. "Open up, Crow, I want to talk to you."

"Go away. I'm on my lunch break."

I hear her heavy breathing out in the corridor; she's torn between ripping the door off its hinges and going quietly. Finally she stomps away. Breaks are sacrosanct in Mercy.

I lean back and close my eyes. The soothing sounds of the ER penetrate my fortress. Wails, moans, unanswered cries for help, beeps, the clatter of metal wheels on tile floors, the drone of the P.A.: my own private Walden Pond. What am I doing here? I wonder. What am I doing with my life? Tears bleed from the rusty faucets of my eyes, staining my face.

Very close to me, a man's voice says softly, "What's wrong, Crow?"

I open my eyes and spy him over by the broom closet. Squatting on the floor with his bony knees poking out of his tweed pants, man looks like a praying mantis, or a Englishman gone native. For some reason, I'm not surprised to see him.

"What are you doin' here?" I ask, wiping my eyes on my sleeve. "Don't you even get Christmas off?"

"I'm Jewish," Elias says. "I come in every year so the Christian ghosts can take off."

"Christian ghosts?"

"Just kidding. Just a little ghost humor."

"Guess you got to be dead to appreciate it."

A smile flashes across his face and disappears quickly, like a radar blip. "What's wrong?" he asks again. "Why were you crying?"

"I've had better Christmases."

"Haven't we all," he sighs, and we sit for a while in comfortable silence.

"I don't know," I say. "It's hard to know what's right. People put things into your head and then you can't get 'em out. I keep wondering, am I doing right by my boy?"

"Ah," he says. "Joey."

I stare at him. I'm certain I never mentioned Joey's name to him; never had cause to. "How'd you know my son's name?"

Elias blushes. Who'd ever have thought a ghost could blush? "I happened to be in the vicinity while you and Dr. Graystone were having your little chat earlier."

"You spied!"

He turns up his hands. "What else is there for me to do?"

"Read a magazine, watch a movie, Christ, I don't know! You can't go skulking around, spying on people."

"I do watch movies, out in the waiting room. They have some good ones. Who's this?" Elias springs to his feet, pointing an imaginary machine gun. *"Hasta la vista, baby!"*

I clap my hand over my mouth to keep from laughing. Looking pleased with himself, Elias slides down to sit Indian-style on the floor.

"Anyway," he says, "I heard. And if you'll allow an unsolicited objective opinion, I think you ought to take the man up on his offer."

Ordinarily I'd have told him to mind his own damn business, but there's a awful weariness laid hold of me today. For once I'm glad for a chance to talk, and talking with Elias is easier than talking with most folks. Death's a great social lubricant. Elias don't hardly seem white to me anymore. I mean, he's still as pasty as ever, but I don't notice it as much. Another thing about the ghost: I know he ain't never gonna repeat what he hear.

"It's hard," I say. "Joey needs a man in his life, a good man."

"Graystone's a very good man!" he says, indignant on his colleague's behalf, so I guess death ain't *that* potent a leveler.

"I know he is. But I can't stand to think of that child gettin' hurt again."

I forget who I'm talking to. ER docs are not impressed by pain, and Elias, by my reckoning, has been haunting this place dead and alive some thirty years.

Sure enough, he shrugs. "Getting hurt is a condition of being alive. You can't protect him from that."

"I know that. It's just I love that child so much, sometimes it feels like that love's gonna rise up inside and drown me. Ever since Blue died, I've been trying to give him twice as much, to make up for what's missing. But it don't work like that. What's gone is gone, for Joey."

"Not for you, though. What's gone isn't gone for you."

His voice is soft, almost hypnotic. It carries me back to the night Blue died. We stayed with Selma in her apartment. Joey couldn't stop crying, so I lay down in his little bed and held him. He curled himself into a ball between my chin and my knees and fell into an uneasy sleep. If I stirred, he roused, or cried out in his sleep.

I didn't stir. I lay unmoving, watching through the night till the earliest rays of pale gray light filtered through the blinds, and in that night I lived a lifetime: our lifetime, Blue's and mine. I saw what would have been; I tasted every portion of the life we should have had, the bitter and the sweet, the passing sorrows and surpassing joys. I saw three children, a little farmhouse outside Paris, with a studio out back where Blue practices with the band. I saw visitors, a garden, a spare room for Selma when she comes to us. I saw our children grown tall and strong; I saw them marry, scatter, and return to us with children of their own. I saw us growing old, Blue and me together. I heard music that was and music that has yet to be, coming from the studio, from clubs and concert halls, heart-tugging strains from Blue's sax. And all the time, as I watched this life unfurl, I knew it would never be. None of it. A single instant, the thrust of a knife, had aborted not only Blue's life, but also our life together, an entire future: children who will never be born, music that will never be heard in this world.

My life contracted around me. Like a woman laboring alone, in silence and comfortless pain I gave birth that night to my stillborn life with Blue. I expelled it, renounced it. I lay down a girl, and rose up a sorrowful woman.

Though I say none of this aloud, Elias seems to understand. He reaches out toward me, then looks at his hand, smiles, and lets it drop. "You have to accept," he says. "You have to let go."

"Why?" I demand, leaning toward him. "Look at you—you're living proof."

"I'm not living proof of anything."

"Before I met you, I thought death was the end, the ultimate Black Hole, total obliteration. Afterwards my point of view changed. I saw that death isn't the end. I started to hope that maybe someday I would find Blue again, and we would be together like we were meant to be."

Elias is shaking his head vehemently.

"I believe," I say, "that love endures."

"I loved my wife—she died before me; we're not together. Blue's story is ended; yours is still being written. You can't wait. You are required to go on."

"I did go on."

"You went home."

"Went home, got a job, got an apartment—what's wrong with that?"

"Home is the place we start out from."

Trouble with telling your problems to folks is they always feel obliged to come back with advice. Advice from a ghost who talks like a fortune cookie is something I personally do not need.

"Man," I say, "you are the *last* person to talk about movin' on."

"You can hardly compare our situations. They're worlds apart."

"Socioeconomically?" I tease him.

"Essentially," he replies huffily. "You're alive. I'm not."

"Just kidding," I say. "Just a little mortal humor."

Again that brief smile. When it passes, his face sags like a basset hound's. He looks, somehow, less substantial today. I don't mean transparent, nothing spooky like that; I mean thinner, grayer, more tired than before. Those bushy eyebrows got a wilted droop about 'em. I get a urge to feed this man, like I'm some kind of Jewish mother. Then I wonder if I'm nuts; but the impulse of pity lingers.

"Tell me, Elias," I say, "how's death treatin' you these days?"

"Same old grind," he sighs, attaching his chin to his knees.

"Don't you ever get tired of hanging around this place?"

"Tired!"

"Well, can't you just leave? Walk out the door?"

"Still trying to get rid of me?" His melted smile makes me think of a clown after the circus is over.

"Now you *know* that ain't it," I tell him.

He stretches his long neck backward and crosses his arms over his eyes. "Don't you think I've tried? I get as far as the exit doors, then something pulls me back. Did you ever have one of those days when you just couldn't seem to get out of here?"

"Plenty of 'em."

"Well," he says bleakly, dropping his arms and looking at me, "I'm having one of those eternities."

I sit back and try to contemplate eternity in the ER, but it don't bear thinking of. Pilar said Elias was a decent man, and so he seems to me—more than decent. Whose justice could be served by such a sentence? It don't make sense. Something's missing from this picture.

It ain't my problem, I know that. But who else has he got?

"Elias," I say, "first time we talked, I asked you why you were here. Remember what you said?"

"Something rude, no doubt."

"Uh-uh. You said unfinished business."

He gazes off, then, with a look I can only call haunted. Goose bumps break out on my skin.

"What was the business?" I ask him.

He gets up and walks to the door. "Isn't it time for you to be getting back?"

"Now wait a minute, Elias. Where I come from, when a person play strip poker, they gotta ante up. I already bared my bones. So what's your story?"

"If you must know," he says, "I murdered a child."

26

·······

A small boy wakes in a strange bed, covered by a quilt as soft and white as a cloud. He lies very still with his eyes shut, until he remembers where he is.

Next to the bed on the polished-wood floor, there is a royal-blue fringed rug, and on the rug a pair of slippers, just the right size, await his feet. The boy slips them on, then follows his nose out of the bedroom, along a corridor, down a winding staircase, through a living room the size of a basketball court (detouring to circle the Christmas tree; the floor underneath is piled with presents bearing his name), and into the kitchen, where Alice is removing a tray of biscuits from the oven. She sets it down on the stovetop, turns, and sees him. No one in his remembered life ever smiled like that at the sight of him.

"Merry Christmas, Noah," she says.

They open presents. Or rather, Noah opens presents while Alice watches gleefully. Like a starving man gorging on sweets, he tears through the packages, ripping one open and hardly pausing to see what's inside before rushing on to the next. She lets him, knowing he'll slow down soon enough. Alice has spent hours combing through Brooklyn Heights toy boutiques and children's clothing stores to choose these gifts, and still she's nervous; what if she didn't get it right? But each discovery is met with smiles and cries of pleasure; he is delighted with everything.

In the middle of unwrapping a box, Noah pauses and looks up at her with stricken eyes.

"Didn't Santa bring you nothing?"

Alice looks at him, sitting in a nest of wrapping paper, ribbons and tinsel caught in his hair. "He brought me you," she says.

He shrugs doubtfully, as if to say *that* wasn't much of a present; then his face brightens. "I'll give you one of mine!" He culls through his pile of toys, selects a shiny red fire engine with blinking lights and a real siren, and lays it in her lap with no more than a sigh and a parting pat. "This here's your present. You can keep it, you don't have to give it back."

It means nothing that she chose and paid for this plaything herself, still less that she is past the age of fire engines. All that matters is his generosity, further proof, if any were needed, of the boy's essential good-heartedness. Moved beyond words, Alice kisses him. Noah doesn't seem to mind.

He returns to his unwrapping. One large oblong box he saves for last, suspecting, perhaps, more clothing. But the last present isn't clothing; it's a pirate set, complete with buccaneers, pirate galleon, treasure chest, cannon, plank for walking, and even a tiny parrot. Noah's delight is complete; he breaks into a spontaneous little dance. Then stops, looks around at the clothes and toys strewn about, and catches his lip between his teeth.

She asks him what's the matter.

"I can't take them to *that place,*" he replies; he does not call the institution home.

"Why not?"

Noah gives her an embarrassed look. "You know. The big kids."

Alice is flustered. Stupid of her not to have thought of this. "Don't you have a private place where you can keep things, a cupboard or a drawer?"

"It don't lock."

She thinks for a moment. "Why don't you take a few things with you, and leave the rest here for when you come to visit?"

Noah agrees. Wistfully says, "I wish I could stay here all the time."

"Do you?" cries Alice, who strange as it seems has never dared to ask. "Do you?"

Alice watches like a hawk but needn't have worried. Her mother's upbringing has rendered her incapable of discourtesy to any guest; nor, in fairness, is Dasha disposed to cruelty toward any child not her own. Beneath the Straughs' tree (a paradigm of trees, small but perfectly formed, sumptuously trimmed with antique hangings, and topped with an eighteenth-century silver filigree angel that the children are strictly forbidden to touch) are as many presents marked NOAH as JASON and AMANDA.

Following an initial period of shyness, Alice's nephew, Jason, and Noah are now fast friends, united in masculine conspiracy against Amanda the doll-player. Dasha and Brooke are engrossed in fabric swatches for the Straughs' country house; John is keeping one eye on the football game and the other on the children. Richard motions to Alice.

They sit in his study, Richard at his desk, Alice in a facing Queen Anne chair. "I have one more Christmas present for you," Richard says, and with a show of something like embarrassment hands her an envelope.

Inside it is a card with a name and a phone number. Alice recognizes the name, Allard Straith, as that of a leading New York attorney with political connections, a man who frequently dines with her parents.

She looks up questioningly.

"I still don't approve," he says. "I think it's a mistake. Nothing against the boy; he's a likable young lad. But still."

"Then what's this for?"

"I know you. There's a stubborn streak in you, Alice. You don't want much, but when you do want something, you get it. Also, I dislike the idea of those pen-pushers at CWA shoving my daughter around." Alice opens her mouth to speak, but he raises his hand to forestall her thanks. "I've

229

spoken to Allard, he's expecting your call. No need to mention this to your mother, dear," he adds with some anxiety.

"I wouldn't," she says. "But I won't need to trouble Mr. Straith. I already have a lawyer."

Silence, except for the ticking of the grandfather clock.

"You went out and hired an attorney?"

"Yes, I did."

He cocks an eyebrow humorously. "Who'd you get?"

Alice says a name, and her father's face changes.

"Well, well," he says.

"I want to win."

"He's expensive."

She nods complacently. "All the good ones are."

"Allard would handle it as a professional courtesy to me."

"He'd *accept* the case as a courtesy; then he'd hand it off to a junior."

Richard can't deny this. It's what he himself would do.

"I'd rather pay," Alice says, "and get what I pay for."

Richard opens up his top drawer and takes out a checkbook. "What's he charging you?"

Her hand descends on his. "No."

"I don't want you dipping into capital. If you're determined to do this thing, I want to help."

"You want to buy me Noah," Alice says. Her tone is factual, not accusatory. "Like you bought me a pony on my sixth birthday. Like you bought me Charlie."

Richard is too flustered to speak. He was prepared for tears, protestations of gratitude from his gentle Alice. This woman is a stranger to him.

"You were right the first time," she says. "This is *my* battle." Then, though he hasn't dismissed her, she leans over, kisses his forehead, and walks out, shutting the door gently behind her.

Richard sits on, thinking, I don't recall saying that.

The next day: Radio City Music Hall, the Christmas Show.

In the middle of the Dance of the Teddy Bears, Joey starts to cry. The two boys sit together, bracketed by Alice and Crow. Crow puts her arm around her son. "What's the matter, baby?"

"It's so beautiful," he sobs.

"Don't worry," says Noah, stroking Joey's arm. "It's just pretend."

They emerge, blinking, into the real world. Two hours of sitting, even for the best of causes, is not easy on little boys. Alice had planned on taking them to a fine restaurant, but allows herself to be persuaded to substitute a fast-food joint with an indoor playground.

Crow, sitting opposite Alice in the restaurant, notices how, like a mother with a newborn infant, her companion's expression reflects Noah's. Their evident and seemingly mutual attachment eats away at the barnacles of doubt that adhere to her heart. It still jars her to see a black child with a white woman. But Selma always said it's a sin to waste good food; and surely unconditional love is a commodity far scarcer than food and every bit as essential to a growing child.

When the boys have finished all of the hamburger and malted they can be prevailed upon to consume, they are permitted to leave the grown-ups for the play area. Crow takes the opportunity to ask about the custody battle.

"My lawyer says I have an excellent chance. They have no better option. His grandmother still refuses to take him, and the mother's out of the picture."

"That fool in jail for what she pulled on Jennifer?"

"She was. She skipped bail."

"Surprised she could make bail, crackhead like that."

Alice busies herself collecting the refuse of their meal onto a tray. "Someone put it up for her."

"Damn generous of someone."

A moment passes in silence. Then Alice meets Crow's waiting eyes. "They would have called me to testify. It would be horrible for Noah to learn someday that I helped send his mother to prison."

"How's her skipping affect his situation?"

"If she makes no effort to contact him, that constitutes desertion. It could open up the door to a permanent adoption."

Crow shakes her head. "You don't mess around, do you?"

"She made her choice. No one forced her. Good riddance, I say."

"What does Noah say?"

"He wants to stay with me."

"Boy's no fool. So what's the problem?"

Alice snorts. "The official version changes from day to day. First they say Noah needs therapy to overcome the trauma of abuse. I tell them I'll get him therapy, I'll hire the best child psychologist in New York City. Then they say I need to take a parenting class, and there are no openings till next September. I'm a registered nurse, for heaven's sake. What are they going to teach me about childcare and nutrition that I don't already know? Next I hear everything's on hold while they try to locate the father. Noah's grandmother told me *and* them: No one ever knew who the father was." Alice runs her hand through her red frizz. "It's all just excuses, excuses and lies, so they don't have to talk about the real reason."

"Which is . . . ?"

"As far as they're concerned, black is black and white is white, and never the twain shall meet."

This being a sentiment that Crow herself subscribes to, or thought she did, she's surprised to find herself in such sympathy with Alice.

Alice leans across the table. "You can't imagine how it feels," she confides, "having people judge you unfit and give you the runaround, purely because of your race."

They walk to Rockefeller Center: the two boys, hand in hand, dancing up ahead, Crow and Alice bringing up the rear. It's one of those brilliant, crisp, preternaturally clear New York days. As the women talk, heads bent together, little puffs of steam escape from their mouths and mingle in the air. The chill breeze brings a glow to their faces; pleasure shines in their eyes. Work on a storefront construction site ceases as they walk by. "Anything you want," one worker groans. "All my worldly possessions. My soul."

Crow can't help but smile. Most of the attention she attributes to the contrast between them, Alice being as pale a specimen of her race as Crow is a dark one of hers; but not all. Alice, flushed with cold air and happiness, looks vibrant, as close to pretty as Crow's ever seen her. As for Crow herself, she sees by her reflection in the eyes of people they pass that she is no longer the Invisible Woman. It's been a long time.

Alice notices nothing. She's talking about Jean Schuyler's offer of the head nursing spot on Ob-Gyn. Time is passing, and she needs to decide.

"I never thought I'd want to leave the ER, but I'm actually tempted," she says, as they reach the promenade overlooking the skating rink. "Not just because of Noah; also for myself. I always liked obstetrics. Delivering babies is about the nicest job there is in a hospital."

"Beats the hell out of delousing vagrants," Crow says.

"The thing is, I'd feel like a deserter."

Crow shrugs. "ER's a bad place to put down roots."

"Pilar did."

"That's her. What'd the man say? I know Pilar, darlin', and you ain't no Pilar."

Alice laughs, but her worried frown lingers. "That's for sure. I just don't know if I'm up to the job."

"What you talking about? Between the two of you, you and Pilar run the damn ER."

"It's not the nursing part, I know I can handle that. It's the other. A head nurse has to be tough; she's got to stand up for her nurses."

"That fool Plummer still bustin' your chops?"

Alice makes a face. "It's his turf. I'd be working with him every day."

"So?" Crow gives her arm a hard squeeze. "Are you a woman or a mouse?"

"I'm a white woman; where does that rank?"

"'Bout halfway between."

In the midst of their laughter—startled, shared laughter it

is—Joey and Noah race back, begging for money for hot pretzels, pleading pitifully, hands pressed together in prayer, as if they hadn't eaten in days. Alice looks helplessly at Crow.

"One pretzel," Crow tells the boys, taking some change from her pocket. "You share. And walk!" she calls after them, because Joey seems winded.

Alice takes the boys down to rent skates. Crow, who's never ice-skated in her life and is not about to start now, remains above to watch.

They take to the ice. Slipping and sliding, squealing with terrified laughter, the boys clutch Alice's hands. The perimeter is crowded with skaters, but she leads them into the center of the rink where the figure skaters practice. Letting go of their hands, she leans down to speak to them, then moves away for a demonstration. Alice skates as effortlessly as she walks, gliding along the ice with the ease of unquestioned privilege, red scarf ends trailing behind. The boys try to imitate her: They skate and fall, get up and fall again. Alice catches their hands and skates with them, swinging them around her in a wide circle. The sound of their laughter floats upward to Crow.

Crow buys a bag of roasted chestnuts, peels one, and pops it into her mouth. Sunlight pours down, glinting off the star atop the great Christmas tree, quickening the wings of the filigree angels that line the arcade. The rink below seems lighted from within, glowing with life. In the center, a girl in a short red skating costume leaps and twirls, arms raised above her head. Around her circle the skaters, brilliant bits of color in a shifting kaleidoscope. A filter falls from Crow's eyes; the world regains its brilliance. The very air seems to vibrate, and a heedless joy seizes her heart.

She searches below for Joey but can't spot him among the skaters. There's a disturbance on the rink, an impediment to the smooth flow: A knot has formed around an unseen nucleus. Amid all the downturned heads, only one is raised: a white face with fiery hair and crimson cheeks. Alice's seeking eyes meet Crow's; she beckons violently. At that moment, Crow spots Joey in the center of the group. He is kneeling on the ice, doubled over, both hands pressed to his chest.

The bag of chestnuts falls to the ground and is instantly set upon by pigeons. Crow flies down the crowded steps, shouldering people aside, fumbling through her purse for his inhaler. By the time she reaches the rink, they're off the ice. Joey is seated on a bench, wheezing, fighting for breath. Alice kneels by his side, supporting his shoulders.

Joey sees his mother. He reaches out, tries to speak, coughs, and vomits. Alice looks up. She's wearing her ER nurse's face, cool and focused. "Asthma?" she says.

27

· · · · · · · ·

Belated coals in his stocking: A week after Christmas, the administration responds to Graystone's budget proposal. Just before submitting it, impelled by desperation and the quixotic hope that those unreachable through reason might be persuaded by emotion, the ER director had appended a personal, handwritten plea. Deliberately he kept no copy, but cannot erase the memory of its abject tone and fervent invocations of God's name, which linger like a bitter taste in his mouth.

He would have forgiven himself if the ploy had succeeded, but it was all to no avail. Not only did the brass fail to restore the previous year's cuts, they slashed the current year's budget by an additional 4 percent. But to prove themselves men of compassion, they also included a personal note, signed by Mercy's director, Boyd Lessing. *Dear Tom: Your points well taken. Wish like hell we could comply. Next year, God and Dinkins willing, we'll do better. Yours ever, Boyd.*

The thing is not to take it personally, Graystone reminds himself. They're assholes because it's their function to be assholes. In their position, he'd . . . No, he wouldn't. An image comes unbidden to haunt him: He sees Lessing and his cronies, the hospital's ruling council, gathered around the first hole on the course of their Gold Coast golf club, discussing him while they wait to tee off.

"Good man," Lessing says in that condescending drawl of his. "Runs a tight ship. Tends to get a bit overinvolved, but that's only natural, considering." And the other wise men nod sagely.

Fuck them. Graystone happens to know that Lessing just redecorated the executive suite at a cost greater than the chunk they've just lopped off his budget. He storms upstairs and pounds some teak and walnut desks, which gains him nothing but a sore fist. Comes back down, closes himself in his office. There's an acrid stink in the air, a miasma of rage, pain, and futile impatience that emanates from the packed waiting room. They'll be dying in there before the new year is out.

Daniel wears a path in Graystone's threadbare carpet. "I love you, man," he says. "You know I love you. But if you won't come with me, I've made up my mind to fuckin' go it alone."

"You're putting a gun to my head, man."

"No, fool, I'm throwing you a life preserver. Stick around here much longer, you'll end up like Elias. They'll use your name to scare young residents: 'Watch out, Graystone's gonna get you.'"

"They do that now," Graystone says.

"I mean, for Christ's sake, what have you got to stay for? And Tom, before you answer, as God is my witness, I swear if you say one word about being needed, I'll kick your black ass."

"It's not that."

"Then what?"

Graystone's head throbs. He wishes Daniel would go away, but not too far and certainly not for good. When he thinks of the ER without Bergman, he envisions a lunar expanse, desiccated, craggy, and lifeless. But when he thinks of leaving, he pictures nothing at all.

Psych patients who land in Mercy ER are given a screening questionnaire, consisting primarily of unfinished statements they are asked to complete. "If you really knew me . . .", or, "If I were to get angry with you . . ." Faced with a similar opening, Graystone draws a blank, flubs the test. "If I were to leave the ER . . ." Nothing comes. There's a hole in his imagination where that possibility ought to fit, and that can't be right. It's a job is all, a job, not a marriage.

Bergman approaches the desk, peers into his face. "It's that girl, isn't it? Goddammit, Tom!"

"No, man," Graystone says. "It's nothing to do with her. You saw her at the party. The woman is not interested. The woman is hostile."

"I saw her. Saw you, too. Ole Love-'em-and-Leave-'em Graystone bites the dust. I don't know whether to laugh or cry."

Graystone says nothing. What can he say? A few days ago he was celebrating his liberation; all it took was five minutes' conversation with Crow to teach him that his cure was merely a remission, and a short one at that. Logic, it emerges, is no antidote to love.

Neither is hopelessness. Crow's indifference is a fact; and in his heart, Graystone believes that if his position and status don't attract her, nothing else about him will. Given that, what are his options? He can order himself to move on, he can prescribe an answering indifference, he can dose himself with other women. What he cannot do is look upon Crow's face without pain.

"Cut the tie," Daniel murmurs like a voice inside his head. "Let her go. Come with me and start fresh."

Oh, he is tempted. A dozen times over the past years, Graystone's father has offered to set him up in private practice, get him privileges and an appointment at his own prestigious teaching hospital. Graystone never even considered accepting. He clung to Mercy as if—it occurs to him now—that job were all that stood between him and the life his parents lead. But this is different; this is Daniel. And there's no faulting the proposition: a clinic of their own, an established practice in a middle-class neighborhood, patients who actually have insurance. The price is affordable, the seller eager. A man would be a fool to turn this down, and Graystone is nobody's fool.

A vision comes to him. He sees himself entering Lessing's

office, shredding his goddamn budget, and dropping the pieces in the man's lap. "Find yourself another boy," he'd say. No more scrounging for money, no more playing politics with patients' lives. Graystone takes a deep breath and says, "Okay. I'll do it."

"What?" At first Daniel looks more surprised even than Graystone; then he begins to glow. "You will? You'll come in with me?"

Graystone grips the edge of his desk. He feels like a man walking in space: emptiness surrounds him, an enveloping vacuum. As if to anchor him, Bergman thrusts out his hand. "You won't regret this."

Graystone grasps the proffered hand. He already does.

Pilar's brisk rap sounds at the door. She sticks her head in, notices their clasped hands, and murmurs, "Ain't that sweet."

"What is it?" rasps Graystone.

"Crow's boy."

Asthma patients are treated at a bank of nebulizers in the corridor opposite the nurses' station. Elsa Kraven's got Joey plugged into treatment already; a mask over his face delivers Albuterol mist directly to his lungs, or would if the airways were not so constricted. The boy's heaving chest and strained neck muscles indicate acute respiratory distress. Crow stands behind him, gray as dust.

"What triggered this?" Graystone asks.

It's Alice who explains. If Crow hears, she gives no sign. One hand rubs Joey's back. Her gaze is focused but remote, like someone staring out the back of a speeding train.

"You came all the way from midtown Manhattan?" the doctor fumes.

"Crow gave him his inhaler. That seemed to resolve the problem, so we drove back to Brooklyn. Then he rebounded."

Graystone lowers his face into Joey's line of sight. The boy's eyes show panic. "Hang in there, champ. You're gonna be fine." He orders a shot of epinephrine. "You'll see a difference within minutes," he tells Crow, who doesn't look at him. Elsa injects the adrenaline, and then they wait.

The only sound is the boy's labored breathing. Five minutes go by, ten. Alice goes off to the waiting room to check on Noah, then returns. Joey, reacting adversely to the drug, begins to squirm restlessly. He bats at the hands holding him in his seat, tears at the mask, and gasps, "Mama, I can't breathe!"

Crow does the right thing—strokes his head, speaks calmly, reassures him—but her eyes are in a land beyond fear, deep, deep into the realm of despair.

It hurts Graystone to look at her, so he doesn't. He can't think about her now. Joey's response is ominous. Asthma's a strange disease. For a life-threatening condition, it's usually extremely manageable. Ninety-nine times out of a hundred, a whiff of Albuterol is all it takes to clear the airways. If that doesn't work, injections of adrenaline and steroids will. Once in a blue moon, though, they get a patient who doesn't respond to drugs. Maybe he's too far gone when he comes in, maybe the onset is too sudden and intense. It's possible to lose a patient like that.

Fifteen minutes have passed since Kraven administered the adrenaline, and Joey is no better; if anything, he's working harder. Graystone doesn't want to think about intubating this child.

"Start an IV," he orders Kraven. "Let's get some amino-phylline going. And oral prednisone. What's his weight?"

Alice wheels over a gurney, and they lay Joey down. Elsa starts the line. In passing she gives Crow's shoulder a squeeze. She might have been squeezing a rock for all the response she gets. Graystone perches on one side of the gurney and talks to the boy about baseball. "Who's your favorite team?" he asks.

Joey gasps something through the mask.

"What's that, champ?"

"Am I dying?" the child asks.

Dr. Graystone blinks back a sudden, shocking spurt of tears. Taking Joey's small hand in his, he traces the veins with his thumb. "No way, honey child. A few more minutes and you'll be breathing easy. Don't we have a date to play ball, you and me? Didn't we make a plan?"

Joey closes his eyes. Crow draws a long, shuddering

breath and sags against Pilar, who gives her a little shake and says briskly, "Pull yourself together, girl. You know that child be safe here."

"I don't know nothing," Crow answers, but softly.

The IV drips. Joey's chest heaves. He has no breath left for crying or talking. "It takes time," Graystone says, but a nerve in his cheek twitches with each ragged gasp. Crow strokes the boy's forehead, hand, hair.

An hour inches by. Alice has to leave; a social worker is coming for Noah, who's been sitting outside in the waiting room. Kraven goes on to other patients. Graystone and Pilar remain with Joey, who despite the medication continues to wheeze audibly and gasp. Every time Daniel Bergman passes by, he looks in on Joey. After one such visit, he signals to Graystone. Pilar follows them over to the nurses' station, where they put their heads together and speak softly.

The head nurse argues for immediate intubation. "I seen kids like this. They maintain, maintain, maintain, then all of a sudden they go south on you. Best tube him while you still got the chance." Graystone, knowing what the procedure can do to a small child's narrow airways and fearful of what it will do to Crow, holds out for more time. Eventually, he says, the steroids have got to kick in. Then Bergman, with averted eyes, says, "I think we should admit him to pediatric ICU."

"What the hell for?" Graystone demands.

"Better ambience," says Daniel. But Graystone won't let it pass; he keeps at him until finally Bergman throws up his hands and says, "You're too involved. I mean, Crow's kid— how could you not be?"

Graystone, having forced him to say it, is furious. "That relationship, such as it is, has no bearing on my treatment of this patient. I'm totally objective, totally detached." He follows Daniel's eyes down to his trembling hands; muttering an oath, he stuffs them into his pockets.

They compromise. Joey is not intubated but is wheeled into trauma room A, just in case a quick procedure is needed. Another drug is added to his IV cocktail. Pilar brings a hospital gown, and Crow undresses her son. Before she can place his street clothes into a plastic bag, Joey retrieves Blue's harmonica from his hip pocket. He hasn't breath enough to breathe, let alone play, but seems to take comfort in the feel of the instrument, which he rubs between his palms like a talisman.

They wait and watch. Nothing harder for the ER doc, who thrives on active intervention, whose instinct says, If a kid has trouble breathing, breathe for him. It took many years for Graystone to accept that sometimes, the best he can do for his patients is to sit on his hands.

Parents are not allowed in trauma rooms, a strict rule, but no one thinks of applying it to Crow. She's one of them, and besides, on the ER scale of things, she's behaving well. Whatever horrors are passing through her mind, outwardly she's restrained and calm. Too calm, indeed, for Graystone's liking. He's not about to forget that one year ago this woman watched her husband bleed to death. While Joey is alert, she speaks to him in a low, constant murmur of encouragement, but whenever he drifts off, she shuts down tight. Outside, the life of the ER follows its accustomed course. Petulant cries, heedless laughter, the clatter of wheels, the bionic buzz of life support, permeate the walls; but Crow, tuned to her own station, wrapped in a dark cloak of solitude, hears none of it. She stares straight ahead with the eyes of a refugee condemned to return, the stolid, affectless gaze of one to whom hope is a foreign word.

He is frightened for her. Seeing that he can't reach her, Graystone suggests calling a friend: Selma, perhaps, or Deacon. Crow shakes her head. "They don't need to see this."

Suddenly there's a change. Joey's restless tossing ceases; his eyes fly open with a startled look. He sucks in a long, shuddering breath and expels it with a gasp.

Crow, remembering the last time she heard such a gasp, lets out a piercing scream.

Pilar, half dozing in a chair, leaps to her feet. Graystone grabs a syringe, pre-loaded with the drug that will paralyze the child while they intubate him.

Joey bats their hands away. "I can breathe," he cries through his mask. "I can breathe!"

Graystone shoulders Crow aside and presses his stethoscope to the child's chest. He listens intently, moving the instrument from place to place.

"Well?" Pilar demands. "You waiting for a drumroll?"

"He's clear," says Graystone.

Crow bursts into tears. Once started, she can't stop weeping. While Pilar tends to Joey, Graystone leads Crow into the adjacent trauma room and shuts the door.

"He's safe now," he says, over and over. "He's out of the woods."

Crow can't believe in her deliverance. "It's my fault," she cries, "all my fault."

"Your fault! How?"

"I was feeling so good, happy as a goddamn fool. I let my guard down. That's what happens."

Graystone is struck dumb. If she really believes that happiness is a lightning rod for disaster, what hope was there for her, or him, for that matter?

"You didn't cause this," he manages at last. "Joey has asthma, like millions of other kids. It's a fact of life, not an act of retribution."

A fit of trembling seizes her. The doctor wraps his arms around her, pretending even to himself that comfort is all he means to offer. Crow clings to him, wetting his jacket with her tears. Shyly, tentatively, he kisses the top of her head. Perhaps it would have gone no further had she not raised her face to his. Even then he hesitates. But once his lips meet hers, he's lost.

His hands splay across her back, drawing her close. Her body molds itself to his; they fit, as he's always known they would. A small, scolding voice inside him carps, "Not here, not now!" but it's drowned out by the roaring in his ears. He lifts her onto the table and presses his mouth to her throat, murmuring her name, whispering endearments. His lips take her pulse and find it elevated; her skin is tangy with dried fear. He would fire any doctor caught in this position, and he knows it; yet he feels no more guilt than a parched man slaking his thirst at someone else's well. Where there is no choice, there can be no culpability.

He slides his hand between her skirted legs, which part at

his touch. Her flesh through silky stockings burns his fingers. Crow moans, cups the back of his head, whispers in his ear.

The words reach his body before they penetrate his mind. His reaction is immediate: He jumps back. "Thank you? Is that what you're doing: thanking me?"

"No, baby," says Crow. "But anytime you save my child's life, you're gonna have to deal with a little gratitude."

A great howl of disappointment rises up inside him. He feels like a child who's just been offered his heart's delight, only to have it snatched away. Knows it's not her fault, but can't help blaming her anyway.

Up to this very moment, he'd thought himself willing to take this woman on absolutely any terms. Though scrupulous in his financial and professional affairs, Graystone has always allowed himself far greater latitude in his dealings with women. All's fair, and so on. How bitter, then, on the very cusp of consummation, to discover that there are limits after all.

He reassembles his old face, cold and dry. "I don't know what got into me. I didn't mean it."

Her skirt has ridden up, and though she's closed her legs, Graystone still sees more than any man in his position needs to see. He shuts his eyes.

"I did," says Crow, reaching out for him. "I meant it."

"No, you didn't. We're both over the edge. Let's forget it happened." And before she can reply, he turns and runs out of the room.

28

·······

Though Joey's recovery is as rapid as the onset of his illness, Graystone admits him to the pediatric ward and puts in a call to Mercy's senior pediatric pulmonologist, Dr. Adrienne Talley. Crow spends a restless night on a cot beside Joey's bed, in a room with five other children and three mothers. Early the next morning Dr. Talley arrives.

She's a pleasant-looking black woman, short and round-faced, with a pocketful of peppermints that she dispenses liberally to the children she sees. "Dr. Graystone asked me to take extra good care of you," she tells Joey, warming her stethoscope on the palm of her hand. "You must be a very special friend of his."

"We're gonna play ball together," Joey says proudly. "He gave me a glove."

"Well then, we better hurry up and get you out of here."

"Can I go home today?"

"Not today, darlin'. Maybe tomorrow. Deep breath now."

After the examination and a thorough history, Crow accompanies the doctor out into the hall. "He's doing great," Talley says. "Now the trick is keeping him that way." She prescribes a three-day course of steroids and an increased regimen of regular preventive medication. "Call if there's any problem," she says, handing Crow her card. "My service can always reach me. And I'd like to see Joey in my office in two weeks."

Crow looks down at the card. The office is in the Park Slope section of Brooklyn, a far cry from Deepside. She's got to wonder what this doctor charges. Talley seems to catch her thought. "You're a hospital employee," she says. "I'll accept your insurance."

Crow nods thanks. But why, if Joey's doing so well, must he stay in the hospital?

"Controlled environment," Talley says. "Less chance of a relapse. Safer all around."

"Yesterday," Crow whispers, "I thought he was going to die."

The doctor's nod acknowledges Crow's fear, not Joey's danger. Crow finds her matter-of-factness reassuring, perspective-changing, just as being on the ward alters the scale of her particular problem. The boy in the bed next to Joey's is a ten-year-old who coughed all night. Cystic fibrosis, his mother told Crow in the morning, by way of apology. From working in the ER, Crow knows the prognosis for cystic fibrosis. So asthma's not so dreadful after all.

After the doctor leaves, Crow phones Selma with a list of Joey's requirements: his teddy bear, toothbrush, and favorite pajamas. Reluctantly she leaves him with a volunteer in the pediatric playroom and takes the elevator down to Mercy's bowels. Entering the ER, she runs into Pilar.

"How's he doing?" the head nurse demands.

"Doing fine now, thanks to you all."

Pilar shrugs. "I told you. Graystone ain't about to let that child go." Deep within the earthy furrows of her face, bright eyes glisten watchfully.

"I better get to work," Crow says. "I swear, I turn my back for half an hour and this place look like a tornado hit it."

"Not so fast, girl. You and me got to talk."

Crow protests, to no avail. Her arm held captive in Pilar's meaty grasp, she is propelled down the hall to the ladies' room, where young Jennifer is applying makeup.

"Nobody come here to look at your face," says Pilar. "Scat."

Jennifer scats. Crow leans her back against a sink and crosses her arms. She feels naked without her mop.

"What's going on with you and him?" Pilar demands.

"Me and who?"

Pilar snaps her fingers. "Graystone. Come on now, I ain't got all day."

"Nothing," Crow says.

"Don't bullshit me, girl. I got eyes in my head. I got ears."

"I'm not shitting you. He was interested; now he's not. End of story."

Pilar snorts. "That why he been moping around like a lovesick pup, 'cause he lost interest?"

Crow shrugs without answering.

"Maybe you just don't like him," Pilar says, ferret eyes fixed on Crow's face. "Everybody else think he's hot, but to you, maybe the man is dogmeat."

"He ain't dogmeat."

"So what's the problem?"

"What are you, his advocate?"

"He's a good man."

Crow echoes Selma. "Then why's he messing with my head?"

Pilar snorts. "That's what I thought at firs'. I put it to him."

"What'd he say?"

"Told me to mind my own damn business. But I was wrong. He ain't the type to shit in his own stable. 'Sides which, any fool can see the man is miserable."

"'Cause he knows it ain't right."

"Never mind him. We're talking about you."

Crow raises her eyes. "Even if he still wanted to be with me, which I know for a fact he does not, I don't need no here-today, gone-tomorrow man."

"Oh," Pilar laughs, "you want guarantees!"

"I've got a child," Crow protests, stung.

"Your child got to take his chances in life, sugar, just like the rest of us. Love don't come with no money-back guarantee. If it did, I'd be retired by now, living in Jamaica and sipping rum." Pilar lets loose her booming, foghorn laugh.

Crow hugs herself. Too late now, she thinks, and with the thought comes a sense of sorrow and bitter waste. The loss of a love that might have been brings back other phantom losses: music that will never be heard in this world, children who will never be born, whose absence is her constant companion. Most galling is the knowledge that she brought it on herself, through stubbornness and pride. She would weep if she could. But Pilar's bosom, though massive, is not motherly; her watchword is not "Come and be comforted" but rather "Heal and begone."

The nurse's eyes have not left Crow's face. Her bulk remains planted between Crow and the door. Finding it necessary to change the subject, Crow asks about Elias.

Pilar's nostrils flare. "What about him?"

"Did he really kill a child?"

Pilar can't keep from looking around. "Who told you that?"

"Is it true?"

Silence.

"It wasn't his fault," Pilar says at last. "He was trying to save her. Child couldn't breathe, had a button wedged down her throat. He was leaning over her with his scalpel in his hand when the bullet struck. Man was dead before he hit the floor."

"He cut her," breathes Crow. So much is suddenly illuminated: Elias's obsession with endangered children, his talk of unfinished business, the faint aura of guilt that accompanies him like a body odor.

Pilar's brown face has taken on a reddish tinge. "Slashed the jugular as he fell. We went to work on him, naturally. Blood everywhere, who was to know? Child bled out before anybody noticed." Her voice is defiant, but her eyes plead for absolution. So maybe they did notice, thinks Crow. Maybe at that moment, the child wasn't the first priority. She's damned if she'll judge them.

"If I thought," Pilar says shakily, "a person could be punished for a thing like that, I'd slit my own throat here and now and be done with it."

"It's not punishment," Crow says. She didn't know she knew this till the words leave her lips, but having spoken, she knows it's true. "He's stuck, like a record in a groove. Man's all hung up."

Pilar sags against the bathroom wall. "What are we gonna do?" she appeals to Crow.

"Nothing we can do," Crow replies. "It's up to him."

She slips past Pilar and goes off to change. All morning long, people keep coming up, asking after Joey. A feeling grows inside her like a slowly expanding balloon, a great indigestible mass of gratitude. The thing she feared is coming to pass: Life is opening its arms to her again. All the time she thought she was just hiding out, she was actually sending down roots. Now she finds herself firmly planted in this garden of weeds, whose ragtag mix of hardy, mismatched folk, black and white and brown, have become her family.

Just as she's fixing to go up and have lunch with Joey, Selma arrives, and with her, Deacon. There was a time, not long ago as the calendar measures time, when Crow dreaded nothing more than just such a collision between worlds. Even now, as Deacon's eyes register her cheap brown uniform and the supply cart, she flinches just a little. But he says nothing, just opens his arms and takes her inside.

"Where is that rascal?" Selma demands.

"Upstairs," says Crow. "Come, I was just going up."

Selma grumbles all the way to the elevators. "Fine thing, scaring everybody half to death. Soon as that child get well, I'm gonna whale the daylights out of him, and it ain't even his fault. Who the hell ever hear of a black child ice-skating? Roller skates was good enough for *my* children. I swear some people ain't got the sense they was born with. Crow," she says in the same querulous tone, "you reckon they got a microwave up there?"

"I'm sure they do," Crow says. "Why?"

Selma pats her big old canvas tote bag. "I made some soup before I come. Ain't nothing clear the chest like good old-fashion' chicken soup."

They get out on the fifth floor and walk down the long, drab corridor toward Joey's room. Deacon holds Crow's arm in his. He's uncommonly silent, and even through his thick woolen sleeve she can feel the tension in his muscles. As they pass the nurses' station, Selma spies a microwave and persuades a nurse to heat her soup. Crow walks on with Deacon.

"What's the matter?" she asks.

His look is full of hurt and indignation. "If I hadn't gotten worried and called Selma, I wouldn't have known. Why didn't you call me, Crow?"

She stops. "I'm so sorry. I wasn't thinking. I was that scared."

He winces. "Who do you turn to when you're afraid? Who's your friend, darlin'?"

"You are." She embraces him, rubs her cheek against his tweedy chest. Being held by Deacon was like being inside a teddy bear. "Don't take it like that, baby. Last night I was so paralyzed with fear, I hardly knew my own name."

She starts to break away, but Deacon holds tight. "It's too much," he mutters into her hair. "It's too hard. You need someone, darlin'. Can't do it all alone."

Something in his voice alarms her. Crow puts her hands on his shoulders and gently pushes him away. Their eyes meet.

"Person do what she gotta do," Crow says firmly. "That's how it is."

"There are easier roads," Deacon begins; she puts a finger over his lips and he allows himself to be silenced, but with a look that says, "To be continued."

There's music in the air, and it's coming from Joey's room. Crow and Deacon stop outside his door to listen. They eye one another in amazement.

"That's never Joey," the old man breathes.

"No way," Crow says. "He's good, but he ain't that good. It's Blue's harmonica, though." She ought to know; that old thing was a fixture in Blue's hip pocket. If the saxophone was his instrument for playing, the harmonica was his instrument for thinking and for feeling, his everyday voice. Now it belongs to Joey, who has so taken Deacon's advice to heart that he not only carries the instrument with him wherever he goes, he even sleeps with it under his pillow.

Joey's learning to play the way an infant learns to talk: in fits and starts, a word, a phrase, a concept at a time. But the sound emanating from his hospital room is no childish concoction. It's pure blues played by someone who's been there: a doleful cry, sound stretched over emptiness, order derived from inchoate pain. Suddenly Crow realizes who's playing. She turns her face to the wall.

Deacon looks at the back of her head, and that great mountain of a man seems to shrink a little. He sighs and says, "No fool like an old fool, eh, Crow?"

She doesn't answer. Deacon opens the door to Joey's room and steps inside.

The player stops in midnote, drops the harmonica onto the bed, and rises from his seat. "Deacon," he says.

"Graystone," Deacon replies grimly. They shake hands like gladiators.

In the hall, Crow straightens and follows Deacon inside.

"Mama," Joey cries, "he can *play*."

Her eyes meet Graystone's. Even as she watches, the softness drains from his face. The surface of his eyes turns bland, matte, nonreflective; he fingers his stethoscope and offers up a cool, professional smile.

"I know, baby," she says. "I heard."

"Seems like the good doctor's got all kinds of hidden talents," Deacon says. "Let's hope he knows how to use 'em."

29

· · · · · · · ·

If Elvira Graystone were the sort of woman to bear adversity stoically, accepting gracefully the portion allotted to her, she would never have achieved the standing and respect she enjoys today. And though it is possible that an ignorant bystander, examining the bare facts of her existence, origins, and destination, might dare to call her lucky, Elvira knows better. Good fortune, she is fond of saying, comes to those who go out and seek it. She didn't just happen, one fine day, to marry a doctor; she worked diligently to find, and having found, to secure her doctor. Though not blessed with genius, Elvira applied her very adequate intelligence, fought her way upstream to win an academic scholarship, and, against all expectations but her own, became the first and only child in her family to go to college, where she met her husband. Though not graced with beauty, she parlayed pleasant features, a fine complexion, innate good taste, and a sweet, petite figure into a superficial but quite effectual prettiness that lasted just as long as it had to. God had bestowed upon her little enough to begin with, but no one could say that Elvira had not made the very best use of everything she was given.

She married well, no doubt about that. Harold Graystone came from a line of businessmen and professionals, a solidly bourgeois black family willing and able to subsidize the customarily lean years of residency. But even after the wedding, Elvira was not content, as she might easily have been, to rest on her laurels. Financially secure for the first time in her life, she went about the business of slowly, steadily eradicating her past. Elocution lessons annulled all trace of her origins. She enrolled in two of the better book clubs, bought season tickets to the Met, took up bridge, subscribed to and rigorously studied *The New Yorker, Harper's, House and Garden,* and *Vogue,* did volunteer work at her husband's hospital, ran the local PTA, and finally, cold-bloodedly and with malice aforethought, joined the Republican party.

When he married her, Harold Graystone was generally considered to have married down. By now, however, Elvira's industrious efforts on behalf of his career and her flair for elegant entertaining have evened the scales. It's an equitable marriage. The knowledge that she has made it so, has hoisted herself by her own bootstraps, is, quite naturally, a source of pride to Elvira, though not one she boasts of to her new friends, most of whom happen to be white (not that it matters, skin pigment being, to her mind, a matter of accident, not essence).

Naturally there is a price to be paid for all this home improvement. Nothing comes free in life, and Elvira of all people knows this. It's a woman's duty, clearly stated in the Bible and many other authoritative books written by men, to cleave to her husband, forsaking all others; and this injunction Elvira, though not a devout woman, has religiously obeyed. Thus has her own family fallen by the wayside; her brothers are lost to her, and with them the last reminder of who she used to be and the world she used to inhabit.

If there is pain in this loss, it is pain she bears willingly for her family's sake. It's a comfort to know she tried; God knows she tried. Every year during the early years of her marriage, the Graystones invited Elvira's family on designated holidays. Harold would take her brothers aside and talk seriously to them, trying to show them the possibilities open to men with good work habits and the right attitude.

But they would not listen; they would not learn. They clung to their old ways as they clung to their music—no doubt the two were related. Playing all night in those clubs, drinking, brawling, constantly exposed to drugs and underworld types: It was clear where they were headed. The humiliation of having the police at her door just put the lid on what Elvira had already decided. For Thomas's sake, the ties had to be severed.

For she has not raised a son of Thomas's caliber to see him lured away by the siren call of black music, the netherworld of dingy cellars, wailing saxophones, and bitter men. Thomas is hers; he belongs to the surface, is meant to inhabit a brighter, wider world.

No. Elvira didn't sit back then, and she's not about to now, when the danger is so much greater. She hasn't had a decent night's sleep since the Christmas party. The worst part is the not knowing. Thomas refuses to talk to her. He stayed away Christmas Day on the transparent pretext of being needed at work, an excuse that Elvira, a doctor's wife, utterly discounted. It could only have been Crow's doing, *her* wicked influence.

Crow: a perfect name for a fierce black predator with sleek feathers and a raucous heart. Somehow this creature has got her talons into Thomas, seduced him, found out his weaknesses, and exploited them. A beautiful widow with a tragic past and a frail child: how pathetic, how tempting. What man could fail to respond? Let alone one like Thomas, always a little too good for this world (witness that dreadful job he clings to).

Elvira makes inquiries, saying nothing to her husband. Why stir up trouble? It's not as if she doesn't know what Harold would say. "Let the boy live his life; it's up to him; blah, blah, blah."

It is their only area of disagreement. Elvira is not of the laissez-faire school of parenting.

Crow is cooking a big pot of chili and Selma rolling out pie dough when the doorbell rings. Rising creakily, Selma wipes her floury hands on her apron. "I'll get it."

Crow hears, without much interest, an unfamiliar female

voice. A moment later Selma peeks in. "A lady to see you," she whispers.

"A *lady!*" Crow laughs. "Show her into the morning room, then." She follows Selma out. The visitor stands in the center of the living room, arms straight down by her side as if loath to touch anything. She turns to face them.

"Mrs. Graystone," Crow says, with the utmost surprise.

"Mrs. Durango," Elvira replies stiffly. They do not smile, nor do they offer to shake hands. Crow, with subarctic civility, offers her visitor a seat, which is declined, and introduces her to Selma and Joey, who has come to investigate. Elvira affords each the flicker of a glance and to Selma a frigid "How d'you do."

Elvira has left her jewelry at home and dressed down for this visit, but her nails are wrapped in rose-colored silk, her jet-black hair is militantly coiffed, and her sleek leather purse and matching pumps register off the Deepside scale. Having refused both a seat and a subsequent offer of refreshment, she stands staring at Crow, expectantly silent.

Crow waits her out. Let Elvira state her business if she chooses; Crow will not inquire.

"I wish to speak to you," Elvira says at last, "privately."

Selma puts her hands on Joey's shoulders. "I was just going home to bake some cookies. Have you got any idea who I could get to lick the bowl?"

"No," Crow says at once and firmly. "There's no cause for you to leave. If Mrs. Graystone wants to talk privately, we can go out. Mrs. Graystone, would you care for a stroll through my garden?"

Elvira maintains an offended silence in the elevator. Mookie, Ray, and Jamal, sprawled across the front stoop, hoot and holler when she emerges but quit at a look from Crow. Mrs. Graystone affects not to hear, but Crow notices her quick appraisal of the boys, her automatic calibration of the threat. No, Crow thinks, no silver spoon in that baby's mouth.

The cold snap's broken at last, and the sun shines brightly, reflecting off bits of broken glass ground into the pavement. The courtyard is full of people venturing forth from their winter dens for a few hours: women in bright-colored headscarfs, bundled toddlers, old folk in folding chairs, soaking up the sun. Crow and Elvira pick their way across the rubble-strewn asphalt, heading toward the playground, where children clamber over cement-and-iron structures dense with graffiti, and women stand sentry around the fenced perimeter like does in a grassy clearing, guarding their young. The women greet Crow and stare curiously at Elvira before shifting their attention outward. Danger in this neighborhood takes the form of roving posses of teenage boys, last year's crop of children pushed from the nest with nowhere to go. Other times it takes the guise of black-and-white patrol cars and cops with itchy fingers and John Wayne mentalities. Inside the enclosure, Elvira spreads a handkerchief along the seat of a bullet-scarred bench and sits stiffly on the edge.

"I have come," she declares, "to tell you something you already know."

Crow sits at the far end of the bench, leans back, and crosses her legs. "It's a long way to come to tell me something I already know."

Elvira frowns. "Don't get pert with me, young woman. I am talking about my son."

"What about him?"

"I am going to pay you the respect of speaking frankly. My son is a distinguished physician, the director of his department. Socially he travels in the finest circles. *You* are a housekeeper; you do not deny, indeed you boast of it. You live," says Elvira, indicating with a wide sweep of her arm the playground, the courtyard, and the slablike project houses that hem them in, "here. What could two such people possibly have in common?"

"Not much," says Crow. "One thing, maybe."

"What's that?"

"We're both real good at what we do."

Elvira looks her up and down. "I'm sure you're very good at what you do."

"Watch it," Crow murmurs. "You're on my turf now."

"I want you to leave him alone."

"Then surely you should be speaking to him."

For the first time, Elvira's assurance wavers. She feels uncomfortable in this playground, exposed to vulgar eyes. Perhaps it had been a mistake, coming here instead of sending for the girl. She'd meant to take Crow unawares, to put her at a disadvantage, but the interview is not going as expected. This person is too self-assured, too—the word comes unwillingly to mind—too poised.

Haughtily, Elvira says, "I don't care to intrude on my son's personal affairs."

"Yet obviously you have no problem interfering in mine!"

"I have come here to be reasonable. I had hoped to find you the same." Elvira's sharp little eyes fasten like teeth onto Crow's face. A hissing sound escapes her. "He'll never marry you, you know."

Crow gasps. Elvira clearly does not know her son's mind, or she wouldn't be worried. But Crow is far too angry to enlighten her.

"In that case," she says, "you have nothing to fear."

"He's engaged, you realize." Elvira produces this plum with a triumphant flourish.

Though a distant tremor of grief runs through her, Crow says coolly, "Then I am all the more mystified by your visit."

"She's a lovely woman, a very successful interior designer, a person from his own world."

"He's kept it very quiet."

A faint hint of defensiveness creeps into Elvira's voice. "They haven't actually announced it yet. There is an understanding . . . everyone expects . . ."

"I see," Crow says. "You're saying you would *like* your son to marry this woman."

"I'm saying that without your interference that is what will happen!"

"My interference!" Crow echoes.

"Do you deny it? What is your relationship with my son?"

Crow produces a polite smile. "If he has not seen fit to answer that, you can hardly expect me to."

Her composure serves only to enrage Elvira, who looks as

if she is about to swoop off her perch and into the air. "I want your word, I want your absolute assurance, that you will stay out of my son's life!"

Now Crow is struck by the kind of horrid curiosity that afflicts rubberneckers at an accident site. "Is there an 'or else' attached to this?"

"I am prepared to do a great deal for you, Mrs. Durango. Regardless of what you may think, I wish you well. You have a child; you want him out of here. I can't blame you for trying. In the event, you've simply aimed too high." Elvira's thin red lips shape her words precisely. "One is not without sympathy. One can be generous."

Springing to her feet, Crow cries, "Shame on you! You don't know who you're talking to."

"I know precisely whom I'm talking to. For the last time, Mrs. Durango: Will you give me your solemn word?"

"I will not. What I do is no business of yours, and as for your son: He must choose for himself."

Elvira glares at her. Framed by the setting sun, Crow seems to glow about the edges. Her shadowed face is all flashing eye and extraordinary cheekbones: They could be natural wonders, those cheekbones, carved by the action of rain and wind over eons, or the product of several generations of obsessed craftsmen. In the set of her long neck and the shape of her head, there is a regality to which, Elvira thinks angrily, the woman has no valid claim. Nevertheless, the image lingers, informing the slender frame of the woman who stands over her. And yet, at the same time, Crow appears perfectly indigenous to this place, solidly at home among these people: a combination of identities that Elvira never even thought possible. It's at this point she realizes, with a sinking heart, the true extent of Thomas's danger.

30

·······

Alice is working triage when the multipara in advanced labor is wheeled in by EMS. The girl who lies clutching the bars of the stretcher doesn't look old enough to have two children, but then they never do to Alice. The girl has reached the stage of labor where surroundings don't matter anymore; she is afloat in a sea of pain, and the only signals she receives come from within. Alice is listening to Percy's report—"No prenatal care, claims to be in her ninth month, water broke a hour ago, overlapping contractions"—when suddenly the patient's soft moaning spikes to a frenzied wail. *"Ai, Dios mío, viene el bebé!"*

Alice and Percy exchange a look; they each grab a corner of the gurney and run for the ob-gyn room. Together they get the patient onto the examination table, where she curls up on her left side, cradling her belly.

Percy goes out to lasso a doc while Alice strips off the woman's pants and drapes her with a sheet. "Ai, ai, ai," the patient cries. Then she grunts, clamps her teeth, and strains hard.

"No!" Alice says sharply. "Don't push." She looks at the EMS sheet for the patient's name. "Don't push, Juanita. Pant." Unsure of the woman's English, she pants in demonstration.

Juanita's blood pressure is 130, low for a woman at term, but who knows what her norm is? With no prenatal records, they have no baseline. Alice takes a fetascope from the OB tray, presses the shallow head to the patient's abdomen, and hears the baby's heart chugging like a train coming in too fast for the station. A small frown collects between her brows. She looks anxiously at the door.

Another contraction collects and breaks. Alice puts her hands on the patient's shoulders and massages them gently. "Pant," she says. "Don't push yet, Juanita. Keep your legs together."

Panting and whimpering, Juanita grabs Alice's hand and clings to it like a drowning man clutching a log. "Good girl," Alice murmurs. "You're doing great." Only thing harder than giving birth to a baby is not giving birth when you need to.

Percy returns alone. "Couldn't get nobody," he says softly to Alice. "They're all doin' procedures and shit."

Flashing him a look of annoyance, Alice bends down to her patient. "I'll be right back, Juanita. I'm going to get a doctor. Keep panting. Whatever you do, don't push. Okay, *señora?*"

"This baby want out," Juanita gasps.

"Just a few more minutes, you'll be holding your baby. Stay with her," she tells Percy as she backs out the door. The corridor is deserted, not a doctor in sight. Amazing, she reflects for the thousandth time, the way they are constantly underfoot when you don't need them and never around when you do. She checks the doctors' lounge and Dr. Graystone's office before hurtling around the corner to the nurses' station.

Pilar looks up from her charts at such unseemly haste.

"Got a baby on the way," Alice gasps. "I need an M.D. stat."

Pilar reaches for the phone. "I'll call upstairs."

"Call, but she's not waiting. Who's around?"

At that moment, like a vision in the wilderness, Douglas Plummer appears at the end of the corridor adjoining the rest of the hospital. He strides along at a no-nonsense pace, eyes fixed on the exit door, camel-hair overcoat slung casually over his arm.

Pilar hangs up the phone. "Never thought I'd be glad to see that sucker."

Alice steps into his path.

The grimace that contorts Plummer's handsome face is quickly pasted over with a smile. "Alice," he says fulsomely.

She says, "I need you."

"How long I've waited to hear those words," he replies, "and how frustrating to hear them now. I'm late for a terribly important meeting."

Alice considers seizing his arm and frog-marching him into the ob-gyn room. He'd resist, of course, but only so much resistance is possible before the scene becomes comic, and Plummer would have a low ridicule threshold. Then an alternate plan occurs to her.

She smiles, enticingly, she hopes, and looks upward through hooded eyes: not a practiced maneuver, but one she has seen successfully performed thousands of times by her mother. It seems to work. Plummer comes to a complete halt and points, like a foxhound scenting prey.

"Could we," she purrs, "talk privately for a moment?"

"Sure," he says, grooming his mustache with one finger. She links her arm in his and vamps him over to the ob-gyn room. Plummer is looking at her and doesn't notice the patient until he's well into the room.

Alice smiles at his suddenly scowling face. "Dr. Plummer," she says, "meet Juanita Perez."

"No fair," he mutters, edging toward the door. "Get someone else."

Alice steps between him and it. "There is no one else, and she's ready to go."

Juanita obliges with an unmistakable grunt.

"Guess you don't need me no more," Percy says. No one answers. He slips out the door and closes it behind him.

"Doctor?" says Alice, reaching for his coat.

Plummer clings to it. "Send her upstairs."

"Too risky."

Too risky for the patient she means, but Plummer takes it as a comment on his liability exposure. Hissing angrily, he lets Alice take the coat. "I'll have a look, but if she's not crowning, she goes up."

Alice helps Juanita roll onto her back and raises her feet to the stirrups. She brings over a towel and gently wipes her face, drenched in sweat. From deep within her pain, the patient's eyes track her. Her dry lips form the word *"Gracias."*

Plummer takes up his position at the foot of the table and aims the overhead light.

"She's crowning," he pronounces with disgust, glaring at Alice as if she were personally and solely responsible for this event. Then Pilar appears in the doorway.

"What's happening here, express delivery? You need help?"

"Call Pediatrics," Plummer snarls as he slips into a gown. "And page Ob-Gyn. I want a resident down here *stat.* Make sure they know the call comes from me, not you people."

Pilar raises an eyebrow but doesn't reply. Before leaving, she approaches the patient. "Is there anyone we can call for you, baby?"

"Nobody," Juanita grunts. Pilar pats her hand and goes out.

"The head's visible," Alice calls nervously.

Plummer shoulders her aside and addresses the patient while staring between her legs. "Okay, dear, you know the drill. When I say push, you squeeze that baby out, like toothpaste. Ready . . . push!"

Three minutes later, the baby is born, a six-pound baby girl with good reflexes and a headful of brown curls. Plummer catches the baby, suctions her, and hands off to Alice, who wraps her in a warm sheet and lays her in Juanita's waiting arms.

Mother and child have four minutes to bond. Then two hearty pediatrics residents arrive to do their drill. "Six whole pounds," says one of them, a redhead who looks too young to drink. "Must be an all-time record for Mercy." They carry the baby away. Plummer and Alice wait for the placenta to emerge.

They wait five minutes, and five more. Plummer looks impatiently at his watch. Too angry at Alice to pursue his usual line of gallantries, he sits seething while Alice and Juanita chatter in the afterglow of birth. Juanita's older children are both boys, she tells Alice, a three-year-old and a one-year-old. She was hoping for a girl. The baby will be named Consuela, after her mother. "It's a beautiful name," says Alice.

Pilar pops back in to inform Plummer, with barely concealed glee, that Ob-Gyn has no one to send at the moment, and their best ETA is thirty minutes.

Plummer fumes. In fifteen minutes, he tells Alice, consulting his Rolex, the board of the East Side co-op he's been trying for six months to buy will be sitting down to meet, with or without him. As is, he's stepping up to bat with two strikes against him: A single man is always suspect, and his job in a city hospital lacks prestige. It is essential that he be there in person to make his case.

Alice listens with an air of sympathetic interest. The way she sees it, he's entitled to his pique. She *did* entrap him, and now he's stuck. Not even Plummer would leave a patient before the placenta is delivered, when the risk of complications is greatest. According to the nurses' grapevine, he's already had the malpractice wolves at his door, before he came to Mercy. He'll stay, if only to protect himself.

"All right, ladies," Plummer says now, springing from his stool. "Break's over. Back to work. Let's get this show on the road."

Alice rises obediently, but with an uneasy feeling. Upstairs Plummer has a rep as a control freak. At the best of times, he tends to micro-manage labor, and this is definitely not the best of times. If she were running the show, Alice would allow Juanita to deliver the placenta when she's good and ready. If her uterus is taking a break, it probably needs one. "No good comes from hurrying," her obstetrics instructor used to say, and during her stints on maternity, Alice has seen plenty of harm done by eager beavers. But of course, she's not in charge. Doctors dictate, nurses implement: That's how it is and how it's always been.

"Push!" Plummer orders Juanita, who looks doubtfully at Alice.

"Bear down, Juanita," urges Alice, who knows the alternatives.

The patient shuts her eyes, scrunches up her face, and bears down.

"Come on, come on," Plummer says impatiently. "You'll have to do better than that."

"But nothing's happening. I mean, I don't get no more pains."

He mimics her accent. "But you still got a placenta, and that placenta's gotta come out. *¿Comprende?* So when I say push, you do it. Push!"

This time he shoves downward with two fists on her belly while she pushes. "No, no, no," Juanita groans. Alice, standing ready with a stainless-steel bowl, sees Plummer's knuckles blanch with exertion. "Doctor!" she blurts.

"Nurse?" His eyes dare her to speak out.

Her first impulse is to back off. Territorial imperative is as potent a force in the hospital as anywhere in the wild, and Alice knows she's encroaching on Plummer's turf. She also knows, quite suddenly, that if she allows herself to be cowed by this man, if she plays little girl to his angry daddy, she might as well march upstairs and refuse the job Jean offered her. A job she's come to think of as hers.

"Well?" Plummer demands.

Alice says, "She needs time."

"We all need time. Time is of the essence." He turns back to Juanita and commands her to push hard.

She pushes and he presses, but nothing happens except that Juanita grows more exhausted, Plummer more frustrated, and Alice more anxious.

Plummer keeps an eye on the clock. So does Alice. She knows the protocol upstairs. If the placenta doesn't emerge within twenty minutes of the baby, it's excavation time; the miners go to work. Sometimes they'll try cord traction first, gently tugging on the umbilical cord to coax the placenta out. Other times it's straight to the OR for total anesthesia and manual removal of the placenta. Manual extraction is the more invasive procedure and so likely to be favored by a hands-on type like Plummer, but it also takes longer. Alice would give odds on cord traction.

Twenty minutes to the second after Juanita gave birth, Plummer calls for ring forceps. Cord traction it is.

Alice takes him aside. "I think we should give her more time," she whispers. "This is her third child in four years. She's just had an intense labor. I'm concerned about uterine atony."

Plummer berates her in a red-faced fury. *"You're* concerned! Who are you to be concerned? I've delivered more babies than you've ever seen, and you're telling me my business?"

"It's my business, too." The words well up from somewhere inside her, bypassing the usual censors. "She's my patient."

He shakes a finger under her nose. "You've changed, you know that, Alice? You're not the girl you used to be."

"Gosh," she says. "Does that mean you don't love me anymore?"

Plummer throws her a murderous look and rushes back to his post. He picks up the ring forceps and waits for Alice to position herself behind Juanita's head, pressing on her shoulders. Cord traction is not as painful as manual extraction, but it's painful in a uniquely intimate way. Some women will jump right off the table if not restrained.

As soon as Alice is in place, Plummer grasps the end of the cord with the forceps and presses down on Juanita's belly with his left hand to anchor the uterus. Slowly he pulls the cord, twisting it as he tugs.

On Juanita's face, an inward look of puzzlement is followed by astonishment, then horror. She shrieks and thrusts out her legs, pushing away from the doctor.

"Hold her still, goddammit," Plummer snaps. He tries the cord again. There's not a lot of give, and for a moment he considers the possibility of placenta accreta, a condition in which the placenta is implanted too deeply in the uterine walls. Unlikely, he decides, and applies greater pressure, more torque to the cord. The patient emits a high-pitched keening, like a teakettle.

Plummer knows he's hurting her. A patient on whom he

performed the procedure once told him that it felt like being pulled inside out. But it can't be helped; she should have had the sense to come in earlier like a normal human being, instead of waiting till the last minute and trapping him here.

Alice's attention has been on controlling and calming her patient. Now, glancing up, she's shocked to see the degree of force Plummer's exerting on the cord. It's absolutely taut, attenuated, stretched to the limit. As she watches, he braces a foot against the rung of the table and tugs sharply.

Juanita utters a piercing scream. The placenta comes free and flies out with a *whoosh*, like a liver with wings. Plummer fields it with the bowl.

"Jesus Christ," Alice breathes. "God Almighty. What did you do?"

"Blasphemy from our Alice? I delivered a placenta is what I did." He glances into the basin. "A lovely, whole placenta. The deed is done." He turns away with a flourish.

Blood spurts from the patient's vagina, splashing onto the floor and splattering Plummer's cuffs. "Shit!" he says, looking down.

Alice palpates the patient's abdomen and finds the uterus flaccid and unresponsive. The bleeding continues, bright red blood, less than a stream but more than a trickle. She tells Plummer, who is wiping his pants cuffs with a paper towel.

"Zap her with some pit," he replies without looking up.

Alice hooks up a bag of Pitocin to the IV. Usually the drug stimulates contractions within minutes. She lays her hand on the patient's belly and feels nothing, no movement. But Juanita's face looks odd, several shades lighter and a tinge greener than when she came in.

"How do you feel?" she asks.

"Bueno," Juanita replies, then turns her face to the side and sighs happily, like a tired child settling into sleep.

All of Alice's alarm sensors go off at once. She summons Plummer in a tone that commands even his fractious attention.

He hurries over and gapes at the flow of blood. "I told you to pit her!"

"I did."

Plummer lowers his voice. "Looks kind of shocky." There's a question in his tone; he hadn't actually looked at the patient's face before.

"She's not contracting."

"Get her pressure." He puts on a fresh pair of gloves, loads a syringe with Methergine, and injects it into the patient's left buttock. Juanita doesn't flinch. She's still conscious but spaced-out. "That'll do it," he says. It sounds like a prayer.

"Want some bodies?" Alice asks, inflating the cuff.

"We can handle this."

"Eighty. Stay with us, Juanita," she calls loudly, but now there's no one home. Without waiting for instructions, Alice goes to the door, throws it open, and hollers at the top of her lungs: "I need a doctor *STAT!*"

The ER seems to pause and catch its collective breath. Is that *their* Alice, that person screaming like a banshee? Graystone comes running, Pilar on his tail.

"She's bleeding out," Plummer cries as they crowd into the room. One fist is deep inside the patient, while the other presses down on her abdomen. His gown is spattered with blood. "Ringer's, stat! Someone start another line."

"What the hell happened here?" Pilar growls, then turns and runs for the Ringer's solution.

Graystone grabs a catheter, tubing, and a wide-gauge needle from the tray. He flicks Juanita's wrist, and her arm, flaccid as a rag doll, quivers. "You've tried Methergine?"

"Of course I gave Methergine," Plummer rasps. "She contracted slightly, but kept on hemorrhaging."

Graystone strikes blood with his first stick and tapes the needle into place. "Ruptured uterus?"

"Fucking Christ knows."

"Want to get her to OR?"

"Gotta push up her BP first. Where's that fucking Ringer's?"

Pilar appears with an armload. She and Alice attach a bag of the fluid to each of the IVs and turn them up full blast.

Graystone's feeling around for a pulse. "I'm not . . . What's her blood loss?"

Plummer avoids his eye. "I don't know, four hundred ccs maybe."

"Five to six hundred," Alice says distinctly. Both men look at her for a moment. Then Plummer tells Graystone, "Put your hand on mine." Plummer still has one fist buried deep inside the patient; the other, reinforced by Graystone's hand, presses hard on Juanita's abdomen, as if Plummer were trying to make his hands meet.

Pilar and Alice shudder and exchange a look. Both suffer from a form of double vision. On a professional level, they see two doctors trying to force the uterus to contract, in order to stop the bleeding. On a deeper level, as women, they can't help seeing a violent assault by two men on an unconscious girl.

After a moment, Graystone lets up. "No good. Better get in there and stop the bleeding."

It's Plummer's patient, his call. Graystone waits for him to make it. But the gynecologist has frozen; he's staring at the BP monitor like a man watching the ball drop in Times Square.

"Come on, man, let's get the lead out."

Galvanized by Graystone's tone, Plummer plunges all his weight down on Juanita's belly. "Contract, goddamn you, contract!"

"That's enough! Pilar, call OR and tell them we're on our way."

They make it to the operating room in record time; the surgical team is scrubbed and ready. But the patient has already lost too much blood. Juanita Perez dies on the table.

The first, informal postmortem takes place half an hour later, in Graystone's office. There will be other inquiries, starting with the hospital's own Mortality Committee, but Graystone is too furious to wait; and Douglas Plummer, who does not want or need Graystone for an enemy, deems it impolitic to plead the pressing engagement for which he's already, in any case, too late.

Alice and Plummer sit facing Graystone behind his desk. The nurse's face is pale, and her eyes are rimmed with red. Graystone pours a cup of coffee and brings it to her.

"Thank you," Alice says. When she lifts the cup, her hand shakes, and a few drops spill onto Graystone's desk.

"I'm so sorry!" She mops at the desk with her handkerchief.

"It doesn't matter," he answers kindly. "Take it easy, Ms. Straugh. No use crying over spilt coffee." The face Graystone shows to Plummer is utterly different, stern and judgmental. "What the hell happened?"

Plummer bridges his hands under his chin. The panic that beset him at the critical moment has passed without a trace. He appears cool and professional.

"The patient presented already crowning. She drops in off the street, no prenatal care, no history. Who knows what kind of problems she had coming in?"

"Just tell what happened," Graystone says.

Plummer tells his story, which is accurate up to the baby's birth. After that, certain elisions appear. The delivery of the placenta and the subsequent hemorrhage are described, but the words "cord traction" do not arise. Throughout his recital, the doctor is careful not to glance at Alice, who stares wide-eyed at him.

"Was the placenta torn?" Graystone asks, when Plummer is finished.

"The placenta was perfect," he replies confidently, knowing it will prove so in the PM.

"Then what caused the bleeding?"

Plummer shrugs. "She ruptured her uterus," he says.

She ruptured her uterus, thinks Alice. Not Plummer; the patient did it to herself. Out of spite for her doctor, no doubt, she exploded her uterus in his face. And the Jews marched willingly to the slaughter, and the Africans chose slavery.

Graystone stares through hooded eyes. "We know she had two previous pregnancies, both normal vaginal deliveries and healthy babies. Juanita Perez came into *my* emergency room very much alive, she gave birth spontaneously to a full-term baby, and you tell me the placenta was whole. Obviously, something is missing."

Plummer flushes. "Her medical history's what's missing. You want answers, Graystone? Look there. As for myself," he says, with grave reproach, "I have examined every moment of the incident in my mind, and I am morally certain that I did everything possible to save the patient."

"You'd better hope so," growls Graystone.

"I wasn't alone in there. Alice will back me up."

Both men look at her. Alice meets Plummer's eyes with cold curiosity. Will they plead? Will they threaten? What she sees is much worse. The man simply looks confident.

She lets a moment pass. Plummer's eyes sharpen, boring into her like lasers. A sense of power suffuses her. Alice realizes that she holds this man's life in her hands, as he held Juanita Perez's. She can be merciful or she can be just; she cannot be both.

She turns to Graystone. "Everything Dr. Plummer told you is true."

Plummer leans back, stroking his mustache with a satisfied smile.

"Up to a point," she adds. "After that, it's bullshit."

Graystone gapes in awe, Plummer in shock. Neither speaks.

"Dr. Plummer neglected to mention that he performed cord traction on the placenta."

"Strange thing to forget," murmurs Graystone.

Plummer cries, "Alice!"

Her tone is calm and factual, that of one professional briefing another. "The placenta was tardy, and Dr. Plummer was late for a very important meeting. Twenty minutes after the birth, the patient wasn't contracting. Dr. Plummer applied ring forceps to the cord. He used *a lot* of force."

"How would she know how much force I exerted? That's a purely subjective opinion," Plummer objects.

"So you *did* perform traction."

"I didn't say that. I refuse to submit to this inquisition."

Alice faces him. "You braced your foot against the table for more leverage."

Graystone gasps. "You saw that?"

"I saw. And I called out to him, but just then the placenta separated, and the hemorrhaging began."

Plummer jumps up, sputtering, "That's a lie!" He grabs

both her arms tightly. "If you ever dare repeat a word of this—" Then two dark hands appear on his shoulders, there's a blur of limbs, and suddenly Plummer is sprawled on the floor, staring up at Graystone with a stultified expression. It all happens so fast, Alice can't quite follow it.

"In my department," Graystone says mildly, shooting his cuffs, "we don't touch the nurses." He turns back toward his seat.

"No," sneers Plummer, "we don't touch the nurses. We prefer the maids."

Graystone stops, turns, and says, "Get up."

But Plummer seems comfortable on the floor; at any rate, he stays there. Transferring his attention to Alice, he says meaningfully, "Better think, Nurse. Remember that what goes around, comes around."

"I hope so," she replies, sick with loathing.

With a wary eye on Graystone, Plummer rises. "It's always distressing to lose a patient. But one has to take a professional attitude toward these things. Patients sometimes have bad outcomes; it's unfortunate, but it happens."

"To some of us more than others," Graystone growls.

Plummer fixes Alice with his dark eyes. "You don't realize what you're saying. You need to stop and think."

"I am. I'm thinking about two little boys and a newborn baby who lost their mother because you were late for a co-op board meeting."

"You don't know that!"

"I know it, and so do you."

"Why are you doing this? What have I ever done to you, that you should turn on me this way?" Plummer's indignation is unfeigned. It's one thing to accidentally kill a patient, quite another to deliberately rat out a colleague. This is a low blow, and from Alice, of all people.

"It's not about you and me," she tells him. "It's about Juanita Perez and her children."

"You *think* it's not about you," he snarls. "Keep this up, and I promise you, you'll never work in Maternity as long as I'm here."

With a humorless smile, Alice asks, "How long is that likely to be?"

31

· · · · · · ·

Graystone stands in front of the hospital's main entrance, hands thrust deep in his pockets, stomping his feet against the cold. He's come to give notice.

He reviews the plan. Straight upstairs to Lessing's swank office. Shut the door. Produce the budget and rip it to shreds. (He's decided against throwing the pieces in Lessing's face—not his style, really.) Give two months' notice, then out the door. If he takes the stairs instead of waiting for the elevator, he might make it down to the ER before the news reaches Pilar. Call her aside. Tell her.

That's the part that's been keeping him up nights. He knows how Pilar will respond; he's seen it before. As soon as Pilar knows anyone's leaving the ER, he's already gone. She can't see him anymore. Doesn't mention his name, except grudgingly and in the past tense. Looks right past him when she needs help. Pilar's respect, so hard-won, turns out to be a bearing beam of Graystone's self-esteem. One never knows, till one tries to remove them, how much weight such structures bear. But what he dreads most of all is the moment of limbo before she shuts him out for good, the moment in which he's no longer a colleague but not yet a stranger. Somehow he knows what he'll see in her eyes. It's

272

the same thing he sees in his own each time he glances in a mirror: desolation, the shame of desertion.

He takes his hands out of his pockets and tucks them under his armpits. The cold seeps through his leather gloves, but he's not ready to go in. He turns and moves away.

Hoping that a walk will clear his head, Graystone wanders through the 'hood. So far, despite Daniel's urgings, he has told no one of his decision. Not even his parents know he's leaving Mercy. Ungrateful wretch that he no doubt is, the anticipation of their pleasure is as awful to him as the certainty of Pilar's disappointment: Each seems another nail in his coffin.

Presently, without noticing how he got there, Graystone finds himself standing on the pavement outside Crow's project. A few steps inward would bring him in view of her window, but he resists the gravitational pull. If she won't play Eliza to his Higgins, neither will he play Freddy to her Eliza.

Besides, she's probably at work.

There's a blur of motion, a streak of red: A little girl on roller skates careens out of the gap between two buildings and crashes headlong into Graystone's legs. He catches her and sets her on her feet. "Shariqua, where you at?" a woman calls; then she appears in the gap, a stork-legged, big-bellied woman in a black ski jacket, with a kinte cloth wound around her head. She takes in Graystone, and a quick note of fear enters her voice. "Get over here, girl!"

He turns the child around and gives her a little push. The mother's wary eyes continue to inspect, consider, and finally accept him. She raises a hand in thanks as she turns back, scolding her daughter in a singsong voice while the child's laughter streams behind like a banner. Graystone walks on. Crow, too, will have to be told. He pictures the scene. With that painstaking formality that is their latest mode of communication, she may make no comment. But she will think, and he will hear her thoughts and be wounded by them. Graystone still hasn't recovered from her sting the first time he asked her out.

"No," she'd said.

"Why not?"

"I'm black."

"And what am I?"

"Black-skinned."

Damn woman. A man has the right to better himself, move up in the world, without being branded an Oreo. Who appointed her the arbiter of blackness?

He turns the corner onto the avenue, passes a bodega, a Laundromat, and a luncheonette. The smell of fresh-brewed coffee draws him back to the luncheonette.

There are no customers. Along the wall opposite the counter stand forlorn racks of yellowing magazines. An old black man with grizzled hair, seated behind the cash register, creaks to his feet as Graystone enters. "Get you something, son?"

Graystone sits on a cracked red vinyl stool at the counter. He takes off his overcoat and lays it neatly across the adjacent stool. "Coffee, please. Black."

The radio, an old-fashioned box stashed on a shelf beside the grill, is tuned to a jazz station. "Bother you?" the old man says, pouring the coffee with a palsied hand. "I'll turn it off, you don't like it."

"No, don't. Coltrane's a favorite of mine."

"Is that a fact. Now me, I favor the big bands. Duke Ellington, Basie, Hampton, that's my bag. Used to hear 'em alla time, back when them bands still played up in Harlem. This here"—he points his chin toward the radio—"sound like scratchin' on a chalkboard to me. Can't tell if they're playin' backwards or forwards or inside out." The old man laughs a slow, wet laugh and pours himself a cup of coffee. "Still, it's better than all that damn hip-hop rap-crap. Can't stand that shit, no sir. Kids come in here with them ghetto blasters blaring, I tell 'em, 'Turn it off or take it on the road, boys.'"

"They listen?"

"Sometime they listen. Sometime they knock me upside the head and empty the till." Again, the rheumy laugh. "Ain't my money."

"It's your head, though."

"That's true, brother. You got a point there."

The Coltrane piece segues into Art Blakey's Jazz Messengers: "Child's Play" is the message. They listen together, the young man and the old, and when Graystone leaves, the tune keeps playing in his head. He walks to a different rhythm now, head up and looking around, seeing through the eyes of the music. Young men strutting, children playing, women hurrying about their business: All seemed touched with grace. Things his eye usually passes over come into focus; the brisk street trade, alley courtships, even the Day-Glo graffiti charge the air with a hectic, vibrant gaiety. Tantalizing odors drift from the Caribbean restaurants and spice shops along the way. People throng the shops, as they do in places where the curfew is lifted for only a few hours a day. Indeed these *are* a people under curfew, for who in his right mind would willingly venture out into these streets at night?

Again and again, as he wanders, Graystone finds his feet tending toward the hospital, his personal lodestone; but the closer he comes, the fiercer the pain in his gut. So he turns and crosses the avenue, moving away from Mercy. As he leaves the shopping street behind, the neighborhood changes, deepens, curves in on itself. He is passing between the outer edge of an eight-story slablike gray housing project and a burned-out supermarket when he hears the footsteps.

Deep shadows fill the pockets between buildings. Crack vials clog the gutters. Here, day is night, and night is something else again. This is no-man's-land between gang turfs, disputed territory. A place Graystone avoids even in his car. Why is he walking here now? Perhaps it's by way of saying good-bye.

Now the street seems deserted, but voices murmur in the shadows. Presently two boys appear behind him, walking in step, one to the right and one to the left. The skin on the back of his neck prickles. Feeling light, energized, strangely unafraid, he turns and faces them.

Two boys. Tall and skinny, sixteen, seventeen years old. They take one more step, then stop in perfect synch, punk

Rockettes. Hands at the ready, brushing their hips like old-time gunslingers. Graystone remembers something his cop friend Feducci once said. "Guns in the hands of adolescents is like poisoned sweets in the hands of babies: guaranteed disaster."

"What is it?" Graystone says in his hospital voice. "What do you want?"

First boy looks at second in amazement. "Here we are playing nice in our own backyard, and he ask us what we doing?"

"The man don't trust us," says the second.

"The man ain't got no faith."

"An' here we just admiring his coat."

"Nice coat. Look warm. How much a coat like that cost, man?"

They're toying with him, checking him out. The coat's not it, just the opening feint. Curiously detached, Graystone wonders about the patter. Do they practice? Their voices are pitched to carry and amuse. Graystone's not surprised when their eyes shift to a spot behind him. He turns. An instinct he didn't know he possessed identifies this boy as the leader. Shorter than the others but absolutely solid, with arms as thick as his calves, a kid who, in another world, would have had the outfielders scrambling backward for position whenever he came up to bat.

The three close in. Graystone keeps an eye on the stocky leader, who says in a soft voice, "Question is what *you* want here."

The voice sounds vaguely familiar. Graystone focuses on his face. There's a scar on his chin: jagged, no work of his.

"Just passing through," he says.

"Jus' passin' through," the other echoes. "This ain't no freeway, brother. This a toll road."

The others giggle excitedly. The stocky boy smirks. "You in Sherwood Forest now, sucker."

"And you're Robin Hood?"

"You got it. We want it."

All three take a step closer. Graystone hears the click of a knife opening behind him. Suddenly the face and the voice come together. "I know you," he says to the leader.

Uncertainty flickers in the boy's eyes, as if he, too, has sensed a connection.

"Mercy ER," says Graystone.

The boy's eyes clear. "You treated my brother!"

"Gunshot wound, drive-by shooting?"

The boy thrusts out his hand. After a moment's hesitation, Graystone clasps it.

The boy laughs. "This the doc saved T.J.'s useless life," he tells the others. "He's okay."

"Nah, this the dude?"

"No shit, I reckanize him. Hey, Doc, what you doing walking out here? Don't you know it's dangerous?"

Graystone smiles. Boy sounds like a mother scolding a child. "No, really?"

"All kinda bad doers 'round here. We gonna walk you back."

"Thanks," he says, "but I'm fine. I know where I am."

Reluctantly they let him go, but as Graystone walks back toward the hospital, the boys trail at a distance, escorting him as far as the avenue.

He finds Bergman in the doctors' lounge, finishing off a bag lunch. His friend jumps up to meet him. "So? How'd he take it?"

"I didn't tell him."

Bergman peers into his face. What he sees there makes him turn away with a groan. "Aw shit, Tom."

Graystone grasps him by the shoulders. "I'm sorry, Dan'l."

"How come I'm not surprised? What happened?"

"Nothing happened." They sit at the table, facing each other. "I came here this morning to do it. But first I took a walk."

"Checking out the old fiefdom."

"Maybe. Somewhere along the way I realized I couldn't go through with it."

Bergman produces a wan smile. "Where, exactly? Could we go back there?"

"I'm sorry, man."

He looks at his hands. "Why, Tom? Because they need you?"

"No," says Graystone. "Because I need them."

32

· · · · · · ·

Tonight is New Year's Eve, and Graystone's in a foul mood. Birthdays have never fazed him, perhaps because when he compares his professional progress to the course he plotted out for himself, he's always registered right on target or ahead. But New Year's Eves are depressing when one's alone with no prospect of a change, and Graystone's custom has long been to smother the night under a raucous good time with his lady of the moment. Tonight, however, he has no date and, worse yet, wants none.

He's spent the morning at home, screaming over the telephone at Mercy's brass. Damn fools are dancing a stately minuet over Plummer's suspension, no doubt at the urging of Ob-Gyn's medical director, Rupal Shanti. Shanti at least, was up-front about his priorities. While the brass mouthed formulas about due process, waiting for the hearing, respecting the man's rights, and similar bullshit, Shanti had the balls to admit straight out that even an incompetent ob-gyn is better than none. "You want Plummer suspended pending the hearing?" he said. "You find me a replacement, I'll suspend his ass."

In the end, Graystone knows, Plummer will be bounced. It's just a question of how many women they allow him to mangle first, and that's a matter that doesn't seem unduly to concern his superiors.

The downstairs buzzer rings.

"What?" Graystone snaps into the intercom.

"It's your mother," is the reply. "Remember me?"

"Thank you, Lord," Graystone mutters. "I needed this." He buzzes her up; what else can he do?

Elvira sweeps past him into the living room, running her finger along the mantelpiece, summing up the place with a glance that snags on Graystone's old easy chair. "I thought you got rid of that hideous thing!"

"Hello, Mother," he says. She is oddly attired, he notices, in a fur coat slung over some sort of plastic smock. "What's wrong?"

"Must something be wrong for a mother to visit her son? It's not as if we speak on the phone." Elvira arranges herself on an antique ladder-back that Michelle picked up for a song at Sotheby's.

"Sorry. Things have been hectic."

"I'm sure they have," she replies with grim emphasis. *"I heard."*

"About Plummer?"

"Plumber, what plumber? I'm talking about Daniel!"

"Oy," he sighs, slumping into his easy chair.

"I ran into Risa Bergman at the nail salon. She told me the whole story. I was so upset, I walked straight out without waiting for the girl to finish. Look!" She holds up her hands. Exhibit number one: The nails on her right hand are blood red, while those on her left are bare, unpleasantly pink and naked, like newborn sparrows. "How could you turn down such an opportunity?" Elvira demands. "And without even telling us, without discussing it. What could you have been thinking?"

"Mother." He interrupts the flow. "It's my life."

"So live it, don't throw it away down that cesspool of a hospital!" Her mouth works, trying to hold back words that will not be held. "It's that woman! I know it is. Don't deny it."

"No woman's going to run my life, Mother, not even you."

Elvira recoils, pressing hand to heart. "Have I *ever* tried to run your life?"

He laughs.

Producing a handkerchief, she dabs at her eyes. "I want the best for you, Thomas, nothing less. Is that a sin?"

"No, dear. But you're going to have to let me decide what that is." Graystone stands and tenders his arm. "I have to go. I'm interviewing this afternoon at the hospital."

Elvira clings to her perch. "Let them wait. I drove all this way to say my piece, and for once I'm going to say it!"

He glances at his watch. "Five minutes."

"Thomas, darling, where does it end? Time is slipping away; in a few years you'll be forty. When do you start getting serious about your life?"

The very question he's been trying to avoid. Graystone crosses his arms protectively over his chest. But Elvira, it appears, is only talking about work. "There is nothing wrong with a little youthful idealism; it's even commendable. But a middle-aged man playing Don Quixote is nothing but a fool."

This is easier; he's on solid ground. "I'm doing what I want to do in a place where I'm needed. That's a gift from God, to work where you're needed. I'm sorry you see me as a soon-to-be-middle-aged Don Quixote, but that's your perceptual problem. For myself, I'm doing the right thing. Thank you for your concern, and have a nice day." He extends his hand.

"It's *her*," Elvira mutters, allowing herself to be hauled to her feet and walked to the door. "You never talked to me like that before. It's her influence."

"You keep saying that, and I keep telling you: It's nothing at all to do with Crow." Graystone grasps the doorknob.

His mother laughs. "Oh, Thomas. You are so deluded. That woman has cast a spell on you."

He replies with cold anger, "The lady cares nothing for me."

"That's true; but she means to have you all the same."

"Really? And you come by this amazing insight how?"

If Elvira did not feel so very upset and threatened, she would have held her tongue. It is not her wish that Thomas should learn of her call on Crow, especially after his unkind and unfounded insinuations about interference. Not that she regrets what she did, precisely. Something had to be done. And yet, on the whole, she cannot think of their encounter with as much satisfaction as she would like. Certain things were said that, in a better world, she might wish unsaid. Though Elvira's intention had been merely to approach Crow on the rational grounds of self-interest, the manner in which her charitable offer was received made it seem, and its maker feel, shabby.

Crow's indignation was fearsome. She'd seemed genuinely shocked and offended by the offer; but of course (Elvira reminds herself) the hussy is after bigger game. It's the fear that she will succeed, and the perception that Elvira's own loss of influence is balanced and indeed caused by Crow's gain, that robs her of her wit.

"I know," she retorts, "because she told me."

He lets his hand fall from the doorknob. *"She* told you! When?"

Too late, Elvira sees her danger. Though she ducks and dodges like an over-the-hill boxer, Graystone gives no quarter; and in the end he has the whole story, or at least as much of it as Elvira chooses to recall.

Her words fall into an ominous well. Thomas's face is set and grim; his eyes are the eyes of a stranger, lacking charity, void of filial regard. All of this Elvira sees as further proof of Crow's ascendency, which so rattles her that she redoubles her calumnies against Crow, knowing even as she does so that it's costing her her son. "Mercenary, ruthless, crafty, ungrateful wretch."

"Ungrateful?" he asks.

Elvira clamps her lips shut.

Suspicions beset him, but in the farsighted interest of preserving some hope of a future relationship, Graystone lets it go. Despite his anger and humiliation, he can't help laughing when he pictures the irresistible force coming up against the immovable object. Elvira has met her match at last.

"I'm surprised you got away in one piece."

"So was I. For a moment, I thought she was going to eat

me. Thomas," Elvira says, heartened by their brief concordance, "this woman is not for you."

"Why's that?" he asks, with deceptive mildness.

"She's so, so . . ."

"Black?"

She compresses her lips and glares at him.

A moment passes while Graystone struggles with his curiosity. Then he gives in. "What did Crow say?"

"She made her intentions perfectly clear. Your career, your standing in the community mean nothing to her. She sees her chance and she's going for it."

"Crow said that?"

"Not in so many words," Elvira replies scornfully. "She wouldn't, would she? No; I asked her straight out to leave you alone. She refused."

"She did?"

"She said it was none of my business. Whose business is it," Elvira appeals, forgetting to whom, "if not mine? She said it's up to you, not me."

"Up to me," he echoes. Then he steps toward his mother with a face so transformed that she gasps and steps backward. Graystone cups her face and, to her astonishment and chagrin, plants a hearty kiss on her brow. "Thank you, Mother," he says, then walks out the door.

"Where are you going?" she calls after him. "Wait!" But it's too late.

CROW

I'm mopping the corridor when Alice comes up and grabs me. "I did it," she says. "I took the job on Maternity."

I'm kind of surprised. Not by her choice—I could see that coming—but that the offer was still there to take. Doctors don't like nurses who tell tales, even on the likes of Plummer. Makes 'em nervous, makes 'em think, There but for the grace of God. Maybe Alice being who she is evened the playing field. It's easier to punish whistle-blowers when they haven't got a straw.

"Good for you," I say.

"I'm going to miss working with you, Crow." She hugs me.

Once I would have pulled away. Now I hug her back. "No, you won't," I tell her. "You'll be too busy catching babies and keeping the doctors in line."

"We'll still meet, though, won't we? Do stuff together with the kids? Noah's coming to me next week, you know."

"No, I didn't know! You got custody?"

"Foster care, for now. It's the first step. So we'll get together, the four of us?" Her eyes show a trace of her old chronic anxiety.

"Are you crazy? Think I wanna be seen around town with a skinny little white girl like you?"

She looks at me, and we laugh.

"Sure we'll meet," I say. "Joey's all the time asking after Noah. We're gonna be the mothers of best friends."

Now Pilar steams into view. "You ain't upstairs yet, buttercup," she tells Alice. "We got customers waiting." Alice tosses off a salute and scurries off. Pilar stares after her with a face as sour as yesterday's milk.

"What's the matter?" I ask. "Ain't you pleased for her?"

"Hell yeah, I'm pleased for her," Pilar grumbles. "I'm just pissed for myself. Workhorses like that don't grow on trees."

"Imagine if they did," says a voice close behind me. I look back, and there's Elias, rubbing his back against the nubby wall like a cat. "Imagine a whole treeful of nurses dangling like plump red apples, just waiting to be plucked."

"That's sick," I say.

"Huh?" Pilar gapes at me.

"Slick," I say. "Floor's slick. Watch your step." I holster my mop and walk slowly back to my closet. Elias comes with me, leaving no prints on the wet floor.

It ain't time for my break but I shut the door and sit down, stretching out my weary legs. Elias perches like a stork on the edge of the sink.

Straight off I lay into him. "Didn't I tell you not to talk to me in front of other folks? Makin' me look like a damn fool."

"Sorry. Didn't think you'd hear me."

I sniff. "Where've you been, anyway?"

"Visiting my aunt in St. Louis," he says.

"Very funny."

"I've been around."

"*I* haven't seen you."

"I know," he says glumly. I stare at him. He forces a smile. "Not to worry. Perfectly natural. Your focus is changing; you're looking ahead, not backward."

I wonder if it's true. I know lately things have felt different to me. When I walk, I feel my body move, like it's coming back to life. People look at me now; strangers speak to me. Men notice me, like in the old days. I'm not invisible anymore.

Elias spreads his hands. "We're losing the tie that binds us."

I ought to be pleased. I never asked to see this ghost, but it happened, and now I can't rid myself of feeling responsible. The man is an interfering, bossy mother of a ghost, always dragging me into situations that ain't none of my business. But somehow or other, I've got used to having him around. Besides which, what's gonna happen to him if I can't see him anymore? He won't just disappear into thin air, will he? Who's he gonna talk to?

That kind of loneliness is something I know about. Never thought I'd feel pity for any white man, but I do pity this lost soul with all my heart, and I would help him if I could.

And then it come to me, maybe I can.

He ain't gonna like what I have to say. Thing is, though, I've noticed these past months that Elias don't ever come or go while I'm watching. Not, I'm pretty sure, because he can't, but because he's ashamed to. A body as down-to-earth as Elias, who never believed in spirits and such while he was alive, don't take well to being one himself. So I fasten my eyes on him and say, "Pilar told me about the child who died."

His face goes slack. I see I'm hurting him, but somebody's got to. Pretty soon he starts writhing and shooting glances at the door like a schoolboy with a terminal case of spring fever. I don't dare blink; I stare till my eyes ache.

"I don't want to talk about that," he says.

"She said you'd blame yourself."

"Of course I blame myself. I killed her."

"You were dead when you cut her," I say.

"I was conscious."

"You're conscious now; don't make you alive. Pilar says the bullet killed you instantly. You're no more to blame for that baby's death than I am."

"Dead or alive, I was the instrument of her death."

"So was your knife, and I don't see *it* haunting the joint."

He presses his hands to his temples. "You can't understand."

"No suh, 'course not: I'm just a ignorant cleaning woman."

"Didn't say that, didn't mean it, don't deserve it," he snaps.

I apologize. "Old habits," I say.

Elias gets up and starts pacing my tiny closet, two steps each way. "If I didn't kill that child, why am I condemned to this worthless, useless half-existence?"

I've thought a lot about this. "You blamed yourself," I tell him. "No offense, Elias, but you fucked yourself over. I bet you could have moved on anytime these past fourteen years if only you'd cut yourself some slack."

"Moved on where?"

"To the great ER in the sky! How should I know where? You're the deceased party, not me."

He runs his hands through his gray hair, which I notice needs a cutting. They do say your hair keeps growing after you're dead. Our eyes meet. The man knows I'm right, I see that. But he's scared to death.

"Didn't you tell me your wife died before you?" I ask.

He nods.

"Don't you want to be with her?"

"I told you: It doesn't work like that."

Suddenly he's an expert.

"You don't know," I tell him. "For all you know, she's waiting on you right now, tappin' her toe and cussin' you for being late again."

The ghost of a smile touches his face.

I say, "You saved two people since I been here, the kid with the spleen and the one who was stabbed. Maybe a third: Noah. So whatever you think you did in life, you made up for. A person's got to move on. This dump is nobody's final resting place. It's a station is all, and, baby, your train has arrived."

"What about your train?" he says.

"Uh-uh. We ain't talkin' about me, homeboy."

"None of that street jive, Miss Crow. I know you now, and I don't buy it. Look at you, hiding in a closet. Didn't you just say that people have to move on?"

"I meant you."

He shakes his shaggy head. "The lady can dish it out, but she can't take it."

I hear him, but it just ain't that simple. When Blue died like he did, it tore a hole in the camouflage net we throw over the world. I couldn't help but see things the way they are, which meant seeing clear through those stories we tell ourselves to make life bearable, stories about who we are, where we come from, and where we're going: well-ordered stories with beginnings, middles, and ends, in which consequences follow like meek little lambs on the heels of their causes. I saw through to what lies beneath, which is nothing, nothing, nothing—no sense, no logic, no just deserts, no punishment, no reward, no beneficent God.

During the funeral service, the preacher talked that shit about not a sparrow shall fall: I believe that was when I got to my feet hollering. Don't remember what I said, but according to Selma, it included suggestions 'bout just what God could do with His goddamn precious sparrows. I do recall Selma clapping a hand over my mouth and hauling me out of church.

Elias is waiting on an answer. "Some things," I tell him, "once you see 'em, you're never the same. How can I pretend I don't know what I know? How can I stick my head back in the tiger's mouth, after I've felt his fangs?"

He shrugs, unimpressed. "You just do it. Life doesn't come with guarantees."

"That's what Pilar said."

"Pilar's a smart woman."

"Then you ought to listen to her. She said you should get your sorry, see-through ass outta here."

"Crow," he says, toying with his stethoscope, "I'll make a deal with you."

"No deals," I say. "What is it?"

"I'll try if you'll try."

A flood of smart-ass answers come to me, but I choke them back. It's true this closet was my refuge for a long time, and a welcome one it was. But now I feel the walls pressing in on me, and I remember the smell and taste of a wider world. Truth is, fond as I've grown of Mercy and the folks who work here, the glory of mopping floors is wearing thin.

"Done," I say, and hold out my hand.

He looks at it, giving me a chance to withdraw, then shyly reaches out to take it. When our hands meet, I feel, not flesh, but a tingle of energy, a muted shock that travels up my arm to my heart.

We walk out together. I bring the cart for camouflage. Down the hallway, past the nurses' station, through the waiting room, which for once is almost empty, to the glass doors leading outside. Elias hesitates.

"Git," I say, shooing him with my mop.

He reaches toward the door, but as he touches the glass, his hand passes right through, penetrating as if it were water. From my point of view, it disappears; I can't see it on the other side. Gasping, Elias pulls back.

"It's okay," I comfort him, as I would Joey. "You can do it."

His knees are shaking, and he's as pale as a ghost ought to be. "I don't know what's next," he gasps.

"Me neither, but it can't be worse than this place."

"Mercy's not that bad."

"It sure as hell ain't paradise."

A siren wails, fast approaching. Elias casts his eyes back.

"No, baby," I say. "You've done enough. No point outstaying your welcome."

"No," he agrees, but still he lingers, looking around. Then (and this ain't something I'd expect anyone else to believe, though it's God's own truth) Elias begins to weep real tears. They roll down his face and splash onto the floor, leaving a damp patch that to this day has never dried.

"God bless you, Crow."

"Go in peace, Elias."

He draws a breath, steps through the glass, and is gone.

I sink into a chair and cover my face. Reverend King's words sing in my head. *Free at last, free at last, thank God Almighty, we are free at last.*

I've just finished changing into street clothes, 'cause me and Pilar are taking Alice out to lunch, when all of a sudden I hear pounding footsteps and a man's voice hollering my name.

I throw open the closet door and peer out. Graystone skids to a halt.

"Crow," he says, huffing and puffing like he ran all the way across town. "May I come in?" Without waiting for an answer, he enters my sanctum and kicks the door to. "Tonight," he pants, "is New Year's Eve."

"Happy New Year," I say, wondering if I ought to draw my mop. He looks that wild-eyed.

"Spend it with me."

"Kind of short notice, isn't it?"

He seizes my hand. "Not just this one; all of them, from now on. I love you, Crow. With all my heart I love you."

I yank my hand away. "Do you have a twin?" I ask. "'Cause last thing I remember, a man looks a lot like you was saying, 'I don't mean it, sorry I started, let's forget all about it.'"

His cheeks turn a couple shades darker. Man looks like a steam boiler about to blow. He mumbles something about what happened to Joey. "As much as I wanted you, I couldn't let it be for that."

"What made you change your mind?"

"My mother," he says.

Now I'm totally confused.

He laughs at the look on my face. "She didn't mean to. She was trying to convince me of your predatory intentions. Instead, she gave me hope. I know you well enough to know that if you truly hated me, you'd have said so to her face."

I can't help laughing. He seems encouraged, takes my hand, and this time I let him. "Crow, you're too good to keep me dangling. One word from you now, and I'll never bother you again."

"What about your fiancée?"

"Fiancée?" he echoes, with a bewildered look.

The relief I feel tells me nothing I didn't already know. "You're not engaged?"

"Where'd you ever get that idea?" He shuts his eyes. "Don't tell me. I am not, have never been, and until this moment never wished to be engaged."

I feel the tiger's hot breath on the nape of my neck. One word, I know, will send him packing; one word will keep me safe. A voice in my ear whispers, "Take a chance." Couldn't be Elias; I saw him leave. It's just the ghost of a ghost I hear.

"I am what I am," I warn him. "What you see is what you get."

"What I see is what I want," he says. Then he wraps his arms around me and kisses me, and instantly all the hurt, all the bad feeling and misunderstandings fade into nothingness. My body wakes to his—it's like my dream only without the guilt, because Blue is gone now, truly gone, and at this moment there's no one in the world but me and Thomas Graystone.

The closet door falls open, but we don't notice till the sound of clapping brings us back to earth. They're all out there in the hall: I see Pilar and Alice, Jennifer and Murchison, Dr. Kraven and Daniel Bergman amidst a crowd of faces, all of them smiling, hooting, and laughing. Alice puts two fingers in her mouth and lets loose a whistle loud enough to wake the dead. Now where on God's green earth does a person like her learn to whistle like that? All I can say is life's full of surprises, and they ain't all bad.